CHILD OF LIES

THE SCION CHRONICLES, BOOK TWO

ERIC KENT EDSTROM

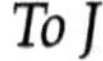

To J

1

____

HER SMALLEST PLANS

Jacey stepped blearily into the dark hallway outside her bedroom in Dr. Carlhagen's hacienda. She'd only gotten a few hours of sleep, and that had come only once the hurricane winds had finally settled deep in the night.

Not enough sleep. Not even close.

She padded down the wide tiles, shoes making a soft scuffing in the quiet. Her whole body ached from the exertions of the past few days. Her fight with Dr. Carlhagen—who had mind-transferred into her best friend Vaughan's body—had left bruises on her legs.

As tired as she was, she needed some physical activity to energize her, to prepare her for the challenges that lay ahead. That's what Sensei would have prescribed if he'd still been there.

Thinking about the martial arts master brought a lump to her throat.

No. She would mourn him later.

She planned to head down to the dojo and get in a light

workout. On the way, she would assess the storm damage. Assigning the Scions to clean-up duty would keep them busy for the day. Soon they would be asking for explanations about where Dr. Carlhagen was, where Sensei and Nurse Smith had gone. And of course they'd all have questions about Vaughan.

She stopped near the entry foyer. The living area lay in darkness to her right, the lumps of wicker furniture vague shapes against the floor-to-ceiling accordion doors making one great window of the far wall. The sky was just lightening as dawn approached. Limbs and leaves blown free in the storm floated in the pool beyond the door.

A trapezoid of light razored through the hallway ahead. It appeared to be coming from Dr. Carlhagen's office. Humphrey must have left a light on the night before. Jacey was happy the electricity was on, but there was no reason to waste it.

She continued down the hallway to turn the light off. The door hung a hand's width ajar, letting the light beam into the hall. She put her hand on the door but stopped when she heard a voice inside.

It was Mr. Justin.

"No, they won't be awake for a few more hours," Mr. Justin was saying. "Have you ever known teenagers to get up early on purpose?"

"I suppose you're right," came a reply.

Jacey waited, poised with her hand against the door. The second voice sounded distant, smaller. She thought it was coming from the holodesk in Dr. Carlhagen's office.

She shifted to make sure the light didn't touch her. All she could see was the mahogany paneled wall and part of the window behind Dr. Carlhagen's desk.

The voice continued: "There's a lot to discuss. I particularly want to know why you ignored my suggestion to put some men on the island."

Jacey placed her hand over her mouth to muffle a gasp. Captain Wilcox had wanted to leave men on campus after he had taken Sensei and Nurse Smith away.

Thinking quickly, she moved along the door to the wall, leaned against it, and slowly slid to the floor. She closed her eyes and listened.

"I don't have to explain myself to you," Mr. Justin said. "I have a better read on the situation here. The Scions are twitchy enough as it is. The last thing I need is for them to see armed men skulking around."

Jacey wanted to remember this conversation. She'd had suspicions about Mr. Justin ever since he had helped her and Humphrey take over the Scion School. He had never sufficiently explained why he worked for Dr. Carlhagen in the first place. And he certainly hadn't done anything to prevent the evil that had gone on in the medical ward.

Her early morning weariness evaporated, replaced by focus as sharp as a thornskipple barb.

On a long exhalation, she fell into her memory concentration. What was said no longer registered as words.

Ehv | ree | thEEng | ahn | mie |

yend | iz | rehd | ee

The sounds flowed to her ears like a melody, and she placed each syllable on a continuous line of falling and rising pitches. If she slipped into comprehension, she wouldn't be able to memorize it. Fortunately, she'd had a lot of practice.

Ehx | ell | int | wee | ll | nEH | ver |

hav | a | bEtt | er | opp | oar | tOOn |

ih | tee | dOck | ter | kArl | hag | in |

iz | sEck | yure | and | said | ATE | ed

The content of anything she memorized in this way always produced emotional reactions. At first she was overtaken with a wave of confusion, and then a strange chill crossed her skin. She attached these emotions to the line of her memorization. Her heart rate increased. Her jaw clenched tight. The voices continued, alternating, rising, falling. She detected anger in them, anxiety, and then they ceased.

Her eyes popped open. She found her fists clenched and her lips twisted in a snarl. One of the speakers was extremely angry at the end. That, or what they had said had evoked anger in her. She wouldn't know until she had a chance to review it.

She got to her feet and crept down the hall toward the hacienda's entry doors. She would still go to the dojo, but instead of working out, she would review the conversation.

She got to the door, grasped the latch, and pushed. She was met with a waft of very heavy Caribbean air.

"There you are, Miss Jacey." Mr. Justin's voice froze her mid-step. "I wasn't expecting you to be awake this early."

"I was just going down to the dojo for a workout." She turned and smiled at Dr. Carlhagen's butler. He returned the smile, crow's-feet at the corners of his almond-shaped eyes crinkling all the way to his temples. He had such a kindly face, one that conveyed infinite patience and calm confidence.

"I'm afraid that will have to wait if you want to be in on the conversation between Humphrey and Captain Wilcox."

Momentary confusion made Jacey hesitate. Had Humphrey been in the office with Mr. Justin? "Is he awake?"

"Not yet," Mr. Justin said. "I was just going to get him. Captain Wilcox called me early this morning. He demanded to speak with Dr. Carlhagen. He's not satisfied with the state of affairs here. Unless Humphrey calms his nerves, we'll have armed men posted here by the end of the day."

Jacey relaxed. That had to be what Mr. Justin had been arguing with Captain Wilcox about.

"I'll be there," she said. "Humphrey's not going to like this."

"He's done well so far." Mr. Justin's hands hung loose at his side, though he rubbed his thumb against his pinky. "I can coach him through what to say. And he's going to have to hold more of these conversations if we're going to continue the fiction that he is Dr. Carlhagen."

"What choice do we have?" Jacey asked, stepping into the entryway and letting the door swing closed behind her.

"I'll go wake Humphrey now and have him suit up."

Jacey snorted. "I think he hates wearing that suit more than he hates pretending to be Dr. Carlhagen."

"As you say, Miss Jacey." Mr. Justin gave a curt bow, then walked down the hall toward Humphrey's room.

Jacey blew out a long breath and pulled her hair from her ponytail. It seemed like even her smallest plans came to nothing.

She went back to her room to change into her uniform, a black top with a mandarin collar, loose black pants. Her hunger faded, replaced by queasiness. They absolutely had to keep Captain Wilcox and his men away from the island of St. Vitus and the Scion School.

Otherwise she would never be able to keep her vow that no Progenitor would transfer his or her mind into a Scion's ever again.

Not ever.

2

5:06 A.M

Belle came awake with a great gasp, sat up in her bunk, and slapped away the hand shaking her shoulder. The predawn gray filtered through the windows of Girls' Hall, sucking all the color from the dormitory.

Someone—a black silhouette—loomed over her. Belle shrank away from it, skin prickling.

"Belle," the figure hissed, "it's me."

Belle relaxed. A continuous chime sounded from beneath her pillow. She dug out her reader and silenced the alarm.

"Go back to bed," she told Leslie, whose face hovered much too close in the darkness. The girl was her Second, and once Belle was gone, she would lead the Nine. Belle didn't have much hope for the girls then. Leslie was none too smart in her opinion.

Belle's bunk shifted as Leslie dropped her weight onto the edge. "Why is your alarm going off so early?"

"A mistake. Go back to sleep." Belle flopped onto her pillow and rubbed her bleary eyes. She had put the reader under her pillow, hoping that the sound would wake her before anyone else in Girls' Hall. As usual, she'd slept right through it.

She listened as Leslie climbed to the top bunk and crawled under the covers. Gauging from the sounds of snoring all around, Belle's alarm hadn't awakened anyone else.

She tapped her reader again and checked the time.

5:06 a.m.

The hurricane winds had settled only a few hours earlier, and Belle didn't think any of the girls had gotten to sleep before that. She waited a few more minutes before getting out of her warm bed and creeping to the bathroom.

Seeing the girls all snuggled under their covers irritated Belle. They were all ignorant and lazy. They had no idea what had really transpired a few days before. Sensei and Nurse Smith carried off in a helicopter, Sarah throwing herself off the bell tower. And Vaughan . . .

She refused to finish the thought.

Though she wanted to rouse the others, kick their bunks, make them go into the quad and begin cleaning up, she left them alone. Besides, she had set this early alarm so she could go out before any of them.

She had something very important to do. Someone very important to see.

3

HORMONAL WHIRLWINDS

Jacey kept a hand pressed to her belly as she followed Humphrey and Mr. Justin into the dark-paneled office that had once belonged to Dr. Carlhagen. The huge mahogany desk sat empty in the middle, and a wide-bladed ceiling fan spun lazily overhead.

The room smelled stale and damp. The wide window behind the desk showed the hazy shapes of palm trees outside. And though the slatted louvers were open, no breeze wafted through. The hurricane had used up all the energy in the atmosphere, leaving the world in silence.

Jacey's stomach churned and her throat felt so dry she thought she could drink a liter of water in one gulp.

"Go ahead," she said to Humphrey. "Let's get this over with."

Humphrey nodded without looking at her. He walked around to sit in Dr. Carlhagen's chair. He wore one of the old headmaster's white suits, the too-wide collar gaping, pants belted so tightly the fabric pleated in odd places. Though they shared the exact same DNA, Humphrey was seventy-five years younger than Dr. Carlhagen and perhaps half his circumference.

She was used to seeing Humphrey in the official Scion School uniform, and the ill-fitting suit looked ridiculous.

At least the bow tie brings out the blue of his eyes, Jacey thought.

She pulled her hand away from her stomach, fingers habitually going to her collar to check the Shark pin.

It wasn't there.

Instead, a lock of hair fell across the collar, another symbol of her rebellion against the old ways. No more ponytails, no more pins. If she'd had anything else to wear—besides the gowns Dr. Carlhagen had given her—she would've put her uniform in the burning barrel by the front gate.

Humphrey nervously licked his lips as Mr. Justin patted him on the back.

"You'll do fine," Mr. Justin said, eyes crinkling. He wore linen pants and a top similar in cut to Jacey's own uniform, although his was white. "Just assure Captain Wilcox that everything is under control."

Jacey's hand returned to her stomach. It roiled as if it couldn't make up its mind over whether she was hungry or nervous. Maybe she should have eaten something.

Humphrey's conversation with Captain Wilcox would be the first contact they'd had with the outside world since the Captain had taken off in his helicopter with Sensei and Nurse Smith. Humphrey had fooled Captain Wilcox once before, convincing him that Humphrey was Dr. Carlhagen. That time he'd done it in person, which meant doing it again over holovid should be easier. That fact didn't settle Jacey's stomach in the least.

Mr. Justin backed up, well out of view of the holodesk's cameras. Humphrey gave one last sigh and placed his hands on the desk. "Captain Wilcox?"

A twelve-centimeter-tall holovid of Captain Wilcox appeared above the desk, the glow of his image lighting Humphrey's face a ghostly blue and casting strange shadows in his sunken cheeks. Jacey thought he might never recover from his days in the pit, no matter how much he ate.

"Good morning, Captain," Humphrey said with a chuckle, an eerie imitation of Dr. Carlhagen that brought a chill to Jacey's skin. She knew Humphrey was a clone of Dr. Carlhagen, but his normal behavior was quite different from the elderly headmaster's. To see him playacting so well . . .

"Good morning, Dr. Carlhagen," Captain Wilcox replied, eyes emotionless, voice clipped. "I hope all is—"

"Yes, yes. Everything is fine. How was your return trip to the mainland?" Humphrey's interruption was a tactic Jacey had suggested—a way for Humphrey to take control of the conversation, just as Dr. Carlhagen would have.

Captain Wilcox stood at attention, hands to his side, chest out. Even as a little holo, he projected a cold air of violence. Not unlike Sensei.

Jacey remembered confronting the man and his gunmen in the rain, begging him not to take Sensei away. Square-jawed and thickly built, Wilcox had the eyes of a predator.

"The return trip was interesting," he said. "Have you ever flown in a helicopter through a hurricane?"

Humphrey laughed. "Can't say that I have. Such adventures are for younger men." He stopped as if realizing what he was saying, and then he laughed louder. "But perhaps I *should* try it now. And what of Mario Rosa and Nurse Smith?"

"They are somewhere in the Caribbean Sea, presumably bloated and decomposing. Or, if we're lucky, already eaten by sharks."

The man's cold words made Jacey's cheeks go hot with fury. Before his transfer, Dr. Carlhagen had instigated Protocol Seven, which called for the removal and murder of

Sensei and Nurse Smith in retaliation for supposed insubordination. Sensei had tried to fight, but Captain Wilcox and his men had taken him at gunpoint. Nurse Smith had gone willingly, having no clue what lay in store for her.

Jacey wanted to grab the little hologram and squeeze the life out of the man.

Humphrey frowned at her, clearly wondering what her problem was. She blew out a long breath and motioned for him to keep going.

"Is something wrong, Doctor?" Captain Wilcox asked.

"No, no," Humphrey said, covering his long hesitation. "I was just thinking that I have to replace Sensei Rosa and Nurse Smith soon."

"I was going to ask you about that. Perhaps I should send a few men to maintain order on campus until you recruit replacements."

"Totally unnecessary. Now that the storm is over, things will return to normal. Classes will resume. The Scions are well trained, I assure you."

"I wasn't referring to the storm. And with all due respect, when I was there, things did not appear orderly. I witnessed a deranged Scion throw another Scion from the bell tower. Not to mention other Scions running about and interfering with my men's duties."

Jacey shivered. Just hearing Captain Wilcox talk about that stormy night brought back visions—of Sarah at the top of the bell tower wearing Jacey's dinner gown. And of Dr. Carlhagen, freshly transferred into Vaughan's body, throwing Sarah over the railing. That had been enough for Captain Wilcox to arrest Vaughan and, at Jacey's urging, sedate him in the medical ward.

Only quick thinking by Mr. Justin had kept Captain Wilcox from posting men there at that time. Mr. Justin had taken Humphrey into the transfer room and positioned him so that it appeared Dr. Carlhagen had just completed transferring to his body.

"I know what you saw, Captain," Humphrey said. "And believe me, I was as concerned as you. But I assure you the problem was specific to a few individuals. With AI assistance, I've already developed an error-checking and correction process for all future transfers."

"And what about the crazy one?" Captain Wilcox asked. "What will you tell his Progenitor? Whoever he is, he won't want to transfer into a mind so obviously unstable."

"That particular Progenitor is dead."

Humphrey chuckled at Captain Wilcox's startled look.

The man recovered quickly. "Still, you have an unneeded Scion. Should I send some men to dispose of him?"

Humphrey's lips moved as he searched for some reason why a deranged Scion shouldn't be disposed of. "He's a valuable subject for study. And I . . . I could prepare him to receive a different transfer, perhaps a client too old to wait for a clone to come of age, someone who wouldn't mind waking up in a different body—a superior body."

Jacey glanced at Mr. Justin, who nodded appreciatively at Humphrey's quick thinking. The butler had been so helpful. But he'd also said it was inevitable that all the Scions would eventually be overwritten. Said it was futile to fight it.

Jacey tried to relax her jaw, which she was clenching so hard it made her head hurt.

Humphrey was on a roll, having caught the flow of his own lies. "Please rest easy, Captain. Everything is under control here. Your Scion is doing superbly well, by the way. And remember, of the last four transfers, three worked flawlessly. I found the source of the problem with the other one, and it will not happen again."

Jacey couldn't read Captain Wilcox's face, but the tension

in his shoulders and the way he clenched his fists conveyed a whole lot of doubt.

After a long pause, he submitted to Humphrey's decision. "Very well. Let me know if you need anything else. Captain Wilcox out."

The holovid disappeared, and Humphrey sagged into his chair, inflating his cheeks on a big sigh. "I don't even know what I just said."

"All that matters is that he believed you and accepted your decision," Mr. Justin said. "You did very well. And you ended the call just in time, because I've just received notice that a VIP Progenitor wants to speak to you immediately."

"VIP?" Jacey mused. "You mean some Progenitors are more important than others?"

Mr. Justin clasped his hands in front of him. "Even the elite have their pecking order."

Humphrey rubbed the corners of his eyes. "I'm not ready to have a conversation with a Progenitor."

"You'll do fine," Mr. Justin said. "You did wonderfully with Captain Wilcox. This Progenitor probably just wants an update since she knows that St. Vitus was in the path of the hurricane. You must take this call."

Humphrey put his hands over his face. "I hate this."

Mr. Justin handed a slip of paper to Humphrey. "Just stay positive. Answer in generalities."

"Who is this VIP, anyway?" Jacey asked. "Why can't she wait?"

"It's Senator Maxine Bentilius. Very important in North American governance. When she calls, Dr. Carlhagen always answers."

"Let's get it over with," Humphrey said. He moved his chair forward and cleared his face of dread. At least, he made an attempt. Jacey thought he looked ill.

"I'm patching her through now." Mr. Justin tapped his

finger on a tablet, and another holovid appeared over Dr. Carlhagen's desk, this one a starkly redheaded elderly woman. She wore a black skirt and charcoal jacket cut to accentuate her feminine curves. A profusion of salmon-colored ruffles blossomed from the throat of the jacket so that her head appeared to sprout from a bouquet of peonies.

"It's about time you answered, Doctor." Her voice was deep, throaty. "I've been on hold for fifteen minutes."

"I'm sorry, Madam Senator," Humphrey said. "I was on another call. We just got through the worst of a hurricane, and there is an endless list of tasks I must attend to."

"I'm sure," she said, though her voice conveyed utter disinterest in the small details of hurricane recovery.

"How may I help you?" Humphrey asked.

"I wish to transfer to my Scion immediately."

Humphrey and Jacey both glanced at Mr. Justin, who seemed just as shocked as they were. He pointed at the slip of paper he'd given Humphrey.

Humphrey cleared his throat and glanced at it. He paled further, then rallied and looked back at the holovid. "But your Scion is not of age. The contract clearly stipulates that transfer can happen no sooner than when the Scion attains the age of eighteen."

"Do you think I'm stupid? My Scion won't be of age for four years, but I have, at best, four weeks to live."

Humphrey hid his confusion by rubbing his temples. "But the Scion's brain at age fourteen is still developing. Transfer would be extremely risky."

Fourteen? That could be only one of two girls on campus. Jacey glanced at Mr. Justin, but his face revealed nothing.

"I know we haven't spoken for a while," Senator Bentilius said. "But don't you follow the news? I have stage-four brain cancer. It's inoperable. So you'll appreciate that I care very little about the risk. What's the worst that could happen? I might die? Same thing that's going to happen to me anyway."

"You might end up a vegetable, or insane," Humphrey said. "We had some difficulty with a recent transfer."

The senator dismissed Humphrey's objection with a slight twist of her lips. "But if it works, the only downside is that I have to endure the hormonal whirlwinds of my teenage years again."

Jacey waved her hands to get Humphrey's attention. He glared at her.

"Stall for time," she mouthed.

"When were you thinking of coming down?" Humphrey asked Senator Bentilius.

"Immediately," the senator replied. "I have a jet standing by to take me to San Juan, and a helicopter from there to St. Vitus."

"Well, as I mentioned before, we are recovering from a hurricane, and our power systems are not yet fully functional. You said you have four weeks. Give us at least three weeks to put things back in order. If we perform a transfer and lose power again, it would mean automatic death for you."

"I'll be there in twelve hours. I will have my security detail with me to offer assistance with the clean up." She turned as if listening to someone off-camera on her side of the transmission. She clapped her hands together and nodded, then turned to address Humphrey. "I'll need the current clothing size for my Scion so I can bring proper attire."

"But—"

"Don't fight me on this, Christof. I can make things very difficult for you. You've escaped public scrutiny thus far. Your clients understand the importance of secrecy. But if I'm going to die, what the hell do I care about secrecy?"

Humphrey sighed. "Very well, Madam Senator. I will

have Mr. Justin send that information to your people. I'll see you soon."

The senator disappeared.

Humphrey glanced at the slip of paper Mr. Justin had given him. He swore and closed his eyes.

Jacey went to him, put her hand on his back. "You did the best you could. Now we need to plan—"

She stopped, realizing where her sentence was leading. They either needed to fight, or they needed to escape. And if the senator's security people were anything like the gunmen who worked for Captain Wilcox, they'd be armed to the teeth.

Humphrey said nothing, merely handed her the slip. She took it. In Mr. Justin's cramped handwriting was the name of the senator's Scion. A fourteen-year-old girl who just days ago had received her Spider pin. A member of Jacey's Nine.

Summer.

4

—————

SENSE DATA

Belle crept out of Girls' Hall and onto the quad. The light mounted above the dojo was off, and only the slightest hint of the approaching dawn stained the sky beyond the eastern hills. She couldn't see what state the hurricane had left the campus in, but she'd seen the aftermath of enough storms to know to proceed with caution.

Even so, her next step came up short, toe smashing into something hard. She pitched forward and fell with a grunt onto the saturated grass of the quad.

Belle cursed under her breath as she climbed to her feet. She brushed at the filth covering her uniform. Her entire left side was soaked, and her big toe throbbed.

Gritting her teeth against the pain, she squatted and felt around for the object she'd tripped over. She found it. A hunk of Spanish tile blown from one of the buildings.

She considered going back to change her clothes but decided against it. She wanted to get on with her plan.

Going even slower, she probed with her feet before committing her steps. As her eyes adjusted, she made out more of the debris littering the quad. Most of it was foliage, leaves shorn from trees. The biggest were twisted tree limbs, which hunched here and there, shadowy and skeletal.

Three days of hurricane rain had saturated the ground, and the grass squished beneath her canvas shoes. Despite the evidence of recent chaos, a quiet lay over the campus. Even the bugs and frogs seemed satisfied to keep the silence for a while.

Belle paused to breathe deeply the island's heady scent, a mélange of bitter greenery, bougainvillea blossoms, and the sea. The smell evoked a feeling of relief. She supposed that was because this particular aroma arose only after big storms.

It's all just sense data, she thought.

An excellent term. *Sense data.*

She remembered a lecture Socrates had given about a brain's perception of its environment. Sight, smell, sound, taste, and touch were all merely data her senses sent to the brain. Preferences for—or aversions to—any particular sensory input were developed by conditioning.

If a smell came along with something pleasant, she would grow to like the smell. If a smell came along with something painful, she would dislike it.

Simple.

And yet . . .

Belle could not figure out what sense data or conditioning compelled her to go to the medical ward at this early hour. She had puzzled over it, theorized about it, and berated herself for not seeing it. All she knew was that Vaughan was there, and that when she was near him, she felt . . . something.

That she didn't understand the feeling irritated her more.

And that she was knowingly giving into the feeling worried her.

Why couldn't she turn away and forget him? And after what he'd said to her . . .

"Unhand me, girl. You have the allure of an eel!"

No, she reminded herself. That had been Dr. Carlhagen talking.

Belle picked her way through more fallen branches and chunks of tile. The noxious, rotten odor of stagnant water hovered over the pit in the center of the quad. She gave its grated maw a wide berth. Another aversion response, she realized. Having spent the better part of a day in the pit, she never wanted to go near it again, let alone smell its smells.

She continued on her way until she came to the medical ward. A chill rose on Belle's skin as she stepped up to the door. The last time she'd been there, something very bad had happened. Another classic aversion response, she decided. Nothing more. Just the brain doing what the brain did.

She slipped into the entry foyer of the ward and felt along the wall for the light switch. She flipped it, not expecting much. Hurricanes usually cut the power.

The light fixture hanging from the ceiling flickered on. The space was small and unadorned. Nurse Smith's desk stood before a steel door that led to the main ward.

Bell pushed on the steel door. It didn't budge. She tapped on the security screen next to it. "Unlock the door."

The avatar of a beefy man wearing a uniform and holstered sidearm appeared on the screen. Chax, the security AI. He was one of the alter egos of Madam LaFontaine's, the school's master AI.

"Password," he prompted.

"It's an emergency."

"Explain."

Belle put a hand to her head. "I have a terrible migraine. I need to find some medicine."

Chax pursed his lips and crossed his arms. "I'll check with

Jacey."

Belle gritted her teeth. It didn't surprise her that Jacey had connived to take over the school, but it made her want to vomit. "Why is it up to Jacey? Why not Mr. Justin?"

Mr. Justin was only a butler, but since Sensei, Nurse Smith, and Dr. Carlhagen were all gone, Mr. Justin was the oldest person on campus. It made far more sense that he take over than Jacey, at least until Sensei's replacement arrived.

"Madam LaFontaine decided Jacey was in charge," Chax said.

Belle cocked her head and considered this. Of course Jacey had wriggled her way into Madam LaFontaine's good graces. It was typical of her. But had she become so favored that she could decide who got into the medical ward? It made no sense.

"Let me speak to Madam LaFontaine."

"She's busy."

A ridiculous statement. Chax *was* Madam LaFontaine or, at least, a version of her. "I guess I'll just have to spend the day in my bed. My head hurts far too much to show up for dance rehearsal."

She turned to go.

"Wait a minute, young lady."

Belle turned to find Madam LaFontaine's avatar had replaced Chax's. The ageless woman wore her black leotard with a gauzy skirt, her hair pulled into a severe bun. One of her pencil-thin eyebrows rose in disapproval. "We've already missed three days with this nuisance storm. And though I no longer *have* to teach you, I've agreed to Jacey's request to continue lessons for a while longer."

"All I need is a couple of ibuprofen," Belle said. "It'll only take a minute."

"Very well."

The door lock clicked and Belle pushed through.

5

CRAZY IDEAS ABOUT FIGHTING

Jacey stood at the window behind Dr. Carlhagen's mahogany desk. Humphrey and Mr. Justin had gone to prepare for Senator Bentilius's arrival, mostly to give Humphrey background on the senator so he could converse intelligently with her without blowing everything.

Except, they were going to *have* to blow everything.

Jacey would never allow the bossy old hag to overwrite Summer.

The only question that mattered was how to prevent it.

Jacey yanked the desk chair back and plopped into it. Scooching forward, she placed her hands on the desk and summoned Vaughan.

His holo appeared above the desk, just as Senator Bentilius's had. The difference was that Jacey wasn't in remote communication with Vaughan. Instead, he appeared as a computer-generated avatar, the only form he could take since he'd been installed on Socrates's server. When Dr. Carlhagen had overwritten Vaughan, the AI had made a backup image of Vaughan's brain. A stroke of luck, since it kept Vaughan alive . . . in a way.

He gazed at her, face as serene and beautiful as a sunset. He wore his uniform, Shark pin on the collar. But instead of the close-cropped hair all Scion boys wore, Vaughan's hair fell over his shoulders in a tumble of brown waves.

"I need you to zap back into your body," Jacey said. "Things are spinning out of control, and I need your help." She explained Humphrey's conversation with Senator Bentilius.

Vaughan blinked as if he hadn't really been paying attention. "I think we'd be best served if I stay where I am for a while."

"You could do both," Jacey said. "I spoke to Greta about it already. She doesn't need to delete your AI instance to overwrite Dr. Carlhagen with the backup she made."

"I don't like it. If she restores me from the backup, that version of me won't know anything I've learned here. Besides, I don't want to propagate the evil of transfers, even if Dr. Carlhagen deserves it."

"Propagate? When did you start using big words like that?"

Like all Scions, Vaughan was extremely intelligent, but his training had been focused on mathematics and economics, not literature. In the flesh, he'd always been plain-spoken, seeking to connect with others rather than to hit them over the head with his genius. Jacey, on the other hand, had received that accusation from her peers more than once.

"Please, Vaughan," she said. "We can't keep Dr. Carlhagen sedated forever, and there are some dangerous people coming. I have no place to hide him."

Vaughan's image began to pace. "I need to stay in this form. There's too much to be learned here. When Socrates was deleted, he left behind a huge amount of knowledge. I've been processing it, trying to defragment the data and put it into some kind of order. Already I've learned how to do this . . ." He snapped his fingers and transformed into Socrates, long white beard and all.

Seeing her old mentor—and the person who had helped her piece together the truth of what the Scions were—brought a lump to Jacey's throat. "Don't, Vaughan. It's not respectful."

He switched back to himself. "Sorry."

Jacey leaned closer to his avatar, wishing she could touch him. "Please. The Scions don't even have an instructor anymore. What am I going to do to fill their days? I need your help."

"I'll teach them."

He said it so simply that Jacey almost started to agree. "Wait. What?"

"I'll teach them. I have access to enough of Socrates's leftover data that I know pretty much where they all left off in their studies."

"You could do that?"

It seemed too good to be true. If Jacey could get things back to normal—at least, some semblance of it—that would give her and Humphrey time to figure out how to protect everyone from future transfers.

"But you can't appear as Socrates," she said. "You'd need to look like someone else."

"How about this?" Vaughan transformed into a tall, gangly man in a strange suit coat and ruffled shirt. His hair fell in long curls over his shoulders. "They can call me Newton."

Jacey leaned back and folded her arms. "I'm assuming this Newton character was a mathematician or something? You still have to teach literature and arts, you know."

Vaughan smiled and spread his arms wide. "I can handle

it. Though I think you underestimate the beauty of physics and calculus."

Jacey had heard other Scions talk about such things, but she'd never been allowed to study any mathematics beyond arithmetic. Dr. Carlhagen had focused her training almost entirely on literature and memorization skills. And dance. Which got her thinking about another problem. "With Sensei gone, there's no one to lead workouts or martial arts training."

"Have Elias do it. He's the best fighter on campus."

Jacey winced, remembering just how good Elias was. It was his kick that had put Vaughan in a coma. And Elias had been an outcast ever since. "He's persona non grata for kicking you in the head. I doubt most of the Scions would tolerate him in that position."

Vaughan morphed back into himself. "There's Sang from Humphrey's Nine. He's not the most talented, but he's solid and probably has the right temperament for teaching."

Sang did everything with precision but without much energy. Also, he rarely spoke. Jacey doubted he'd be able to control the more boisterous and aggressive Scions. But there weren't any other good options. Except . . .

"What about Leslie?"

Vaughan stroked his chin and nodded. "Her tai chi forms are very good. Not sure about actual fighting skills, since Sensei never let girls spar with us."

That had been another of Jacey's complaints. She had taken dance with Madam LaFontaine, but the only martial arts training she'd gotten was tai chi. Sensei only had her go through the slow forms, never at speed, and she had never sparred with anyone.

"I'm going to change that," she said. "From now on, girls will be trained to fight."

"I don't disagree," Vaughan said. "But nobody should get

any crazy ideas about fighting with hands and feet against people with firearms."

He was right, of course. Sensei had succeeded in taking down two gunmen when Captain Wilcox had come for him. But there had been too many of them. And a man with a gun could kill a martial arts master as easily as he could kill a novice.

"I think I'll assign Sang and Leslie to teach together," she said. "Sang for the technique and Leslie for the discipline. And I will tell them to start training the girls."

Until Jacey could figure out what to do about the whole mind transfer problem, the Scions needed to stay occupied. Training would help use up their energy, which would otherwise turn toward mischief. After all, she'd been the worst offender about breaking the rules recently.

Vaughan started to respond, but stopped when Mr. Justin stepped into the room.

"Miss Jacey," the butler said, "I just received notice from Chax that Madam LaFontaine has admitted Miss Belle to the medical ward. I'm not sure what—"

Jacey was out the door before he finished the sentence.

6

REVENGE MADE HER SLOPPY

Belle's steps rang hollowly in the main medical ward. The windows were shut, and the slow spin of the ceiling fans did little to stir the heavy air filling the huge room. The dark forms of cots lining the walls were mere shadows in the gloom.

Though she moved quickly, Belle's heart beat much faster than her exertion demanded.

A nervous response, she thought. She didn't know what was going to happen when she saw Vaughan.

She approached the steel door at the back of the room, put her hands to the latch. She paused a moment, willing her pulse to slow.

It refused.

Hands trembling, she opened the door and stepped into a corridor with rooms to the right and to the left. At the end of the hall stood another door, which she knew led to the transfer room.

Belle quietly stepped to the third holding room on the left.

Vaughan's room. She unlocked the door, slipped in, and flipped on the light.

Squinting against the piercing brightness, she went to Vaughan's side.

Vaughan didn't wake up. An IV bag hung from a stand next to his gurney, the tube snaking down to where it connected to a needle stabbed into a vein on the top of his right hand.

Belle had seen Jacey adjust the drip before and did likewise, turning it off entirely. Vaughan's eyes fluttered open, and he shifted his eyes to stare at her. His vision seemed bleary. He didn't recognize her. But then his pupils shrank and his brows came together.

"Belle?" His voice was raspy, and he licked weakly at his dry, flaking lips. "Why are you here?"

Belle didn't answer right away. She didn't know how to answer. All she knew was that she had loved Vaughan since they were Dolphins. Even before that.

Vaughan had always been closer to Jacey. The thought made Belle's shoulders tighten. She didn't understand why everyone thought Jacey was so great. She was always breaking the rules and strutting around with that smug look on her face.

But now, impossibly, Jacey had rejected Vaughan and turned her lascivious eyes on Humphrey.

And the story Jacey had concocted about Vaughan—that his mind was gone, replaced entirely by Carlhagen's—was beyond belief. That whole transfer thing might work on weak-minded people like Sarah and Dante, but on Vaughan?

Not a chance.

Belle believed Dr. Carlhagen had *tried* to overwrite Vaughan. After all, Vaughan had acted very strangely that night when Sarah had jumped to her death. He'd certainly said some awful things to Belle then, too.

Surely all Vaughan needed was a bit of rest. He was the strongest Scion, and if anyone could fight off Dr. Carlhagen, Vaughan could.

He gazed at her with those lovely, intense eyes. His face was perfectly symmetrical except for a prominent vein on one temple. And Belle thought he was more beautiful for it.

She placed her hand on his forehead, tentatively at first. He closed his eyes and sighed.

"How are you feeling?" she asked.

"My head is killing me. But my mind is clearing. Belle, I'm —" He clamped his mouth shut.

Belle waited. She knew that he remembered the horrible insult he'd thrown at her. It had to be eating him up, because Vaughan was generous and kind.

And then he proved it. "I'm sorry for what I said to you. After Elias knocked me out, my thinking has not been that clear. And Dr. Carlhagen was playing very strange games with me. He had me strapped to a bed in the hacienda, and he kept coming in and telling me all the horrible things he was doing to you and Jacey and Humphrey. It just made me crazy."

That was so Vaughan, to be thinking of everyone else while he suffered. If this boy before her were still Dr. Carlhagen, he never would have apologized.

"I forgive you," she said softly, allowing her face to match her words.

"Would you unstrap me?"

Her hands went to the strap around his chest and started loosening the buckle. She caught herself and stopped. "I should probably talk to Jacey about it first."

The words were out of her mouth before she realized what she was saying.

Vaughan's eyes widened, and he laughed humorlessly. "Since when have you ever listened to her?"

Belle wanted to let Vaughan go just because of what she had said, but she had to be careful. Acting out of emotion could make things worse. Over the past few days, she had done some impulsive things, and they had all gone very poorly, including her attempt at punishing Jacey.

Lashing the girl with the thornskipple branch had been so satisfying. Jacey had certainly deserved it. But Belle realized the mistake in it. She shouldn't have reveled in it, shouldn't have made it personal, because then it wasn't justice. It was revenge.

Revenge made her sloppy.

She resolved that at the next opportunity to punish Jacey, she would remain cool, would box in her wrath and not wallow in it.

At least, not until it was over.

She folded her hands behind her back to keep them from caressing Vaughan's hair. She had to be logical. She had to make sure.

"Jacey and Humphrey say you are Dr. Carlhagen," she said.

Vaughan closed his eyes and cursed under his breath. "Dr. Carlhagen did try to overwrite me. I can feel him fighting to take control." His eyes popped back open and his lips thinned. "But I'm winning. I'm in control."

"I believe you."

"So you'll release me?"

"Not yet."

There was another reason not to let Vaughan go without talking to Jacey first. Having Jacey as an ally, at least on the surface, would be more effective than having Jacey as an enemy. It would give Belle more freedom of movement until the time came for her to act.

So why not let Jacey manage things until a new martial

arts master showed up to take charge? The whole mess with Livy in the pit and Jacey negotiating with the helicopter gunmen had given her credibility among the other Scions.

Belle tightened the strap. "I'm sorry. I would love to let you go, but I can't do it yet."

He started to object, but she put a finger over his lips and bent close to him.

"Don't worry. I will set you free soon, but right now there's no place for you to hide. Jacey would send the entire campus after you, and you'd be back here in an hour or less."

"But we could escape," Vaughan said, his voice rising in pitch and volume. "I know where the keys to the Jeep are kept, and I know how to open the front gate."

Belle took a step back. "How do you know all this?"

"I—I guess I sometimes see Dr. Carlhagen's thoughts, his memories."

"Oh," Belle said, taking another step back. She supposed that made sense, though it chilled her to think of it. A little thrill zipped down her spine at the thought of running away with Vaughan. "Where would we go?"

"I just need to speak to the AI. They believe I'm Dr. Carlhagen, right? I'll have them summon Captain Wilcox."

"The AI is loyal to Jacey now. Madam LaFontaine has struck some kind of deal with her to preserve the status quo."

Vaughan uttered a series of vile curses, a clear case of Dr. Carlhagen fighting to the surface. With visible effort, he calmed himself, brow smoothing. "We'll go to Mother Tyee-sha's. I can contact the outside from there without going through Madam LaFontaine's filters."

A footstep sounded in the hall. Belle spun and found Jacey swinging the door open. She stood in the doorway, tall, blond, and curvy. The girl seemed incapable of keeping a sultry look off her face. Perhaps it was her full lips, or her aqua eyes, or the habitual way that she cocked her head to one side. Even more brazen, she now wore her hair down. It was typical of Jacey to so blatantly flaunt school dress code.

"What are you doing here?" Jacey demanded.

Belle uttered the exact same words at the same time. She straightened and turned back toward Vaughan's bed. "It's obvious isn't it? I came to check on Vaughan."

"That's not Vaughan. That's Dr. Carlhagen."

Jacey stomped into the room and gave each of Vaughan's straps a sharp tug. "I almost fell for his act, you know. He pretended to rescue me from the pit and took me into the medical ward. I was so relieved to see Vaughan alive and well, so relieved to be out of the pit. Do you know what he did then?"

Belle wanted to run out of the room, wanted to plug her ears to keep from hearing. But the girl pressed on with her hateful story. "He kissed me, said he loved me, took advantage of the fact that he had stripped the gown from me before putting me in the pit, took advantage of my weakened state, of my fear and my relief of being rescued. I had to fight him off or who knows what else he would have done."

The way Jacey said it made it clear that she knew exactly what he would have done. Belle had witnessed some of the altercation, which had happened just outside the room they were currently standing in. But Dr. Carlhagen had been in control of Vaughan then. Once rested, Vaughan had resurfaced. Anyone who truly knew him could see it on his face.

Belle said, "Vaughan is back in control."

Jacey's eyes narrowed. "Dr. Carlhagen is trying to trick you the same way he tricked me." She flipped her hair back with one hand, even more annoying than her old habit of tossing of her ponytail when she was angry.

Belle would have rather swallowed a baby gecko whole

than to say what she said next. But she could see the future forking in many different paths before her. Outright defiance of Jacey's authority would inevitably lead her to place greater controls over the medical ward, making it harder to free Vaughan.

Belle dropped her gaze and looked at her own feet, pretending to be chastised. She wasn't as good of a faker as Jacey, so she couldn't summon tears on command. She made an effort to turn the corners of her mouth down. "I know you're right. It's hard for me to accept that Vaughan is gone. I had to see for myself."

Jacey's body lost its tension, and she touched Belle's shoulder. "I showed you the video of the dogs. You know how mind transfer works. There's nothing left of Vaughan."

"But Sarah fought off Janicka," Belle said. "At least somewhat. And Vaughan—he's so much smarter and so much more capable than Sarah ever was. He's a fighter."

Jacey's eyes shifted to Vaughan. He'd been watching the exchange carefully, eyes darting between Belle and Jacey.

"Jacey's right," Vaughan said to Belle. "Perhaps you shouldn't trust me. I'm not feeling one hundred percent myself. I thought it was the sedative, but maybe it's best to keep me under observation for a while longer."

If Jacey had been suspicious before, her eyes narrowed to mere slits. "You can't fool me, Doctor."

"I'm not trying to fool you," he said. "I wish I could convince you somehow."

"The only thing that will convince me is when we put you in the transfer machine and the AI re-overwrites you with Vaughan."

Jacey's lips broke into a smile when she saw Vaughan's face fall, mouth opening with a look of horror. She stepped closer and put her face close to his. "That's right, Doctor. The

AI retained Vaughan's full brain scan at the time of your transfer."

Vaughan's face turned thoughtful, sorrowful. "I'd always known you to be full of compassion, always thought you were the opposite of Belle in that regard. But now I'm beginning to wonder."

His eyes shifted to Belle's, and his face looked so sad. "I was beginning to see this lovely girl in a new light. It's a shame that will be erased in the blink of an eye." He looked away.

Jacey turned up the IV drip, and Vaughan's eyes instantly unfocused, and his mouth fell open. His breathing slowed.

"Come on," Jacey said. "We're meeting with Humphrey in the hacienda."

"Why should I care?"

Belle instantly regretted her tone. Pretending to be Jacey's ally was going to be harder than she thought. "I mean, why do you need me there?"

Jacey went to the door and held it open, waiting expectantly for Belle to leave. "We Sharks have many decisions to make."

Belle wanted to refuse, but she decided it best to bide her time and not raise too much conflict. She left the room, and Jacey locked the door behind her. Together they left the medical ward and passed back into the quad.

The breeze had picked up, bringing warmer air with it. Golden sun broke over the eastern peaks, casting morning shadows across the campus. A curly-headed girl emerged from Girls' Hall and scurried toward the bell tower. It was Livy, the Dolphin from Jacey's Nine.

Jacey's demeanor changed when she saw the girl. Her face softened, and a fond smile played on her lips. Why Jacey adored Livy, Belle would never understand. Maybe it was because the new Dolphin was as willful and disrespectful of the rules as Jacey.

They stepped over a fallen limb and continued up the gravel path to the hacienda, skirting along Dr. Carlhagen's prized bougainvillea hedgerows.

Jacey looked at Belle and touched her arm again. "We worked together once. When we thought Vaughan was dead, we searched the campus for his body, and then we cooperated to force Nurse Smith to let us into the medical ward."

Belle winced at the mention of Nurse Smith, remembering another time she'd let her emotions take charge of her body. She'd felt so powerful, so full of righteous fury when she'd struck that woman's face.

Belle pulled away from Jacey's touch. "You said there are decisions to make." She barely made it a question, but Jacey must have heard it as such, for she stopped to glance at the quad. The path to the hacienda had taken them high upslope, giving them a wide view of the campus below them.

Jacey said, "There are thirty-six Scions here. Only a dozen of us are thirteen or older. And then there are the little ones at Mother Tyeesha's compound. That's another thirty-six. The great destiny we were promised was a lie. We are just a farm, really. A farm for human bodies. We have to plan, Belle. And we don't have much time. The next Progenitor will arrive in less than twelve hours."

Belle's blood turned to ice. "But that's not possible. We're not set to graduate for nearly a year." The next graduating class included her, Jacey, Vaughan, and Humphrey, and three of those Progenitors were dead.

That left Belle's Progenitor, who would arrive in 360 days.

Jacey started walking again. "It's an emergency transfer. The Progenitor is deathly ill."

"So it's not my Progenitor?" Chills crisscrossed Belle's skin as relief washed over her.

"No."

"Whose is it?"

"Summer's."

The Spider from Jacey's Nine.

Belle relaxed. *There's still time.*

7

THE LINE BETWEEN HERO AND CRIMINAL

The hacienda's carved mahogany entry doors swung inward as Jacey and Belle approached. Mr. Justin stood just inside holding a tray of pastries. The smell of them made Jacey's stomach growl.

The butler bowed slightly, smiling.

He's always so friendly, Jacey thought. *Always so helpful.*

So why wasn't he more forthcoming about how Dr. Carlhagen compensated him? Why did he insist that resisting future transfers was hopeless?

"Is Humphrey in the office?" she asked.

"Yes, Miss Jacey. I had a hunch you'd return with Miss Belle, so I prepared an arrangement of breakfast items."

"Good. I'm starving." She didn't wait for Mr. Justin to lead her into Dr. Carlhagen's old office. Humphrey stood at the window, still in the white suit, staring out at the turquoise sea.

Mr. Justin set the tray on the edge of Dr. Carlhagen's desk. Jacey snatched up a piece of buttered toast and took a bite.

Belle ignored the food. She fell into an at-rest stance, blue eyes straight ahead, porcelain face betraying no emotion. She wore her nearly-white hair in a severe ponytail. It was bound even tighter than usual. Jacey wondered if Belle was trying to make up for her own lapse in form.

Humphrey turned and forced a wan smile at the sight of food. He poked through the items and absently selected a bagel. "I was just thinking that the hurricane might have damaged the fence somewhere along its length. Perhaps it's no longer electrified and we could climb over."

"Oh, the fence is quite intact," Mr. Justin said. "We have sensors mounted along its length that tell us if trees fall against it or if sections become compromised in other ways."

Humphrey swallowed and dabbed crumbs from the corner of his mouth. "I guess we'll have to search Sensei's villa again for the gate control. I wonder if he had it on him when he was taken. Is that coffee?" He pointed at a sliver urn.

"It is, indeed," Mr. Justin said. He swept up a cup and poured the aromatic drink. Humphrey accepted the cup with a grim smile and sipped. He let out a contented sigh.

Jacey had never had coffee until Sensei had made some for her. Since then, she had gotten Humphrey hooked on it as well.

She took a cup from Mr. Justin and carried it to the window. She sipped and peered toward the fence line. Its razor wire top sparkled in the morning sunlight.

She hated it.

Its only purpose was to keep her and the rest of the Scions trapped inside of this small section of the island. Now that Sensei and Dr. Carlhagen were gone, it was only a matter of time until the Scions started clamoring to be let out to explore the rest of the island.

Not that they'd be getting out anyway. No one could find the gate opener, and Madam LaFontaine absolutely refused to open it.

Just as well the gate stays closed, Jacey thought. The last thing she needed was Scions sneaking out and getting lost.

She sipped more coffee, then took the seat behind the desk, skin warming under Humphrey's gaze as he followed her movements. Though his cornflower eyes looked just like Dr. Carlhagen's, she welcomed his attention.

He was like coffee in a way. Bitter at first. But once she'd acquired the taste, his presence filled her with warmth and energy.

She'd never felt anything from a boy's stare before. But now she was hooked.

Belle clamped her lips tightly together, clearly disapproving of Jacey's presumption to sit in the position of power. But somebody had to sit there, and Jacey was too tired to stand.

Mr. Justin stood patiently by the door. She glanced at him. "That'll be all."

His smile faded to impassivity. With a slight flash of one brow, he backed out of the room and closed the door behind him.

Jacey turned to Humphrey. "I've updated Belle about the situation with Summer. We need to figure out how to protect her. The only weapons I know of are Mr. Justin's rifle and Dr. Carlhagen's pistol. We'll have to ask Mr. Justin to bring them out from wherever he's got them locked away. I have no idea how much ammunition is on hand."

Humphrey's lips parted, and he set his cup on a sideboard. "Are you seriously suggesting we shoot Senator Bentilius and her guards?"

"I told you. I will not allow another mind transfer."

"This Senator Bentilius woman seems especially important. Kill her and her guards, and someone out there will miss them. Then we'll be overrun with outsiders."

"What do you suggest?" She took another bite of toast,

but her mouth had gone dry, making the bread as tasteless as stone.

"Run. Take Summer and hide her until Senator Bentilius succumbs to her disease. She said she only has four weeks to live."

"That would invite even more outsiders for search teams," Belle said. She lifted the coffee urn, pulled off the lid, and sniffed. Shrugging slightly, she poured herself a cup. "Not a smart move at all."

Jacey was surprised Belle had spoken, since she'd made a point of not looking at either her or Humphrey this entire time.

Belle went on, "They'll search the campus millimeter by millimeter. There's no place this side of the fence to hide, and no escape unless you're stupid enough to try building a raft." She took a sip and made a face. "What *is* this?"

Trying to escape by raft would be tantamount to suicide, Jacey knew. The pounding surf made any escape by sea impossible, especially for Scions who had never swum farther than twenty meters from shore, let alone been on a boat.

"If we could get past the fence, there's the whole island," Humphrey said. "There has to be somewhere to hide. A cave or something."

"There's Mother Tyeesha's," Jacey said, tossing the remainder of her toast onto the desk.

"That's the first place they'd look," Belle said. She lowered her eyes to the floor, thin brows furrowing as she puzzled over the problem. "The most obvious answer is probably the best."

"And that is . . . ?" Jacey prompted.

Belle lifted her gaze to meet Jacey's. "Let this Senator person have Summer. It's regrettable, but Summer's been a troublesome Scion anyway. The Progenitor and her guards would come and go, never knowing that Dr. Carlhagen is no longer in control here."

Jacey stood, hands clenched into fists. "You can't be serious."

Belle's face remained expressionless. "You must take the emotion out of the equation to solve it."

"But what if it were you instead of Summer?"

"It *will* be me in a year. Summer's sacrifice will buy us time to prevent any further transfers."

Jacey flopped back into the chair. She saw Belle's logic. But if she took the emotion out, it became too cold of an equation. People weren't numbers.

Besides, math had never been Jacey's forte. "We have less than twelve hours before the senator arrives. I'm not willing to give up just yet. And there's one more issue. I want to get the school back to some semblance of normalcy."

Belle smirked. "Semblance of normalcy? Why don't you speak in plain English for a change? Socrates is no longer here to praise your elocution."

She's trying to bait me, Jacey thought. Whether it was intentional or reflexive, she didn't know. Reacting to Belle would just make things worse, so she kept her face smooth. "What did you tell the others about what happened the other day?"

"I told them that Sarah committed suicide and Dr. Carlhagen died."

"Suicide? I thought everyone saw Vaughan throw her from the bell tower."

Sarah had been overwritten by Janicka, her Progenitor. But something had gone wrong in the mind transfer, and Sarah's awareness hadn't been completely obliterated. As a result, Janicka/Sarah had been disoriented and panicky, which had led her to ascend to the top of the bell tower. But she hadn't jumped. Her fall had been Dr. Carlhagen's doing. Because Sarah had been wearing Jacey's discarded gown, Dr.

Carlhagen—newly transferred into Vaughan's body—had thought that Sarah *was* Jacey. Desperate, he had raced to the top to save her. Enraged upon finding Sarah, he had thrown her over the railing.

"That's not what I saw." Belle said flatly. "Vaughan tried to save Sarah. She broke free and jumped. Vaughan was so overwrought by it that he had to be sedated in the medical ward."

Humphrey laughed quietly to himself. "Excellent lies, Belle. And they believed that?"

Belle's thin brows lowered a fraction of a centimeter. "I told no lies. That's what happened."

Jacey and Humphrey exchanged glances.

"Did anyone actually believe that Sarah jumped of her own volition?" Jacey asked.

"She did jump 'of her own volition,'" Belle said, again mocking Jacey's choice of words. "And the others are very concerned about Vaughan. They know he probably blames himself, though he was the only one who thought fast enough to try to rescue Sarah."

Either Belle was in flat denial or she was lying. Jacey didn't see why Belle would knowingly lie about the events, since it would gain her nothing. That meant Belle was delusional, which actually made more sense. The pale girl had been in love with Vaughan. It also explained her behavior in the medical ward just now. Jacey would have to keep a close eye on Belle.

"So, you said nothing about us being clones?" Jacey asked. "Nothing about mind transfers? Nothing about Dr. Carlhagen overwriting Vaughan?"

"No," Belle said. "And Vaughan is *not* Dr. Carlhagen. Not anymore."

"So you see nothing erratic about his behavior? You're not

the least bit startled that he admitted to being Dr. Carlhagen?"

"I'm not saying that Dr. Carlhagen didn't try to overwrite Vaughan. I'm not stupid. I saw the transfer machine and the dog video." She lifted her chin and looked down her nose at Jacey. "But I know Vaughan. If Sarah could resist being overwritten, then Vaughan certainly could."

Jacey had to admit that if anyone could do it, Vaughan could. But she'd seen no glimmer of Vaughan in those eyes. Even his facial expressions had twisted to resemble Dr. Carlhagen's.

"He just needs time to heal," Belle said, "and he'll be himself again." Her voice was all confidence, but she twisted her coffee cup in her fingers.

Instead of arguing the point, Jacey placed her hands on Dr. Carlhagen's desk. "Vaughan? Would you mind talking to us for a moment?"

He appeared, a glowing hologram above the desk. He wore his uniform, Shark pin on the collar.

He smiled at Jacey. Without turning, he greeted Humphrey and Belle.

Belle's face, always pale, went white as a frangipani petal. Her cup clanked on the desk and nearly toppled as she set it down. She came around to stand next to Jacey. "Socrates, stop it. This isn't funny."

"I'm not Socrates," Vaughan said. "I'm afraid our old mentor and teacher was deleted at Dr. Carlhagen's order. When Dr. Carlhagen transferred from his body to mine, the transfer AI retained a digital image of my brain. It was Jacey who discovered this and came up with the idea to have me installed on Socrates's server."

Jacey said, "Vaughan, would you tell Belle what you discovered?"

"Socrates was working on the Sarah/Janicka problem

before he was deleted. He traced the bug back to a synapse count mismatch. Simply put, Janicka didn't have enough gray matter to completely overwrite Sarah, so a significant proportion of Sarah remained. When the AI conducted Dr. Carlhagen's transfer into my body, the AI made sure to blank out any such leftovers."

Jacey laid a hand on Belle's arm. "That means nothing of Vaughan is left. He can't regain control over his body. "

Belle snatched her arm away. "I can't believe it. I won't believe it." She pointed an accusatory finger at Jacey. "You put this—this machine—up to this."

"I'm sorry," Vaughan said, "but the human form you knew as Vaughan is now completely Dr. Carlhagen."

Belle snapped her mouth shut. All emotion drained from her eyes. Jacey had seen this phenomenon before. It seemed that every time Belle got too emotional, she flipped an internal switch and became stone. There had been a few exceptions. Jacey shivered to remember one in particular, when Belle had lashed her with a thornskipple branch.

Mr. Justin stepped into the office and cleared his throat. "Since you asked me to leave the room so you could futilely discuss ways to protect Summer, I took the opportunity to find the list of Progenitors Dr. Carlhagen entrusted to me." He extended a piece of paper to Jacey.

She took it. Printed in fine black letters was a list of Scions and Progenitors. She found her own name right away. Her Progenitor's full name had been Jacqueline Buchanan. Just above it was Charles Buchanan, Vaughan's Progenitor. Their surnames were the same. An odd coincidence.

Humphrey stood behind her, reading over her shoulder. "Dr. Carlhagen is not on the list."

Mr. Justin shrugged. "Dr. Carlhagen created the list. He knew you were his Scion."

Belle crowded close to Jacey's other shoulder. She slid a finger from her name to her Progenitor. Korra Bolelli.

She grunted, as if dissatisfied with her Progenitor's name. "After my transfer, would this Korra person have returned to the world as Belle Bolelli?"

"That depends on the cover story," Mr. Justin said.

Jacey looked up. "What do you mean 'cover story?'"

"Ah, you've had such amazing educations, and yet there are so many gaps. A cover story is a kind of lie. The Progenitor can't transfer into a Scion's body and then just return to his or her life as if nothing happened. People would notice they had become fifty or sixty years younger overnight. They are all quite wealthy, so they invent a fiction, a lie, that they had an illegitimate son or daughter—or in some cases grandson or granddaughter—that they'd kept secret or hadn't known about. After they transfer into their Scion, they return to the world as that son, daughter, grandson, or granddaughter, having inherited the entirety of their Progenitor's wealth."

"So you're saying that Korra Bolelli is rich?" Belle asked.

"Very."

Jacey leaned back in the chair. "It is difficult to accept that the outside world is not the wasteland Dr. Carlhagen told us it was. But to think that so many have accumulated masses of wealth . . ."

"It is not so many, Miss Jacey. Perhaps a thousandth of a thousandth percent can afford to sponsor a Scion. And of those, Dr. Carlhagen tried to screen out the more despotic types. For the most part, we have no war criminals or dictators amongst our Scions."

"For the most part?" Jacey asked, frowning.

Mr. Justin raised and lowered his hands as if weighing one against the other. "When considering the character of a politician or a general, the line between hero and criminal is a matter of perspective. As for Korra Bolelli, she is among the poorer of the rich. But she's enough of a celebrity that one could find out much about her on the net. I happen to know she was the wife of a very famous racecar driver, Eduardo Bolelli, who was killed in a crash. Dr. Carlhagen told me that Korra hadn't known about her husband's plan to sponsor a Scion at the school until she was going through his paperwork and found the contract. It hadn't been signed yet, but Eduardo had made a deposit. Korra contacted Dr. Carlhagen and asked to sponsor a Scion in her husband's place. Dr. Carlhagen was only too happy to oblige, since at the time he needed the cash."

"Race cars," Humphrey mused. "You mean like the Jeep?"

Mr. Justin let out a dry, raspy laugh. "Only in that both vehicles have four wheels. No, the Jeep is a very specialized vehicle designed for rough terrain. The company that manufactures it has been in business in many forms for well over two hundred years now. Racecars are generally custom-designed. They're low, sleek, and they go over four hundred kilometers per hour on a straightaway."

It was difficult for Jacey to grasp that there was an entire activity around racing cars. It seemed frivolous and wasteful. She struggled to accept that the outside world wasn't a disaster area where humans barely scraped out a meager existence. In fact, Dr. Carlhagen had told the Scions that their purpose was to go into the world and help bring humanity back from the brink of extinction.

All lies, it turned out.

The Progenitors lied, too. Jacey wondered if anyone in the outside world told the truth.

She scanned the list until she came to Summer's name, and there across from it was Senator Bentilius. "There's nothing to indicate this individual is more important than the others. Would you be able to mark the ones on the list who are as important as the senator?"

"I could, but my knowledge is incomplete. And even if I research some of these names, I'm certain that many are pseudonyms. Perhaps even Dr. Carlhagen didn't know their true identities."

"Then how could he screen them out?" she asked.

For the first time that Jacey could remember, Mr. Justin had no response. He pursed his lips and considered the question, though he didn't seem particularly concerned about it.

"I suppose it doesn't matter much right now," Jacey said. "But I'd like to be prepared in case another VIP decides they want to transfer early. This makes it even more important that we not allow Summer's transfer. If Senator Bentilius returns to the outside world as a fourteen-year-old girl, the other Progenitors may get wind of it. They may decide that they also want to transfer early."

Mr. Justin took a slight inhalation as if preparing to respond, but he abruptly closed his mouth.

"What is it?" Jacey demanded.

Mr. Justin said nothing.

"What Mr. Justin is not saying," Belle said, "is that we have to let Senator Bentilius have Summer."

The butler nodded.

Jacey ignored the comment and the nod. A thought nagged at the back of her mind. "Mr. Justin, you just said that the Progenitors want to keep the school and its technology a secret. That means they know it's wrong."

"That's one interpretation," Belle said, though her voice made it clear she thought it ridiculous. She snatched the list from Jacey. "It seems more likely that these people want to keep it secret in order to keep the advantage to themselves. You can't have everyone transferring to a Scion when they get old. If I had access to that type of power, I would keep it secret, share it only among my allies."

Jacey snorted at the idea of Belle having friends. But then, she supposed, allies weren't exactly the same things as friends.

"I hate to say it, but Belle's right," Humphrey said. "I'm guessing these people don't really care if it's wrong. It has more to do with power. It's like our training here on campus. The more time that goes by, the more knowledge we have, right? The more training we had with Sensei, the better our fighting skills, even for those of us who weren't particularly gifted in that art. Now imagine you had lived seventy or eighty years and during that time you had accumulated a vast hoard of knowledge and ability. In addition, you'd also amassed wealth and influence. By transferring to a Scion, you could hold onto all that. With a new young body, you'd give yourself an extra lifetime to build upon what you've already established. Yes, a smart person would want to hoard that ability and make it very difficult to share in it."

"What about right and wrong?" Jacey said plaintively. "The act of overwriting a Scion—a person—is wrong. They *all* have to know that."

Jacey had to believe her own Progenitor had known it was wrong. And how could Livy's Progenitor produce a clone so full of love and wisdom without possessing those qualities, too?

She sighed. The answers to those questions weren't going to help Summer or anyone else.

Mr. Justin clasped his hands and shook his head sadly. "I know it's difficult for you. Believe me, I have not enjoyed watching all of you grow up, knowing that you will be over-written by people who in most regards are your inferiors. But it is as inevitable as the rise and setting of the sun."

With that, he left the office.

His comments irritated Jacey, not only because they were true, but also because he wasn't willing to fight. Now she suspected he had a Scion of his own. It was the only thing that made sense.

She scanned the list again. No one named Justin was on the list, but he had said that some Progenitors used pseudonyms. He must have done the same himself. Could it be that Dr. Carlhagen hadn't even known that Mr. Justin had a Scion?

Which Scion could it be? Offhand, Jacey couldn't think of anyone who bore the slightest resemblance to Mr. Justin.

Jacey stood, conscious of the time flying by. "I'm going to speak to Summer. She has a right to know what is happening. And a right to make a decision for herself about whether she will fight or flee."

Belle grabbed Jacey's elbow to stop her. "She has no such right."

Jacey snatched her arm away and spun on Belle. "How can you be so cavalier about the life of one of your sisters?"

"She's not my sister. She's not even in my Nine. But even if she were, I'd give her up. Any resistance that you or Summer make has consequences for all the other Scions you claim to care so much about. If Summer fights or runs away and it brings down a troop of gunmen on this island, don't you think it'll make it that much more difficult to save the rest of us?"

Jacey opened her mouth, but no argument came out. She couldn't find one.

Belle gave Jacey one last long stare. "Think before you act for a change, Jacey." She brushed past her and out of Dr. Carlhagen's office.

Humphrey collapsed into a side chair as if he'd been struggling to stay upright while Belle was in the room. "I hate to say it again, but she's right."

8

A PURELY LOGICAL STANDPOINT

Belle pocketed the Progenitor and Scion list as she left the hacienda. Fortunately Jacey and Humphrey were so involved in themselves that they hadn't noticed her walking off with it. She'd taken it on a whim, on instinct. Perhaps it would be useful once she was off the island. She didn't know exactly how, but she'd rather have it than not.

She threw nervous glances behind her as she hurried down the gravel path from the hacienda to the campus. It was clear from the conversation in Dr. Carlhagen's office that Jacey wasn't going to allow Senator Bentilius to overwrite Summer. She was far too emotionally attached to the other Scions to see reason. Belle knew there was nothing anyone could do to stop Progenitors from overwriting Scions. That meant her Progenitor would arrive on St. Vitus in a year—probably with a force of armed men—and Belle, too, would be overwritten.

Fortunately, Belle thought she saw a way out, for herself at least.

The first objective was to get back into the medical ward.

Belle assumed Jacey would give the guardian AI fresh instructions to keep her out. That Jacey had become such a busy body was no surprise. She'd always been bossy with everyone, so full of herself. It made Belle want to hit something.

But no. This was not the time to release her fury. For the moment, she needed to keep her thoughts clear. Jacey was predictable. She'd run directly to Summer and drag her to the medical ward to show her how the mind transfer technology worked.

That presented an opportunity—if a somewhat risky one — for Belle to get back in.

Belle got to the bottom of the path and scanned the quad. It lay empty. Apparently the students had been summoned to class. She cut left and darted up the front steps of the medical ward. Inside, Nurse Smith's metal desk sat in front of the steel door that locked off the rest of the ward.

Belle knew better than to argue with the AI again. Instead, she ducked under the desk. She sat cross-legged and fell into one of the deep-breathing exercises Sensei had taught her. She had never enjoyed them, but if there had ever been a time for her to meditate, this was it.

Now all she had to do was wait for Jacey to do her part.

∘ ∘ ∘

A long silence stretched in Dr. Carlhagen's office as Jacey considered the dilemma facing them. Unused to wearing her hair down all the time, she found it made the back of her neck uncomfortably hot. She was tempted to pull it up, but refused out of sheer stubbornness.

She had never wanted off the island more than she did at that moment. She vowed that someday she'd go somewhere it snowed all the time.

Mr. Justin returned, clearing his throat. "Perhaps the best thing would be to make Summer's last days more comfortable. You could excuse her from classes. Perhaps we could put together some of her favorite meals. I believe she is particularly fond of swimming at Isaac's Beach."

"So you're saying I shouldn't even tell her," Jacey said, realizing that it might be crueler for Summer to know the truth.

She took a croissant from the tray but tossed it back. Her appetite was long gone, killed by her frustration and the uncomfortable warmth in the office.

"Belle *is* right," she said, staring at the doorway through which the pale girl had recently departed. "From a purely logical standpoint," Jacey continued, "Belle is completely right. But I can't be logical about this. Summer is in my Nine, and I am responsible for her."

Humphrey walked around to face her, put his hands on her shoulders, and looked into her eyes. She welcomed the warmth she found there. The support.

He urged her into his arms. She went reluctantly at first and then sagged, letting her weight rest against him and pressing her cheek to his chest. He stroked her hair for a while, then leaned away from her until she looked up at him.

Despite their closeness, a strange unease made them awkward together. Jacey knew that Humphrey loved her. She loved him too. She thought she did, anyway. But it was hard to think about such things when there were life-and-death issues to confront.

"I don't see how we can stop it," he said.

For a moment, she thought he was talking about their feelings for each other. But he went on, "Even if we could keep the senator from overwriting Summer, it's going to be Belle next. And a year after that, four more."

Jacey stiffened and pulled away. "We can't worry about

that. We have to deal with the current issue, and the only answer is to get Summer away from campus and let the senator's disease take its course."

Humphrey kissed her forehead. "I knew that would be your decision from the start." He kissed her cheek. "I'd never try to talk you out of it. But I want you to be sure."

"I'm sure."

Mr. Justin cleared his throat again. "I shall retire to the kitchen. Call if you need anything."

Humphrey grinned before kissing Jacey. She returned it. They lingered there for another minute before Humphrey broke free. "Go. But don't tell me where you plan to hide. I'll do what I can to stall the senator, and it's easier for me to lie if I'm telling the truth."

Jacey gave him one last kiss, then fled from the office, cursing the situation that kept her from spending the time she needed with him.

She shoved Humphrey from her thoughts. What she had to do next was miserable work and lingering on her own problems wouldn't make it any easier.

9

———

I WISH I COULD SEE A REAL DOG

The classroom building stood next to Girls' Hall on the far edge of the quad. Like all buildings on campus, wide windows let in Caribbean breezes.

The girls stood sweating before their desks in the still air. Each desk was a pane of glass set atop height-adjustable legs. Socrates had always insisted that Scions stand during their lessons, claiming it improved their cognition.

Wanda, Jacey's Second, stood at a desk in the front of the class, facing toward the other girls. If things had been normal, Jacey would have been in that position. But things were anything but normal, and the day-to-day management of Jacey's Nine had fallen to Wanda who, at sixteen, was a year behind Jacey.

Upon seeing Jacey, Wanda moved her hand reflexively to her Eagle pin, checking to make sure it was correctly positioned. It was.

Jacey figured she owed Wanda some sort of explanation, since she hadn't been to Girls' Hall for several days.

"I need to take Summer out of class," she told Wanda in a whisper.

Wanda's red locks were always slipping loose from her ponytail and falling over her eyes. She blew them away absently and nodded. She didn't ask anything, though her expression did.

Jacey wanted to tell the girl what was going on. Wanda was the only one of them who knew they were clones, but she didn't yet know about the mind transfer part. Jacey wanted to tell all of the Scions the truth about their lives. But now wasn't the time.

"It's too hot in here for full uniforms," Jacey said to Wanda. "After I've left, send the girls to change into exercise clothes. Let them wear them until the breezes return."

Relief softened Wanda's face. "Thank you."

Jacey moved down the aisle, stopping next to the youngest girl in her Nine. Livy was doll-like, with blond curls and wide green eyes. Despite her age, the nine-year-old's expression could be very grave, as it was now.

Jacey patted her back. "How are you doing, sweetheart?"

"Good. I'm learning a lot from Newton. He's very friendly."

Newton's small holographic avatar crossed his arms and looked down his nose at Livy. "She's very intelligent. Has a good head for figures."

"Are you coming back to Girls' Hall tonight?" Livy asked Jacey. "I want to tell you a poem I wrote for you."

The question caught Jacey off-guard. She didn't know where she was spending the night. So much depended on Summer.

"I'm not sure. But even if I don't stay, I'll try to stop by. I'd love to hear your poem."

Livy seemed satisfied with that. Jacey kissed her head and

continued down the aisle, making a show of checking the girls' sigil pins. They were perfect, of course. Wanda was doing an excellent job.

At fourteen, Summer was pretty with raven hair pulled into a ponytail according to school dress code. In evenings at Girls' Hall—when it was permissible to wear it down—Summer's hair fell like a silky black curtain across her face and shoulders. She was slender, olive-skinned, and had large, brown eyes that constantly glimmered as if on the verge of tearing up. When Summer was happy, those eyes and her pert nose made her as adorable as a baby animal. When angry, she tended to grin humorlessly, like a nymph intent on some mischief.

Today, she wore a cutely curious expression. It broke Jacey's heart to have to bring fear into those eyes.

Summer was deep in conversation with another iteration of Newton. He was going over some aspect of math that Jacey had never been taught. It involved a lot of numbers, parentheses, and arcane symbols. Next to it was a three-dimensional image of a bridge spanning a chasm. Summer adjusted her calculations and studied the design.

"I think that'll work," she told Newton. "Let's drive the truck across."

A vehicle pulling a boxy trailer behind it appeared and zoomed silently from behind the floating calculations. Summer tensed as it approached her bridge.

"It's going to make it," she said.

The truck zoomed across and disappeared into nothingness on the other side.

"Excellent work, Summer," Newton said. "Your choice of materials concerned me at first, but you have a natural insight into forces and support structures."

Summer beamed. "That one was easy."

"Excuse me, Newton," Jacey said. "I need to take Summer out of class."

He twisted his lips in obvious disapproval. Jacey thought Vaughan was playing the role a bit too on the nose. He said nothing before disappearing in a waft of mist.

Summer and Jacey had always had a somewhat strained relationship. Over the past few days, Jacey had flaunted school rules and had, temporarily at least, completely lost her reputation when Dr. Carlhagen had accused her and Vaughan of an impropriety in the bell tower. Since Sarah's death, Summer had become a little more cooperative.

Very little.

"Come with me, Summer."

Summer hesitated, then snatched her reader from the desk and followed Jacey. She kept glancing at her expectantly as they walked across the quad. Jacey tried to keep her face passive so as not to cause alarm, but the effort seemed silly considering what she was about to tell the girl.

"What is it?" Summer asked.

"I have to show you something. In the medical ward."

"Is it Vaughan? Belle says he blames himself for Sarah's death. Because he couldn't get to her in time."

Jacey ignored the propaganda Belle had been spreading. "This isn't about Vaughan. It's something else, and it has to do with you."

Summer licked her lips and hugged her elbows. "It's not a bad result on one of my medical tests is it?"

"No, nothing like that."

I wish that's all it was . . .

o o o

Jacey held the door of the transfer room open for Summer,

then let it swing closed with a hushed click. A sense of doom crept over Jacey, as if the door closing somehow committed her to some irrevocable decision she hadn't even realize she was making.

The cool air made Summer shiver. She spun in a slow circle, wide-eyed. "What is this place?"

Everything was a clinical white, the tiled floors, the painted concrete block walls, the ceiling. In the center crouched the transfer machine, two cots pushed head-to-head inside a sort of hollow wheel. Jacey didn't know how it worked, but when two people's heads were inside the wheel, knowledge transferred from one to the other.

Summer's eyes locked on the machine. She walked around it, rapped on the wheel, and peered inside. "What is this thing?"

Jacey rubbed her nose, which itched from the dry, sterile air in the room. It smelled faintly of bleach, probably used to sanitize everything. "This is called the transfer room," she told Summer. "It's part of what I wanted to show you. I'll explain the machine in a minute."

She tapped a dark screen on one wall, and it flickered to life. She then pressed play on a video that showed a man training a dog to do tricks. Over the course of the video, the man put the dog that knew tricks into one side of the machine and a dog that didn't know tricks into the other. At the end of the video, the dog that had known all the tricks was dead, and the other dog now knew all the tricks.

"Do you understand what you just saw?" Jacey asked.

"Amazing," Summer said, smiling broadly. "I wish I could see a real dog." She hugged her reader to her chest as if it were a dog.

This was going to be harder than Jacey had thought. "Summer, I didn't bring you here to show you the dogs. I want to know if you understand what you saw happen to the dogs."

"It looked like the knowledge of tricks passed from one dog to the other. They're sooo adorable! They remind me of —" Summer cleared her throat and looked away.

Jacey knew why Summer stopped. Girls her age didn't talk about the stuffed animals they had received at Children's Villa, didn't talk about how they'd been forced to burn them on arrival at the Scion School.

Summer recovered her composure. "I get it. The machine here looks like the one in the video. Are there dogs here somewhere?"

"No."

Jacey decided to just say it. Like how Nurse Smith always pulled a bandage off in one, swift yank. "Dr. Carlhagen has raised us Scions to be like the dog that didn't know the tricks."

She led Summer through another door and into a walk-in freezer. Five body bags lay on a wooden pallet. Four were the Progenitors of the first graduating class. The last was a new addition. It contained Dr. Carlhagen's ninety-two-year-old body.

Jacey knelt by one of the bags. "Be strong, Summer. I'm going to show you something very disturbing. Don't run away." Jacey unzipped one of the bags and opened it to show the forehead, nose, and eye of a dead elderly woman with white hair. The face, saggy and pale, stared past Jacey as if seeing some great horror just over her shoulder.

Summer covered her mouth.

"This woman looks a lot like Vin, doesn't she? Just older," Jacey said.

Summer bobbed her head but kept her hand clamped over her mouth. Her huge eyes glistened with confusion and fear. "Why are there dead people in here?"

∘ ∘ ∘

Belle sucked her fingers and squeezed her eyes tightly. The pain in her fingers throbbed like jolts of electricity.

Damn Jacey and damn that door!

Belle took some breaths and struggled to stifle her moans.

After Jacey and Summer had gone into the ward, Belle had scrambled from beneath Nurse Smith's desk to thrust a hand between the door and the jam. Only her absolute determination to get to Vaughan kept her from screaming in pain when the door slammed on her fingers. Every heartbeat had been an eternity of agony while she waited for those slowpokes to get through the door on the other side of the ward.

Belle tucked her injured fingers into her opposite armpit as she slunk through the door to the holding room corridor.

In three seconds, she slipped down the short hall and into Vaughan's room. She left the light off, relying on the illumination streaming in from the hallway. Tears streaked her cheeks, and she sucked air through her teeth. She needed to ice her fingers, but there was simply no time for that.

She fumbled with the IV stand, followed the tube to Vaughan's hand. Jaw clenched, she yanked the needle free. Vaughan groaned as the sedative dissipated from his system. "Is that you, Belle?"

She shushed him, hand searching his body for the strap buckles. One by one she undid them. "We have to get out of here and away from the campus."

"Thank God you've finally seen sense."

Belle hesitated, surprised by Vaughan's use of the word "God." It must have been one of the figures of speech he'd picked up from Jacey.

"We have to move quickly," she said. "Do you really know how to open the gate?"

"Of course I do."

She helped Vaughan sit up. He swung his legs over the side of the gurney and then stood, though shakily.

She peeked into the hallway. It was clear. "Come on."

o o o

Jacey zipped the body bag shut and stood, wiping her hands on the pants of her uniform. "A few days ago I told you that the graduates met their parents after the ceremony. I was wrong. This woman is not Vin's mother. She is what Dr. Carlhagen called a Progenitor. Vin was her clone."

"A what? That's not . . . That doesn't seem . . ." The effort to deny what Jacey was saying played across Summer's features the way dappled sunlight swept over the quad as a cloud bank crossed the sun. The sun did not return with Summer's pained smile. "How?"

"I don't know. But somehow Dr. Carlhagen discovered a way to take the DNA from that woman," Jacey pointed at the body bag, "and make a new baby, identical in every respect."

Summer's hand fell away from her trembling mouth. A tear formed in one eye and tumbled down her cheek. "And he put Vin in the machine, didn't he?"

"Yes."

"And that woman died. Like the dog."

"Yes."

"So what happened to Vin? She knows everything that old woman knows?"

"Yes, and in the process, the girl we knew as Vin was destroyed."

Jacey guided Summer out of the freezer, put her arms around her. At first, Summer was stiff, balled up with her arms hugging her reader against her chest. After a moment, she threw her arms around Jacey and clung to her. "That's horrible. Why would Dr. Carlhagen allow such a thing?"

"Dr. Carlhagen not only allowed it, he started this school in order to do it."

"But how could a mother do that to her daughter?"

"I told you, that's not Vin's mother. Vin was a clone of that woman."

It was clear that Summer didn't understand, not because she was too stupid to get it, but because she was overwhelmed. They went back into the transfer room, Summer wiping tears from her face and shivering. "Why are you showing only me this? Everyone needs to know this. We have to get away."

"You're right. We do have to get away. But we can't take everyone. Not right now. But you have to go now."

Summer's mouth quirked with realization. "Someone's coming for me. Some woman is going to try to overwrite my mind."

"I just found out this morning. Normally, it doesn't happen until a Scion turns eighteen. But in this case there was an emergency. Your Progenitor is deathly ill, and she's coming here with armed guards to oversee the transfer. She'll be here tonight."

"How will I get away? Where will I go?"

"I don't know," Jacey said. "We have to find a way out of the campus first. We have to search the island, find some place we can hide out. The woman, Senator Bentilius, says she has only four weeks to live before her disease kills her. I figure we can find some place for you to hide until then. After that, it won't matter."

To her credit, Summer found the internal mettle to straighten up and square her shoulders. She wiped her tears on her sleeve and clamped her mouth so tightly her jaw bulged.

Jacey felt a rush of pride. Summer was in her Nine, after all.

She wondered if Dr. Carlhagen realized just how successful the school was at training Scions. It had produced young people of particularly strong resolve. It seemed to Jacey that, in perfecting the Scions, Dr. Carlhagen had made the Progenitors obsolete.

"Let's go," Jacey said. "We don't have much time."

o o o

The sun was well up as Belle guided Vaughan across the quad. There were no Scions about as they were still in classes. "Where do we go?"

"The garage," Vaughan said. He squinted against the bright sunlight. He staggered and nearly fell, but Belle caught him.

"You'll have to be my crutch for now," he said.

She wrapped an arm around his waist to support him. If the need to get away hadn't been so urgent, she would have enjoyed the physical contact. Belle stood a head shorter than Vaughan, and with his arm draped over her shoulder, she felt small, almost childlike.

He's so warm! she thought. She felt her face go hot and hoped he didn't notice.

They crossed the quad as fast as Vaughan could manage in his slow shuffle, cutting past the dojo and through the mango grove to the garage. The structure was nothing more than a large shed open on one side.

The Jeep stood in shadows, its headlights and grill looking like a determined face. Vaughan climbed into the driver's side and Belle into the passenger side. She had never ridden in the Jeep before, but she'd seen Sensei drive it a number of times.

Vaughan muttered under his breath. "I hope Mr. Justin returned it. Ah, here it is." He grabbed a key fob from a storage compartment in the dash. He pressed a button, and the Jeep's engine roared to life.

"What about the gate?" Belle asked.

Vaughan jabbed at a control screen in the middle of the dashboard. It flashed up a menu. "I can open it from here."

He revved the engine and tore out of the garage.

10

NO FOOD, NO WATER

"If we're going to get past the gate," Jacey said as she led Summer out of the medical ward, "I've got to find the remote. I think you should go back to Girls' Hall. Get some extra clothes for both of us, toothbrushes, that kind of stuff."

"Hurry, Jacey. I'm scared."

"I know."

Summer headed toward Girls' Hall, head down and rubbing her arms. She turned frequently to look at Jacey, who waved encouragingly.

Wishing she felt as confident as she was pretending to be, Jacey headed toward Sensei's villa, determined to turn it upside down until she found the remote.

A siren squawked from beyond the mango grove. For a moment, Jacey feared that Senator Bentilius was arriving already. But she had been in holo communication with Humphrey that morning. No way she could travel to St. Vitus that fast. Which meant somebody else was arriving.

Mr. Justin hadn't mentioned a supply delivery.

Jacey peered down the main drive from the gate. The Jeep sped into view, obviously coming from the garage, wheels spitting up gravel behind it. Belle's pale profile flashed in the sunlight through the passenger window.

In three heartbeats, Jacey put the pieces together. Belle wasn't driving. And the only other person it could be was Dr. Carlhagen. Somehow Belle had set him free, and now they were leaving the campus. Beneath the whoop of the siren, Jacey heard the rattle of the chain-link gate grinding open.

She shoved concerns about Dr. Carlhagen and Belle from her mind. This was her chance.

She turned and shouted, "Summer! Summer!"

Calling on all the speed in her legs, she raced toward Girls' Hall. Summer stood at the doorway, facing back toward Jacey. The gate siren must have stopped her.

Jacey waved for her. "Summer, come on!"

Summer just stood there, shielding her eyes from the sun with one hand and staring.

Jacey stopped running and jumped up and down, waving her arms. "Come now, Summer. Run!"

Summer started forward. Jacey waved her arms even harder and started backing toward the gate. "Come on!"

Summer fell into a jog, reader tucked in one hand.

"Faster!" Jacey cried.

Summer picked up speed, ponytail streaming behind her. "What's going on?"

Jacey pointed ahead. "The gate."

They pounded down the path, past the dojo, past the mango grove on their left and Boys' Hall blurring by on the right. The Jeep was just passing through the gate. Together, Jacey and Summer sprinted toward the opening, footsteps crunching on the gravel.

The gate stopped its opening crawl, shuddered, then reversed course.

Three years older than Summer, Jacey was bigger and faster. She could hear the girl's heavy breathing and footfalls behind her.

The opening in the fence shrank second by second.

Too fast.

Jacey's feet slid on the gravel as she stopped in the opening. She braced herself to take the ten thousand volts. She'd do anything to stop it long enough for Summer to get out. She tensed and threw her shoulder against the edge of the gate as it continued to crush closed.

Nothing happened. Apparently the gate wasn't electrified while it was open. Jacey pushed with everything she had. Her feet found no purchase on the gravel. She spun, putting her back to the gate, pressing her feet against the steel riser at the opening of the fence. A groan escaped her as she slowly lost the battle against the unstoppable power of the gate. Her knees buckled.

Summer dove at the opening, falling to her hands and knees with a cry. She squeezed beneath Jacey's legs to the outside. But then she stopped and wriggled back through, shooting out her hand to grab something.

Her reader.

"Just go!" Jacey groaned as the gate squeezed the wind from her lungs.

Summer grabbed the device and slipped back out. Jacey twisted and wrenched herself free, falling next to Summer, gasping. The gate rattled shut and the siren cut off, leaving the world in a silence disturbed only by their heaving breaths.

Jacey scrambled to her feet. "Quickly, we have to get away from here before someone sees us."

She helped Summer to her feet and started down the gravel road. This was the first time she'd been outside the campus grounds since she'd arrived seven years before.

"Where are we going?" Summer asked, brushing the dust from the knees of her uniform.

Jacey didn't answer right away. She didn't have an answer.

They had nothing with them. No food, no water, no familiarity with the terrain. But if they were going to survive for four weeks, they would need all three.

The answer came to her then. The only answer she could offer.

"Forward."

11

VERY MUCH LIKE CHESS

Belle twisted in her seat to watch the gate closing behind them. Two figures stood on the road, but the Jeep rounded a turn before she could see who they were. Belle guessed Jacey and Summer. She smiled at the thought of them running away on foot. Searching for them would provide a nice distraction for Senator Bentilius while Belle and Vaughan found a way off the island.

The dusty road climbed a hillside in a series of precipitous switchbacks before cresting and descending toward the coast. Ahead, the white line of the southern shore trailed into the distance.

Belle rubbed her arms and tried to shake off the feeling she'd crossed some invisible barrier that had taken her a thousand miles from the campus. She had never seen this part of the island, and she was surprised by how different it looked. Scrub brush, wildflowers, and hardy, tall grasses blanketed the rolling landscape. Occasional trees, bent and wind-gnarled, reached skyward.

Vaughan steered the Jeep westward, plunging them into

cool shade. Natural fences of impenetrable thickets paralleled the road on either side, their leafy tops arching overhead and, in places, forming a tunnel through which the Jeep rushed.

"They were supposed to prune these when they came for supply deliveries," Vaughan said. A very Dr. Carlhagenish sourness colored his voice.

"Are you okay?" Belle asked, eyes narrowing.

"I'm fine." He patted his cheek and widened his eyes in an exaggerated manner. "It's strange. I *feel* Dr. Carlhagen's memories in my mind as if they were my own. The pruning is part of the procedure during supply delivery. There's a team that's supposed to keep these limbs in check."

Just as he spoke, they drove through a section so overgrown that limbs slapped against the windshield. Vaughan slowed the Jeep and patted his pants pockets. "Where are they?"

"What are you looking for?" Belle asked.

"My pills. Mr. Justin brought me my pills."

"Mr. Justin came to see you in the medical ward?"

Vaughan jerked his head as if coming awake. "No, no, no. I asked him to fetch my pills. He gave them to me after—"

Belle knew what he was going to say. Mr. Justin had given him some pills right after Dr. Carlhagen had transferred to Vaughan. Jacey had mentioned something about Dr. Carlhagen's addiction to painkillers.

"Never mind," he said. "Jacey surely confiscated them while I was unconscious." He scratched at the thin growth of beard on his chin. Having been strapped down for several days, he'd had no opportunity to shave. "I need to eat. What did you bring?"

"Bring?" Belle gave him a long, exasperated stare. "I didn't *bring* anything. I came straight from a meeting with Jacey."

Vaughan swore, then clamped his mouth shut. "I'm sorry. I'm starving. What was this meeting with Jacey about?"

"Apparently an important Progenitor named Senator Something-or-Other is coming to transfer to her Scion."

"Bentilius?" Vaughan asked incredulously. "What the hell is she thinking?"

Belle studied Vaughan closer. She'd never known him to curse. Clearly he was still struggling with the residual effects of Dr. Carlhagen's persona.

"The senator is apparently very ill. Near death. You know who she is?"

"Yes! Well . . . not exactly. I remember her, but I've never met her before. Dr. Carlhagen did, though, many times. She's a powerful political operator in North America. Her Scion is . . ." Vaughan rapped his knuckles on the steering wheel, then snapped his fingers. "Summer! Is that right?"

"Yes. When I came to get you, Jacey was taking Summer into the transfer room to explain to her what was going on."

"Why would she do that? It seems cruel."

"I'm pretty sure she means to have Summer escape or hide someplace."

"The senator's people will find her eventually," Vaughan said. "I know it sounds cruel, but the best thing would be to let the transfer happen."

"That's what I said!" Belle allowed herself a thin smile, enjoying the fact that Vaughan agreed with her for once. "But Jacey's so idealistic. She doesn't understand the chess game."

"Ah yes," Vaughan said. "It's very much like chess. So knowing that, you came to free me to get away because . . ." He considered it, then smiled and gave her an approving nod. "Because you know that once the senator discovers her Scion has gone missing, she'll lock down the whole island. And even after she's overwritten Summer, the armed guards will never leave. And you're next to be overwritten."

"You said you knew a way off the island. I want to get away from here. And since you have access to Dr. Carlhagen's memories, you can help. Jacey still wants to overwrite you, by the way."

Vaughan wasn't listening. His head drooped forward, and the Jeep slowed.

"Vaughan?" Belle said, patting his shoulder. His head lolled to one side. Fighting down a flush of panic, Belle took hold of the wheel and kept the vehicle aimed straight down the road.

"Wake up!" She shoved him harder.

No response.

She studied the lever Vaughan had used to make the Jeep go forward. Not knowing what she was doing, she shifted it backward. The engine roared, momentarily waking Vaughan. He mumbled something and removed his foot from the accelerator. The Jeep coasted to a stop.

"Vaughan, wake up."

He slumped forward, face mashing on the center of the steering wheel, causing the horn to blare. She jerked him back. His breath came in the long, slow cycle of deep sleep.

He's exhausted.

And probably half-starved, she realized. If Dr. Carlhagen's addiction played a part, he was also in the grips of withdrawal.

She shifted the lever into the bottom position, aligned with the P, which is where she thought it had been when they'd first gotten into the Jeep. She got out, studied the road. It continued into dense inland foliage. A glance at the sky told her it was midmorning.

She climbed into the Jeep and tugged Vaughan toward her. He let out a moan but didn't awaken. She leaned him onto the passenger seat, then hooked her arms around him and pulled.

He was dead weight. She braced her feet on the side of the seat and tugged with all her strength. Slowly Vaughan slid across the shift lever and into the passenger side.

It took another five minutes of tugging, pushing, and shoving, but she got him out of the driver's seat.

She bound him to the passenger seat with a strap she found. It had a buckle that snapped into a shorter strap on the other side of the seat. *Clever design.*

Heaving a great breath to work up her nerve, Belle climbed into the driver's seat and closed the door. There were two pedals. *One to go and one to stop*, she thought. *Couldn't be simpler.*

After a few failed attempts, she figured out the combination of pedals and lever shifts to get the Jeep creeping forward.

"What are you doing?" Vaughan mumbled.

"We can't stay here." She pressed the accelerator down, and the Jeep lurched. She let out a vile curse and stomped the brake. She nearly slid out of her seat. Vaughan jerked forward, but the strap she'd affixed to him kept him secure.

She found the strap on her side and snapped it in place. "Now I know what that's for."

She tried again, and soon they were under way, creeping forward. According to the gauge under the steering wheel, they were going twenty kilometers per hour.

It was nothing compared to the speed Vaughan had driven, but she didn't intend to run off the side of a cliff after coming this far. She kept the speed low, slowing to a stop at every sharp turn.

After twenty minutes, the interior of the vehicle grew too warm. She fiddled with a few buttons until she found one to lower the windows. The breeze blowing against her face relaxed and cooled her as she drove. Though her confidence in the machine grew with every kilometer, she occasionally applied the brakes just to make sure they still worked.

She didn't know how long she'd been driving when the road turned south again and descended a hill among thicker trees. It came out along the coast on an area paved with concrete.

"The docks," she said, smiling to herself.

The Scions had speculated that boat docks existed somewhere on the island, but none had ever seen them. In her studies, Belle had seen pictures of harbors and docks and piers. These were similar. A broad concrete quay ran parallel to the shore and longer concrete piers jutted into the bay.

A huge machine with an appendage sticking out over the longest pier stood on its own platform. A metal cable dangled from its tip, and at the end of that hung a huge iron hook. She recognized it immediately as a hoist mechanism, probably used to unload the supply boats.

Farther along was a small jetty. A white boat was tied up alongside it. It was small, but it was something. How it operated she hadn't the faintest idea. Hopefully Vaughan would be able to summon a more substantial watercraft to take them off the island.

Across the road from the docks stood a bank of open-sided sheds very much like the Jeep garage on campus. She slowed and studied the machines inside. One was a huge contraption with six wheels. Beneath it was slung an angled blade that appeared to drag upon the ground. Another machine had a big, flat implement on the front that was slightly scooped. She didn't know what either of them were for.

Between the sheds stood a sign with arrows pointing in opposite directions. The one pointing the direction they'd come was emblazoned with: St. Vitus Retreat Center. The other arrow read: Groundskeeper's House.

"Retreat Center?" she mumbled. She supposed that the signs were intentionally misleading. If a wayward boat docked, Dr. Carlhagen wouldn't want anyone seeing the words "Scion School."

Mother Tyeesha's had to be the Groundskeeper's House. Belle gripped the wheel and continued on her way.

12

IT'S NOT REASONABLE. IT'S OBVIOUS

Jacey had always wondered why Dr. Carlhagen had made their uniforms black. She now fervently believed it was to slow the Scions down if they ever happened to escape the campus.

The long trudge up the hill and down to the southern coast took most of the morning. The low wind-gnarled trees along the way offered little shade, and by the time Jacey and Summer had descended to the southern slopes, the wind had died.

Now they boiled beneath their uniforms as the black fabric drank up the sun's heat.

Jacey drew her sleeve across her brow to wipe away the runnels of sweat streaming into her eyes. "I wish I had a rubber band for my hair." She supposed it served her right for defying school dress code and wearing it down.

Summer walked to the edge of the road, snagged a long length of vine, and returned to Jacey. She used her fingernails to split and draw the vine into thinner sections of fiber. "Here," she said, holding one out, "use this."

Jacey stared at Summer, surprised by the girl's initiative. "I should've thought of that." She drew her hair back, but fumbled with the strand, then botched the job by tying it too loosely.

"Let me do it," Summer said, pressing Jacey's shoulders.

Jacey knelt. Summer's hands gently but efficiently pulled her hair back and cinched it into a ponytail with another strand of vine. A gust of breeze swept down the hillside as if the island itself had been waiting for Jacey to take this sensible step.

At least one problem was solved.

During their flight from the school Jacey had been playing out all the possible bad things that could happen. First of which was that they would get lost—which they had.

Her second worry was that they would exhaust themselves just as Senator Bentilius's guards started to search the island.

And then there was the problem of food and water. She licked her dry lips and tried not to think about how wonderful a cool drink would be.

She didn't know much about the geography of St. Vitus. She had spent the first eight years of her life at Children's Villa but left there the day she turned nine. She didn't remember much about the landscape around Children's Villa, except that it stood at the top of a rise surrounded by trees. Since arriving at the Scion School, she had always assumed Children's Villa was on the opposite end of the island. The trees there had been taller and lusher than any at the Scion School. One thing she did remember quite clearly—it rained a lot at Children's Villa.

On the day that she had traveled to the Scion School, Mother Tyeesha had gotten her and the others out of bed before the sun rose. They had gotten into a vehicle that everyone called "the old Jeep."

She'd been so nervous during that long, winding drive, staring at the darkness. Seeing the road rush at them in the headlights had revealed almost nothing about the nature of the island, and she certainly hadn't remembered all of the turns and twists.

After what had seemed like hours of driving, they had gotten out of the vehicle and waited in front of the chain-link fence. It had opened, and she'd been greeted by Dr. Carlhagen and Sensei. And that was all she had seen of the island.

Jacey and Summer continued onward. Summer's initial panic had subsided. She gazed around curiously, commenting on how the plant life had changed. The road along the southern shore had climbed into dense forest, which brought new smells. Damp earth, moss, floral scents half-remembered that evoked feelings of safety, fun, and innocence.

Jacey hadn't taken any biology or botany classes, but Summer apparently had. She pointed out acacia trees and a stand of fragrant bay rum.

After several hours of walking, they passed a mango tree. The fruits were not quite ripe, but they took them anyway, biting into the soft skin and relishing the moisture, if not the taste. They sat in the shade while they ate their mangoes. When Jacey finished hers, she threw the pit into the woods. "We have to find water."

"We may not have to wait long," Summer replied, eyes lifting to the sky. A band of black clouds was blowing in from the southeast, a veil of gray rain hanging below it.

Jacey welcomed the rain, was ready to let it soak her to the skin. Anything to quench her thirst.

The squall blew in fast, sending a strong breeze across the road. "We're never going to catch enough rain water in our mouths," Summer said. "We need some way to funnel it." She drifted to the side of the road and pressed her fingers on the various wide leaves hemming in the road. She stopped, peering into the thicket. "There we go."

She pushed aside stalks of weeds and the thumb-width trunks of scrub trees and disappeared.

"Summer!" Jacey called.

Eyeing the foliage for insects, Jacey pressed after the girl. "Hold on. I don't want us separated."

Once past the initial barrier, the undergrowth thinned. The tall trees, vine-covered and mossy, stretched high overhead, their branches intertwining and blocking the sun.

Summer stood next to a stand of rambling bushes bearing leaves as wide as her head. They were concave and facing up. Some still held water from past rains. Summer got to her knees and burrowed her way deeper into the thicket. "Maybe these'll protect us from the worst of the rain, too."

Jacey scanned the ground, but didn't spot any creepy-crawlies. The first rain hit the canopy above, followed soon after by a furious downpour. The sound of it battering the leaves grew moment by moment, each drop making a sharp crack. A minute later, the first drips penetrated the canopy and runnels spread across the forest floor like wandering serpents.

They sheltered under the bush, arms wrapped around their knees. Water coursed down a slight rise behind them, and soon they sat in a puddle, bottoms wet and cold.

"Do you ever wish you'd never figured it out?" Summer asked.

"What do you mean?"

"About the Scions and the transfer machine. And what happens to us." Summer put her chin on her knees. "Maybe it would be better not to know, to just go in dumb and have it happen without realizing it."

"No," Jacey said. "I don't ever wish that."

"I do. Sort of."

"We'd be dry inside of Girls' Hall right now, if that's what you mean."

Summer hunched forward and rubbed her nose. Jacey couldn't see enough of her face to tell if she was trying to sleep or hide tears.

The rain fell harder, and the trees swayed above them.

Just as Summer had predicted, the leaves of their shelter filled with water. Their stalks bent under the weight so that streams poured to the ground right in front of Jacey and Summer.

Once they had drunk their fill, Jacey wished aloud for a container to collect more water. Summer immediately set about stripping one of the leaves down and weaving it into a bowl.

"That will never hold water," Jacey said.

"Not like this it won't," Summer said. "But I have an idea."

The squall passed while Summer was weaving her bowl. It wasn't large, perhaps as wide as Jacey's hands cupped together. Summer plucked another leaf, but kept it whole and tucked it down inside the bowl.

"It won't hold much," Summer said, "but it's something."

In another burst of ingenuity, Summer wound a length of vine around the rim of the bowl and drew it tight so that it formed a sort of handle allowing them to carry the water without spilling any.

Jacey smiled at the girl and patted her back. Summer shrank away from Jacey's touch and brushed past. "Let's get going."

"You did a good job."

No answer.

Summer retreated through the thick foliage by the road and disappeared.

The shift in Summer's mood infected Jacey. She didn't know what she'd said or done to provoke the behavior.

Jacey joined Summer on the road and they continued west. Three minutes later they rounded a bend and discovered boat docks, across from which stood metal-roofed sheds.

Summer uttered a string of curses Jacey was surprised the girl even knew. As a Nine leader, Jacey should have scolded her for that. Considering the circumstances, Jacey laughed it off. They'd suffered twenty minutes getting their butts soaked when shelter lay so close by.

Summer said, "At least we found a roof for the night."

"I don't think so. We won't be able to stay here long. When they start searching for us, they'll look here first."

Summer trudged forward. "You mean when they start searching for *me*."

They headed to the nearest shed and peeked in. "What do you suppose this machine is for?" Jacey asked, hoping to ease the growing tension.

The vehicle was ten meters long and had six wheels, each as tall as Summer. The thick treads looked perfect for gripping the dirt road they'd traveled. A monstrous metal blade hung from its belly, dirty and chipped.

Summer squatted and studied the blade. "This is meant to be dragged on the road. To scrape it, make it level."

Jacey eyed the machine. "Sounds reasonable."

"It's not reasonable. It's *obvious*." Summer stood and stepped onto the road.

"What's wrong with you?"

"That monster in the other building must be meant to push stuff," Summer said, pointing at a machine with a flat blade mounted on its front. It crouched upon steel tracks. "That would be fun to drive."

Summer's attention went to the docks and a huge

machine standing on its own concrete pier. "They use that thing to hoist things out of the supply boat."

She started toward the water's edge, but Jacey blocked her way. "Summer, why are you being a brat all of a sudden?"

Summer folded her arms across her chest. "I'm not."

"You're acting like you're mad at me. Did I say something?"

"No. I'm just tired." She side stepped around Jacey and continued to the pier.

Jacey made a neck-strangling motion behind Summer's back, then took a deep breath and forced a smile onto her lips. Adding energy to Summer's mood wasn't going to help them at this point. To be fair, the girl had a lot to deal with. This morning Summer had woken up an innocent Scion, believing Dr. Carlhagen's lie that she was important to the future of humanity. Now she was homeless and would soon be the object of an island-wide search.

Jacey joined Summer on the pier. She hadn't expected to find a ship, and even if she had, she didn't know the first thing about driving one. They would just as likely drown or be captured by someone loyal to Senator Bentilius or Dr. Carlhagen.

They retreated and walked along the quay. Jacey made a face as the smell of rotting fish wafted from the shoreline. The thought of fish stopped her. She eyed the water, considering how they might catch some of the long, silvery fish sheltering in the shade of the pier.

Summer suddenly dashed away, running onto a smaller jetty. She let out a high-pitched squeak and clapped her hands together.

Jacey followed. "What is it?"

"This is it. This is our way off the island."

Summer had discovered a wooden skiff tethered to the

jetty. It stretched four meters from bow to motor. It was empty, except for three flat, wooden bench seats that appeared to be part of the structure. Two weather-splintered oars were tucked along one side. It sat low in the water, partially flooded with rainwater.

Summer crouched and rapped her knuckles on the hull. "It's wood."

"And old," Jacey said. More bare spots showed than white flakes of paint. If it was sea-worthy, which she doubted, Jacey thought they might manage to drive something of its size. But not for leaving the island. "It doesn't look like it's meant for long voyages."

Summer threw an irritated sneer at Jacey. "It's obviously for fishing and moving along the coast. Probably faster to get around the island than to cross it. But it could get us to Turtle Island."

Turtle Island was a small hump of land a few kilometers off Isaac's Beach. Jacey doubted there was any shelter there at all.

Summer moved to the rear of the skiff, stopping to thump the black metal housing of an outboard motor. "I bet I could get this started. Socrates covered the details of internal combustion engines. This one is simple."

Jacey glanced at the sky, trying to gauge the time of day. She guessed they'd been off campus for four or five hours. And that meant they had about seven before Senator Bentilius arrived by helicopter.

Not wanting to douse Summer's enthusiasm, Jacey nodded noncommittally at the boat. "I think we should rest for a little while, see if we can find some more food, maybe some more mangoes. And then I think we should scout down the road a bit farther."

"Why?" Summer's face grew sullen, and her arms wrapped around her middle.

"Because the more we know about what's down there, the better prepared we'll be to—"

A strange heartbeat sounded from the west. She didn't recognize it at first, but a shift in the wind brought the sound to her more clearly. She spun. There was nothing in view, but she knew what made the sound.

A helicopter. The senator had come early.

"Quick," she said to Summer. "Into the shed. We've got to get out of sight!"

Summer didn't move, but she'd turned her gaze to the sky.

"It's the senator. Move!"

Summer's mouth parted with fear as she leaned into a sprint.

The beat of the helicopter blades grew behind them, but Jacey didn't spare a glance. They burst into the cover of the scraper machine's shed, not stopping until they collided with the rear wall. Panting and exchanging terrified glances, they crouched behind the road machine and listened to the roar of the helicopter as it passed overhead.

Summer clung to Jacey's arm. "Did it see me?"

"I don't know. I don't think so"

The sound faded to the east.

Jacey waited, hoping it didn't return. But would they bother to circle back even if they had seen two girls running? They couldn't know Summer was missing yet. Jacey didn't know how much space a helicopter needed to land, but a quick look outside showed her several relatively open spaces.

The pilot and passengers might have seen them. She had to assume they had. And once they discovered Summer missing, they'd remember.

"Now we really can't stay here," she said.

Summer nodded, then cast about, looking for something.

Eyes flashing, she crawled under a workbench and pulled out a small, dented bucket. "Perfect."

"What is that for?"

"To bail out the skiff."

Jacey smiled and tried to offer understanding. "That's a good idea, but we just don't have time."

"It won't take that long."

"We can't risk it. We need to search for what supplies we can find, and then get moving. I want to be five kilometers from here before they realize we're not on campus."

"But—"

Jacey smacked her hands together. "Don't argue with me!"

Summer's face paled and her nostrils flared.

Jacey calmed herself. She had only been the leader of her Nine for a few days. She hadn't encountered a discipline issue like this before. "Trust me, Summer. You go out in that boat, the helicopter will spot you in two seconds." She didn't wait for agreement. "There's a smaller shack over there that might have something we can use. Come with me."

She strode out of the machine shed and headed to the shack.

Soft steps trailed after her and caught up. Jacey adjusted her pace so that Summer could walk beside her.

I need to change the mood.

"The senator told Humphrey she'd arrive in twelve hours. Apparently she lied."

"And this person," Summer said, "this Senator Bentilius— she's . . . me?" Gone was the cuteness in her eyes, replaced by a hunted look.

"No." Anger at their situation flamed in Jacey's gut. "Your body may be the same, but that doesn't mean you *are* her." Her hand went to the back of Summer's head and stroked it gently. "What's in here is unique. That's why we're doing this."

Summer grimaced and slipped her head away from Jacey's touch.

"It's okay to be scared," Jacey said. "Fear will keep you alive."

13

SHAPED LIKE A DAGGER

Humphrey slammed his hands on the desk. "No more, Mr. Justin. I'm sick of going through this." The butler had been feeding him facts about Senator Bentilius for the past half-hour, and it was all too much to remember. "I don't have Jacey's ability to memorize everything."

Mr. Justin stood impassively, hands clasped behind him. The smile crinkles at the corners of his eyes smoothed. "I just wanted to impress upon you, Humphrey, that the tiniest slip will jeopardize not only your encounter with Senator Bentilius, but possibly the future of the Scion School. If she realizes that you're not Dr. Carlhagen, you can be sure she will summon a force to take control of the school."

"I just don't see why I need to talk to her that much. If the woman is sick, she should go to the medical ward." He snapped his fingers. "Yes! That's perfect. We'll keep her there."

"Oh, no. That won't do," Mr. Justin said, picking an invisible piece of lint from his sleeve. "The senator will be staying here at the hacienda, and you will be having a nice quiet dinner with her this evening."

"But why? If it's so risky for me to talk to her, isn't it smarter to keep me away from her?"

"That's not how client relationships work. You don't understand how business in the outside world is conducted. When a customer visits, you entertain them. It's called schmoozing, and Dr. Carlhagen was a master at it. You would only insult the senator if you avoided her. And believe me, she is not to be trifled with."

Humphrey tugged at his hateful bow tie, wishing he could rip it off and destroy it. "Damn thing is suffocating me."

"A few more hours and you can remove it."

"Fine." Humphrey tried to buck himself up by remembering that he'd endured Dr. Carlhagen's unbelievably uncomfortable dinner parties at the hacienda before. How much worse could this be?

"Just don't make me drink wine," he said.

Mr. Justin arched an eyebrow. "It would hardly be believable that Dr. Carlhagen wouldn't drink some. Anyone who knows him well would find it odd if he turned it down."

Humphrey shrugged. "Maybe I'm turning over a new leaf. You know, to keep my new, young body healthy."

Mr. Justin nodded thoughtfully, and Humphrey thought he was going to concede the point, but then he pursed his lips and said, "The Scions' whole purpose is to allow one to live without consequences. You won't have to drink much, but I caution you to do nothing that will raise suspicion."

"I understand," Humphrey said through gritted teeth, putting as much disgust into it as he could muster.

The thumping sound of a helicopter beat against the hacienda and drew his eyes to the window.

"She's early," he said.

Mr. Justin looked very pale all of a sudden. "Are you ready?"

"Does it matter?"

o o o

At Mr. Justin's suggestion, Humphrey declared a lockdown for Senator Bentilius's arrival. By the time the roar of the helicopter's arrival grew loud enough to draw attention, the Scions were all inside their residence halls. Humphrey stood at the edge of the quad as the flying machine circled the campus and hovered over the quad like a monstrous mechanical insect before coming to rest on its skids in the grass.

A hatch on the side, hinged at the bottom, folded open. Up popped a short ramp of stairs. Four men in dark fatigues and sunglasses descended. They wore sidearms on their waists, but their hands were empty.

Good, Humphrey thought. *They're being cautious, but at least they're not expecting trouble from the start.*

They dispersed and formed a perimeter around the helicopter and Humphrey.

A colossus of a woman appeared at the top of the steps. She had a narrow face, bony, as if carved from stone, her grim expression a blend of anger, suspicion, and hatred. She, too, wore black fatigues, sleeves rolled up to expose bulging biceps. She hopped down, ignoring the steps, then turned a slow circle, studying the quad. Her eyes barely registered Humphrey's existence. Satisfied that Humphrey and Mr. Justin were no threat, she reached back toward the door with a black-gloved hand.

A lily-white hand materialized from darkness and took it. Senator Bentilius emerged, blinking, into sunlight. Humphrey was instantly struck by how frail she looked. Much worse than she'd appeared on the holovid.

No wonder she's insisting on transferring now. A strong wind might blow her away.

The enormous bodyguard held the senator's hand as she descended to the grass.

Putting on his best Dr. Carlhagen smile, Humphrey spread his hands wide. "Welcome to the Scion School, Senator Bentilius!"

The senator's face resembled Summer's somewhat, despite their difference in age—which Humphrey judged to be at least 60 years. The senator wore her hair short, dyed a shocking red, which made the sickly pallor of her skin even more pale. She had the same huge eyes as Summer, and they widened further when she locked eyes with Humphrey.

"Christof," she said, thrusting forward both hands. He took them, awkwardly, and held them, barely keeping the smile painted on his face at the feel of her papery skin. She seemed so different than she had on the holovid.

"Ah, Maxine, so nice to see you." Humphrey was glad that Mr. Justin had told him the senator's first name.

Another individual emerged from the chopper. She wore an ill-fitting jacket and narrow skirt that stopped just below her knees. Dark glasses made her eyes a mystery, but judging by her black hair and skin, she was no relative of Senator Bentilius'.

"You remember Miss Dayspring, my nurse, don't you?" She turned to the huge captain of her bodyguards. "And Alice."

Humphrey smiled and withdrew his hands from the senator's so that he could extend one to the nurse. "Of course, welcome."

The woman clasped his hand for a second. Her weak grip

left behind a film of sweat, which he surreptitiously wiped on his slacks.

Miss Dayspring held her head low, as if she might smack it on the helicopter blades, as impossible as that would be. She stood two hands shorter than her boss.

Alice barked, "We must take the senator somewhere she can rest. The travel has exhausted her."

"Of course. Of course," Humphrey said. He turned to Alice. "I welcome you and your men. They can bunk down in the medical ward. I've instructed the AI to admit them."

Which wasn't really true. Mr. Justin had taken care of that.

"And isn't that where we're going?" Miss Dayspring asked, voice tremulous and squeaky. "We must conduct the transfer immediately."

Mr. Justin had prepared Humphrey for this. But rather than address the nurse, he turned to the senator. "For your sake, Maxine, I recommend you have a full night's sleep before we transfer. Things will go much smoother. And the chances for success will be much higher. Surely you can wait another twelve hours. Mr. Justin has planned a wondrous meal for us."

Miss Dayspring's lips twisted with disapproval, and Alice's jaw muscles twitched as she grimaced. Alice's head turned side to side in three precise and very quick movements. "There must be no delay."

Humphrey pressed, still addressing the senator. "I invented this technology. If you won't trust my recommendation to delay your transfer into a Scion who is too young, at least take my advice in this. You are obviously well enough to wait another day. Please understand, the transfer will deconstruct your brain in whatever state it's in. Wouldn't it be best to wait until you're rested so that nothing important is lost in the transfer?"

Miss Dayspring tried to squeeze between Humphrey and the senator, but the old woman put a pasty hand on the nurse's chest and pushed her back. "I'm fine, Miss Dayspring. And I quite agree with Christof. As eager as I am to get this over with, I do need to psych myself up for it. A quiet dinner and good night's rest would do wonders for me."

Mr. Justin had told Humphrey that the senator was aggressive, assertive, but nobody's fool. She had built a powerful political career on her negotiation skills, always cinching deals that made it look like she was winning even when she had conceded major points.

"I apologize that our Jeep isn't available to drive us up to the hacienda," Humphrey said, "but it's a pleasant walk." He turned, and began to lead the senator toward the path to the hacienda. The guards followed. "Surely you don't need all of your guards. Mr. Justin has not prepared meals for them."

Without looking, the senator ordered, "Alice, tell the others to stand down."

Alice made the barest head tilt, and her men faded back to the helicopter and started tossing down duffle bags.

Alice and Miss Dayspring followed after Humphrey and the senator. "Dr. Carlhagen," Alice said, "I would like to secure the senator's Scion immediately. Where will I find her?"

Thinking quickly, Humphrey waved a dismissive hand. "Oh, leave her to her routine. She's not expecting the senator to arrive, and with you barging in, all of the Scions will be thrown into a tizzy."

"I insist."

"It's fine, Alice," Senator Bentilius said. "Leave the Scion for later." She put a hand on Humphrey's shoulder. "Now that it's come to it, I am rather glad we can wait until morning. I'm so tired from the travel. Miss Dayspring, you go with the guards to the medical ward."

"Madam Senator," Miss Dayspring said, shuffling sideways alongside her, "I must come with you. If you have another one of your spells—"

"I'll be with one of the finest doctors in the world. Now run along and do as I say."

Senator Bentilius hooked elbows with Humphrey and together they walked up the path. Having never seen the woman before, Humphrey didn't know whether she looked better or worse than usual, but she certainly didn't look well. A deep crease cut between her eyebrows, as if she struggled to bear through a tremendous headache. Though she was shorter than he expected, the way she wore her hair, like flames jutting from her skull, gave her an imperious presence.

"Lovely flowers," she said, as they passed one of Dr. Carlhagen's bougainvillea hedges. She cast a quick glance over her shoulder. Alice kept pace with them a few meters behind. "And never mind Alice. She's overprotective. She once broke a sixteen-year-old boy's arm when he asked me to sign a photo at a campaign rope-line."

"His pen was shaped like a dagger," Alice said. From the sound of her voice, Humphrey wondered if she was capable of parting her teeth when she spoke.

"It was a gag pen," Senator Bentilius said with a giggle that sounded so much like Summer that Humphrey did a double-take. Despite the awkwardness of pretending to be Dr. Carlhagen, he thought he preferred entertaining the senator to spending the same dinner with Summer. The girl was a shameless flirt, and had not given Humphrey a moment's peace for several months.

Alice picked up her pace to stride next to the senator. "I won't let you be injured again, Madam. Absolutely will not allow it. You are too important. The world needs you."

The senator giggled again. "A lot of good I'll be able to do the world as a fourteen-year-old girl."

"Better than dead, eh?" Humphrey said, trying to inject some humor into the conversation.

The senator grinned, exposing yellow teeth marred with lipstick. "You have a definite point there, Christof."

"I still say we should do the transfer immediately, before you have another one of your spells," Alice said.

Why won't that woman just shut up?

It took all of Humphrey's will to keep his jovial smile in place. "The senator will live the rest of her life based upon the quality of that transfer. A solid night's sleep can account for as much as five percent greater memory and skill retention post-transfer. I agree that Madam Senator is truly too important to let die, but please let's preserve everything we can."

The senator stopped and tugged on Humphrey's arm, forcing him to face her. "I thought my Scion was supposed to be even better than me."

"Oh, she is. She is," Humphrey said. "Or at least, she would have been if we could give her a few years to develop."

"I don't like this," Alice said.

"I don't either," the senator said. "But I don't see what other choice I have."

They walked the rest of the way to the hacienda in silence. By the sound of her huffing and puffing, the uphill trek was taking a toll on the old woman.

Mr. Justin met them at the door, giving the senator a deep bow and offering to guide them to the room he'd prepared for her.

"Of course, you'll be dining with me this evening," Humphrey said, as he stopped in her doorway. "Mr. Justin has planned something delicious." He turned to go, but stopped, snapping his fingers. "Is there a particular wine you prefer?"

"Oh, you know me, Christof. If it's red, I'll drink it."

Mr. Justin offered a room to Alice, but she declined with a grunt. "I'll sleep there." She pointed at an armchair next to the senator's bed.

"Until six o'clock, then." Humphrey gave a curt bow and walked away, wishing the dinner were already over.

14

LIKE A BRATTY LIZARD

Jacey sniffed at the musty air inside the shack. Little more than a metal-sided pavilion, its walls didn't even reach the ceiling, leaving a ten-centimeter gap open to the outside all the way around. According to Summer, it was designed to allow wind to pass through rather than blowing the shack over during the hurricanes.

A filthy lighting fixture dangled from chains off the ceiling. Jacey flicked a switch by the door and the two long white florescent tubes flickered to life. They buzzed and hummed disagreeably, as if irritated to have been awakened from their long nap. They cast a bluish glow over the dirty concrete floor.

Jacey ran a fingertip across a hose slung over a hook on one wall. It came away black with grime.

Several slender poles leaned in the corner. They must have been there for a decade to collect so many cobwebs. Summer pulled one free and held it to the light. She twisted the crank handle on a reel of greenish filament. "A fishing pole." She squinted at the mechanism. "Interesting."

Jacey agreed, but not for the same reason as Summer. The girl's head for mechanical things didn't necessarily make her practical-minded. "Do you think you could make it work? We need to eat something, and fish would be great."

"It needs bait."

"Like what?"

"I don't know. Another fish?"

"Let's keep looking."

A few bare wooden shelves held rusty bolts, a broken bottle, and a dish filled with ash and little white half-burned cylinders. They had foamy ends and they stank.

"We need to get moving," Jacey said.

"We'll hear the helicopter coming," Summer said, no hint of concern in her voice. She continued to fiddle with the pole, wiping off the dust and studying a hook dangling from the line.

Summer had a fair point. And since Belle and Dr. Carlhagen had taken the Jeep, whatever search parties were dispatched would be on foot. As long as she didn't hear the helicopter, the ground search couldn't be very close.

Summer put the fishing pole back and snatched up a tarp. "I'm going to lie down and take a nap."

"No you're not. We have to get out of here."

Summer dropped the tarp and stared at Jacey with those huge eyes. "To where?"

Jacey scooped up the tarp. She shook it out to make sure there were no scorpions in it, then refolded it. Satisfied, she handed it back to Summer. "We're probably going to have to sleep in the rainforest tonight. So look around for things we can use to shelter ourselves from the rain. And insects."

"What about the boat? I can get the motor started. I know I can."

"That'll put us right out in the open."

"If the helicopter comes, we'll head to shore someplace where the helicopter can't land."

"We're not taking the boat. I'm not discussing it anymore. Now look around for anything else we might use."

Summer said nothing but made her opinion known in other ways. She poked through the junk in the shack, kicking over rusty bits of machinery, tossing metal cans, and slamming down trays filled with washers and nuts so hard the bits and pieces scattered all over the shelves.

Jacey searched with more deliberation and forced herself to project an outward serenity at complete odds with her inner rage. Only by repeatedly telling herself that strangling a Spider was poor form for a Shark did she refrain from tackling the thankless girl.

A small pile formed in the middle of the shack as she collected potentially useful items. A coil of very thin metal wire, a slender, razor-sharp knife in a carved leather sheath, a roll of rough fabric with frayed edges, and a sturdy strap with clips on each end. She didn't have much of a plan for the items, but most were small and lightweight.

She found a pair of binoculars and two ponchos hanging from pegs behind the door. The ponchos were a thin, flimsy plastic, but they had hoods.

Summer had stopped her dissatisfied noises and stood motionless, watching Jacey and making a show of not helping.

Jacey thrust the binoculars and ponchos at Summer. "Here. Find something we can use to carry all this stuff in."

Summer let out a final huff of dissatisfaction, then turned and began to search for real. Jacey wanted water jugs but didn't find anything suitable. There was one plastic container, red with a strange flexible hose attached to it. She unscrewed the cap and took a sniff. "Ugh."

Summer peered over her shoulder. "What is it?"

"I don't know. It's horrible."

Summer sniffed and nodded knowingly. "That's fuel for the motor boat you won't let us use."

Jacey hefted the container. She considered emptying it, but from the smell of the fuel, she assumed it would contaminate any water she tried to put in it.

"Over there," Summer said, pointing at a white plastic jug. She made no move to get it from the high shelf it rested on.

Jacey managed to knock it down with one of the fishing poles. Dust coated the outside of the container, but a screw cap had kept the inside clean. Jacey sniffed, but it smelled of nothing but plastic. She handed it to Summer.

Jacey moved to the assorted bolts and junk on a lower shelf, stopping by the tray filled with ash. Behind it was a flimsy package. She plucked it up.

"What's that?" Summer asked.

"Cigarettes," she said, reading the label. An idea occurred to her, and she removed one of the slender cylinders. "Socrates said that people used to eat packaged food."

She sniffed the object. It didn't smell like food. And then she noticed that the stub end of it was the same as the charred ends in the tray of ash.

"Looks like something they use to start fires." Jacey put the cylinder back in the package and noticed another object, this one oval-shaped and as long as her index finger. She pressed the black button on one end, but it didn't do anything. She shrugged and tossed the package and device to Summer.

The girl seemed to have gotten over her most recent bratty streak and had turned her ingenuity to fashioning a backpack from the tarp and a length of rope she had found piled in one corner.

Jacey studied Summer's invention and shook her head in

amazement. Apparently, the lack of any practical application for Summer's talents at the Scion School had kept them hidden.

Summer's gifts shouldn't have surprised Jacey, she realized. All of the Scions were designed to be superior to their Progenitors—smarter, healthier, better trained. Jacey's thoughts turned momentarily to her own Progenitor, about whom she knew almost nothing other than that her name was Jacqueline. And that she was dead.

She offered Summer a nod and a smile, but the girl refused to return the gesture, instead deliberately looking away from Jacey and hefting the backpack over her shoulders.

"Let's go," Summer said, sighing.

They left the shack and continued down the road. A sign pointing in that direction said "Groundskeeper's Residence." But Jacey saw the lie in that immediately. Mother Tyeesha's had to be in that direction. Not that they could go there. Searchers would check every building on the island first. Fortunately, the forest thickened as they journeyed west, and Jacey didn't intend to stay on the road for long.

As they walked, they enjoyed the shade cast by the towering trees. The smells changed, became earthy and moist, heavier with humidity, and filled with the buzz and chatter of billions of insects. Jacey shivered to think of bedding down among them. She didn't know that much about the fauna of the island beyond what she had seen around the Scion School. That was on the east end, the drier side of the island. There were lizards and mongoose there, a few birds and butterflies. Lots of mosquitoes when the wind died down. And the occasional shaddle spider.

They walked in silence for an hour, stopping only once to refresh themselves with the remaining water in Summer's improvised water carrier. Jacey was about to suggest they turn into the depths of the rainforest when they came to a slight clearing. An overgrown pathway led to the right. It looked like the remains of an old road though grasses and brambles grew over it. But the way was clear of trees, which would make it easy to follow without getting turned around.

Even better, the old road disappeared into a denser band of rainforest, which would make them invisible to searchers in a helicopter.

A chill crept over Jacey's skin as she took her first steps into the unknown wilds. Summer straggled after, mumbling something about the boat under her breath. Jacey thought the girl wise to keep her thoughts quiet, because Jacey's tolerance lessened with every step.

But then one word rose from Summer's grumbling. *"Stupid."*

Jacey spun on Summer, coming nose to nose with her. "What is your problem?"

Summer stumbled back a few steps as if desperate to get out of striking range. As if Jacey would ever hit a Scion, let alone a member of her own Nine.

Jacey stomped a foot and jabbed a finger at Summer. "Why do you have to make this so difficult? I'm trying to help you."

Summer shifted the weight of her makeshift backpack and straightened. "And why *are* you helping me?"

"Because it's the right thing to do. Because I care about you." Jacey put her hands on her hips and blew out a long breath. "But you don't seem to appreciate it."

"I do appreciate it."

"Then why are you behaving like a bratty Lizard? What did I do to deserve your attitude?"

Summer looked at her feet and mumbled something.

Jacey stepped closer. "What was that?"

The girl's head snapped up, eyes blazing. "I said *because of you and Humphrey*."

Jacey closed her eyes and let out a long breath, cursed herself for not seeing what was so plain. Everyone knew that Summer was in love with Humphrey. Before the whole island had been turned upside down by recent events, Humphrey was the only subject Summer ever talked about. It had been a sore point for Humphrey, who had been mortified by the attention.

With the senator coming and the urgency to get away rising every moment, Jacey hadn't thought about that at all.

Summer sniffed and wiped wetness from her eyes. "Why couldn't you just love Vaughan like you're supposed to? Why did you have to take Humphrey from me?"

Jacey resisted pointing out that Humphrey was never Summer's to begin with. She also bit back the argument that their feelings for Humphrey had no bearing on the current crisis involving Senator Bentilius.

Summer was fourteen, and, to her, both issues were life-and-death problems.

Jacey turned it around on her. "And why can't *you* love Vaughan instead of Humphrey?"

Summer's lips moved, but she didn't say anything at first. She was obviously taken aback by the question. Finally, her shoulders drooped and she made a wry face. "Because Vaughan is too good, too perfect. I don't think I deserve someone like him." Petulance flared again, and Summer's eyes flashed. "And neither do you."

Jacey couldn't argue with that. Vaughan *was* too perfect.

He was also dead.

Summer sighed and wiped her wet cheeks with the back of her hand. She suddenly looked like a Dolphin, small, vulnerable. Her lips trembled. After another few breaths she mastered the flood of emotion and laughed as if her own thoughts didn't make sense to her. "Humphrey is different," she said at last. "He's less beautiful than Vaughan but more . . ." She shrugged, giving up her search for the right word. "I don't know. He's more real. You know? Like you can actually touch him."

Jacey understood. "I'm sorry, Summer. I didn't mean to steal Humphrey from you. But you have to understand a boy isn't property that you can give or take. That kind of thinking is what Dr. Carlhagen promotes with the Scion School."

Jacey risked putting an arm around Summer. She didn't resist. "And you're not someone who can be taken or given either. I understand you're upset about Humphrey and me, but trust me, I don't know how I feel about him. Yes, we've grown close over the past few days, but we've been through some really terrible things together. Let's just focus on surviving tonight and the next day and the next and get through this."

Summer sniffled. "I know you're right. But still, I could never compete with you. You're older and . . . I've heard the boys talking about you. I've seen how they look at you. Including Humphrey."

Jacey didn't know how to respond to that. She didn't like the idea that it had to be a competition. They were in the same Nine, the same family. They should be able to support each other.

They continued walking, picking their way through the thick foliage that covered the old abandoned road. It climbed steadily, and soon they were huffing and sweating. Jacey started to question her decision to come this way.

They topped a rise, and a gap in the trees showed that they had climbed one of the lower hills. They couldn't see the ocean behind them through the thick rainforest, but ahead lay a clear, grassy valley. A few tall tamarind trees dotted the lower reaches, and closer by stood a grove of mangoes.

"Look," Jacey said. "Mangoes. At least we'll have something to eat." Just seeing them made her stomach rumble.

Summer didn't respond. She was frozen, hands shading her eyes, leaning slightly forward.

"Summer?" Jacey said. "Let's go gather some mangoes."

"Yeah. Yeah, that would be good," she said. But she didn't move.

Jacey stepped next to her and tried to see what she was staring at. Summer pointed. "You see there, right at the edge of where the valley meets the tree line, you see that big mound? It looks like rock."

Jacey saw it, but it looked like part of the hillside, perhaps a thrust of rock covered with vegetation.

"Give me the binoculars," Summer said. "I think that's a building."

Jacey didn't agree, but she handed the binoculars to Summer.

Summer scanned the valley with the binoculars. "I'm pretty sure that's a building." She started off the road directly toward the structure, which lay at least a kilometer away.

"Summer, come on. Let's go get some mangoes. We can look at that rock pile after."

But Summer wasn't listening. She was marching straight off.

Jacey didn't want to split up, so she ran forward and grabbed Summer by the elbow and turned her around

"Listen to me. We're going to get the food first. Then we'll investigate what you found."

Summer's petulant look returned, but only for a moment. "Yes, you're right. Of course. That would make the most sense."

o o o

They stopped to rest in the shade of a tamarind tree, sweaty and thirsty. The valley was much bigger than it had appeared from the rise behind them. And there was no breeze here at the bottom. Jacey squatted to preserve energy and undid the catch at the throat of her uniform top. She would have loved to roll up her pant legs, too, but it seemed every other weed and bush bristled with thorns.

Jacey gnawed the last bit of mango flesh off the pit, then tossed it into a bush. Three mangoes had taken the edge off her hunger and had given her a burst of energy. But her stomach roiled. If they didn't eat something more substantial soon, they'd be helpless against searchers.

More than that, they needed water.

A glance at the sky showed nothing but blue. Hopefully the rainforest would live up to its name. Jacey would feel much better once the water jug was full.

"I think it's the ruins of an old windmill tower," Summer said, more to herself than to Jacey. Ahead, right at the edge of the forest line, the heaping mound of vine-covered rock hunched on the landscape. It looked a giant bucket of stone had been dumped upside down, holding its form like damp sand.

"It *is* a windmill tower," Summer said, voice full of conviction. She trained the binoculars to the left and fiddled with the focus. "And there is part of an old house. We should keep going."

Unlike Jacey, Summer had eaten a full breakfast. Jacey wished she'd eaten all of the pastries Mr. Justin had laid out that morning.

"Lead the way," Jacey said, thrusting herself upright.

The final stretch to the windmill tower offered no cover. If the helicopter appeared, they'd be spotted for sure.

Summer chose the easiest path, but the going got difficult

as they started upslope. Jacey kept scanning the skies for the helicopter.

The mound of stone slowly drew nearer. When they finally reached it, Jacey bent over, hands on knees, heaving huge breaths. She consoled herself with the fact that any pursuers would have to cross the same terrain. And with it so open, she and Summer would see them coming.

Unless they come at night . . .

Jacey blocked the thought. One could only worry about so many things, she decided. If she was going to expend the energy to worry, it might as well be about something she could control. Like getting into cover.

"We should move into the forest," she said.

"But there has to be an entrance," Summer said. "An archway, like in the bell tower."

They circled the vine-covered stone, looking for the entrance that had to be there. A few moments' prodding showed that the mound was made from stacked stone.

"Here it is." Summer wrenched a gap in a section of thick vines, exposing a dark opening. A second later, she had thrust her head and shoulders through.

"Wait, Summer," Jacey said. But the girl was gone

Jacey poked her head in. Faint light beamed through holes in the wall above them, providing just enough illumination to see a tumble of dead vines and limbs covering the floor of the structure.

A thick wooden beam ran from wall to wall overhead. A section of loft still remained on one side. If there had ever been stairs or a ladder to get up there, it had long since moldered away into nothing.

Summer walked the perimeter of the great stone circle. "This will do well, assuming we don't find a better option." She shrugged off the backpack.

The tower felt wrong to Jacey. She didn't know why, except that it made chills creep across her skin.

"Let's keep looking," she suggested.

They squeezed out of the tower and headed into the trees. Tumbled stone humps, the fallen walls of several structures, stood around an area of several hectares. A curved wall was the only remaining piece of what once had been a house of stone. A wide gaping window stood in it, and at its base lay the rusty hinges from the shutters. The wood had long ago disintegrated and now nourished the rambling plants that surrounded the wall.

They edged past the wall and into the deeper shadows, climbing over more mounds where only the cut square stones poking from the turf told that a manmade structure had once stood there.

"What's that?" Jacey asked, pointing.

A rectangular stump five meters high stood among the trees, its top jagged and broken. And beyond it, a ridge covered with fallen leaves and soil and moss showed where the remains of the tower had collapsed

"I think it was some kind of chimney," Summer mused.

Nearby, thrusting through the vegetation was the top half of a great iron wheel, toothed and mated to another gear attached to long iron shafts. The bones of some long-dead machine, they reminded Jacey vaguely of the torture devices from the Middle Ages Socrates had taught her about.

Summer studied the gears, running her fingers along the teeth. "People lived here. Worked here. This is old technology. There must have been another windmill at some point. These gears were wind-powered. They would spin and turn the shaft. But I don't know what purpose they served."

Jacey knew.

And it explained why she felt such dread in the windmill tower and such darkness seeping from the ground here.

"Socrates said St. Vitus was once a major sugar plantation. This has to be one of the farms. I don't know how they processed the sugarcane, but this must have been part of it."

She didn't want to stay there, but she knew they had no choice. They needed to rest. They needed to find more food.

The hushed crash of the surf came to her ears then, and she realized that they had made it nearly to the north shore of the island. That meant they might be able to find crabs or clams. With cover available and shelter in case of rain, she couldn't abandon this location. And it was very well concealed. She would never have noticed it. Only Summer's sharp eyes and awareness of construction and mechanical things had revealed it at all.

"Why are you hesitating?" Summer asked.

"It's . . ." Jacey rubbed her upper arms and lead Summer away from the rusty wheel. "We're not going to leave here. Not yet. It's just that if this is a plantation, it means that most of the people who worked here were slaves."

Summer shrugged. "They're gone now. This whole place is dead. I want to get back to my backpack. I think I might be able to make a snare."

"A snare?" Jacey said as they walked. "What do you think you're going to catch?"

"I don't know for sure, but I'm hoping a mongoose. Maybe a lizard."

Jacey suppressed her instinctive sneer, not wanting to discourage Summer's efforts. Despite herself, her stomach rumbled at the thought of mongoose meat. She would eat a lizard, too, if it came to it. She would do anything to survive. Anything to make sure Summer and all of the Scions survived.

She reflected on the amazing things a person could do when their life depended on action.

Maybe that's how Dr. Carlhagen and all of the Progenitors

had come to justify what they did with the Scions. Perhaps, little by little, they were corrupted by forces outside their control.

Jacey welcomed the protection of the windmill tower then. She wished it could keep out the great wide world beyond the shores of St. Vitus. Because if that world could pressure people into accepting such evil, perhaps it was best if she and the Scions stayed away from it.

15

DEAR, DEAR CHILD

The Jeep powered up a rutted gravel road that carried Belle and Vaughan higher and higher. Belle's knuckles whitened as she gripped the wheel. The road was barely wider than the Jeep. One bad rock or hole could make the machine tip and tumble down the scrub-covered hillside.

She summited the hill—more of a mountain, really—and descended toward a tree-shrouded valley. Seeing the tall, vine-covered trees brought up memories of Children's Villa. It had to be close.

Vaughan's head lolled against the window. Belle let him sleep, though she wished he were awake. The farther Belle drove, the more anxious she became, worrying she'd missed a turn.

The road smoothed out once she got to level ground and plunged into the forest's shadows. Where the landscape around the Scion School lay brown and dry in the winter months, this side of the island stayed green year-round. Even as she thought about the oddity of the climate differences from one side of the island to the other, raindrops spattered on the windshield.

The air thickened as she drove deeper into the rainforest, growing heavy with a scent she could only describe as "green."

The Jeep emerged from darkness. A growing patch of blue sky stretched overhead as rain clouds raced away to the east. She stomped the brake, bringing the Jeep to a sharp stop.

Small, tidy buildings stood all around her, white stucco walls and red-tiled roofs shining cheerfully in the fresh sunlight.

"It's so small," Belle said to herself. The tiny campus, known to every Scion simply as Children's Villa, seemed to have shrunk during the years she'd been away. Belle unlatched her restraining strap and stepped out of the vehicle.

There was no one around.

Mother Tyeesha's villa squatted nearest to Belle, its white-plank porch hugging the house. The old white rocking chair sat upon it. Attached to the house on either side were the Girls' and Boys' Halls for children four and up.

Belle stopped herself, realizing she'd taken a few unconscious steps toward the propped-open red doors of Girls' Hall. She fought the silly urge to find her old cot and think back on simpler—and safer—days. The childish impulse irritated her.

She pressed her lips together and turned to face the schoolhouse, where the sound of a woman's voice bubbled from open slatted windows. Birds responded from the trees, as if they were the pupils.

Though Belle couldn't make out what the woman was saying, the high, singsong voice belonged to Mother Tyeesha.

Eagerness rose in Belle's breast, constricted her throat, and caused her heart to gallop. A sudden need to embrace and be embraced by the schoolmistress propelled Belle toward the entrance.

She forced herself to stop.

Yes, she needed to speak to Mother Tyeesha, but she would not allow herself to indulge in emotional—and, there-fore, weak—urges. Besides, to throw herself into the woman's arms would be admitting subservience. Belle had had enough of that recently, what with all the playing along with Jacey's fantasy of running the Scion School.

Belle straightened her top, fingers automatically going to the Shark pin on her collar. Pulling her face into dead passiv-ity, she climbed the three steps to the schoolroom and stepped inside.

The woman she remembered had shrunk even more than the school grounds. Gone was the thick black cloud of hair that haloed Mother Tyeesha's face in all of Belle's memories. Instead, a short-cropped fuzz of gray carpeted her skull.

The face, once smooth, had eroded into a terrain of dry riverbeds and deltas. Only the eyes were the same. After a moment of confusion, those familiar eyes softened.

Belle's control wavered for a second, but she regained it, balling her fists and taking a deep breath.

Mother Tyeesha's face sagged in shock before suddenly crinkling even more. Finally, a smile split her wide, pursed mouth, stretching to reveal a tremendous expanse of white teeth. It was the widest, most welcoming smile Belle had ever seen.

Children from four to eight years old sat in various circles, hands on the study materials they'd taken from tidy shelves all around the sparely appointed room. Every eye lifted and focused on Belle as if she were a mythological being descended from heaven in a column of light. Their curious stares unsettled Belle even more than the time-wrought changes in Mother Tyeesha's face.

One girl in particular, a narrow-faced and lovely little elfin girl, seemed to drink Belle in. The look reminded Belle of how Livy sometimes looked at Jacey.

Belle shivered and forced down all thoughts about the destiny that awaited these children.

I just need to get away from this island, she reminded herself. *Jacey's the savior. I'm the survivor.*

"Children," Mother Tyeesha said, breaking the long, strange silence that gripped the room. Her voice rose an octave. "This is one of my first Scions. Please offer cheerful greetings to Miss Belle."

As one the children said, "Welcome, Miss Belle." The chorus of voices, high-pitched and burdened with unskilled youthfulness, sent another chill along Belle's skin. They sounded alien to her. She hadn't heard a four-year-old speak in a long time.

They're just babies.

Mother Tyeesha took slow steps forward, pausing once to snap her fingers at a pair of squirrelly boys who whispered to each other in the too-loud way Dolphins did when they first arrived at the Scion School.

The old woman spread her arms wide. Belle almost gave in, almost let herself be drawn into that promise of comfort and safety. But she held herself back. There was no safety here. What could the affection of an old woman do to prevent Belle's Progenitor from overwriting her? Love could do nothing practical; it had no might. Love was an illusion, as insubstantial as Belle's own memories of Children's Villa.

"We need to talk," Belle said, keeping her voice cold and flat. "Things at the Scion School are . . ."

Mother Tyeesha wasn't listening. Her gaze had shifted, fixing somewhere over Belle's shoulder. Belle turned, expecting to find one of the children misbehaving. Instead, she discovered Vaughan silhouetted in the doorway.

Mother Tyeesha gasped.

Vaughan staggered into the room, smiling in his impossibly beautiful way. Without a word, he swept Mother Tyeesha into his arms.

She closed her eyes and pressed her cheek to his. "Oh, my dear, dear child. You've returned to me at last."

o o o

Belle didn't know how she'd gotten outside, didn't remember walking out of the schoolroom. She was just there, staring at the Jeep, which blurred as tears formed but did not fall. She angrily blinked them away.

What did it matter that she was not a "dear, dear child?" Those sentiments had no true meaning.

Her feelings were nothing but a conditioned response to sense-data input.

She associated the old woman with a vulnerable, innocent time of her life. That was all. Mother Tyeesha's thoughts were nothing but morning mist.

"Nothing can touch me," she said to her distorted reflection in the hood of the Jeep.

She leaned against the vehicle, determined to wait for Vaughan and Mother Tyeesha's joyous reunion to end. Then they'd figure out how to contact the outside world, figure a way off the island.

Just her and Vaughan. Together.

They would survive.

And then—only then—would she consider indulging in love.

16

FULL OF OAK AND PEAT MOSS

umphrey had very little time to relax before the evening meal with the senator. At Mr. Justin's insistence, he had changed out of one white suit and into a different white suit. The blue bow tie Mr. Justin brought out might have been a slightly different shade, but Humphrey didn't see the point.

"One dresses for dinner," was all Mr. Justin would say for explanation.

When the senator came into the dining room, Humphrey apologized for the ill fit of his clothes. "I haven't yet had time to visit a tailor." He patted his flat stomach and smiled wanly. "I fear I was quite corpulent before the transfer."

Senator Bentilius had changed into a loose-fitting pants and tunic with short sleeves that revealed her slender, but spotted, arms. "You look dashing as always, Christof."

The use of Dr. Carlhagen's first name puzzled Humphrey. He wondered if the senator had known Dr. Carlhagen personally. Mr. Justin hadn't known anything about it, and

Humphrey had not uncovered any clues among Dr. Carlhagen's papers.

Humphrey guided the senator to a chair next to the one at the head of the table where Dr. Carlhagen traditionally sat. Mr. Justin came in, bearing salads on a silver tray. Humphrey tried not to dwell on memories of a similar meal just days earlier, when Dr. Carlhagen had entertained him and Jacey at this table. Two such dinners had taken place, the most uncomfortable of Humphrey's entire life.

Mr. Justin poured out half-glasses of the red wine. Humphrey gave it an appreciative sniff, though in truth he would have rather poured it out the window. He dampened his lips with the smelly liquid, but didn't let it touch his tongue.

The senator took a much longer swig, the whole time eyeing Humphrey over the brim of her glass. She swallowed and patted her lips with a white napkin. "I envy you, Christof. What freedom it is to be able to step forward as yourself after your transfer."

Humphrey nodded as if he understood her point.

The senator smiled. "I've been able to track down your first graduating class, you know." She flashed a mischievous look at him. "Don't act so surprised. When four of the richest people on earth die within a short period of time, and then suddenly have heretofore unknown relatives emerge as heirs, it's easy for people like me, who know your secret, to put the pieces together. The handsome young man, Dante, is certainly Silvio Silva. The girl Vin is Elizabeth English, and young Ping, who now studies art in Paris, has to be Han Cheng. I have not yet been able to track down the fourth, though. I assume it's a woman. Whoever she is, she is laying very low. But given the mysterious disappearance of one Janicka Howard, I am watching certain bank accounts very carefully."

Humphrey cleared his throat to make a show of being caught red-handed. "I can't comment on details of my other clients, Maxine."

The senator winked at him. "I appreciate your discretion, but you know you can confide in me."

More than ever, Humphrey wished that Jacey were there. She had always been able to read people so well. He didn't like the trajectory of the conversation, so he decided to change the subject. "I was distressed to hear about your illness. I hope you're not feeling too poorly tonight."

"My medication is good," the senator said, stabbing a cherry tomato from her salad. "It suppresses the worst symptoms, but I do have memory lapses and occasional bouts of dizziness."

"Do let me know if you need to return to your bed. Don't be polite on my account."

"I'm fine, dear." The senator popped the tomato in her mouth and sighed appreciatively. "Do you know how much a tomato like that would cost in Indianapolis?"

"Cost?"

"Of course you don't. You're rolling in it. I have a pretty good idea what you're raking in from this little operation." She took up her wine glass and drained it. "And to think, a billion dollars will be walking-around-money for you soon."

Mr. Justin bustled in with the wine bottle and topped off their glasses. Humphrey tried to make eye contact, desperate for some sign of what he should say. The butler ignored him and departed.

Humphrey stammered a response. "I don't care to discuss money at the table."

"Oh? What would you like to discuss?" The senator's foot rubbed against Humphrey's calf. He froze with his fork halfway between his plate and his mouth. The realization that the senator was flirting with him sapped what remained of his poor appetite. It was Summer all over again, except a million years older.

The senator winked. "I know I'm going to be a bit too young after the transfer for our relationship to be public, but I am looking forward to trying out my new body."

The room felt suddenly quite warm, and Humphrey wiped his brow with his napkin. Without thinking he took a deep swig of wine, which made him cough. "That wouldn't be appropriate," he said, eyes tearing. "Your Scion is only fourteen."

"Come now, doctor," Senator Bentilius said, leaning on her elbow and sliding closer to him. "I know you're a bit of a prude, but *I* won't be fourteen, no matter what body I'm wearing." She flashed a painted-on eyebrow. "I plan to prove that to you many times over."

"But, Maxine!"

"No one has to know. Besides, I'm not asking you to marry me. Where's the harm enjoying each other's company? Besides, we'll be spending so much time together now that we're in business together."

Business?

Humphrey covered his shock with a cough. "Oh, of course. How are things going on your front?" He stuffed his mouth with bitter greens and chewed with great vigor. Maybe if he kept his mouth full, he wouldn't be expected to say anything more.

The senator pushed her salad aside, and leaned back in her chair, dangling the wine glass from her fingers. "The new facility is almost done. Much has been accomplished since you returned here and got out of my way. I know how to twist arms. I think we'll be ready to receive the first Scions by the first of the year. What progress have you made in recruiting a martial arts master for the new Scion School?"

Humphrey's lips moved, but nothing came out.

Another Scion School?

Clearly, Mr. Justin hadn't known of this or he would have said something.

Wouldn't he?

"I am, um, reviewing possible candidates. As you know, I like to recruit those who I have complete control over. The most competent people keep the skeletons in their closets locked up tight. I have a number of candidates in mind, but I'm still searching for sufficient leverage over them."

The senator took a long, languid sip of her wine, swallowed it, swirled the remainder in her glass for a moment, then tossed it back. "Delicious!" she exclaimed. "You know, Christof, I want to apologize for how stern I was in our holo communication earlier. You understand, don't you? I had an audience off-camera, and I need to keep up my reputation as a tough broad."

"Oh, of course. No offense taken at all, my dear. But I must reiterate, transferring to your Scion now is fraught with risk."

The senator didn't let her sultry smile fade, though her words came out like stone. "And of course you understand I have no alternative."

Humphrey was saved from responding by Mr. Justin's entrance. The butler noted the senator's empty wine glass. "I'm afraid the bottle is empty. Shall I go to the wine cellar and fetch another?"

Humphrey opened his mouth to decline, but before he could utter a word the senator clapped her hands. "No, no. Let me and Christof go down to find something. Wouldn't that be delightful? I'm so interested in seeing your wine cellar."

The prospect of going down there alone with the senator filled Humphrey with dread. And irritation. All he really wanted was to go to bed. But seeing no alternative, he patted the table and stood. "All right," he said, tossing his cloth napkin down. He made a great show of going to the senator's chair and pulling it back so she could stand. She wasn't too steady on her feet. Humphrey couldn't gauge if it was due to her illness, the wine, or perhaps a combination of both. He steadied her by taking hold of her elbow. She leaned into him as he guided her to the door.

"Dr. Carlhagen?" Justin called to him. Humphrey left the senator holding onto the doorjamb and followed Mr. Justin toward the servers' entrance of the dining room. Mr. Justin extended a small shiny object.

The key to the wine cellar.

Humphrey grabbed at it. "Oh, thank you."

Mr. Justin didn't relinquish it.

"Far left row, in three shelving units, third shelf down, is a decent Alexander Valley Pinot. You're choosing it because it is among the rarest in your collection and you've been saving it for a special occasion. It tastes of blackberries, oak, with hints of morning dew on grass." Mr. Justin smiled broadly, and cut a glance at the senator before meeting Humphrey's gaze. "Be careful, sir."

Humphrey returned to the senator and tried to brush past. She caught his elbow and slipped an arm into his. "Oh, this is a wonderful house," she said as she tottered down the hallway. "I'm going to enjoy spending much time here with you

"Time did you say? You'll be spending *time* here?"

A cackle burst from the woman's throat. "As you continue to point out, I'm going to be a fourteen-year-old after all of this. I can hardly return to my duties as a senator."

"Oh, yes," Humphrey said. "About that . . . What is your cover story?"

"Same thing as all the others'. I'll be the long-lost daughter I gave up for adoption."

Humphrey did the math in his head. The senator could be

no younger than sixty-four, which would mean that Summer, at fourteen, would have to have been born when the senator was fifty years old. He had no idea if that was possible or not.

He didn't pursue it. He remembered something Jacey had told him. To keep a conversation going without having to contribute anything, ask about the other person's interests. "I don't recall if you were in politics yet when you were fifty."

She patted his arm playfully. "Christof! You flatterer. Of course you know that to have a fourteen-year-old, she would have to have been born when I was seventy—and in my second term as senator."

Seventy?

That meant the senator was eighty-four. He glanced at her appreciatively. His only reference point for judging ages was photographs he had seen in the various history lessons Socrates had provided. That, and Dr. Carlhagen himself, who had been in his nineties before transferring into Vaughan. For all her hideous frailty and shocking red hair, it seemed the senator had aged quite well.

They came to the wine cellar door. He disentangled his arm from the senator's and placed the key in the lock. Suddenly, the senator's arms wrapped around him and she hugged him close, hands exploring his chest. He let out a cough and wriggled free, turning to face her.

"Excuse me, Maxine. The door swings open into the hall." They shuffled backward. He opened the door and hurried down to the steps, flicking the light switch as he passed it. His youth got him to the bottom well before the senator had gotten halfway. He didn't wait for her before jogging down the aisles of wine racks.

He called over his shoulder, "The vintage I'm looking for is over here." He moved left and hugged the stone wall, which was moist with condensation. The low ceiling made every step and breath reverberate. The crisscrossed wine racks were densely packed with bottles, so that each was effectively a wall.

"Ooh. It's cold down here," said the senator.

Humphrey turned with a start. The senator wasn't there, but the strange acoustics had made it sound like she was speaking in his ear.

"Where are you?" The senator's voice echoed in the great chamber.

"Over here," he said, searching quickly for the bottle Mr. Justin had told him to fetch. He counted down three shelves. He pulled out a bottle. "This must be it."

"There you are!" The senator oozed close to him, then something in her demeanor changed. She moved past him. "Where does that lead?"

"Where does what lead?" He spun the bottle to read the label. The last thing he needed was Mr. Justin scolding him for bringing the wrong wine.

"That door."

He glanced up from the bottle and moved to look over the senator's shoulder. And there it was, a steel door set in the stone wall. To one side of it, mounted chest high, was a numeric keypad.

Not having the first clue where the door led, he improvised. "Ah, it's just a supply closet.

"Strange for a supply closet to be locked with a security system. Or is Mr. Justin always stealing your towels?" She giggled like a mere Dolphin.

Humphrey didn't answer and turned back up the aisle. Remembering to put on his Dr. Carlhagen joviality, he said with a laugh, "I've been saving this bottle for a special occasion. A Keno Boir. Full of oak and peat moss, with a hint of seaweed." He barely listened to his own words. The door puzzled him, and he wondered what Dr. Carlhagen might have locked up in there.

"Sounds delightful," the senator said, again sneaking and arm around his waist. She cast a glance at the stone floor. "Pity the floor is so damp and hard. It would be cozy down here otherwise."

"Ah yes, you're right. We should return to the dining room immediately." Humphrey nearly dragged the senator after him, as she refused to let go of him. He propelled them both toward the stairs, fuming at her intrusion and her unwelcome advances. The woman could not get the hint.

He got to the bottom of the steps, and then, in a burst of inspiration, swept his arm around the senator and gave her a slight hug. "It is good to see you, Maxine, but I forgot a dessert wine I thought we should try. Why don't you run along? I'll be right up."

Her eyes glistened at his warm gesture. A stab of guilt passed through Humphrey's chest. As much as he hated the woman, he didn't like lying to her.

"That's a good idea," she said. "I need to use the little girls' room anyway."

She started up the steps, supporting herself with a hand against the one wall and the other grasping the railing.

He spun and darted down the rows of shelving, back to the door. He studied the keypad and wracked his brain for what code Dr. Carlhagen might have used to secure it. His mind turned to the puzzle of why Dr. Carlhagen had employed such a low-tech system when the AI could have watched over the door.

The only thing he could think of was that Dr. Carlhagen didn't trust Chax to guard this room, which seemed odd since he guarded everything else about the campus. Humphrey's hand went to the keypad and he was about to enter a random string of numbers when he snatched it back. Entering the wrong code might produce an alarm somewhere.

The last thing he needed was Mr. Justin running down and wondering why he was trying to get into the room.

But how to get in?

He tapped his lips with a finger and studied the door. The hinges were attached to the stone wall with fat bolts. Even if he had a wrench, it would take hours to wrest it free and the door itself would be too heavy to move out of the way without help. Unless he had some explosives, or some huge excavating machine, he wasn't going to be able to break the door free of the wall.

He thought about the floor plan of the hacienda and what lay directly above the door. As far as he could tell, whatever lay beyond was carved out of the bedrock of the island. There would be no way to dig his way in. The only way was to figure out the code.

He swore in frustration and tapped his toe in irritation. Agitation built, and he unconsciously crossed his arms and hugged his shoulders, as if to contain it.

A lump in his jacket drew his attention. *His reader.* In a burst of inspiration, he pulled it free from his inside pocket and glanced up at the wine racks behind him. There, along the right wall, was a shadowy area. He placed his reader in this dark patch, leaning it atop the rack and against the wall, its camera aimed directly at the door and the keypad.

"Vaughan?" he asked. His friend's face appeared on the screen. "Do you have a good view of the keypad?"

"I do," Vaughan said, "although the optics in this camera aren't good. I can't zoom in very close."

"It's the best I can do right now. Keep watch in case Mr. Justin accesses the room. I'll try to find the key code among Dr. Carlhagen's things, but my guess is that it was something he memorized."

Vaughan didn't seem very interested. "Why do you need to get in there?"

"I don't know that I do. It's just . . . it's a locked door, so I presume that Dr. Carlhagen had something of value in there. Maybe something that can help us."

"Very well. I'll task an instance of myself to keep an eye out."

"I've got to go." Humphrey hustled down the aisle, pulled a second bottle from a rack at random, ascended the stairs, flipped the switch off, closed the door, locked it, and returned to the dining room.

Humphrey slowed his steps as he approached the entry to the dining hall. He took several deep breaths and pasted the old Dr. Carlhagen smile on his lips. He lifted the wine bottles as he stepped through. "And here we are," he said, adding a guttural laugh.

"I was starting to get worried, Christof," Senator Bentilius said. "I was just about to send Mr. Justin down to fetch you. Isn't that right, Mr. Justin?"

"As you say, madam." Mr. Justin swept forward and took the bottles from Humphrey, flashing him a questioning look.

Humphrey gave a little shrug, and whispered, "She was getting very handsy. I needed to get away from her for a few minutes."

"Of course, sir," Mr. Justin said, adding a curt bow. He glanced at the label on the second bottle of wine. "An excellent choice, sir."

Humphrey made a show of eagerly sweeping around the table to take his position, even though inside he felt like he was walking to the gallows. The senator scooched her chair closer to his and placed a hot hand on top of his.

"Like old times, isn't it?" she said

"Yes, just like. So how long do you think you plan to stay on the beautiful island of St. Vitus?"

"I don't know," she said, waving a lazy hand. "It's been so

long since I've been on holiday. I think I'll just enjoy my new youth, the sunshine . . . your warm company."

Improvising, Humphrey smiled and placed his hand on top of hers. "But surely, Maxine, you can't stay away from the political intrigues. The Scion School is beautiful, I'll grant you that, but it's not where the action is."

The senator arched an eyebrow and leaned even closer. "There's action, my dear, and then there's *action*. Besides, proximity will be useful as we work out the final details of the new school. I hate coordinating over holovid. It seems half my life has been spent talking to little translucent people. I'm far more interested in flesh and blood." She smiled evilly, and Humphrey struggled not to snatch his hands away.

Mr. Justin brought in the main course. Humphrey wanted to hug the man for interrupting the very uncomfortable intimacy that was starting to suffocate him.

"And how about things on your front, Christof?" Senator Bentilius asked. "Has being in this new, strong body distracted you from your part of the work?"

"Distracted?" Humphrey said, trying to sound offended. "I may enjoy the pleasures of life, but ninety-some years have taught me that I only enjoy a thing to the extent that I have endured its opposite. Hard work begets delightful pleasure." He lifted his fork and jabbed a hunk of the mango from his plate and popped it in his mouth. Then, pulling his other hand away from the senator, he lifted his wine glass and took a tiny sip. "Just as the bitter wine makes the sweet sweeter."

The senator's face flushed and her eyes glistened. "And a cold shower makes for a warm bed."

Humphrey nearly choked on the mango and had to wash it down with another slug of wine. "Indeed, Madam."

As if his coughing was a cue, Mr. Justin entered again. "Dr. Carlhagen, I hate to interrupt your dinner, but you have an important call waiting in the office. I really do believe you should take it."

"Of course, of course," Humphrey said, eagerly pushing away from the table and standing. "Excuse me, Maxine. I'll be back directly."

He followed Mr. Justin out of the room and into Dr. Carlhagen's office. The butler closed the door and turned to face Humphrey. Gone was the usual smile and crinkling eyes. Instead, he bit his lip and began to pace.

As Humphrey expected, there was no call at the holodesk. Mr. Justin had called him away in order to get him out of earshot of the senator.

"I think I should have been better prepared for this dinner, Mr. Justin," Humphrey said, coolly.

"Trust me, Humphrey, the senator's revelations this evening came as a shock to me as well. I had no idea of Dr. Carlhagen and Senator Bentilius's past romantic relationship. And I certainly had no idea about this other Scion School."

"I thought you were Dr. Carlhagen's right-hand man. Why would he conceal the other school from you?"

The butler pursed his lips and then shrugged. "I have no idea. Perhaps he grew mistrustful of me because I knew as much as I did. After all, as you know, he wasn't himself in the final weeks of his life. He was so addicted to the andelprixin."

"That's a sedative, right?" Humphrey said, an idea coming to him. "Do you think you could slip a tablet or two into her wine?"

"That's not a bad idea," Mr. Justin said. "Except for that giant bodyguard of hers might come up to speak with the senator, and it wouldn't do to find her drugged unconscious."

"Very well. I think I'm going to go insist that she gets to bed. You know, get rest and everything for the transfer tomorrow. What we're going to do to prevent it, I have no idea."

"It's certainly not going to happen first thing. It seems

Summer and Jacey are missing. I got a worried message from Wanda that neither has returned to Girls' Hall this evening.

"Does Alice know?"

Mr. Justin gave Humphrey a what-do-you-think look. If Alice had found out, she would have already stormed into the dining room and trashed the place.

"I can't say it surprises me," Humphrey said. "I knew Jacey was up to something, but I wouldn't let her tell me what it was. Though hiding seems futile. Alice will turn the campus upside-down."

"Oh, I don't think they're on campus," Mr. Justin said. "You see, Belle managed to release Dr. Carlhagen from the medical ward and drive right out the front gate in the Jeep."

"She did what?" Humphrey gasped. "That's the last thing we need. Wait—do you think Jacey and Summer went with Dr. Carlhagen and Belle?" The idea seemed preposterous.

"No. I think that Belle and Dr. Carlhagen took the Jeep and Summer and Jacey slipped out while the gate was open."

Humphrey put his face in his hands. Relief battled with anxiety. He was glad that Jacey and Summer were gone. He was horrified that Dr. Carlhagen was loose and that Belle was with him. And even more pressing than that was the prospect of facing Alice when she learned of it all the following morning.

"I'm going to play stupid as long as I can," he said. "Delay, delay, delay. Give Jacey and Summer the chance to get far away and find some place to hole up."

"That's not going to help the situation here at the Scion School," Mr. Justin said. "The longer Summer is missing, the more likely it is that the senator will call in a larger search team. Our control of the school will be ripped away. Soon after, your true identity will be discovered. Nothing I can do will protect you then." Mr. Justin went to the window and gazed out. "And the island will offer no long-term safety for Jacey, Summer, or even Dr. Carlhagen. There is no way off."

"This is just getting worse and worse," Humphrey said. "What do you think I should do?"

Mr. Justin looked at his feet, clearly not wanting to say what came next. He raised his head then, expression cold. "You must tell the senator before Alice finds out. And then you need to hope they find Summer and get the transfer over with."

17

GUILE IN HIS EYES

Belle lifted the dainty white cup to her lips and sipped the hot tea. She didn't care for it, but at least it was wet.

Vaughan sat across the small round table from her, frowning at his own cup, eyes at half-mast. Mother Tyeesha bustled by the sink of her small kitchen, drying a mahogany bowl with an embroidered towel.

Vaughan tipped his cup, draining the last of it. He set it down and let out a satisfied sigh. "That was wonderful, Mother. Thank you so much." His lips spread, and his eyes crinkled with what might have been delight if he hadn't looked so weary. He really needed to get to bed, but had so far refused Mother Tyeesha's offer of her own room.

Mother Tyeesha put the bowl in a cabinet, nesting it inside a stack of identical ones. "I'll have to introduce you to the nursery staff and the assistant teachers."

Vaughan pushed back his chair and stood. He had to press his hands to the table to stay upright. "Oh, how are Robin and Marcus doing?"

Mother Tyeesha froze momentarily, then turned off the water and wiped her hands on the towel. "They're marvelous. Such a sweet couple. And they dote on the babes."

"That's excellent," Vaughan said. Belle could tell by his sagging face that his smile was a work of will, and not much else. He backed out of the kitchen. "I'm going to go use your holodesk, if you don't mind."

Not waiting for permission, he disappeared down the short hall and into Mother Tyeesha's tiny office. It was barely more than a closet, from what Belle had seen.

She watched the door where Vaughan had been standing. They were so close now, so near reaching freedom. All Vaughan needed to do was contact someone to come pick them up.

Mother Tyeesha sat in the chair that Vaughan had vacated, carefully dried the rim of his cup with the towel, then poured herself a cup. The wooden chair creaked beneath her, but from the way she looked, the sounds could just as easily have come from her bones.

So this is what an old woman looks like, Belle thought. *No wonder the Progenitors buy Scions.*

"What happened to Vaughan?" Mother Tyeesha asked, still intent on her cup.

Belle kept her face smooth. Mother Tyeesha couldn't have known the truth, but the woman had always been intuitive. She had watched Vaughan grow up, so maybe she remembered his mannerisms and expressions. Belle squirmed inside to think of how much Mother Tyeesha knew about her. She had witnessed Belle's unguarded emotions before Belle had learned to properly mask them.

"I don't know what you mean," Belle said.

Mother Tyeesha hunched up her shoulders and shifted in

her chair. "There's a stiffness in Vaughan's arms, a perfunctory quality to his words. As if he's playacting."

"It has been nearly nine years since you've seen him," Belle said. "We've all changed."

She wondered what Mother Tyeesha expected after so long. And after they had endured the rigorous physical and mental training Dr. Carlhagen had prescribed for them.

"Vaughan was always such a warm, loving boy." Mother shook her head as if she couldn't figure it out.

Belle didn't understand what the old woman was talking about. Vaughan had been nothing but warm to Mother Tyeesha since arriving.

"It's as if it's not even him," Mother Tyeesha said. "There's too much guile in his eyes." Her dark gaze lifted from her cup and met Belle's.

Belle wanted to withdraw from that stare. It seemed to drink her in and at the same time weigh her on a scale. "Maybe it's because you sent us off to a fate worse than death." She kept her hands clasped tightly in front of her and refused to allow herself to fidget. Every instinct urged her to move out of Mother Tyeesha's sight, which at Belle's words had intensified to a knife-sharp focus.

"I sent you off to have the finest education on the planet," Mother Tyeesha said, her voice lifting just enough at the end of the sentence to make it a question.

She doesn't know, Belle realized. All these years, Mother Tyeesha had believed Dr. Carlhagen's lie that the Scions were being prepared for a great destiny.

18

MY REMAINING $25 MILLION

Humphrey unbuttoned his white suit coat and yanked loose the blue bow tie, letting the tail ends fall across his lapels. With a great sigh of relief he undid the top button on his shirt. As loose as it was, it seemed to strangle him. He let out a sigh.

Even Dr. Carlhagen's tie is trying tried suffocate me.

The irony of his situation—that he had to pretend to be the old man—grated on him. That he was apparently quite skilled at it made him queasy. If there was anyone he wanted to be unlike, it was Dr. Carlhagen.

He sighed and rubbed his eyes. Fending off the senator's surprisingly energetic advances and getting her to bed had taken a lot more physical effort than it should have. He'd done so only with the help of three more glasses of wine. He'd practically had to carry her down the hall, until Alice appeared and took charge of the old woman.

Humphrey headed back towards Dr. Carlhagen's office, planning to go through the drawers and search for information about the new Scion School the senator had mentioned.

As he approached, he heard a voice coming from inside. It was Mr. Justin speaking to someone.

The door was closed. Humphrey pressed an ear to it. Vaughan's voice came to him then, though he couldn't understand what was being said. He decided that if Mr. Justin was talking to Vaughan there'd really be no reason to keep Humphrey out. He rapped a knuckle on the door and turned the knob and stepped in.

Mr. Justin stood behind the mahogany desk holding up a hand to silence Vaughan.

"Hello, Humphrey," Mr. Justin said.

Humphrey shrugged off the suit coat and tossed it on a chair. He could hardly wait to be rid of the damn thing. Stretching until his shoulders and ankles popped, he paced around the room. "That was awful. Did you tell Vaughan what we learned?"

Mr. Justin's face pinched in an odd way. "This is not Vaughan."

Humphrey's eyes snapped up. He stepped around to stand beside the butler and stared down at the twelve-inch-tall hologram. Realization made his jaw clamp tight.

"Dr. Carlhagen," he said through gritted teeth. "What do you want?"

"He is demanding to speak to the senator," Mr. Justin said. "I refused him."

On closer inspection, it was clear from the holo's face that he was Dr. Carlhagen. On the surface, he looked like Vaughan, but somehow, his expression had twisted in a way peculiar to the old man.

"So," Dr. Carlhagen said, "my erstwhile Scion is playing at being headmaster. And you, Mr. Justin, are a traitor. I know what you're up to. But if you think you can use my Scion as your puppet, you have no idea the contingencies I have in place."

"I only serve the best interests of the Scions," Mr. Justin said. "I have nothing else to say to you." With that, Mr. Justin left, shutting the door quietly behind him.

"What have you done to Belle?" Humphrey demanded.

"Done to her?" Dr. Carlhagen said, smiling. "I don't want to do anything to her. She is very valuable to me. In less than a year she'll be overwritten and I'll get my remaining twenty-five million dollars from her Progenitor." Dr. Carlhagen frowned at that. "I never should have discounted so deeply for the early Progenitors." He shook off his momentary disappointment and looked Humphrey up and down. "I see you're wearing my suit. You're such a disappointment. You could never fill it."

"Your disapproval of me," Humphrey said, "is the best thing I've heard all day. Speaking of which, this has been a long one and I want to go to bed. You're not going to speak to the senator. She just passed out in her room, quite drunk."

"And what are you going to do when they find her Scion has gone missing?"

Humphrey froze. How did Dr. Carlhagen know that Summer was missing? Humphrey had only found out himself a half hour earlier. Had Mr. Justin told him?

"I'm going to deny all knowledge of it," Humphrey said. "And from the state of the senator's health, I don't expect her to live more than a few weeks, and then it will be a moot point."

"I cannot impress upon you enough," Dr. Carlhagen said, "how critical it is that you secure her Scion and transfer the senator. She's perhaps the second most important Progenitor of the lot. If something happened to her . . ."

"What?" Humphrey asked, but Dr. Carlhagen had clamped his mouth shut. Humphrey wanted to demand more information about the new Scion School, but he didn't feel that revealing that knowledge would be wise. Dr. Carlhagen wouldn't confide anything to Humphrey.

He wondered where Dr. Carlhagen was that he could communicate by holodesk. The answer followed right after. Mother Tyeesha's. That was a fine place for him, Humphrey thought. As angry as Dr. Carlhagen was, he had no power to do anything about what happened in the Scion School. Once the senator and her people were gone—however that came to pass—then he could worry about Dr. Carlhagen.

Smiling at the pleasure of it, he disconnected from Dr. Carlhagen and set about searching through his papers.

19

SEEMS AN ODD TOPIC

"**Y**ou've had suspicions about the school, haven't you?" Belle said to Mother Tyeesha in a bare whisper.

"Suspicions that something was not right?" Mother leaned forward and grasped Belle's hands, forced them apart. Mother's palms were hot, dry and rough. "Always. But no proof."

Belle closed her eyes and barely resisted squeezing those hands and holding onto them like a lifeline.

"Tell me, child," Mother Tyeesha urged.

Belle pulled a hand free and took a long sip of the tea, grimacing as the bitter liquid eased her dry throat. She swallowed again, trying to pull back the bitterness she felt toward Mother Tyeesha. And yet, why shouldn't she feel bitter? If the woman had suspicions, why hadn't she sought answers?

"You're telling me you don't know what happens at the Scion School?" Belle said. "You don't know that we're clones?"

"I did know that. Dr. Carlhagen said that the wealthy and privileged had entered a secret program. He said that you children would one day be welcomed back into their families and raised as their children."

Belle let out a humorless laugh. "I don't think you will even believe the truth."

"Try me," Mother Tyeesha said. "Please."

Belle explained it all. About how the Progenitors arrived on the Scions' eighteenth birthday, were introduced as the Scions' parents, and then taken for a "medical test," one which transferred the mind of the Progenitor into the Scion. "It erases the Scion from existence, Mother. All so the Progenitor can live another life."

As Belle told the story, Mother Tyeesha's grip hardened on her hand. Her craggy face tightened, and tears streamed down the wrinkly waterways of her cheeks. Belle wrested her hand free and gripped her sides, shivering. "I've seen the machine. I've seen the bodies of the dead Progenitors. That means that Vin, Dante, Sarah, and Ping . . . They're all gone."

They fell into a long silence, and only Vaughan's voice, a baritone rumble down the hall, disturbed the quiet.

"So why did Dr. Carlhagen let you leave the campus?" Mother Tyeesha asked.

Such a simple question. Such an obvious one. Belle berated herself for not having figured out an answer already. She opted for the truth. "Dr. Carlhagen is dead. Vaughan and I decided to find a way off of the island. That's why he's using your holodesk. He's trying to contact someone to come get us."

Mother Tyeesha's lips turned down, and an eyebrow arched high on her forehead. "But that's impossible. There's no communication connection to the outside from here. Even with all his leverage over me, Dr. Carlhagen never trusted me. He figured I would reveal the school's existence."

The woman seemed to shrink before Belle's eyes as the weight of her part in the Scion School settled over her shoulders.

"What kind of leverage did he have?" Belle asked.

Instead of answering, Mother Tyeesha straightened and cast a glance at the hallway toward her office. "Tell me something. Did Vaughan spend much time alone with Dr. Carlhagen?"

Belle didn't know what had happened after Vaughan had been knocked unconscious by Elias. Vaughan said that he'd been strapped to a bed somewhere in the hacienda and that Dr. Carlhagen had come to him occasionally.

"Not by choice," Belle said.

"And did Dr. Carlhagen ever talk to you about Children's Villa and the nursery and teaching staff?"

"Not to me. Why?"

"Well, I found it odd that Vaughan asked about Robin and Marcus."

Vaughan couldn't have known their names unless Dr. Carlhagen had told him. Or unless Dr. Carlhagen was him. Belle kept the realization under wraps. "Dr. Carlhagen must have told him, I suppose."

Mother Tyeesha's eyes crinkled. "Seems an odd topic to bring up at all." She was going to say more but clamped her mouth shut as Vaughan's footsteps came down the hallway. His jaw was clamped tightly and a muscle beneath one eye twitched with barely suppressed fury.

He forced a smile. "Would you excuse us, Mother Tyeesha? I need to speak to Belle privately."

Mother Tyeesha clapped her hands together and grinned. It, too, looked forced. "Certainly. I need to go check on my classroom. Hopefully the children haven't torn it apart."

She cast a long, cautioning glance at Belle, then left.

By the look on Vaughan's face, his conversation hadn't

gone well. Belle drank the rest of her tea, this time savoring the bitterness on her tongue.

20

WHOEVER POSSESSES HER

"So?" Belle asked Vaughan. "Did you reach the outside? Is a boat coming?"

"No. Things are complicated."

Belle imagined they were, since Mother Tyeesha had told her that there was no outside connection from her office. "Who did you talk to?"

Vaughan threw up his hands, nostrils flaring. "That traitor Mr. Justin. He's using Humphrey to take control of the school."

"We're not going to be able to do anything about the school from here anyway," Belle said. "We have to get away, find a place of safety. Maybe we'll just have to get off the island ourselves. Driving here, I saw a skiff by the docks."

"Don't be an idiot," Vaughan barked, eyes blazing. "We can't take some little boat across seventy kilometers of open water. You have no concept how big the ocean is." The twist of disgust on Vaughan's lips was pure Dr. Carlhagen.

Belle's face burned, and she looked away.

"I'm sorry," he said, his voice suddenly soft and warm. "It seems like every time I get angry, *he* creeps back to the surface. I hate this. I hate being two minds in one body."

He slipped off his chair to kneel next to her. Just as Mother Tyeesha had done, he took her hands in his.

She refused to look at him. He leaned low, nearly putting his head in her lap until she had to meet his eyes.

"Forgive me," he said. "I need you. You're the only reason I'm getting this chance to prove myself. With your help, I know we can get away from here. Together."

Sense data, she thought. *Such sweet, welcome sense data.*

She wondered why resisting this flow of input was even harder than turning away from his abuse just moments before. She lifted her head, holding Vaughan's gaze, commanding herself to stay rational. His beautiful face hovered so close to hers. His large hands held hers, making her feel small.

As hard as it had been to decline Mother Tyeesha's embrace, this was a thousand times harder. She wanted nothing more than to pull Vaughan's lips to hers. But if she gave in, if she dipped below the surface of that desire, she would never come up for air.

With great effort, she gently pulled her hands free of his. "What do you propose we do?"

His jaw thrust forward, betraying a slight irritation, but then he stood and paced the floor.

"There's only one way out of this for us, I think. I have to convince Senator Bentilius that I am Dr. Carlhagen. Then we ride out on her helicopter."

"That should be simple enough," Belle said. "You seem to know a lot that Dr. Carlhagen knew. The problem is getting in contact with her."

"Yes. Yes, it is. Damn that Mr. Justin!" He stopped at the

kitchen counter and held onto it, swaying. "And damn this dizziness." He licked his lips. "I just need a few andleprixen, and I'll be able to think more clearly."

"We don't have any. Why don't you get some sleep? You'll be of no use if you pass out."

He nodded absently, staring at her as if he'd never seen her before. He shook it off. "We have to get out of here."

"Why?" Belle demanded.

"Because once they realize Summer is gone, they'll search here right away. They'll search the docks, too."

"What does it matter if they find us? You want to talk to the senator, don't you?"

"Her guards won't listen to me at all if they think I'm merely another escaped Scion. I need leverage." He brightened and snapped his fingers. "Summer. The senator's Scion is the key to this whole thing. Whoever possesses her has the bargaining power."

Possesses? That choice of words sounded even more like Dr. Carlhagen than Vaughan's burst of rage earlier. Was she going to have to put up with these erratic swings the rest of her life?

But what choice did she have? She needed him to get off the island.

She needed him. Period.

Vaughan sat down heavily and put his head in his hands. "Ugh, this cursed headache. I *must* have my pills." He pressed his palms to his temples. "If Summer sneaked out of the gate behind us, she's probably to the docks by now. We've got to go get her. And we need to do it now, before the senator's people realize she's gone. Yes. And once I have her, I can force Senator Bentilius to talk to me. I'm positive that I can convince her that I'm Dr. Carlhagen. I know things about her that Mr. Justin doesn't even know. And that means

Humphrey can't know them either. We'll turn Summer over in exchange for a ride back to North America."

"Do you really trust the senator that much? What's to stop her from pushing us out of the helicopter?"

Vaughan smiled. It was a strange smile, oddly filthy, as if he had some salacious secret. "Trust me, my dear. If Maxine believes I'm Dr. Carlhagen, she'll want to keep me around." He looked at his hands, admiring them. "Especially in this packaging."

Belle stood and moved to the opposite side of the room, covering her retreat by taking a quick look out the front door. Vaughan was clearly losing his battle with Dr. Carlhagen at the moment. "Why?"

"Because Senator Bentilius and I—I mean she and Dr. Carlhagen—have had a longstanding love affair."

Belle covered a flinch by fidgeting with the rubber band holding her ponytail. What she didn't need was another competitor for Vaughan's attentions. If the senator ended up in Summer's body and then sought to rekindle her relationship with Dr. Carlhagen . . .

She gritted her teeth. Summer had been a shameless flirt, fawning over Humphrey at every opportunity the past few months. It hadn't worked on him because—for reasons Belle would never understand—he'd been head over heels for Jacey. But if a woman in Summer's body focused that kind of obsessive adoration on Vaughan . . .

No. Summer is barely more than a child.

Vaughan is too noble to succumb to such temptations. Isn't he?

The thought that he wasn't completely Vaughan returned to her. She wished she could have just a few weeks of uninterrupted quiet with him. She was sure that, with enough rest, he could recover completely. In time, he would come to appreciate Belle's better qualities even more.

"I have another idea," she said. She dug in a pocket for

the paper she had surreptitiously taken from Dr. Carlhagen's office. She unfolded it and spread it on the kitchen table. "This is a list of all the Progenitors and Scions. Using Dr. Carlhagen's memories, you should be able to tell me which Progenitors are less important. Isn't there another Scion we could give to the senator? Perhaps one that belongs to a Progenitor who isn't so powerful in the outside world. Maybe one who's a bit older? In fact, the senator might enjoy a change for her next go-around at life. Someone prettier than Summer."

"Prettier?" Vaughan said doubtfully.

That irritated Belle. Summer managed a certain cuteness, like a stuffed animal, but that was the best Belle could say. "What about Leslie?" she asked. Leslie was the Second of Belle's Nine.

"No, no," Vaughan said with a nervous laugh. "We're not messing with *her* Progenitor." He scanned down the list. "You have an interesting idea, though. A couple on here would work. Wanda's ideal, actually." He chuckled to himself and continued under his breath, "That old hag deserves it."

Belle wasn't sure if the hag he was talking about was Senator Bentilius or Wanda's Progenitor. She didn't care, either. Vaughan obviously needed to get some sleep. She couldn't tolerate this much Dr. Carlhagen coming through.

Vaughan folded the paper and handed it back to Belle. "The problem is that I'm in no position to offer the senator anything. If I can't talk to her, the point is moot. To even get into the conversation, I have to have Summer in my possession."

"Listen to yourselves!" Mother Tyeesha's voice cut across the little kitchen. She stood trembling in the doorway, hands balled into fists. Her face had crumpled until her eyes were black pinpoints. Her lips pulled back to show her white teeth, but this time in a snarl. "You're talking about one of your sisters. How could you think of giving one of them up to that horrible woman?"

"I know it's difficult, Mother," Belle said. "But it's a complicated situation."

"No!" She smacked her hands together. "There is nothing complicated about it. If all you care about is protecting yourself, then you're both just being cowards. I thought I had raised you better than this." Mother Tyeesha stared at Vaughan, tears welling in her eyes.

Belle recoiled from the obscene display of emotion. Even worse was the fact that Mother Tyeesha had addressed her disappointment only to Vaughan, as if she didn't expect better of Belle.

"You don't understand," Mother Tyeesha continued. "If the outside world knew about what happened at the Scion School, it would be the greatest scandal of all time. Why, if the net media knew about it, the story would blow up. There would be trials. Executions maybe."

The old woman tottered to the table and sank into a chair. "I never should have taken this job. I just wanted to care for children. I believed in the great destiny that Dr. Carlhagen talked about." She clasped her hands beneath her chin and lifted her eyes to the ceiling. "There is so much evil in the world. He convinced me that you children would be the antidote. But I see now that you are a distillation of that evil. You are poison!"

Vaughan went to Mother Tyeesha, but she wouldn't let him touch her.

"I'm sorry, Mother," he said, voice soft and tender. "I don't like this any more than you do. I really don't. But sometimes we have to set aside our emotions and consider what's practical for survival. Our outrage won't do anyone any good if we're dead. The greater good requires a few sacrifices."

Mother Tyeesha shook her head and got up. She moved as if her years had doubled. "I must go check on the nursery."

She shuffled out of the house, the door clunking shut behind her.

Belle clamped her mouth shut, tried to control her breath. She refused to let the emotional charge the old woman had left in the air infect her. "If I'm going to find Summer, I should go now."

"You?" Vaughan said.

"You obviously can't go. Summer and Jacey believe you're Dr. Carlhagen. Do you think they'll get into the Jeep with you in it?"

"I hadn't thought of that. But I'm sure I can overpower them."

Belle went to him, but stopped a meter short, not daring to enter that tempting zone of warmth. "You need rest. You look very tired and pale. I know how to drive the Jeep well enough, and with the top down, they'll be able to see that I'm alone. I can even tell them what a mistake I've made setting you free. Jacey will eat that up."

A smile crept over Vaughan's face. "That she will. That she will. And I *could* use some sleep. If only I could get some of my pills. But hurry. If you find them, bring them back here. Watch out for the helicopter, and if you even suspect it's been here, don't come back. I will flee into the woods, and I will find you."

She turned to go, but Vaughan caught her waist, swept close, and planted his lips on hers. An inrush of sweet warmth threatened to take away her breath, take away her heartbeat. Overpowered, she collapsed into him, returned the kiss with ravenous desire.

And then he pulled away.

She trembled more than he did and had to cover her mouth with a hand to keep in a moan of disappointment. But she was also thankful that he'd released her because she never would have let go of him otherwise.

She stumbled out of the little villa and into the Jeep, breath coming in deep gasps, heart racing.

Sense data she told herself. *It's just sense data.*

21

DEAD MONGOOSE DANGLING

Jacey shuddered to think what insects or other creatures might be living among the dead vines that littered the floor of the old windmill ruin. But she wanted to collect all the dry debris she could to make bedding for her and Summer. As the afternoon lengthened, less and less light beamed through the gaps high on the wall.

She grabbed a handful of the rough stalks and gave a yank. Fortunately, they were brittle enough to easily rip free. She had wanted to clear away more of the vines that covered the archway but didn't dare do more than create a slight opening to let in more light. It wasn't enough. Her next handful stung her palms. *Thornskipple.* She snatched her hand away and sucked at the wounds. Deciding she had created enough of a cushion, she unfolded the tarp and spread it over the pile of debris. She knelt on it and patted it down with her hands, mentally preparing herself for an uncomfortable night.

She wiggled her jaw to relax the tension that had built into a sharp headache. It was made worse by dehydration. A brief rainsquall had helped, but she still felt like she could drink five liters in one go.

A constant pulse of anxiety wore on her, too. Summer was outside somewhere trying to snare a mongoose. The girl's brilliance with mechanical things didn't give Jacey much confidence in her judgment.

Summer had promised to stay under the cover of the rain-forest. But the mere separation made Jacey antsy.

The sound came to her ears gradually. *Not the helicopter,* she thought. It was low and distant, but not an animal, not natural.

She stood and went to the gap in the vines at the entry. The noise was louder.

A shift in the wind made the sound instantly clear.

It was the Jeep.

The entrance faced north, away from the coastal road and docks. But the Jeep sounded closer than that.

Jacey squeezed out of the tower and crept along the wall, keeping low. She peered around the edge until she could see the length of the overgrown plantation road that she and Summer had followed most of the way here. There was no way the Jeep could traverse that. At least, she didn't think so.

She heard the Jeep again, the sound of the engine revving as if straining to overcome some obstacle. And then the hiss and crush of tires spinning.

Thinking that she might see farther from a higher a vantage point, she began climbing the outside of the tower. She found easy handholds and footholds among the vines and bits of the stone block thrusting out.

Soon she was five meters up, hugging the face of the ruin and inching her way back around so she could see the planta-tion road. She hoped that the helicopter didn't show up while she was so exposed.

Leaning away from the wall, she scanned the faint trail of

road.

Very far away she spotted a flash of red metal and part of one headlight as the Jeep thrust over a rise and came to a stop. It had to be Dr. Carlhagen and Belle.

Jacey realized it was the same rise she and Summer had stood upon when Summer had first spotted the tower. She wished she had the binoculars, but Summer had taken them with her when she left on her mongoose hunt.

Jacey hastily made her way back around the side of the windmill and descended.

She didn't think Dr. Carlhagen or Belle would spot the windmill. It had taken Summer's particular talents to see it. But still, she wanted to be prepared just in case. She wasn't afraid of Belle, but Dr. Carlhagen was in Vaughan's body, and he was the best fighter in the school. Dr. Carlhagen didn't have as much control, but he had nearly subdued Jacey just a few nights before in the medical ward. She had no intention of being in that position again.

Jacey jumped the last few feet to the ground and gazed into the depths of the rainforest. No sign of Summer. Jacey was tempted to shout for the girl, make her come back so they could hole up inside the tower, but she realized her voice might carry to the Jeep. Besides, there was no reason to voluntarily corner herself inside the structure.

Keeping the windmill between her and where the Jeep had been, she went into the rainforest and took shelter behind the old plantation house wall. From there she'd be able to see anyone approaching by peeking through its window.

The sun angled lower, and the wind rose, though not enough to chill her.

She huddled there slapping at mosquitoes and occasionally lifting her head enough to peer out the window. Her headache deepened as she strained to hear the progress of the Jeep.

After fifteen minutes of waiting, she was just about to head back to the windmill. But Summer approached from behind. Jacey waved to her, and the girl darted forward. Jacey motioned for her to keep low.

In whispers, she explained what she had seen. Summer nodded, face going pale. Jacey noticed then that Summer held a length of wire, a dead mongoose dangling from a loop on one end. Her snare had worked.

"Give me the binoculars," Jacey whispered. "I'm going to go see if they've gone or not. You stay here."

Jacey crept from behind the wall and back to the windmill. She had just reached its stone foundation when a bunch of foliage rustled behind her.

She squawked and spun, barely glimpsing the wriggling tail of an iguana as it darted from one patch of shrubbery to another. Body vibrating with adrenaline, Jacey ascended the wall, then crept around to check the road.

She stopped where a plume of leaves offered some camouflage. Winding a vine around her left forearm and digging her feet in, she lifted the binoculars with her free hand and scanned the road.

No sign of the Jeep. The binoculars showed her there was no way it could have gone any farther.

She was just about to descend when a movement caught her eye. She trained the binoculars, fingertips adjusting the focus. A figure in black stood atop the same rise where the Jeep had been earlier. A nearly white ponytail fluttered behind. It was Belle.

Jacey hugged closer to the wall, though she doubted Belle would be able to spot her from that distance. She swung the binoculars left and right.

Where is Dr. Carlhagen?

She framed Belle in the field of view again. The pale girl held a hand to shield her eyes, clearly searching the valley.

What is she looking for?

Jacey wondered if Belle and Dr. Carlhagen were searching for a hiding place, too. Maybe they worried the senator's people would snatch them up in their search for Summer.

Jacey wouldn't mind that one bit.

After a few more minutes, Belle turned away and disappeared. Jacey waited until she heard the Jeep start up and its motor fade to nothing.

By the time Jacey's feet touched the ground, Summer was there.

"I told you to wait," Jacey said.

"I heard you," Summer said. "But I also heard you squawk." There was nothing petulant about Summer's statement. It was just a fact.

"I got startled by a lizard."

Summer's eyes brightened. "Really? Where? Maybe I can catch it."

Jacey eyed the mongoose dangling from Summer's wire snare. "What's the point? We can't cook anything without a fire."

"You're right. I'll build a fire."

"How?"

"With the fire starter you threw at me in the shack."

Jacey had no idea what Summer was talking about.

○ ○ ○

The mongoose meat was utterly delicious, Jacey decided as she licked the grease from her fingers. If only there were more of it.

Summer had cleared an area on the floor and dug an indentation in the dirt. To Jacey's astonishment, Summer had easily started a fire using the small oval device with the black button on top. According to Summer, it was filled with a flammable liquid, and pressing the button created a spark to ignite it.

The fire had been nice while it lasted. But once the mongoose was cooked, they doused the flames. Smoke had filled the interior of the old ruin, and Jacey worried that what escaped through the cracks in the walls would signal their presence to the senator's guards.

She and Summer had both served in the kitchens at the Scion School, but the recipes had been a step-by-step process using ovens and stoves. The meat had all been pre-butchered cuts of chicken, pork, and beef. They had occasionally cleaned a fish Sensei had brought in, but never a mammal.

Summer had only the vaguest notion of how to skin and clean the creature, and they lost quite a bit of the meat in the process. They didn't have any experience roasting meat over an open flame, which resulted in a burnt and tough meal. And yet, it was the finest Jacey had ever had.

Their water had run out, so they sucked on mangoes and waited for the inevitable rain shower to sweep in and refill their jug. Summer had set it outside beneath some leaves positioned to funnel water directly into it.

Showing even more initiative, the girl had fashioned a roll of rough fabric they'd brought from the shack into a sort of droopy satchel.

"When did Socrates teach you how to make things?" Jacey asked.

"He didn't." Summer looked up from her work. "I just sort of see it. You know?"

Jacey did not know. "Let's get some sleep."

Fortunately, the residual smoke helped to keep the mosquitoes at bay. Despite the lumpiness of their bed and the loneliness of their sorrowful state, Jacey expected to fall asleep easily. Yet her mind wouldn't stop thinking. She clung to the desperate hope that they could hide until the senator passed away. But she and Summer wouldn't necessarily be safe then. If the senator died without a transfer, an invasion of greater force would sweep the island, searching for answers.

Jacey needed a distraction. She rolled onto her back and prodded Summer. "I'm going to review something I memorized this morning. I'll try to keep quiet."

No response. Jacey heard the girl's soft breathing. Poor thing was exhausted.

A few deep breaths sank Jacey into the focus she needed for memory recall. She pictured the hacienda hallway, the light coming through the door. There it was, a man's voice. Captain Wilcox's.

Ehv | ree | thEEng | ahn | mie | yend | iz | rehd | ee

She spoke quietly, mimicking without effort the tone and emotion of each speaker.

Captain Wilcox: "Everything on my end is ready."

Mr. Justin: "Excellent. We'll never have a better opportunity. Dr. Carlhagen is secure and sedated."

Captain Wilcox: "That was a very fortunate development."

Mr. Justin: "Fortune had little to do with it. You have no idea how long I worked to hook him on those pills. Months crushing up pills and slipping them in his cake."

Captain Wilcox: "This worked out better than I'd ever imagined. You have his Scion under control?"

Mr. Justin: "Oh, yes. Humphrey shares Dr. Carlhagen's obsession with Jacey. As long as she's around, he's happy. She's a bit of a handful, though."

Captain Wilcox: "Her Progenitor is dead, right? I'll take care of her when I arrive."

Mr. Justin: "You'll do nothing to her until I say so. I'll still need Humphrey to stand in for Dr. Carlhagen once the boat leaves, and he won't cooperate at all if Jacey is harmed."

Captain Wilcox: "Speaking of the boat . . ."

Mr. Justin: "Yes. What's the schedule?"

Captain Wilcox: "Now that the storm has passed, I can have it there tomorrow evening. It's loaded up. The bus is in place. I'm worried about the crane at the dock, though. If it's not operational, we're going to have a problem."

Mr. Justin: "It's perfectly functional. The supply boat used it just a few days before the storm."

Captain Wilcox: "Did they offload a fifteen-ton bus?"

Mr. Justin: "No. But it can handle it. Dr. Carlhagen spared no expense on this operation."

Captain Wilcox: "Nice of him to make all these Scions for us, wasn't it?"

Mr. Justin: "It was indeed. Now, what are you going to do about Captain Wilcox?"

Jacey's eyes popped open, losing the thread.

If the man Mr. Justin had been talking to wasn't Captain Wilcox, who was he? A noise to her left drew her attention. It was Summer, hand over her mouth, staring at Jacey in shock.

"Don't say anything," Jacey warned. "I need to get back into it or I'll lose the rest."

She closed her eyes and took long, calming breaths. Letting her mind go, she searched for the line of rising and falling pitches.

Mr. Justin: "It was indeed. Now, what are you going to do about Captain Wilcox?"

Man: "Assuming things go to plan, he'll never know we've been to the island until we're long gone. The tricky part will be keeping him away for a few days after we've left to let our trail grow cold."

Mr. Justin: "I suppose you're right. I have to keep things looking normal. I hate leaving any of the Scions behind. So much missed opportunity there."

Man: "How many were you thinking? Maybe we could come back for them."

Mr. Justin: "I'll need the oldest ones in order to keep up appearances. I'm thinking six or seven." (sighs) "But the Eagle girl, Leslie, is too important to our plan. . . . You'll have to take her."

Man: "We'll move the little ones first, then bring the bus up for the rest. You'll have to sort them out for us so I don't take the wrong ones. Now, what about the equipment?"

Mr. Justin: "I don't think the machine will fit through the doors."

Man: "How the hell did they get it in there?"

Mr. Justin: "It's quite simple, Orson. They built the medical ward around it."

Summer's voice cut through Jacey's concentration. "His name is Orson!"

"Shush. You'll make me lose the rest."

Orson: "That's going to slow us down."

Mr. Justin: "I'll think of something. Now, I need to get going. I've got to prepare my puppet to speak with Captain Wilcox. That bastard is pressing hard to post men here."

Orson: "Don't let that happen."

Mr. Justin: "I won't."

Orson: "See you tomorrow."

And that was it.

Jacey opened her eyes and discovered she was trembling.

Summer moved closer to her. "I'm not sure I understood all that. Who was Mr. Justin talking to?"

Jacey had no idea. But it didn't matter. All that did was what the man had said. *"We'll move the little ones first, then bring the bus up for the rest."*

"We have to warn Mother Tyeesha and Humphrey," Jacey said. "Mr. Justin is planning to steal the Scions. And it sounds like he and this man Orson have been planning it for a long time."

"Why?"

"We're valuable. You're the Scion of a very powerful person in North America. We have to assume that the others must also have important, powerful Progenitors. Once Mr. Justin controls us, he can go to those individuals and demand . . . anything. And once he's hidden us away, the Progenitors will have no choice but to give him whatever he wants."

She clenched her fists, berating herself for not heeding her suspicions about the butler. She desperately needed to sleep, but her thoughts kept spinning in useless circles. "Orson said he's arriving tomorrow and that he's going to Children's Villa first. We have to warn Mother Tyeesha. Maybe she knows where to hide the little ones. After that . . ."

She had no idea. Once the search for Summer started, even going to Mother Tyeesha's was a huge risk. But maybe the search would work in their favor. Mr. Justin hadn't known the senator was coming when he had his conversation with Orson. It did explain his insistence that they allow the transfer, though. He wanted the senator in and out before his boat arrived.

"Get some rest, Summer. We'll figure out what to do next in the morning."

Summer rustled on the tarp as she settled in. She lay much closer to Jacey than she had before.

Jacey took some satisfaction in the current situation. Mr. Justin had believed there was no way off campus for Jacey and Summer, so he hadn't tried to restrain their movements. He hadn't counted on Belle running off with Dr. Carlhagen. He hadn't counted on the gate being open for Jacey and Summer to slip through.

"Mr. Justin must be worried," Jacey said to herself.

"What?" Summer mumbled.

"Let's try to sleep. I think we're going to need it."

22

A CLOAK OF FROZEN STILLNESS

Belle rose early, not that she had slept much on the loveseat tucked along one wall of Mother Tyeesha's tiny front room. The east-facing window in the little kitchen showed just the barest glimmer of blue horizon beyond the trees.

She crept to Vaughan's room and peered in. He lay bare-chested among the twisted sheets, arms out to either side. Fear carried her in a rush to his bedside. With a rush of breath, she relaxed. It had been too dark to see clearly, and she'd thought for a moment he wasn't breathing. She wrinkled her nose at the smell of sickness in the air.

She glanced at the window, thinking to open it and let in some fresh breeze, but the hurricane shutters were still in place. If they were like the ones at the Scion School, they locked from the outside.

Vaughan moaned and shifted his position but didn't wake. His forehead burned to the touch. Belle wiped the clamminess from her hands and quietly retreated from the room.

Vaughan's withdrawal from the pills was worsening.

Belle felt her way down the hall and to the kitchen. She went to the refrigerator, intent on pulling together some food to fuel her continued search for Summer. She stopped mid-step, startled by the tiny figure sitting at the kitchen table.

Mother Tyeesha held her hands folded in her lap, eyes closed. Belle thought the woman was asleep, but her eyes popped opened and locked on Belle. "Going back out to capture Summer."

It wasn't a question.

Belle opened the refrigerator and began assembling the fixings for a few sandwiches. "Do you have a container I can take water in?"

"Summer is your sister," Mother Tyeesha said. "Maybe not by blood, but by any measure that means anything. You've grown up together. You've lived together. You've endured the same experiences."

"Yes," Belle said. "And should we both be overwritten?"

"You think that's the only choice, don't you?" Mother Tyeesha said. "That it's her or you. You've always thought that way, Belle. That life is win or lose."

"Yes, yes," Belle said, opening a package of sliced meats. "Life is a zero-sum game. I'm quite familiar with the concept."

She assembled a few sandwiches, barely paying attention to how much meat and cheese she mashed between slices of bread. As long as it sustained her in her search, it would do.

"Do you have a container or not?" she asked. "Preferably something with a cap."

Mother Tyeesha pointed vaguely to one of the lower cabinets in the tiny kitchen. Belle swung open a door and found a plastic jug with a screw cap. She began filling it from the tap.

"I can accept that you disapprove of my plan," Belle said

over the hiss and gurgle of the filling jug. "But you haven't offered an alternative."

"Haven't you considered the obvious one?" Mother Tyeesha asked. "How about you find Summer so that you can help her?"

Belle turned off the water and screwed on the lid. "I don't want to help her." She dug through the cabinets until she found plastic bags to stuff her sandwiches in.

"That boy in there is not Vaughan," Mother Tyeesha said quietly.

"How could you possibly know? You haven't seen him for nine years. None of us are the same as we were when we left here."

"You're the same, Belle. Exactly the same." The words were so laden with disappointment that they hit Belle like a slap in the face.

She spun on the old woman. "You don't have the right to judge me. It's easy for you to give in to sentimentality and emotion, easy to let weakness guide your choices. But any time I do something out of emotion, it ends up a disaster. Reason is the only sane path to follow in this world, and reason demands hard choices. Reason demands that I survive."

If Belle's outburst had any effect on the woman, she hid it completely. Her face was a wrinkled mask of equanimity, and she met Belle's cold, hard stare as if studying a curious shell she'd found on the beach.

"And so you survive," Mother Tyeesha said. "What happens then? What do you do? What gives your life meaning, if not emotion? You're in love with that boy," she said, waving her arm toward the hallway. "Does reason guide you in defending him? Does reason blind you to the fact that he is not Vaughan, but is, in fact, *entirely* Dr. Carlhagen? Does reason reveal to you that he is using you to get what he wants? That he has no intention of leaving the island with you? That all he wants, aside from regaining control of the Scion School, is a bottle of painkillers, and that he will trade you, Summer, or even me, to get what he wants?"

Belle pulled a cloak of frozen stillness around herself. Forced the heat in her blood to cool. It was always about Vaughan. Everyone wanted Vaughan, and if they couldn't have him, they painted him as some sort of monster.

She flung open the front door and left, carrying her sandwiches in one hand and the jug of water in the other. She drew in deep breaths of heavy, humid air, trying to hold onto the ice in her mind. But the inferno inside raged, breaking through her will.

She climbed into the Jeep and fired up its engine, stomped the accelerator to make the engine roar. And as she drove away from the school, she gave vent to her anger by pounding a fist on the steering wheel and screaming.

After a moment, her fury passed, leaving behind a core of cold determination, the same thing she had clung to since she had come to the Scion School all those years ago.

Mother Tyeesha's ploy was obvious. She was trying to plant a seed of doubt about Vaughan in Belle's mind.

Belle knew that Dr. Carlhagen had attempted to overwrite Vaughan. She knew that at one point, the old man had been in control of Vaughan. She knew that Vaughan appeared to have regained some control. She knew that Dr. Carlhagen's addiction was making it harder for Vaughan to stay in control.

And so, she had a question to answer. Could all of those kind things that Vaughan had said, the smiles that he had given to her and to Mother Tyeesha, the kiss he had granted her the day before, could all of those things have been fake? Was Dr. Carlhagen that good of an actor?

She didn't think so.

The source of Vaughan's worst behavior was the andleprixen withdrawal. A double-edged sword for sure, but one she needed if she was going to cut him free of his addiction.

If she had Summer, she'd be in the power position in any bargaining. She could get an endless supply of the drug, then. The problem was that there was no guarantee she could find Summer. And even if she could, was there enough time? Vaughan worsened by the minute.

If he dies . . .

Belle wouldn't let herself finish the thought. The only things she needed to focus on were finding Summer and getting some pills for Vaughan.

23

YOU MEAN THE JEEP?

Pain flared across Humphrey's scalp, and he let out a high-pitched shriek. His arms flailed, coming free of the blankets. His hands went to his head and found a fist there, grasping his hair. His fingers followed it to a thick arm and beat against it.

"Let me go!"

"Where is she?" Alice's grating voice cut through Humphrey's panic.

He blinked the sleep out of his eyes and looked up at the huge woman. An animalistic snarl contorted her face. Just behind her, the senator's nurse Miss Dayspring wrung her hands. She glared at Humphrey, dark eyebrows forming a V of worry.

Mr. Justin's voice floated from near the door. "I'm so sorry, Dr. Carlhagen, but these women would not listen to me. They just barged right in."

Alice shook Humphrey's head. "Where is she?"

It had been bound to happen. Alice had figured out Summer had run away.

"She's . . . I think she's . . . I don't really know."

"I'm right here." The voice, soft and calm, startled Humphrey.

Alice released his hair, and he fell back onto the bed. Alice's face had shifted to wide-eyed surprise. Just beyond her, Mr. Justin looked utterly shocked. Humphrey turned to find Senator Bentilius standing at the doorway of his bathroom, her red hair flattened on one side from sleep, a shockingly short robe draped over her shoulders and gaping to expose far more bosom than Humphrey wanted to see.

He sat up, pulling the covers up to his chin. "What? Wait, no. This isn't what it looks like."

"Oh, let them gape, Christof," Senator Bentilius said as she approached the bed. Humphrey noticed then that the blankets on the other side of his bed were wrinkled, the pillow indented. He put a hand to his head and wondered how much wine he'd drunk. But no, he'd been very careful. The senator must have slipped into bed next to him in the night.

"Are you insane?" he asked the old woman.

Alice had backed up a few steps and was looking at the floor. "I'm sorry to have intruded, Madam Senator," she said, full of contrition. "I know how you value your privacy."

"She didn't value mine," Humphrey said, voice rising in pitch.

"Shall I prepare breakfast, Dr. Carlhagen?" Mr. Justin asked, emphasizing the name.

Humphrey quickly slipped back into his Dr. Carlhagen impression. He took a deep breath and put on an ingratiating smile. "If you would be so kind."

"It shall be waiting in the dining room." The butler departed.

Humphrey smoothed the blankets over his stomach.

"Madame Senator, I really must protest. This isn't seemly conduct for the Scion School."

Senator Bentilius wavered were she stood, suddenly putting her hands on the bed to stay upright. Alice started forward, but the senator urged her away. She turned her most lascivious smile on Humphrey. "Oh hush. The Scions are all tucked in their dormitories. Who's going to know? Besides," she slipped under the covers and sidled up next to him, "I was cold."

Humphrey cleared his throat and squirmed out of bed.

Senator Bentilius's hungry expression disappeared in a flash and she put a hand to her face. "Perhaps I don't feel well, after all."

Alice was at her side in a second, hands going to the senator's wrist to feel the pulse there.

Seizing on the senator's momentary dizzy spell, Humphrey leaned across the bed and placed a hand on her forehead. "You see, all the wine and excitement is getting to you. This is not good for you in your condition."

Senator Bentilius closed her eyes and took a deep breath. "Do you have my medicine, Alice?"

"No, I left it in your room."

"You should take her back there," Humphrey said. "Make sure she takes her medicine and let her rest for a while longer."

Despite the senator's weak protests, Alice scooped her from the bed and carried her away. Miss Dayspring trailed after.

Humphrey slumped back onto his pillows. He didn't feel at all rested, having spent the small hours of the morning rifling through all of Dr. Carlhagen's papers. He'd found nothing of true interest. Nothing about the new Scion School he was building with Senator Bentilius.

"The senator is very fragile," Alice said, pushing her way

in. "We must get on with the transfer. Now if you'll tell me where the senator's Scion is, I'll go fetch her."

"She'll be in Girls' Hall now. I'll summon her to the medical ward. Please move the senator down there."

Alice glared at him, clearly not happy with him issuing an order. But since it was sensible, she gave a curt nod, spun, and stormed away.

Humphrey took this rare bit of privacy to pull one of Dr. Carlhagen's white suits from the closet. He drew on the white trousers, cinching the belt to its tightest hole. Dr. Carlhagen had really gotten a bit big around the waist toward the end. Humphrey clicked his tongue, wondering if he'd share the same fate since he was genetically identical to the old man.

Once dressed, Humphrey went to Dr. Carlhagen's office, closed the door, locked it, and summoned Vaughan. His old friend's image materialized above the desk. In a few sentences, Humphrey summarized the situation: Alice demanding an immediate transfer. Summer, Jacey, Dr. Carlhagen, and Belle missing and presumed off-campus.

"I'm sorry you have to face this alone," Vaughan said. "What are you going to do?"

"I was hoping you'd have some ideas."

"She can't transfer if she doesn't have Summer. It seems to me all you need to do is wait. Let Alice search the campus and then she'll move on to searching the island. The bigger concern is what might happen after that. I don't have any information from the outside to know what the implications would be if something happened to the senator."

Humphrey knuckled the table, and let out a grim sigh. "All right. I guess I'd better go down to the medical ward."

Vaughan held up his hands. "Wait. I wanted to tell you that Mr. Justin went down to that door you found in the wine cellar last night. I think he was suspicious that you might have touched it when you went down there with the senator."

Humphrey grunted and jabbed a thumb into his chest. "*I* was the only thing that got touched down there."

Vaughan let out a distracted laugh, and said, "That door puzzles me."

With all his other worries, Humphrey had forgotten about the door. And he had no time to think about it now. "Just keep watching it. I'd better get down to the medical ward and continue this farce. The game is to see how long I can delay the truth coming out." He straightened and gave himself a little shake. "And I guess I do have Plan B."

"Oh really?" Vaughan said. "And what is it?"

"Never mind. You don't want to know."

"Humphrey—"

"Goodbye, Vaughan."

Humphrey didn't wait for Vaughan's holovid to disappear before striding to the door and leaving. He checked down the corridor, stopping to listen to see if he could tell where Mr. Justin was, but he heard no sounds of activity nearby. With slow steps, he forced himself to the front door and started down the bougainvillea-lined pathway.

It had always seemed like a long walk before. This time it seemed too short. All he really wanted was to turn away from the medical ward, head toward one of the paths and just keep walking. Maybe go out to Isaacs' Beach or Jacque's Point. Anything to avoid the inevitable confrontation awaiting him in the medical ward.

He found Alice and Miss Dayspring in the main ward. The bodyguard stood like an iron statue in the middle of the room. The nurse sat on the edge of one of the cots next to Senator Bentilius.

"Please," he said, motioning to the back of the room. "The transfer room is this way.

"Where is the Scion?" Alice demanded

"She isn't here?" Humphrey asked, looking around as if she might be sitting in a corner somewhere. He turned his gaze to the senator. "She's looking terribly unwell. I think perhaps we should delay. She had way too much wine last night, despite my protestations."

"It's not the wine," Miss Dayspring said. "It's the illness. She's been having more and more of these episodes."

"We will transfer now," Alice declared and scooped the senator up.

Seeing that Alice would not be put off any further, Humphrey guided her through the rear door and into one of the side rooms.

The room he chose was the one he had been locked in just days before. The antiseptic smell of the room brought a wave of fury crashing through Humphrey's heart. It was there that Dr. Carlhagen had verbally abused him, then smashed him in the legs with his cane. Humphrey wanted to burn the whole place to the ground.

Alice laid the senator on the gurney and drew the covers over her. Miss Dayspring crowded in to fluff the senator's pillow.

Humphrey pointed to a cabinet. "There are gowns in there. Please help her change into one while I go retrieve the Scion." Humphrey's stomach flipped as his simple, elegant Plan B came to mind. He took a step backward into the hall, grabbed the edge of the door and pushed it shut.

Hands shaking, he fumbled with the lock.

Too slow.

Alice grabbed the handle and pushed the door open. "What are you doing?"

She stepped into the hall.

"Uh, just making sure it wasn't locked."

Humphrey shouted a silent curse in his mind. If he'd

gotten it locked, he could have just left all three of them in there and waited them out.

"What are you waiting for?" Alice demanded. "Let's go get the Scion."

o o o

Humphrey kept his steps short and slow while he and Alice crossed the quad toward the Girls' Classroom.

His pace clearly irritated Alice, whose long strides covered nearly twice as much ground as Humphrey's. "Let's move, Doctor."

He darted a dark glance at her. "It's bad enough that you are coming with me, but I won't disturb the rest of the Scions by rushing across the quad as if there is some emergency."

They got to Girls' Classroom and he stopped at the door, positioning himself to bar Alice from entering. He held up his hands. "You must stay outside. If we barge in there and drag Summer out like a criminal, it's going to cause all kinds of chaos that we do not need."

"Your concern about the other Scions means nothing to me." Alice shoved him aside and went in. He could hear her calling for Summer.

Humphrey followed after. "I insist that you leave this classroom at once!"

Alice didn't listen. She went to every girl old enough to be Summer. "Are you Summer? Are you Summer?"

Each one shook her head and stepped back in fear. The younger students crowded away to hide behind the older ones. All except Livy, who stood by her desk watching Alice with a look of curiosity on her face. Leslie and Wanda stepped forward. With Belle gone, Leslie was in charge of Belle's Nine, and with Jacey gone, Wanda was in charge of Jacey's.

"Who are you?" Leslie demanded. "And what do you think you're doing, coming in here like this?"

Humphrey rushed forward. "There has been an emergency with Summer's mother."

He stared straight at Wanda who, alone among the girls, knew the truth of what the Scions were. Just days before, Jacey, Humphrey and Vaughan had come to believe that upon graduation the Scions were introduced to their parents. That turned out not to be true, but in the interest of keeping the peace and preventing panic, the three of them had agreed not to tell the rest of the Scions the truth. But Wanda knew some of it.

"Summer's not here," Wanda said. "Jacey came to collect her yesterday, and I haven't seen either of them since."

"Who is this Jacey person?" Alice loomed over the girls, hands flexed into claws, as if she considered picking them up and smashing their heads together.

Wanda looked to Humphrey but kept her mouth shut.

Humphrey said, "Go ahead and answer the question."

To her credit, the red-haired girl stood firmly under Alice's glare and calmly reported that Jacey had removed Summer from class. It was assumed that they were going to the medical ward and that was all she knew. "We figured that Jacey and Summer spent the night at the hacienda." She turned a questioning look toward Humphrey. "Isn't that the case?"

"No," Humphrey said.

"We must find Summer immediately," Alice said, spinning to face Humphrey. "Did you know she was missing?"

Her eyes narrowed to bare slits. She towered over him, and though Humphrey was a reasonably accomplished fighter, one clean blow from her and he'd be knocked unconscious, or worse.

"Obviously not," Humphrey said. He turned to Wanda

and Leslie. "Organize a search. Scour the campus. As soon as you find Summer, escort her to the medical ward."

He snapped his fingers at Livy. "Dolphin, run to Boys' Hall and tell Elias and Sang to organize their search parties. Tell them to search the running paths."

Livy darted away, and Wanda and Leslie busied themselves dividing their Nines, who shuffled out of Girls' Hall in particularly poor form.

Alice followed Humphrey out, and placed a huge hand on his shoulder. "The only reason this Jacey would have run off with Summer is if she knew Senator Bentilius was coming. How could you let this happen?"

"I assure you that Summer had no notion of what was going on. And, for that matter, neither did Jacey." He tapped his lips with his fingers, as if trying to imagine what on earth could have gotten into their heads. Pretending to a hit an idea, he brightened. "Jacey's the head of Summer's Nine, and there have been reports of some discipline issues. My guess is that Jacey took Summer out to the East End for disciplinary purposes. It is not unusual to make a Scion spend a night out in the elements doing pointless tasks like carrying rocks up a hill to get through to them. I suggest we return to Senator Bentilius and make sure she's comfortable."

Alice glared at him. "You're the doctor. You see to the senator. I'm going to turn this campus upside down until I find that Scion." She stormed off.

Humphrey let his breath go. It took all of his strength not to slump to the ground and cover his head with his hands. Instead, he stumbled across the quad, watching as groups of Scions searched the buildings, the bougainvillea hedges. Several faces peered down from the top of the bell tower. A girl from Jacey's Nine even peered into the pit.

Two boys from Humphrey's Nine, Kirk and Horace, headed into the mango grove that stood between the dojo and the garage. At least the Scions were putting on a good show of looking, though he suspected Horace intended to loaf somewhere out of sight.

Humphrey ambled toward the medical ward, not really wanting to go there at all. Wanda caught up to him. "Humphrey, what is going on?"

"Long story. Summer is in danger from these people."

Wanda's lips parted, but to her credit she kept her composure. "I don't suppose you'll tell me why."

"Like I said, it's a long story. Make sure everyone searches thoroughly and very slowly."

"But we don't want to find them, right?"

"Oh, you won't find them," Humphrey said. "They're no longer on the campus."

Wanda's shoulders drooped with relief, but a second later she squared them. Her gaze shifted across the quad where Alice's form burst from the dining hall, headed toward Boys' Hall. She shouted at two of her men, ordering them to search the dojo.

Wanda said, "I'm sure I can talk the boys into doing something about that woman."

Humphrey was tempted. With numbers, they could certainly overwhelm Alice and her men, but they bore weapons. It only took one bullet to kill someone. The whole point of protecting Summer was to save a life. The effort would be wasted if one or more of them died trying to delay the search.

"No," Humphrey said. "Not yet."

A cry rose from the mango grove. "It's gone! It's gone!"

Alice stopped and turned toward the grove. Her voice boomed across the quad like a crack of thunder. "What?"

Horace burst out of the trees and ran up to her, panting. "The Jeep! It's gone."

"That idiot!" Wanda hissed.

Alice's head swung toward Humphrey. And though he stood nearly fifty meters from her, he thought he could feel the heat of her rage burning his face. She stalked toward him, and at the same time lifted something from her belt to her mouth.

Humphrey pretended not to notice her, and picked up his pace toward the medical ward. Alice caught up with him, jerked him around with her iron grip. "Why didn't you tell me you had a vehicle missing?"

"A vehicle? You mean the Jeep?" He stammered for a moment, at a loss for any reason it might have disappeared.

"Mr. Justin often takes it off campus," Wanda said. "Perhaps it broke down. I do recall seeing him walking through the gate a day or two before the storm. I thought it odd."

Humphrey stared at the red-headed girl, amazed by the absolute sincerity she infused into her abject lies. "Did you see that? Interesting. I remember him coming to the villa in a bit of a mood. He was quite a sweaty mess. That would explain it." He chuckled. "That's Mr. Justin for you. He never likes to burden me with minutiae like misbehaving motor vehicles."

Alice's jaw worked like some great animal crushing a mouthful of bones. "Then it won't be too difficult to find the vehicle from the air."

"From the air, you say?" Humphrey looked at the cloudless sky.

Alice glanced at a timepiece on her wrist. "Yes. I've radioed for the helicopter. It will be here in a few minutes."

Humphrey decided that playing dumb was his only remaining strategy. "It's quite generous of you to go retrieve our Jeep, but what about your search for the senator's Scion?"

Alice gave him a flat look. "I suspect I'll find the Scion with the Jeep."

Humphrey straightened and dropped his jaw, feigning

shock. "You think Mr. Justin removed the Scion from campus?"

"Stop pretending I'm an imbecile, Dr. Carlhagen. I don't know what part you've played in this debacle, but two Scions go missing at the same time as a Jeep? I can easily fit the puzzle pieces together. Surely you can, too."

The thump of helicopter blades cut through the air and grew louder. Soon the insect-like machine swooped close, passed the bell tower, and descended toward the quad. It had barely touched down before Alice and three of her men ran forward and disappeared into its side. The helicopter lifted off and flew out of sight.

"What now?" Wanda asked.

"Get everyone back into the residence halls. I've got to go find Mr. Justin."

Wanda scurried off and began shouting orders to Scions of every Nine, girl and boy alike. They listened to her, which surprised Humphrey. In just a few minutes, he stood alone upon the quad, and the whole world was silent save the sigh of the breeze rustling through the nearby trees.

His eyes went to the mango grove and to the gate beyond. He hoped Jacey was lying low.

24

A VERBAL HAMMER

Crouching among the tall grasses at the windswept edge of the beach, Jacey lifted the binoculars and scanned the coast. A narrow band of sand stretched along this northern shoreline littered with twists of pungent seaweed. At the waterline, waves curled across jagged black rocks and pooled among boulders as tall as Jacey. The water in the curved inlet was relatively calm, protected by a break farther out where whitecaps rolled in and collapsed in ribbons of foam.

To get to the water's edge, she and Summer would have to cross an open expanse twenty meters wide. But that's where Jacey expected to find the crabs they intended to devour for breakfast. After that, they'd follow the coast west and hope to find some sign of Mother Tyeesha's compound.

A gust blew from the sea, and Jacey turned her face to greet it, welcoming its cool caress. She would have loved to strip off her clothes and dive into those waters. Not only to get her skin something close to clean, but the salt water might soothe the ceaseless itching of the innumerable bug bites covering her legs and ankles. Both she and Summer had been harried mercilessly in the night by invisible little bugs that left tiny red welts on their skin. The bites itched way out of proportion to their size.

"We can't risk much time in the open," Jacey said, letting the binoculars hang around her neck. "Let's grab what we can and get under cover."

She unfolded one of the plastic ponchos. "We'll put our catch in this."

Summer had made it very clear she wasn't putting nasty crustaceans in her satchel, which she wore over her shoulder, strap crossing her chest. Jacey had to agree, since it held Summer's reader, among other bits and pieces Summer thought she might need. If the search for Mother Tyeesha's compound didn't pan out, Jacey had a mind to head back toward the Scion School and see if they could get in range of the reader network. Maybe she could get someone to toss food over the fence. That would be the last option, though. She didn't want to be anywhere near the school as long as the senator was there.

Realizing there was nothing to do but just go, she stood and ran across the beach, Summer close behind.

Tiny sand crabs darted away from her and disappeared into pencil-width holes that perforated the short, damp stretch of sand. Jacey didn't care. She was after more substantial quarry.

She and Summer kicked off their shoes and walked barefoot across the damp stone, crossing to a tidal pool still filled with shallow water.

"Found one," Summer said and snatched up a gray-shelled crab by its hind legs. Not very big, but better than nothing. The pincers snapped and wriggled. Summer tossed the creature into the poncho, and Jacey folded it shut. A moment later, Jacey found another. She'd never enjoyed such hunts, but Sensei had extolled the virtues of fresh seafood in their diet. All Scions went on crab hunts from the time they were Dolphins.

The girls continued around the tidal pool, occasionally bending to snatch up another wriggling crab. Summer found a few mussels. An octopus squiggled into an impossibly tight hole among rocks. Jacey knew they'd never get it out.

They came to a jut of rock blocking their way east. Summer climbed atop it to see if more tidal pools lay on the other side.

Jacey hefted the poncho. She knew most of the weight was inedible chitin, so she wanted a lot more before they headed back to the plantation.

"There's something over here," Summer said. She stood on tiptoes, shading her eyes with one hand. Jacey picked her way up the rocks to join her. Close by on the other side, a dozen birds covered a shapeless hump on the sand, obviously feeding upon it.

"A dead fish. It's huge," Summer said. "Too bad we didn't find it before the gulls did."

"Yeah," Jacey said absently, lifting her binoculars. She eyed the birds, not really concerned about the fish. "Could we capture one of them?"

"No," Summer said matter-of-factly.

"Stay here," Jacey ordered, handing Summer the poncho full of crustaceans. She quietly descended the thrust of rock and tiptoed forward, not sure exactly what she planned to do. Her mouth watered just thinking about roasting a bird over a little fire.

She crouched and picked up a stone, thinking she might try to hit one of them. Maybe if she threw it while they were crowded over their breakfast, she would get a lucky shot. She crept closer, taking great care to place her weight and find her footing before stepping forward. A rock slipped beneath her feet, producing a hollow clank. The birds squawked and took to the air.

Jacey cocked her arm back, ready to make a desperate throw.

She froze when she saw what the birds had been feeding upon. It wasn't a fish.

It was a person.

Jacey stepped closer, horror filling her throat, blocking the groan that needed to come out. Her hand went to her mouth to suppress a gag. Behind her, Summer shrieked. Jacey knew who the figure was. She edged around the body, caught a slight glimpse of the bloated and crab-eaten face, before turning to fall on hands and knees, convulsing with sickness. Little came up. She had nothing left in her stomach.

"Who is it?" Summer called, voice rising in panic. Footsteps clanked over stone as she joined Jacey.

Jacey wiped her mouth and stood, turning away from the corpse. "It's Nurse Smith."

Summer tugged on Jacey's arm. "Let's get away from here. Now."

Jacey didn't allow herself to glance back at Nurse Smith. A part of her wanted to study the rest of the beach to find out if what she suspected was true. Captain Wilcox had said that Sensei and Nurse Smith had both been thrown out of the helicopter. If Nurse Smith had washed up, then perhaps Sensei had, too.

"We have to go," Summer said.

The firmness in the girl's voice caught Jacey's attention. A second later, she heard what was behind Summer's urgency. The faint beating sound of the helicopter.

Jacey darted straight away from the shore and into the tall grass. She didn't feel much protected by it. Another three hundred meters of grass separated them from the denser rainforest to the south. She stopped, torn for a moment between lying low and making a run for it.

"Our shoes," Summer said. "We have to go back for our shoes."

"Shush," Jacey said, kneeling in the grass. She held her breath, tried to will her pounding pulse to silence as she listened. The crash of the waves became a roar in her mind, and she tried to pick out the sound of the helicopter.

Next to her, Summer kneeled with her hands on her thighs, looking to the sky. "I don't think it's coming this way."

Jacey waited for another fifteen seconds, then began working her way parallel to the shore, occasionally stopping to peek out until they came even with the spot they had left their shoes. Before she could make a move, Summer darted onto the rocks, grabbed both pairs and sprinted back.

Jacey wanted to berate the girl, but there was no point. It was clear that Summer was going to do what Summer wanted to do. But Jacey was grateful to have her shoes, which she slipped over her sand-crusted feet.

Summer fiddled with the poncho. She rolled it up, creating a pocket for their catch, then twisted the ends until they were thin enough to tie around her waist. "Let's go."

Jacey led the way, deciding to take a straight route for the trees and hoping that it wouldn't leave too distinct a path in the grass behind them.

"This is too slow," Summer said. "We've just got to run."

Summer was right. The grass simply wasn't tall enough to conceal them from the air.

Jacey ran, her hands outstretched to block the stiff stalks that tried to snap her face. She hoped she wouldn't stumble across a thornskipple patch or turn an ankle on the countless hidden stones among the weeds.

The tree line grew closer, but the way grew steeper, and soon she was clawing with her hands to pull forward.

"It's coming," Summer said.

Jacey glanced over her shoulder, saw nothing in the sky. She heard the thump of the blades much louder now. Then it appeared to the east, a black dot in the sky heading straight for them.

Jacey thrust her legs, forcing herself up the slope, careless now of what she grabbed onto. The binoculars swung wildly around her neck and thumped painfully against her chest. The sound of her own breath, ragged and loud in her ears, was soon drowned out by the thump and roar of the helicopter.

"They see us!" Summer moaned.

The breeze coming from the ocean was suddenly replaced by a wind blowing straight down, and the grass flattened all around them. Summer cried out. Jacey spun to see the girl flailing to keep her balance. Jacey grabbed Summer's collar, pulled her forward.

Summer's wide eyes seemed to take up half her face. There was nothing sullen or cute about them now. They conveyed only pure panic.

"Go," Jacey urged.

Together they scrabbled up the rest of the slope, making the tree line, which instantly cut off the force of the helicopter's downdraft. The slope steepened further, but in the shade of the trees the undergrowth was thinner.

"We've got to get over this hill," Jacey said between gasps for breath.

Summer didn't say anything and kept moving. The exertion was wearing on her, though. Every few steps, she groaned plaintively as if she was at the end of her endurance.

The sound of the helicopter abruptly changed, and Jacey sensed that it was lifting higher. A quick glance at the canopy told her that they were well concealed, and she paused by the bole of a thick tree, leaned against it, and helped Summer the last few steps.

The girl put her hands on her knees and bent at the waist, heaving in air. Jacey was tired too, but she had spent far more time running the Scion School paths than Summer had.

The helicopter's sounds grew fainter, as if it was backing away from the forest.

"It must be looking for a place to land," Jacey said.

"How many people do you think are onboard that thing?" Summer asked, voice shaking.

Jacey thought it looked big enough to hold at least five or six. Seven if she included the pilot. Once on foot, they would spread out to cover more ground. But they'd be slower.

She glanced back toward the ocean, which she could make out as a thin blue line between the gaps of the trees. She turned away from the ocean, getting her bearings. The plantation lay a bit farther west and to the north. Their heading on entering the rainforest had actually been a bit easterly. Hopefully that would throw off the pursuit.

They went slower, taking care to be quiet and not leave any sign of their passing. The helicopter had moved off a great distance, though they could still hear its pulse on the wind. The hills and the trees played tricks on their ears. There was no telling in which direction it was.

They made it to the top of the ridge and began the descent toward the plantation. Another five minutes brought them within sight of the great house ruins and fallen chimney.

"Finally," Summer said in a tearful voice. "I need to lie down."

"They won't give up," Jacey said. "They're going to find this place. We can't stay here."

"Where can we go?" Summer sounded very young. Very afraid.

Jacey couldn't begrudge her that. Their pursuers were after Summer. If they caught Jacey, the worst that would happen was a quick flight back to the Scion School and her locked in Girls' Hall. But if they caught Summer . . .

"Stay here," Jacey said, guiding Summer to the shelter of the remaining wall of the house. "If anyone approaches, run."

"Where are you going?

"I'm going into the windmill. I don't know where we're going to end up staying tonight, but we're going to want that tarp and our water jug."

Summer crouched, leaning against the wall just beneath the window. Jacey crept toward the fringe of the forest, senses alert, heart pounding. She paused there, hugging close to the trunk of a tamarind tree and studied the landscape through the binoculars. She didn't see any movement, didn't hear voices or footsteps. The helicopter sounded even farther away, muffled by the rise of the hill. Realizing there was never going to be a better time, Jacey dashed toward the windmill and shoved her way through the vines and into the cool shade inside.

She scrambled to roll up the tarp. "Where's the rope?"

She cast about, heart falling. Evidence of their presence was everywhere, the most damning being the little fire pit Summer had made. If the searchers found this place, they'd set up a trap and wait for Summer and Jacey to return.

She kicked some vines over the pit, hoping that anyone who came in would only give a cursory look. With one last look behind, she pushed through the vines and into the open.

A voice cut across the air, freezing Jacey to stillness. "Circle 'round."

It was a woman's voice, hard-edged and full of command.

Jacey hugged her tarp bundle to her chest, head turning this way and that, trying to find the source of the voice. She saw nothing.

She edged around the windmill, then dropped to her stomach atop the tarp. A figure dressed entirely in black picked its way twenty meters from her, head turning back and forth as it scanned the ground. It was a man in all-black clothes. He reminded her of the armed men from Captain Wilcox's squad.

She crawled backward until the curve of the windmill was between her and the man. A noise came from behind her. Very close. She stood, holding her breath. With painfully slow movements, she slipped back among the vines and into the windmill. She set the canvas down and carefully pulled the vines around the entrance.

"Alice! Thought I heard something over here." A man's voice.

"That was probably me, you idiot," said the woman. "I told you to search over there."

The woman, Alice, was obviously in charge. Even in low tones, her voice managed to be a shout, as if long years of command had compressed and shaped it for use as a verbal hammer.

Jacey backed away from the entrance. It seemed to her then that an enormous amount of sunlight cut through, as if every gap in the vines were a meter wide. She remembered how hard it had been to find the entrance just the day before. But she and Summer had been going in and out. Jacey worried that they'd left evidence of their passing on the ground outside.

Jacey took a step back. Her foot fell on something that gave a little too much. Crouching, she felt around her feet. It was the rope that Summer had used to fashion the backpack out of the canvas tarp.

She lifted it and felt along its length to the loop Summer had tied in one end.

"There are ruins over there," another man said.

Jacey coiled the rope in her hands, leaving the end with the loop free. She paused to listen, but heard nothing. With a great heave, she threw the loop into the air, arcing it over the rotten old crossbeam overhead.

"Yeah, I noticed," Alice barked. "Focus on your own patrol, Simpson."

A pause. "What is this thing anyway?" The woman's voice was very close.

The loop had made it over the beam, but just barely. Not good enough. Jacey tugged it free. It fell with a crunch onto the dry foliage on the floor.

"This looks like a structure," Alice said. She was just outside, but not directly in front of the entrance.

Jacey tried to control her breath. It shook more from fear than the exertion. The same fear drove her heart to its top speed. She threw the loop again. This time it made it well over the beam, but it still hung out of reach.

She flicked the rope to create more slack and it lowered a bit more.

"This is definitely a structure." The voice had come from just outside the entryway. Loud. Almost as if the woman was standing next to Jacey.

Jacey fed the end of the rope through the loop and drew it tight against the beam. The vines covering the entry rustled.

"Hey Simpson, bring your machete over here."

Jacey's eyes went to the tarp. There was no way she could carry it and climb the rope at the same time. She pulled the binoculars from her neck and shoved them among the dead vines, then launched herself upward. She grabbed the rope, sweaty palms threatening to slip.

Squeezing with all her might and pinching the rope between her ankles, she struggled her way up.

The vines at the archway shook. The woman outside grunted as she hacked at it.

New energy coursed through Jacey's veins, and she pulled the last centimeters up the rope. She flung a hand out to catch the edge of the beam. Splinters dug into her skin as she hefted herself up and swung a leg over the beam.

More blows shook the vines, each letting in sharp rays of light.

"I see something!" Alice said.

Jacey sat up, straddling the beam. Her hands feverishly sought the loop below her. She loosened it and pulled the rope free, then brought it up in a messy coil and draped it over her shoulders.

"Something on the floor."

Jacey swallowed, then put one foot on the beam and slowly stood, flailing for balance with wide swings of her arm. Flakes of wood and dust fell, glistening like mist as they drifted to the floor.

Jacey brought her other foot down to the beam, desperate to strengthen her balance. She glanced over her shoulder at the ragged edge of the rotting loft floor. It would conceal her. If it held.

She tried to take a step backward, but her foot couldn't find the beam, and her weight suddenly shifted to one side. She flung her arms out again and, for a long second, hung frozen on the edge of falling before slowly tipping back and gaining her balance. Not giving herself time to process the fear, she turned a half-pirouette. Without thinking about it, she took five quick steps *en demi pointe* and crossed past the edge of the remaining loft floor. She fell into a crouch, then lowered herself onto the mossy planks.

The hacking stopped, and the woman let out a groan. Her footsteps fell heavily on the floor below, directly beneath Jacey.

Jacey held her breath, braced her hands on the slimy boards to either side.

A second later, she heard the sound of the tarp being unrolled.

"They've been here," Simpson said.

"Obviously." Alice's voice filled the windmill ruin with a palpable disgust. "They have to be close by. They've probably been holed up in here like scared animals."

A burst of static blasted from a walkie-talkie, followed by a tinny voice. "We saw one of them. Lost her in the trees. In pursuit."

The woman swore and soon her voice was barking from outside the windmill ruin, ordering her men into an orderly search group.

Jacey lay back, chest heaving as she surrendered to her body's need for air. "Run, Summer," she whispered. "Run."

25

TEN PER DAY

Belle drummed her fingers on the steering wheel as she motored closer to the Scion School. She had covered the road twice already, first creeping along at a crawl, then faster.

Things were looking bad. Jacey and Summer were hiding somewhere, and now a helicopter was flying over the island. Belle was running out of time. If she didn't find Summer first, she'd have no bargaining power. No leverage to get the andleprixen for Vaughan, and certainly none to get off the island.

She had no alternative, so her search continued. Her remaining hope depended upon the one positive quality Belle saw in Jacey: tenacity.

Jacey wouldn't give up. She and Summer would not be easy to find and, once found, not easy to catch. Since they were Scions, the bodyguards would have no option but to capture them alive and unharmed.

They were both fit, strong, and resourceful. But the island was small, and given what Belle had seen of it, the only possible hiding spot was the rainforest, most of which covered hills with no roads. At the western extreme of the island, some areas looked utterly impenetrable, even on foot.

She slowed to a stop. If she kept on, she would be at the front gate of the Scion School in minutes. She no longer cared that she was out in the open. The helicopter had disappeared to the west and south. If it happened to come into view, she would easily be able to escape among the trees. Unless she ran out of fuel, of course.

Her eyes went back to the gauge. The little pin stood three notches above the E. She didn't know how many kilometers that would take her, but it had already fallen one notch, and that had taken three trips of driving from the Scion School all the way to Mother Tyeesha's. When she had last left, she had checked on Vaughan. If anything, his condition had worsened. He had raved about pain, sweat beading on his forehead, eyes wild with suffering.

And that decided it for Belle. Vaughan needed the pills.

This was the perfect time to go back to the campus, since the senator's bodyguards were all hunting for Summer. At least, Belle hoped they all were.

She pressed the accelerator down. Her confidence in driving had grown tremendously over the past day, and she flew up a hill and down the switchbacks without slowing, finally heading straight for the gate. Her hands reached out to the touch panel in the dash, barely having to look to find the command to open the gate. She slammed the brake and skidded to a stop as the gate slowly slid open. Its red light flashed and its siren whooped.

She didn't see any Scions about, and as soon as the opening grew wide enough, she powered through. She tore across the quad, past the medical ward, and wound her way up the wide gravel path to the hacienda.

Belle slid the Jeep to a halt at the top of the path just a few meters from the carved mahogany doors of the hacienda. She leapt out and raced to the doors. Barging through, she dropped low, just in case one of the senator's bodyguards was posted there.

Her skin prickled at the unusual silence filling the huge house. The silhouettes of wicker chairs and a long sofa hunched directly ahead. The space felt closed in with the far wall closed up. Usually Mr. Justin kept the span of folding doors wide open, letting in the easterly breezes.

Belle stopped, looking down both hallways. One led to Dr. Carlhagen's office and the dining room. The other direction led to the bedrooms.

She went right, glancing in each doorway until she found the room that had to be Dr. Carlhagen's. It was the largest and had sliding doors that opened onto a private patio looking out over the raging ocean far below.

She pulled open all the drawers in the bureau, digging through Dr. Carlhagen's clothing. Nothing.

The bathroom cabinets were next. There she found a bottle. She snatched it up, shook it. It was empty. Enraged, she threw it at the mirror. It bounced off and rattled on the floor.

"What's going on?"

She spun, hands out in a defensive pose.

The tension rushed out of her. Humphrey stood in the doorway, looking ridiculous in one of Dr. Carlhagen's white suits with a blue bow tie.

"I need andleprixen for Vaughan," she said, then shouldered past him into the hallway.

"Wait. Where's Summer? Where's Jacey?"

"I don't know," she called over her shoulder. With quick steps, she ducked into Dr. Carlhagen's office and began rifling through the drawers in his desk.

Humphrey followed her. "Didn't you see any sign of them?"

"The senator's guards are searching for them now. I saw the helicopter," Belle said, absently.

"Are you *sure* you don't know where they are?"

"I swear I do not know. Now, do you know where there's andleprixen or not?" She pulled open the last drawer and found another bottle. She snatched it up and shook it.

It rattled.

Fingers fumbling with the lid, she popped it open and looked inside. She uttered a curse under her breath. There were only three pills.

"I hope they're okay," Humphrey said. He gazed out the window and fidgeted with his tie. He turned on her. "That huge woman dragged me out of bed by my hair this morning."

"What woman?" Belle restarted her search, tossing handfuls of pens, notepads, paper clips onto the floor as she emptied each drawer.

"The captain of the senator's bodyguards. She's a beast," Humphrey said. "She must be two meters tall and has muscles like I never imagined would be possible on a human."

Belle looked up. "A woman?"

"Yes. Her name is Alice. I managed to delay the transfer overnight, telling the senator she needed rest in order for the transfer to work safely. I insisted her guards leave Summer alone so as not to alarm her. But this morning, that woman realized Summer was missing. I bluffed my way through it, but then that idiot Horace told her the Jeep was gone."

"What did you do?"

"I played stupid."

"I guess that wasn't a stretch for you."

"Ha ha," Humphrey said sourly. He snapped his fingers. "Alice had that helicopter here in thirty seconds."

Belle arched an eyebrow. "Thirty seconds?"

"Well, it seemed like it." Humphrey rubbed his throat as if remembering a hangman's noose. "Let me tell you, I'm going to have a tough time explaining how Summer knew to run away when Alice returns."

Belle emptied the last drawer. No more pills. "There has to be more in the hacienda."

"I wouldn't be so sure," Humphrey said. "Mr. Justin told me that Dr. Carlhagen was taking as many as ten of those per day. He might have used them all up."

Ten per day, Belle thought. And she only had three.

"Mr. Justin knows where they're at then," she said. "Where is he?"

Vaughan waved at the window out toward the campus. "Mr. Justin suggested I call for a lockdown because of the helicopter activity. He went down to count the Scions in Boys' and Girls' Hall and then lock the doors and shutters."

Belle dodged past Humphrey and out the door.

"Wait, where are you going?" he called.

Belle raced out, jumped into the Jeep, and tore down the path. She turned a particularly sharp corner and had to slam the brakes to avoid running over several Scions who were working their way up the path. The Jeep slid sideways into a bougainvillea hedge before coming to a stop.

Wanda rushed up, red hair flying free from her ponytail. Behind her were Elias, Horace, Dajeet, Bethancy, and Tytus.

"Belle!" Wanda cried. "Have you seen Jacey and Summer?"

Belle ignored the question. "Where's Mr. Justin?"

Wanda frowned and pointed down the path. "He said he's stopping at the medical ward."

"I thought there was a lockdown. What are all of you doing here?"

"Mr. Justin sent us to the hacienda. He said he is going to tell us what's going on with the helicopter and the visitors."

That seemed very odd to Belle. Dr. Carlhagen and Sensei had certainly never explained lockdowns before. But she had the answer she needed from Wanda, so she threw the Jeep in reverse and backed out of the hedge.

The Scions scrambled to get out of her way. Except for Wanda, who stood firm, fists planted on her hips. "Do you know where Jacey and Summer are or not?"

"No, I don't," Belle said, snapping her fingers. "Now do as you are told and go."

Wanda stood firm for another two seconds, face flushed red with anger, before stomping away.

Belle put the Jeep in D and pressed the gas pedal. The Jeep lurched forward, and she whipped the wheel back and forth to guide the machine down the twisting path. She came out between the bell tower and the medical ward and cut left.

Mr. Justin stood at the entrance of the medical ward, looking her way. She stopped the Jeep and waved him over.

He stepped forward, hands clasped behind his back. "I see you have returned. Did you bring Summer?"

Belle frowned at the man. Why on earth would he think she knew where the girl was? She held up the nearly-empty bottle of pills and rattled it. "I need more andleprixen for Vaughan."

The butler smiled and held his hands out to the side. "I'd be happy to provide more if you return with something of value to exchange. Summer, perhaps?"

"I don't know where she is."

Mr. Justin's eyes drifted away, looking over the campus, past the dojo, past the gate. "The senator's guards are in a helicopter combing the island. It'd be a pity if they found Summer first."

"So you'll just let Vaughan die?"

Mr. Justin laughed, eyes crinkling. "Vaughan is already dead. The person you're aiding is Dr. Carlhagen." He held up a hand. "I know you don't believe me, and quite frankly, I don't care. If you want the andleprixen, you'd better find Summer before Alice and her men do."

He turned to walk away but paused to look at her over his shoulder. "And do drive carefully, Belle. I would hate for you to get killed in this machine. You are far too valuable to lose merely for Dr. Carlhagen's sake."

With that, he walked off as calmly as if it was any other day in the Scion School. Belle gunned the motor, tore across the quad, and through the gate.

26

SOME ANCIENT WAR GODDESS

Jacey lay panting on the rotten remains of a loft in the windmill ruins. She counted thirty heartbeats. It didn't take long. She counted thirty more, then slowly shifted her weight. The loft floor creaked and sagged. Light streamed from a crack in the stone wall to her right. Muffled shouts came from outside.

She rose up and pressed an eye to the crack. The field of view was narrow, but it faced the right way. Curses streamed out of her mouth at her first sight of Alice. The woman was enormous. She wore all black, rolled up sleeves straining around her biceps. Her carriage reminded Jacey of Sensei's. Every move looked dangerous.

Alice was stomping toward the tree line. Two similarly dressed men marched to either side. Counting the voice on the walkie-talkie, that made three men and Alice. There could be more, Jacey knew. But they were likely deeper in the forest, looking for Summer.

Alice stopped, lifted her walkie-talkie to her ear and said something. A second later she raised her left arm and pointed. The man on her left darted in a wide arc. Alice and the remaining guard picked up their pace. She had sent a man in a flanking maneuver.

She scooted on her butt to the edge of the loft until her feet dangled over the edge. The platform shivered with every movement. With a crack, the section to the left of the beam gave way and crashed to the floor. Jacey rolled right, spreading her arms wide, face planted against the mossy planks. She sought the beam with her toes.

Nothing.

But it had to be there or Jacey would have fallen already.

She eased herself up on all fours, grimacing as the floorboards shifted beneath her. She looked back through her knees and spotted the beam.

She crept backward, sweat dripping into her eyes. The loose coil of rope dangling around her neck threatened to unbalance her.

With painstaking care, she secured the rope around the beam and dropped the rest to the floor. Before she could think too much about it, she grabbed hold and swung off the beam.

Her hands flamed with pain as she slid. The ground rushed toward her, and drove her knees to her chin. She fell backward with a grunt, breath bursting from her throat as her back struck the floor.

She lay in frozen time. Dust motes spun a lazy vortex, as slow and meaningless as the swirl of stars in the galaxy.

No sense of pain penetrated that eternal moment. No thought disturbed the utter silence of her mind.

Her body convulsed in panic as she fought for air.

The struggle broke on a great, raspy inhalation, filling her lungs and returning time to its normal, ceaseless clip.

Summer!

Still fighting for breath, Jacey climbed to her feet. She left the rope hanging, but quickly retrieved the binoculars, thankful Alice hadn't discovered them. Looping the strap over her head, she tucked the binoculars inside her uniform top to keep them from swinging.

Vines hung askew from the opening, their severed ends ragged and coiled like decapitated snakes. She pressed through.

The guards were gone, having slipped into the forest. Jacey staggered away from the windmill. She glanced over both shoulders, searching for the helicopter. There was no sound except her feet through the grass and the distant roar of the waves. The insects and birds had gone silent, scared to stillness by the intruders.

Jacey tried to run toward the thick trunk of a tamarind tree but managed little more than a fast shuffle. She reached it, exhausted and aching. She twisted her neck and rolled her shoulders, wincing as every muscle screamed in protest.

Hoping the searchers wouldn't bother to look backward, she started forward again. She made the tree line and slunk from tree to tree, heading to where she had left Summer at the old house's wall.

She froze when she spotted a guard. He had been standing so still she might not have seen him at all, but a slight movement of one of his hands as he signaled to someone had caught Jacey's attention. Alice rose into view like a black ghost from where she'd been crouching among a thicket of foliage. Together, the two crept forward. Alice lifted the walkie-talkie to her mouth, but if she said something, it was too quiet for Jacey to hear.

The fact that they were still sneaking meant that Summer hadn't been captured yet. Jacey didn't know where the girl was, but with two other men out there searching it seemed likely she was hiding. A burst of static and a squawking voice came through the woman's walkie-talkie. She began to sprint toward the rusted iron gear Jacey and Summer had found the day before.

A flash of black darted from behind the wheel and headed straight for Jacey.

It was Summer, her ponytail flying behind her, her legs blurring with speed. Alice moved to cut Summer off, but the girl fell to the ground and rolled right past the woman's legs. Summer popped up and continued to sprint.

Men appeared from behind her out of the trees. The woman screamed at them to spread out. They began to circle. Jacey saw they would soon cut off all retreat.

Jacey wouldn't allow that. She had no choice but to try a little deceit. She stepped from behind the tree. "Run, Jacey!" she cried at the top of her lungs. She waved her arms, gesturing Summer south. Summer stumbled to a stop, confusion and fear warring on her face.

"Jacey, go!" Jacey cried.

Summer got it then and took a few tentative steps away, but then stopped, hands held out, clearly not understanding where Jacey wanted her to go.

"To the docks," Jacey hissed. Then, raising her voice, "Please, Jacey, run."

Summer ran then, weaving her way among the trees, heading to the thickest part of the forest before disappearing from view. Jacey had a moment to feel pride that the girl didn't head directly for the docks, but instead headed due west.

Jacey's trickery had worked. Only one man pursued Summer. The others continued toward her.

She backed away as Alice approached. Jacey could see the woman's face now, all hard angles and fury.

"Surrender, Summer," the woman said, voice pounding through the trees like a club. "I don't want to hurt you."

Jacey continued to backpedal and soon was in the open air

beyond the rainforest fringe. She had a vague notion to go back to the windmill. To her left and right, the armed men began to close in. She turned and sprinted.

But the fall from the beam had taken its toll, and she could barely jog. The man to her left headed straight for the windmill, too, and his angle made the distance shorter.

Jacey counted three more paces before cutting hard to the right. The man stopped and shuffled sideways to intercept her, hand going to the side arm on his belt.

"No weapons, Simpson!" shouted the woman. "Tackle her."

Jacey ground her teeth and headed straight for the man.

He widened his stance and held his arms out. He must have seen Summer's move, and he crouched low on the chance that Jacey would try the same thing.

All the better, she decided.

She picked up her speed, putting all the power of her legs into the final steps, then launched herself straight at his head. His eyes widened in surprise and he straightened.

At the last moment, she tucked her head and threw her shoulder into his chest. They tumbled to the ground, and he wrapped her up in his arms.

She kicked out and got some separation. Without thinking, she crushed her knee into his groin. He let out a squeal. His grasp loosened.

Jacey rolled free and clambered to her feet. She would head east and lead these fools away from the docks and buy Summer time to hunker down.

But she hadn't taken one step before a huge hand grabbed her collar and jerked her back. Before she knew what was happening, she was slammed onto the ground, face to the sky.

Alice towered over her, expression as angry as a hurricane front.

Jacey tried to sit up, flailed her arm weakly at the woman's leg. The huge guard just stood there and looked down at Jacey.

"How old are you, girl?"

"Fourteen," Jacey rasped.

"You're awfully mature-looking for fourteen." Doubt colored the woman's face, and she glanced over her shoulder to where Summer had disappeared. She lifted her walkie-talkie. "Status, Garcia?"

A moment later the man's voice came back. "Lost her in the woods. Still searching."

Jacey realized it wouldn't take long for them to figure out her trick. Summer had dark hair. Jacey's was blond. Summer had dark eyes. Jacey's were a bluish-green.

Alice straddled Jacey, looking like a colossus of some ancient war goddess. She kneeled and pressed a hand to Jacey's neck.

Jacey felt a sharp pinch and cried out, hand going to a small pinprick of pain the woman had made. Her fingertip came away dotted with blood.

The woman looked at a device in her hand, waiting. It beeped and the woman swore. "This is not the senator's Scion."

She stood, dragging Jacey with her, manhandling Jacey's wrists behind her. In seconds, Jacey's hands were bound.

"Pederson, stay with her." Next she stabbed a finger at the man Jacey had knocked over. "Simpson! Come with me if you can breathe."

"I wasn't expecting her to attack," Simpson whined.

The woman grunted and strode off toward the trees. Moments later the beat of the helicopter came back. Pederson grabbed Jacey's wrists and twisted, forcing her around. She lost her balance and fell to her knees.

The helicopter swung overhead and began a fast descent. With a roar and a rush of wind, it landed forty meters away.

"Get up!" The man yanked on Jacey's wrists, and it was either stand or have her shoulders dislocated. The man's grip felt like iron shackles as he guided her toward the helicopter.

The fall from the beam and the tussle with Simpson and Alice had left Jacey trembling. Mostly from weakness, but also from anger.

Refusing to make her capture go easily, she intentionally stumbled and fell. The man let go of her wrists. He swore. "Get up."

Jacey refused.

"You want me to carry you? Fine, I'll carry you."

He bent low, hands outstretched. Jacey rolled onto her back and swung a leg hard against his neck, simultaneously bringing the other leg around and clamping him in a sort of *retiré passé*, which ended with his neck clamped between her thighs.

He choked and pulled at her legs, face going red. She squeezed harder until he fell onto his back. She released him with her legs and kicked down with a heel, striking his jaw. Something cracked, and he went still.

She rolled onto her knees, got to her feet, and glanced back at the helicopter. She could see the pilot's shocked face through the windshield. He began to unbuckle the straps holding him in his seat, but she started away, stumbling at first and then picking up speed.

She cursed the band that kept her hands behind her back, because it made balancing as she crossed the uneven terrain almost impossible. But she went forward anyway, heading straight for the docks.

Chancing a look back, she spotted the pilot. He had jumped out of his helicopter, the blades still blurring above it like hummingbird wings. He went to his fallen comrade, pulled the walkie-talkie from the man's belt, and shouted at it. Whatever response he got, he wasn't ordered to pursue Jacey on foot.

He lifted his compatriot, stuffed him in the helicopter, then climbed in. Jacey continued to run. Fiery fear coursed down her spine as she heard the helicopter take off. Soon it was hovering twenty meters above her. The wash of its blades brought with it the acrid stench of motor exhaust. She coughed and stumbled.

But she kept going.

It seemed the pilot was keeping an eye on her, his only objective to make sure she didn't escape.

Fine, she thought. She veered away from the docks. Why lead them to where Summer was going?

She made her way back to the old plantation road where the way was slightly easier. Too late she realized that, from the air, they would be able to see the path of the old road and know where it led. She stopped and considered heading back uphill to the north side, putting more separation between the helicopter and the senator's guards. Not that it would matter. It could cover that distance in minutes.

With a roar of power, the helicopter lifted higher and charged ahead. It flew to the docks and descended behind a band of trees. Out of its view, Jacey realized she had a chance to escape. But the fact it had left her could only mean that Summer had been captured at the docks. It was going there to collect her.

Jacey groaned with frustration at her inability to help Summer or to even help herself. But while there was fight left in her, she would not allow one of her Scions to be overwritten. She marched down the plantation road, screaming for Summer, hurling curses at the helicopter, at Alice, and at her men.

Sweating and panting, she finally reached a patch of cover near the docks just as the helicopter lifted off.

It was too late. They had Summer.

She kept close to the trees, well hidden by the canopy overhead. The helicopter circled once, twice, and then disappeared to the west.

Tears streaming down her cheeks, Jacey staggered toward the concrete quay lining the shore. The water sparkled a deep blue, serene and eternal. It stretched to the horizon, a fence of a different kind.

Jacey was so sick of being trapped here.

She dropped onto the rough ground and struggled to draw her arms beneath her, but they were bound so tightly she couldn't squeeze through. The temptation to give up, to lie back and let sobs take control of her, nearly got the best of her. But instead, she got back on her feet and continued forward. If the helicopter returned, it would not find her there.

She came to the road between the docks and the machine sheds. Her eyes scanned for any sign of struggle, but a strange peace lay over the world.

And then she saw what she'd first missed. Tears came freely then. She made no effort to stop them.

The skiff was gone.

Summer had escaped.

27

HAVE A NICE SWIM

Jacey laughed and fell to her knees, drawing in ragged breaths. A burst of pride filled her. That Summer, a fourteen-year-old girl, had managed to get the boat motor started and slip away, was nothing short of amazing.

A crunch sounded behind her. Not footsteps. It was accompanied by the roar of an engine.

She turned to see the Jeep crawl into view and stop. The top was down, and Jacey saw Belle's pale face turning robotically. The girl spotted her and jumped out of the vehicle. Jacey didn't care. She hung her head. The door slammed. Belle's footsteps scuffed across the gravel and stopped somewhere behind Jacey.

"Where's Summer?" Belle asked, voice flat.

"I don't know."

"Did the helicopter take her?"

"I don't think so," Jacey said. She lifted her eyes, smiling despite the tears. "The skiff is gone. She went out to sea."

"There's still a chance," Belle said. More footsteps on the

gravel, retreating. They stopped. Then, as if it was an afterthought, "Are you coming?"

Belle made no offer to help Jacey up, so she got to her feet and followed after. Belle got in the driver's side and waited. Jacey gave her a look.

Belle grimaced, reached across, and opened the passenger door for her.

Jacey didn't get in. She looked at the pale girl, realizing the game Belle was playing.

Fine. It would cost Jacey nothing to ask.

"Belle, would you please unbind my wrists?"

Belle hesitated as if she were actually considering the question. Finally she sighed, got out of the Jeep, and opened the hatch in the rear and dug through a box.

She approached Jacey holding a small pocketknife. There was a tension in the girl's muscles. Jacey felt a momentary chill at the thought that Belle might stab her.

"Turn around," Belle said.

Jacey did as instructed, and in moments, Belle had cut her free.

Sucking air through her teeth, Jacey winced at the pain in her wrists and hands as circulation returned.

"Now let's stop wasting time and get Summer. Which way would she go?"

"West, I think. We were trying to find Mother Tyeesha's, and the forest is thicker that way."

Jacey climbed into the passenger seat, rubbing her aching wrists. Belle confidently took her position, started the engine, threw it into gear, and swung the Jeep in a wide circle. They tore west along the gravel road, the wind whipping through their hair.

Jacey soon forgot her pains as she was forced to cling to the Jeep's roll bar. Belle tended to steer with jerky twists of the wheel that made the vehicle swing side to side. At every corner, the whole machine leaned so hard, Jacey was sure it would tip. But she couldn't ask Belle to slow down. If anything, she wanted to go faster.

The coastline blurred by on their left. They burst from the trees and sped along a curving road that hugged the shoreline. Huge waves crashed against black rocks, sending up spouts of mist. Sunlight cut through, sparking rainbows over the raging foam.

"There it is," Belle said.

The helicopter hung a kilometer off shore. Beneath it bobbed a white speck. The skiff.

"Stop," Jacey said.

Belle complied, instantly, throwing Jacey against the dashboard. Pain shocked through every muscle at the impact. Groaning, she pushed back onto her seat. "Couldn't you stop more gradually than that?"

Belle tugged on a strap crossing her chest. "That's what these are for."

Jacey got to her feet and climbed onto the seat. She dug her binoculars out from her uniform top. But even with their magnification, the helicopter and the boat were small in the field of view. Jacey could barely make out the tiny figure of Summer, moving first from the bow of the boat and then back toward the motor. She made several sharp jerks with her arm.

"Out of fuel, I think," Jacey said. "She's doing something to the motor."

The helicopter hovered lower. A slender white ladder unfurled, and a black-clothed figure began to descend. Summer continued her jerking movements as if she was pulling something out of the motor.

The guard neared the bottom of the ladder, and the helicopter swung around to bring him over the boat. He lowered himself farther, dangling by his arms, feet waving. Suddenly a gout of water shot up from behind the skiff, and the boat lurched forward. Summer nearly fell out the back, but she held on. The skiff carved a sharp arc in the water, turning for shore.

Jacey fell back into her seat. "She's headed somewhere west of us. Go."

Belle stomped the accelerator, and the Jeep shot forward. The helicopter pursued Summer, the man still dangling from the ladder.

Summer angled the skiff toward a point on shore farther ahead. The boat disappeared behind an outcrop of rock.

"Faster!" Jacey cried.

The helicopter swung in and lowered until all Jacey could see was the blur of its blades above the rock. And then it lifted off.

The Jeep topped a rise and seemed to leap into the air before descending with a crunch and swaying violently. Belle got it under control and continued down the road until the beach came into view.

The skiff lay on its side, motor still churning in the surf. Ahead of it the guard chased after Summer. Jacey saw one flash of the girl's black hair flying behind her, and then she vanished behind a stand of trees.

"Keep going," she ordered Belle.

Belle turned the Jeep's wheels off the road and pressed through the thick grass that separated it from the rocky shore. The tires spun on the wet stone and, for a moment, they were perched there, one tire atop a boulder, two others suspended. But then the traction caught, and it jerked over the obstacle. Belle steered around the promontory and onto the beach.

"What the . . . ?" Belle skidded to a stop.

The helicopter circled overhead. Another figure began to descend the ladder. Jacey didn't care. She had fixed her binoculars on a form lying face down on the sand. It was the guard.

She scanned the entire length of the beach. No Summer.

The chopper swept lower.

Belle stood in her seat next to Jacey. "He looks dead."

"We need to get off this beach," Jacey said.

They sat back down, and Belle turned a wide circle, this time picking more carefully through the rocks and back onto the roadway.

The helicopter descended over the fallen guard, but Jacey and Belle ignored it and continued along the road.

"Summer had to have crossed here somewhere," Belle said. Tension drew her pale face into a tight frown. Her eyes darted nervously as she scanned the grass and trees on either side of the road.

But the road climbed steeply and came to an abrupt end. A long water-worn defile led down to a different section of beach. The helicopter lifted and began to circle.

"At least they don't have her," Jacey said.

"How do you know?" Belle demanded.

"If they had her, they wouldn't stick around."

The chopper drew near, though there was no place close by it could land. Jacey was concerned that they might use the ladder to drop a guard.

"Let's get out of here," she said.

Belle didn't make a move. Instead she stood, scanning all around. "Where did she go?"

Jacey realized Belle was asking her. "I have no idea. We were separated at the . . ." She stopped herself. She didn't know how much she could trust Belle. She didn't want to tell her about the plantation. "We were separated. We didn't have time to coordinate anything."

"You were searching for her at the dock. You knew she was going to take the skiff."

"It was a guess," Jacey said. "Summer wouldn't stop talking about the boat."

Belle didn't look convinced. Only the helicopter drawing nearer convinced her to move. She dropped into her seat, swung the Jeep around, and sped down the road.

The aircraft kept pace, but high up.

"Maybe they think she's with us in the Jeep," Jacey said. She glanced at the back seat, which was exposed to the sky. Farther back, the canvas top lay in a rolled up heap.

"They suspect something," Jacey said. "They think Summer's with us, and that's good. We'll lead them away from wherever she's hiding. Head for the rainforest."

Belle gave Jacey a look. "I thought we'd just go to the beach and have a nice swim."

Jacey ignored the sarcasm and turned her binoculars back to the aircraft. With the jerking of the Jeep, it was nearly impossible to frame it for more than a second. But she could see Alice's cropped blond hair shining just inside the open side hatch.

Jacey's breath caught. The woman was sighting down a scope attached to a sleek, black rifle.

"She has a gun," Jacey said.

"Calm down," Belle said. "She's not going to shoot us. They can't shoot us."

"Speak for yourself," Jacey said. "My Progenitor is dead."

Belle said nothing more. Ahead, the road turned away from the shoreline and into the trees, and soon they were under cover. Belle wound along the road and then came to a stop. Before Jacey could ask why, Belle threw the machine into reverse and started backing off the road into a gully.

The descent was so steep Jacey was sure the Jeep would roll upside down. To Belle's credit, she got them to the bottom safely. She jumped out. "Grab some vines. Let's get this thing covered. I'll put up the roof."

In ten minutes, they were back inside the Jeep, and Jacey was confident it was completely obscured from the road.

Even if the helicopter did land guards to patrol the road on foot, they would never see it.

"Where did Summer go?" Belle asked, unscrewing the lid from a water jug.

"I don't know," Jacey said. "I already told you that. And why do you care all of a sudden?"

"I'm not heartless, Jacey. Just practical." She smacked her forearm and flicked away the corpse of a dead mosquito.

"How long are we going to wait here?" Jacey asked.

"The helicopter can't run forever. It will have to go back to wherever it's based to refuel."

Jacey hadn't thought of that. "How will we know?"

Belle had been staring through a gap in the vines that covered the windshield. At Jacey's question, her eyes narrowed, and her head turned slowly until her cold gaze met Jacey's. "We won't. But I have no intention of sitting in this vehicle with you for longer than I have to."

o o o

Belle regretted her cutting remark to Jacey the moment she said it. Not that it wasn't true, but there was nothing to gain by irritating Jacey at the moment.

Jacey stared at her for a long time, her head tilted slightly to the side, hand absently stroking her ponytail, which to Belle's eyes appeared to be tied back with a strip of plant fiber.

The sultry girl bit her lower lip and touched Belle's shoulder. "I know you're in pain. But I didn't do anything to you."

Belle looked away. She wished she had Jacey's guile, that ability to fake affection. But that was too much to ask of herself at the moment. Nothing had gone according to plan, and it was all Belle could do to keep from screaming and punching Jacey in the face.

"How is . . . ?" Jacey looked away. "How is Vaughan doing?"

"He's not well," Belle said. She knew Jacey had been going to call him Dr. Carlhagen. How deceitful she was.

"Is he sick?"

"It's a leftover from the transfer. He seems to have Dr. Carlhagen's addiction to pills."

"Oh no," Jacey said.

It sounded false. Because it *was* false. Jacey didn't believe Vaughan was Vaughan, and she would love nothing more than to see him dead.

But Dr. Carlhagen was already dead. Belle had seen his old body, which was now zipped up in a black bag and lying a freezer in the medical ward.

"There must be something we can do to ease Vaughan's discomfort," Jacey said.

Belle saw right through that. The girl always used questions disguised as statements to extract information people didn't want to share. She was probing, trying to learn more about Vaughan's condition.

"I'm doing all that can be done," Belle said. "I don't need your help."

A heavy silence filled the Jeep. Jacey shifted in her seat and looked behind her. She reached back, and Belle heard the shuffling of a plastic bag.

"Food," Jacey said excitedly. "May I?"

"I have no appetite," Belle said, shrugging. "Help yourself."

Jacey dug into the bag and brought out two sandwiches. She offered one to Belle, but Belle declined.

Jacey glugged down more water, stopping occasionally to take gasping breaths. It reminded Belle of how Dolphins and Pelicans gulped water after being put through one of Sensei's workouts.

"I am so dehydrated," Jacey said. She attacked the first sandwich, taking a huge bite and chewing it with her mouth open. She swallowed and heaved a great sigh. "This needs some mustard or something."

"What do you think I am," Belle snapped, "a Spider on kitchen duty?"

"That's not what I meant. The sandwich is great. I was just saying . . . forget it." The rest of the sandwich went in her stupid mouth.

Belle leaned her head back, closed her eyes. "I'm impressed with Summer's fighting skill. She took down that man on the beach very quickly. Did Sensei train her?"

"No," Jacey said, mouth still full. "We all would have known if he had."

Belle grunted in agreement. Sensei didn't teach girls how to fight, apparently on Dr. Carlhagen's orders.

Jacey swallowed and took a sip of water. "I've learned that Summer is very resourceful, though."

Belle's eyes popped open, and she studied Jacey's face.

"I'm serious," Jacey said, then started in on the second sandwich. "Maybe she found a weapon in the boat."

That seemed utterly unlikely to Belle. Summer was a shameless flirt, a chatterbox, and a troublemaker. "Where do you think she went?"

"I told you," Jacey said irritably. "I have no idea. Why would you think I'd keep her from you?"

"Because you don't trust me."

Jacey swallowed the last bite, slammed more water, then wiped her mouth on the back of her hand. She tucked the jug between her thighs and leaned her head back, yawning hugely. "You're right, I don't trust you. You don't trust me, either. Though I've never given you any reason not to. I'm just trying to help people. I'm trying to keep everyone safe."

"You've done a great job of that. Helicopters flying all over, armed men chasing after Scions."

Jacey's eyes had fallen closed. "You know what I mean."

Belle said nothing more. Jacey's breath slowed, became more even, her mouth open slightly. Belle studied that face, one she had known her entire life. She was surprised to see how young it looked. She angled the rearview mirror so she could look at herself. There was no sign of youth in her reflection.

She twisted the mirror back into position. Looking at herself always made her uneasy. The reflection never matched how she thought she looked.

Decision time.

If they left their hiding spot and went back onto the road, it would almost certainly wake Jacey up. But the girl seemed so tired, she might just fall back to sleep and that would give Belle a few moments of peace. She considered heading back to the Scion School. Maybe she could figure out some way to talk to Mr. Justin, maybe work out a trade.

Belle bit her lip. But that was far from a sure thing. Mr. Justin clearly wanted Summer, not Jacey. Belle didn't know if Jacey was lying about not knowing where Summer was or not. It seemed like she wasn't.

Fingers tapping the steering wheel, she considered another option. Time kept slipping by, and Vaughan would need another dose of andleprixen soon.

Belle didn't like the idea of taking Jacey back to Mother Tyeesha's. She didn't want Jacey anywhere near Vaughan. Then again, Jacey was convinced Vaughan was entirely Dr. Carlhagen, so she would probably keep her distance.

The final snag was that Belle didn't know if the senator's guards had gone to Mother Tyeesha's while Belle had been away. If so, they might have found out enough to know Belle would return. They'd lie in wait, hoping Belle had picked up

Summer. If the guards hadn't been there, they would likely show up soon.

There were no good options. But the priority was clear. She had to help Vaughan.

She got out of the Jeep, cleared away the vines, then clambered up the slope on foot to check the road. It was empty, and the rainforest sounds had all returned—the birds, the bugs, and the wind in the trees.

She skidded down the slope and got in the Jeep. Jacey didn't awaken at the sound of the engine, and amazingly, slept through the rather harrowing climb up the slope to the road.

Decision made, Belle turned down the forest road toward Mother Tyeesha's.

28

SO THE TRUTH WAS OUT

"I still don't see why you can't tell us more," Wanda said, glaring at Humphrey with her bright green eyes. Wisps of red curls had escaped her ponytail and fluttered around her head like flames. The other Scions—Elias, Horace, Dajeet, Bethancy, and Tytus—sat before him in the hacienda dining room, most giving him the same glare as Wanda. Everyone except Horace, who appeared to be staring at Wanda's chest.

Humphrey tugged at his bow tie. "I really don't know what Mr. Justin intended to discuss with you."

Dajeet, a Snake from Belle's Nine, unfolded her hands and placed her palms on the long mahogany dining room table. She leaned forward slightly, drawing the eyes off all present. She rarely spoke, so people noticed when she was about to start. "Mr. Justin was going to tell us why there are armed men and women swarming over the campus. And I suspect he meant to tell us why you are wearing one of Dr. Carlhagen's suits."

Dajeet was small for fifteen, and her round face gave an impression of childishness. And yet Humphrey had always been shy of meeting her gaze. Her black eyes held a strange luminosity that gave her an air of elderliness. "So why are you wearing his suit?"

"It's a long story."

"We've got nothing better to do," Elias said. He sat closest to Humphrey, separated from the others by two empty chairs. From what Humphrey had heard, the Scions' resentment toward Elias for kicking Vaughan in the head had eased somewhat. But it seemed Elias hadn't forgiven himself.

"Where did Belle go?" Bethancy asked. She crossed her arms over her chest and pasted a bored look on her face. "And why didn't Mr. Justin send Leslie up here, too?"

"I don't know," Humphrey said. He blew out a long breath and pulled a chair out. Collapsing into it, he put his elbows on the table and rubbed his temples. Now that these Scions were confronting him with all these questions, he wished he and Jacey had just told them everything from the start. But Jacey hadn't wanted to panic everyone with the truth. "Give me a moment. I need to think this through."

Why had Mr. Justin sent this particular group to the hacienda . . . ?

He looked at each in turn, trying to put together the puzzle. Wanda and Elias at sixteen years old were Eagles. But so were Leslie and Sang, and neither of them were present.

The rest—Bethancy, Dajeet, Horace, and Tytus— were all Snakes, fifteen years old.

Humphrey himself was the only remaining Shark on Campus. So here were all of the older Scions, minus Leslie and Sang. What did that signify?

Footsteps pounded down the hall. Humphrey turned just as Sang burst into the room.

Breath heaving, he came to an abrupt stop, eyebrows bunched with worry. "Did I miss it?"

"Miss what?" Wanda asked wryly. "Humphrey doesn't even know why we're here. Where were you?"

Sang's face relaxed with relief. "I was searching for Summer on the east path. I came back and found the quad empty. Leslie came out of Girls' Hall and sent me up here. She said Mr. Justin wanted to tell us something. She was not happy about being excluded."

"Have a seat," Dajeet said. "Humphrey is thinking through how he's going to tell us he doesn't know anything."

Sang took a chair next to Elias, which drew an odd look from Elias. The two had been good friends when they were little, but since Elias had excelled so much in the martial arts, Sang had been a bit jealous. The two rarely spoke, and never spent time together if they could avoid it.

"Where's Mr. Justin?" Sang asked.

"He stopped at the medical ward," Wanda said. "It's been a while."

Humphrey wondered if Mr. Justin was talking to Senator Bentilius. The thought worried him. Had the butler decided to switch sides? Maybe he was telling the old woman how the man she thought was Dr. Carlhagen was just a seventeen-year-old boy wearing a big suit.

But no. The senator's bodyguards would already be there if Mr. Justin had done that. Or maybe not. Maybe they had all gone off in the helicopter in search for Summer and Jacey.

Humphrey met Wanda's eyes. She nodded encouragingly, making her opinion clear. She knew a bit more than everyone else here. She knew that the Scions were clones and probably thought that was all Humphrey had to tell. "There's more to it than that, Wanda."

Her head shot back, chin going down. "I suspected as much."

"What are you two talking about?" Bethancy hissed. "Why does Wanda know something the rest of us don't?"

"Because Jacey ordered her not to tell. But Jacey's not here, so I'm going to tell you what I know."

He had never seen such intent looks on his fellow Scions' faces. They'd certainly never been this interested in anything he'd had to say before. He couldn't help but relish the attention a little bit.

So this is what it felt like to be Vaughan.

Except, Vaughan had gotten this all day, every day. Jacey too, though to a lesser extent. It felt odd.

"A few days ago, Jacey, Vaughan, and I learned that the graduating Scions met their parents in the medical ward just after the Birthday ceremony."

"We knew that already," Tytus said under his breath.

Humphrey gave the boy a sharp look and received a sullen sideways stare in return.

"We were wrong. The people that Dante, Ping, Vin, and Sarah met were not their parents."

Shock and disappointment gave way to disbelief, laughter, and finally stunned silence as Humphrey related all he and Jacey had learned about the cloning and mind transfer process. He marveled at how he'd already moved beyond his own disappointment. But then, he was in a unique position among the Scions.

"Clones," Sang said, shaking his head. "And we've been raised just so we could serve as new bodies for these Progenitor people? That's . . . horrific."

Wanda's face flushed bright red and her nostrils flared. "Why did you keep this from us? We deserved the truth as soon as you learned it."

"Jacey thought it best to keep things calm due to the hurricane coming. She meant to tell everyone the truth as soon as we'd figured out what to do."

"As soon as *you* figured out what to do." Wanda shouted, jabbing a finger in Humphrey's direction. "What gives you the authority to make those decisions? Do you think just putting on Dr. Carlhagen's suit makes you the headmaster?"

"No. I'm wearing this in order to keep those on the outside from learning that Dr. Carlhagen has been deposed. I'm doing that because if the wrong people learn of it, we'll have more armed guards on campus. And that will make it impossible for us to escape."

That silenced them. But only for a few moments. Horace had finally begun to really think about what was being said. "It's stupid to think that anyone would believe you are Dr. Carlhagen. You're too young."

A moment after his words were out, true understanding transformed Wanda and Dajeet's expressions. The latter showing a look of disgust, the other softening into a warm compassion.

Wanda spoke first. "I understand now. Humphrey is Dr. Carlhagen's clone."

So the truth was out. Humphrey had expected the revelation to overwhelm him with shame. And even though Dajeet was repulsed by the idea, Humphrey didn't care. He actually felt lighter all of a sudden.

He put on his Dr. Carlhagen impersonation, smiling and chuckling. "Right you are, my dear. Right you are. And since the people I've been speaking with know what the Scion School is all about, it was easy for them to believe that a ninety-two-year-old man had decided to transfer into his Scion a year early." He patted the table and leaned back in his chair. "Now. I've got more to tell you. We have a guest on the island. A Progenitor who also seeks to transfer early."

"Into Summer," Wanda said, voice cold with certainty.

"Exactly!"

He dropped the Dr. Carlhagen bit, which had made

Dajeet's eyes go wide with horror. "I've been being Dr. Carlhagen so much, it's become second nature. Ha ha!"

"So Jacey and Belle helped Summer escape?" Elias asked.

"Jacey did. As for Belle . . . I need to step back a minute and talk about what happened to Vaughan. You see, Dr. Carlhagen is not exactly dead."

29

STARVING FOR ANOTHER KISS

It was midmorning by the time Belle rolled into Mother Tyeesha's compound. By then she'd decided to put Jacey in one of the little villas where the nursery and assistant teaching staff lived. That would keep her out of Vaughan's sight.

She turned off the engine and shook Jacey's shoulder.

"What's going on?" Jacey said, sitting bolt upright. "Where are we?"

"Mother Tyeesha's."

"Why did we move? Why did you . . . "

She was looking through the passenger window toward Mother Tyeesha's villa. Belle followed her gaze and groaned. Standing there, hand on a support column of the front porch overhang, stood Vaughan. His uniform was bedraggled and clung to him from sweat.

Jacey opened the door and stepped out. She took slow steps toward Vaughan. Belle hurried out and ran to Vaughan's side. He ignored her. His eyes bore into Jacey's.

"I see you are upright, Dr. Carlhagen," Jacey said. "Belle led me to believe you were unwell."

Belle stepped between them and pointed toward a villa across the square. "You can rest over there, Jacey. Leave Vaughan and me alone."

"You're welcome to Vaughan," Jacey said, "but this is Dr. Carlhagen. Just look at his eyes."

Against her will, Belle looked over her shoulder at Vaughan's face. His eyes *were* strange, but it was because of his feverish drug withdrawal. Jacey continued to move closer.

"So tell me, Vaughan," she said, emphasizing the name, "after Humphrey left us alone together in the bell tower, what did we talk about?"

"That's not a fair question," Belle said. "He was kicked in the head shortly after that."

"Okay. Let's go back further in time. At the Birthday celebration, Dante gave you a signal. What was it?"

"Jacey," Belle warned.

"Okay, let's go further back. When we were Snakes together on kitchen duty, what did Dante put in the chili?"

Belle knew the answer to this one. She had been there. Dante had been put on kitchen duty with the Spiders as punishment for attempting to swim around the fence line. Though he'd nearly drowned, Sensei didn't think that sufficient discouragement. Dante, who had always been up to no good, thought it funny to put in five times the recipe's amount of habanero peppers. Vaughan had thrown out the batch after nearly choking on a test bite.

Vaughan didn't answer. And why should he? Jacey's disgusting accusations didn't merit a response.

"Let's go further back," Jacey said. "What was the name of your stuffed animal? The one Dr. Carlhagen forced you to burn in the barrel?"

Vaughan didn't answer. But Belle knew. It was Leroy, a stuffed seal.

"Let's go further back. Who did you get into a fight with right behind that building?" Jacey pointed at the schoolroom. Belle knew the answer. Vaughan had gotten into a fight with Humphrey, though she didn't know over what.

"You see, Belle?" Jacey said. "He doesn't know any of the answers because he isn't Vaughan at all."

Vaughan wavered and sagged to his knees.

Mother Tyeesha bustled out the door. She saw Jacey and stopped, mouth open, eyes wide. She sighed and lowered her head as if she couldn't keep it up under the weight of events.

Jacey stared back at the woman. And then the spell broke. In three rushed steps, she ascended to the porch, skirted around Belle and Vaughan, and embraced Mother Tyeesha, engulfing the tiny woman in her arms and letting out a long, laughing sob.

"Oh Mother, it is so good to see you."

Belle knelt by Vaughan, fumbling with the pill bottle. She popped the lid, dumped a pill into her hand, and thrust it under Vaughan's nose. His eyes slowly focused on the tablet. With trembling hands, he brought her hand to his mouth and pulled the pill away with his lips. He swallowed and released her hand.

She pressed her palm to her cheek, relishing the faint dampness he'd left there.

Vaughan shifted his weight to rest his back against the column. "How did I get outside?"

That explained why Vaughan hadn't answered Jacey's hateful questions. He hadn't even known where he was. He probably hadn't even realized what Jacey was asking him.

A strange twisting feeling remained in the back of her mind. She gave herself a shake. The truth would be easy enough to assess. Once the pills kicked in, Vaughan would be lucid, and she could ask him all of Jacey's questions. He would prove to her that he knew everything Vaughan did.

Not that she needed proof. It was just that Jacey was so good at creating doubt. She was always manipulating people with such tricks.

Vaughan's eyes cleared, and he got to his feet. He swayed. "Jacey? How did you get here?"

Jacey released Mother Tyeesha and stepped away. "Mother, is there someplace we can talk alone?"

"Yes, dear. Follow me."

As Mother Tyeesha passed Belle, Mother nodded back to the door. "Get him inside and put to bed. And if I were you, I'd block the door."

Jacey followed Mother Tyeesha, who led her toward the nursery. Belle guided Vaughan back inside and down the little hall to Mother Tyeesha's bedroom. He collapsed onto the bed with a groan.

"Oh Belle, thank you so much. I hate being in the grip of this drug. I was sure I was going to die." His eyes went to the door. He stared hard, as if he could see far beyond it. "What's Jacey doing here? What's happening with Summer and the senator?"

"Summer is still missing. Now get some sleep." Belle drew the thin sheet back over Vaughan, but as she started to step away, he grabbed her wrist and pulled her close. He looked into her eyes. Gone was that strange haunted look he had given Jacey. His face was full of softness.

"Thank you," he whispered. His eyes dropped to her lips, making her throat and face flush with heat.

"You're welcome," she said. It came out a whisper. Her throat was suddenly very dry. She closed her eyes and leaned closer, starving for another kiss.

But Vaughan didn't rise to meet her. "Do you have more?"

She opened her eyes. The strange, fevered look had

returned.

"I have more," she said. "But I'll be doling them out as I see fit."

His lips pulled back in a snarl. His fingers tightened on her wrist, and he yanked her onto the bed. In a second he had rolled her over. He sat astride her, one hand still crushing her wrist, the other searching her body. "Where are they?"

Reflexively she twisted and flailed her legs. A lucky blow to his stomach curled him into a ball, and he fell away. She scrambled off the bed and darted through the door, slamming it behind her. She put her weight against it, but Vaughan didn't try to open it. From the groaning coming through, she figured she had immobilized him.

She turned away from the door and studied the knob. It locked from the inside. With stiff, jerky steps, she collected one of the chairs from Mother Tyeesha's small kitchen. She carried it back down the hall and tucked it under the doorknob, hind legs firmly wedged against the wood planks of the floor.

Leaning against the corridor wall, she lifted the back of one hand to her mouth to stifle the sobs bubbling in her chest. Why couldn't she be in control of herself? Why did emotion always explode in her and ruin everything and make her feel so utterly alone?

In that moment, she hated Jacey more than ever. Not because of Jacey's ruthless questioning, but because Jacey had been right.

Belle had been fooled by Dr. Carlhagen.

And she had fooled herself. She had used her own rationality to convince herself of things that weren't true. She stumbled into the living room and collapsed onto Mother Tyeesha's tiny sofa.

And there, curled into a ball and sobbing, she gave vent to a lifetime of disappointment and loneliness.

30

RAINDROPS ON ROCKS

"Mother, I need to tell you something." Jacey walked alongside the old woman, twisting her thumb in her fingers.

"If it's about Vaughan, you can save your breath. Belle told me how Dr. Carlhagen tried to overwrite him. She says that's why he behaves the way he does."

That wasn't what Jacey had wanted to talk about at all, but she stopped and stared at the little woman, muscles tensing. "So you knew? All this time, you knew what was happening to us?"

"Of course not," Mother Tyeesha said. "I only found out when Belle filled me in."

"Oh." Jacey's shoulders relaxed, and she heaved a sigh.

Mother Tyeesha took her arm, and Jacey was reminded how much the old woman had changed. For one thing, she had shrunk.

"Are you feeling okay, Mother?"

"I'm fine. Just old. And it feels like I've aged ten years in the past twenty-four hours." Her eyes went to the schoolroom and then to the nursery. "I thought I was doing something good here, something the world needed."

"If it hadn't been you, it would have been someone else," Jacey said. "And for my part, I'm glad it was you. Besides, we didn't turn out all that bad."

Mother Tyeesha gave a non-committal grunt. "I can't say I'm surprised about Belle," she said after a long pause. "Such a closed up little girl. Whip-smart, gifted in many ways, but I don't think I ever once saw her smile. Let alone giggle. Even when she played, it was serious business."

"She's an unhappy girl," Jacey said. "She always has been. She takes it out on everybody, especially me. You know, she once—" Jacey cut off. There was no point in telling Mother Tyeesha that Belle had lashed her with the thornskipple branch.

"I have a confession to make," Mother Tyeesha said. "When the Jeep arrived just now, I was filled with dread. I knew Belle was searching for Summer. When I saw that she had found you instead . . . I was relieved."

They continued winding through the buildings, Jacey marveling at how small everything had gotten. "There has to be a way off the island for all of us. Some way to protect all of the Scions."

"If you could get off the island," Mother Tyeesha said, "and land somewhere relatively safe, it might be possible to use the news media to create a scandal. There are billions of people on Earth, most struggling just to get by. I don't imagine they would relish the idea of the richest and most powerful being able to live another life by murdering teenagers."

"That's the thing," Jacey said. "I don't know anything about the outside world. Until a few days ago, we'd all been told it was a wasteland. You told us that yourself."

"I did, I did." Mother Tyeesha squinted and shook her

head. "Dr. Carlhagen instructed me to. He said it was very important for your education that you believe you were special and had an important destiny to fulfill. I didn't like it. But he told me it was all part of a great experiment to produce people who were fundamentally good and extraordinarily gifted, who would selflessly go out into the world to fix what was broken. I was fooled."

She slowed and tilted her head toward the nursery. "Would you like to see the babies?"

"Yes," Jacey said. "Of course." She needed to tell Mother Tyeesha about the boat and Mr. Justin's plan to steal the Scions. But at the same time, she didn't want to spoil this reunion.

Mother Tyeesha guided her into a long white stucco building with a red roof. A pleasant-faced woman in a floral sundress sat reading to a group of children in one corner.

"Hello, Veronica," Mother Tyeesha said. "Where's Robin?"

"She asked me to fill in for a few minutes. She said she had to check on something."

Mother Tyeesha frowned but continued toward a rear hallway. From down the hall came the tiny cries of babies.

"Birthday was just a few days ago," Mother Tyeesha said. "Four new babies arrived."

That had been the day everything had changed, the day Dr. Carlhagen had arrived back at the Scion School. The day she and Vaughan had eavesdropped on the Scions and their Progenitors.

"Did you meet their mothers?" Jacey asked quietly.

"No. When the infants arrive, they're already two weeks old, according to Dr. Carlhagen. Though some appear to be a week or two older than that."

"Of course," Jacey said. "Birthday is a fiction too. They're all born at different times."

"True," Mother Tyeesha said. "But not too far apart. I was

always curious how he managed to time it so well, but now I suppose it isn't that hard to accomplish using the right technology."

They pick their way through the squirming and giggling mass of toddlers, Jacey waving her fingers and smiling at each as she passed. They went through a rear door, down a short corridor, and into a quiet section where a man in a linen tunic and pants sat in an armchair feeding an infant from a bottle.

"That's Marcus," Mother Tyeesha said.

"Morning, Mother," he said. He returned Jacey's nod with a slight smile.

Jacey peered into one of four little bassinets along one wall. An infant looked up at her, eyes blue and distant. But so bright.

Mother Tyeesha lifted the infant. "Would you like to hold her?"

Jacey gently took the child from the old woman's arms. A tiny hand grasped her pinky, and Jacey felt a great wave of awe.

"What's her name?"

"That's Ariana," Marcus said.

"Hi, Ariana," Jacey said in a small voice, marveling at the tiny features.

She had once been like this child, she realized. Innocent.

A child didn't ask to be born, didn't have any choices. None of the children here could control the circumstances of their lives. Someone had to protect them.

Jacey's awe shifted to anger. She gently set the child back in her bassinet and backed out of the room with Mother Tyeesha.

"I need to rest," Jacey said. "I need to think."

"It isn't safe here," Mother Tyeesha said. "As long as

Summer is missing, they'll continue their search, and they will certainly come here."

Jacey's head shot up. "They haven't been here yet?"

"No," Mother Tyeesha said in a worried tone. "But it won't be long."

They stepped out of the nursery, closing the door behind them.

"Mother . . ." Jacey began. Seeing the babies made it tougher to say what she had to say. But time was running out. "I overheard a conversation between Mr. Justin and someone off-island. A man named Orson. He was on holovid. Mr. Justin and this man are planning to steal the Scions. A boat is going to dock today, and they're planning to come here first. I could recite the whole conversation for you if it would help."

Mother Tyeesha's face tightened, lips protruding in consternation. Though old, she was wiry and her steps full of vigor. "No need."

"You don't seem surprised."

The woman laughed. "I'm shocked. But after what's been happening, what Belle told me yesterday . . . Mr. Justin, you say?" Her mouth twisted in disgust, like she'd just taken a big bite of unripe mango. "I never trusted that man." She leaned close to Jacey. "Truth is, I barely trust my own people here. All were hired by Dr. Carlhagen without my input. They do a good job, but they know who's paying them."

"I was thinking you could take the children to the Scion School. It would take six or seven trips with the Jeep packed full, but if we could get them there before the boat came, maybe . . ."

But Jacey only had half of a plan. Putting the children in one of the dormitories or the dining hall would do nothing to protect them. And with the senator and her guards based there, the school wasn't particularly safe.

"Not much safer than here," Mother Tyeesha said, as if reading Jacey's thoughts. "But it's a little safer. And I'll take what I can get. That's probably the best choice we've got. You've got a good head on your shoulders, child. But I don't expect Belle will help us. Do you know how to drive the Jeep?"

Jacey squared her shoulders. "Don't worry about Belle." She'd make Belle help, even if she had to drag her to the Jeep by her long white ponytail.

Mother Tyeesha gave a skeptical grunt and led Jacey around the corner of the classroom toward her own villa.

From behind, a steely arm wrapped around Jacey's waist. Another clamped across her throat. She recognized the black fabric of a Scion's uniform sleeve.

Dr. Carlhagen.

She tried to scream, tried to warn Mother Tyeesha, but Dr. Carlhagen's arm was too tightly wrapped around her throat. It was all she could do to breathe. She flailed her legs, wriggled with all of her strength, but her arms were bound to her sides by his. He tightened his grip around her throat, forcing her to stop moving.

His breath burned her ear. "Stop struggling. Everything will go a lot easier for you if you relax."

Mother Tyeesha finally noticed Jacey wasn't keeping up. She turned and her eyes went wide. She shrieked and ran forward to pound against Dr. Carlhagen's arms with her small, bony fists. Her blows had no more effect than raindrops on rocks.

Vaughan backed away from the old woman, dragging Jacey with him.

"Let her go," Mother Tyeesha shrieked. "Let her go."

Dr. Carlhagen said nothing and kept pulling Jacey backward. She relaxed, let him bear her weight until her feet were dragging. Now that he was in Vaughan's body, Dr. Carlhagen was too strong to fight. Even the days he'd spent sedated hadn't weakened him enough for Jacey to break free.

In a minute, he had moved her to the Jeep. "Open the passenger door, Mother Tyeesha."

"I will not."

Dr. Carlhagen squeezed Jacey tighter, until she began to choke for breath. "Do it or so help me, I will kill this girl."

Mother Tyeesha tottered forward and opened the door. She trembled with rage, mouth gaping as she drew in heaving breaths.

The pressure on Jacey's throat loosened and she sucked in air. "I'll cooperate. I'll cooperate."

She had no intention of cooperating.

"Of course, you will, my dear," Dr. Carlhagen said. His grip loosened around her arms, and she tried to turn and throw a punch toward his face. He deflected it easily, countered with a silencing slap across her cheek.

The world went quiet, and Jacey staggered. Pain bloomed on her cheek. Dr. Carlhagen spun her. His arm clamped across her chin, forcing her head to the side.

He gave a strong jerk and daylight turned to darkness.

31

THE COMPACT AND DEADLY FORCE

Cold water splashed across Belle's face, eliciting a gasp of shock. She welcomed its bracing effect, though. The tears had run out, leaving her eyes puffy and hot. Surprisingly, the spell of self-pity had left her muscles loose and her breath deep and relaxed, the way she felt after a long run on the Scion School paths.

She glanced at herself in the bathroom mirror, ashamed at the redness around her eyes, ashamed of so many things. But mostly for being tricked. She blotted her face dry, then left the small bathroom.

Mother Tyeesha met her in the corridor. The woman's face was as pale as Belle had ever seen it.

"What is it?" Belle asked.

Mother Tyeesha strode past her, yanked the chair from beneath the door, and pushed it open.

"What are you doing? There's no other way to lock it." Belle snatched the chair from Mother Tyeesha, ignoring the woman's mutterings of, "Too late, too late, too late."

Belle started to yank the door shut when she saw that the

bed lay empty. Just above it the hurricane shutters swung open in the breeze. The remains of the screen, bent and torn, lay on the floor. "You unlatched the shutters!"

"I did no such thing, fool." Mother Tyeesha toed the remains of the screen. "But someone did." Her eyes lifted to meet Belle's.

"You can't think I did it! I locked him in."

Mother Tyeesha's lips pressed tightly together. "No. Someone else. Someone loyal to Dr. Carlhagen. I suspect one of the new nursery staff. Robin had the opportunity to do it. Somehow Dr. Carlhagen must have spoken with her—probably through the window itself—and gotten her to open it up."

She turned to storm away, and Belle knew she was going to confront the culprit.

"No, don't do it," Belle said. "If you back them into a corner, they might . . ."

"Attack me? Kill me? So what if they did?"

It shocked Belle to hear Mother Tyeesha talk in such a way. "Stop, Mother," she begged. "The children need you. Stay here in the villa. I'll go find Dr. Carlhagen. If something happens to me, it won't matter. Do you have any weapons?"

Mother Tyeesha gave Belle a flat look. "Weapons? In a school for small children? But you won't need any. Dr. Carlhagen took the Jeep."

Belle ran through the house and out the front door. The Jeep was gone.

The door opened and closed behind her, and a warm hand pressed against her back. Belle didn't jerk away from it, but she didn't lean into it either. She never liked being touched, except by Vaughan. But she felt something in the old woman's gesture, a sort of support, she thought. Not literal support, not helping her stand up, but a different kind. It struck Belle as a strange idea, and she couldn't fully grasp it.

"Jacey's going to throw a fit," Belle said.

"Jacey is with him."

"She went with him?" Belle screamed, turning on Mother Tyeesha. "Why didn't you tell me?"

"She didn't go with him voluntarily. He kidnapped her."

"Oh." Belle ran a hand down her ponytail and gave it a tug. "That makes more sense."

She sat on the bottom porch step and folded her hands between her knees. Mother Tyeesha descended on shaky legs and plopped down next to her with a moan.

A single thought swirled in Belle's head. She considered it, looked at it from all angles, and surprised herself by deciding she hated it. The thought—that maybe Jacey was getting what she deserved—did not come from Belle's sense of justice. Only her desire to hurt Jacey.

Belle berated herself for entertaining the idea at all. "Back at school, right after Dr. Carlhagen transferred into Vaughan . . . he tried to rape Jacey." She said it softly into the evening air. "He kept calling her Jacqueline. I guess that was her Progenitor's name."

Mother Tyeesha made a low grumbling sound. Belle turned to find the old woman's face contorted in fury. She was actually growling.

"Jacey escaped that time," Belle continued. "So she's got a better chance than most to get away from him now."

"He knocked her unconscious, then tied her into her seat."

Belle had no answer to that problem. "How long have they been gone?"

"Five minutes," Mother Tyeesha said. "I can't believe you didn't hear the racket."

"I was in the bathroom washing my face." Belle felt the tears welling again. This time she had no idea where they were coming from. If anything, she supposed it was from her sense of utter powerlessness. Even if she ran as fast as she could, she had no hope of catching up to the Jeep.

She hated Jacey, but she hated Dr. Carlhagen more. Whatever he possessed, Belle wanted to take.

She put her head in her hands, and though the tears flowed, she managed to keep her sobs inside. Mother Tyeesha rubbed her back. Belle did not pull away.

"Maybe there's hope after all," Mother Tyeesha said after a long spell.

"There's no hope for any of us," Belle said, wiping her nose on her arm, no longer caring about the state of her uniform.

"You can't know that," Mother Tyeesha said, her voice rising, a strange quality coming into it. Her hand was gone from Belle's back, and she was standing. "Look. Over there."

Belle looked up. Her mouth fell open.

Summer strode across the little square between the buildings. But it wasn't the willful Spider that brought new tears to Belle's eyes.

For behind Summer strode an image Belle never thought she would see again. The breath went out of her, and a spark of hope flared in her heart.

It was a man. The compact and deadly force Belle had known her entire life as Sensei.

32

THAT WONDERFUL JACQUELINE BUCHANAN

The surf tumbled Jacey, crushing her into the seafloor, spinning her until she lost all orientation. The need for air drove her to panic. She struggled to claw for the surface, but her hands wouldn't move. Lost in the spinning crush, roar crescendoing, she flailed for air. Doom descended upon her, pressed her beneath its merciless talons, bashed her beneath the seabed and into utter blackness.

Air rushed into her lungs with a rasp. Her eyes flashed open from the nightmare. Her body jerked. Heart pounding, she moaned. Wind whipped her face and the world continued to bounce.

She was in the Jeep as it barreled along the coast.

Dr. Carlhagen sat behind the steering wheel, eyes intent on the road speeding toward them. Desperate, Jacey went for the door handle. Her arms wouldn't move.

She looked down to find her wrists bound tightly together with a length of nylon rope. Dr. Carlhagen had also wound it around the restraining strap crossing her chest.

She kicked out, but her ankles were also bound and

secured to a support strut beneath the seat. Only her head remained free.

"Relax, my dear," Dr. Carlhagen shouted over the wind. "I don't want you damaging yourself."

"Where are you taking me?"

"Isn't it obvious? I'm taking you back to the Scion School." He seemed smugly sure of himself, exactly the way Dr. Carlhagen always behaved.

"They're looking for you," she said. "As soon as you appear, Humphrey will have you detained. He'll put you back in the medical ward, strapped to a gurney and sedated out of your mind."

"An interesting theory, my lovely. But you're quite mistaken."

Jacey gave up arguing and continued to struggle against her restraints. But Dr. Carlhagen had tied them securely. Though it took all of her will, she forced herself to calmness. She couldn't exactly relax, but a stillness came over her purely out of the will to preserve her energy.

She gazed at the landscape to gauge how far they'd come from Mother Tyeesha's. The thick canopy of the rainforest was far behind, and they traveled through the open scrublands along the southern coast. That meant they would be turning to climb the hills and then head down to the school gate at any moment.

Jacey scanned the sea but didn't see any sign of an approaching boat. There was still time to get the children away from Mother Tyeesha's if she could just get control of the Jeep. She eyed Dr. Carlhagen, heart burning with hatred at the sight of his face. What would he say if she told him Mr. Justin's plan?

He'd probably laugh at her. She toyed with telling him anyway but stopped herself. If Mr. Justin was around when they got to campus, maybe she could play them off each other. A desperate hope, but it was all she had.

"I have no idea where Summer is," she said. "Torture me all you want."

"Summer?" Dr. Carlhagen said as if trying to remember who Jacey was talking about. "Oh yes, her. I have no interest in our errant Snake."

Either he was telling the truth or bluffing extraordinarily well. And if he was telling the truth, that meant that he wanted something else from Jacey.

She knew what that would be. Memories of him chasing her through the medical ward flashed before her eyes. "I'm surprised at you, Doctor," she said. "Taking a woman by force . . ."

He didn't look at her, but his smile soured. "I have little memory of that night except that a madness came over me. I can only attribute it to the transfer into this young body. I was temporarily overwhelmed by its surplus of virility."

"That's no excuse."

He became serious. Gone was the arrogant mocking tone. "I am sorry, my dear." But his eyes gave the lie to his statement, for they dropped from her eyes to her chest.

She looked away from him. "You disgust me."

"Not for long," he said. "You see, I have a solution to this little dilemma, one that will satisfy my desire for you, and one which will satisfy your very correct point that it is despicable and unforgivable for a man to take a woman by force."

Panic rose again in Jacey. She knew what he meant. "If you think drugging me will get me to offer myself to you, you don't know me at all."

He laughed. "My dear, you have never enjoyed andleprixen. You know nothing of which you speak."

The Jeep descended the long winding mountainside, and he barely slowed as he approached the gate. She was sure they were going to crash through. But then he tapped something on the center screen, and the gate began to slide open, its red light flashing and the siren sounding in the late evening silence. The tires crackled over the gravel as he guided the machine past the mango grove and to the quad.

He had barely brought it to a stop when several black-garbed men appeared, waving handguns.

Dr. Carlhagen lifted his hands from the wheel and slowly got out of the Jeep. "I am Dr. Carlhagen," he said. "I am here to see Senator Bentilius."

One of the men shouted toward the medical ward, "Get Alice!" Another rushed forward and forced Dr. Carlhagen to his knees, pulled his hands behind his back, and secured them with a strap.

Jacey cried out, "Help! Please let me out."

A man came to her side, limping and grimacing. He opened her door, and her heart sank. It was Simpson, the man she had knocked the breath out of by the plantation.

"Don't loosen her bonds," Dr. Carlhagen called. "She is a fugitive Scion and extraordinarily important."

The man stopped and looked at the guard standing over Dr. Carlhagen, clearly not knowing what to do.

"I'm sorry I hurt you earlier," Jacey whispered. "But let me go. That boy is insane. He's been claiming to be Dr. Carlhagen for days."

The man backed away. "We'll wait for Alice."

They didn't have to wait long. The huge woman who had wrestled Jacey to the ground at the plantation stormed out of the medical ward and trotted toward the Jeep. "What's going on?"

"I am Dr. Carlhagen. The young man *pretending* to be me is a fraud. I can prove it."

Alice stepped very close to Dr. Carlhagen, toes just inches from his knees.

He stared straight up at her, still wearing his usual jovial smile. "You must be Alice. Maxine has spoken fondly of you. I assume she arrived with Miss Dayspring in tow."

Alice's eyes narrowed.

"We've got one of our runaways over here," said Simpson.

Alice stared at Jacey through the windshield, then grabbed the front of Dr. Carlhagen's shirt. With an easy motion, she curled him from his knees to his feet, and then to his tiptoes. "Do you know where Summer is?"

Unperturbed, Dr. Carlhagen said, "I'm afraid I do not. Everything went to hell in a handbasket during the mutiny. I fear when all of this is corrected we will have to have a much larger force here. But please take me to see Maxine. She will vouch for me."

"She isn't well," Alice said. "And she's fading fast."

She glanced at the sky. "The chopper should have refueled and been back by now. We're losing daylight."

"I'm afraid you're about out of time, my dear," Dr. Carlhagen said. He made an effort to pull free from Alice's grip. "Please unbind my hands and let's go talk to Maxine. I do think I can save her."

Alice clearly didn't like this development, but Jacey saw she was uncertain enough to give Dr. Carlhagen a chance.

"Don't trust him," Jacey shouted. "He wants to kill the senator."

"She's a noisy one," Dr. Carlhagen said. "I suggest you gag her."

Alice nodded at Simpson. He shoved a band of cloth into Jacey's mouth and tied it tightly behind her head. He produced a long, gleaming knife from a sheath strapped to his leg and cut her free from the Jeep.

"I hope you try something again," he said, twirling the blade in his hand. "I hear Scions heal fast."

"Let's go," Alice said.

Jacey was forced to walk behind Dr. Carlhagen. She wanted to tackle him, stomp on his head, but she didn't think she would get two steps before the guard knocked her to the ground and stabbed her.

They entered the medical ward, passed between the cots, and walked into the short corridor with the holding rooms. Inside of one lay Senator Bentilius, apparently asleep. A meek-looking woman with dark skin and limp shoulders sat next to her. She jumped up as Alice entered, dragging Dr. Carlhagen behind her. "Oh dear!"

"Senator Bentilius?" Alice said. "Are you awake?"

The old woman opened her eyes. "Have you found my Scion yet?"

"No, but this young man claims to be the *real* Dr. Carlhagen."

Senator Bentilius's eyes slowly shifted to Dr. Carlhagen. "He looks nothing like my Christof. We've known each other since our twenties."

"Yes, we have, my dear," said Dr. Carlhagen. "But I transferred into a different body than I had originally intended. Do you remember Paris, how we walked in Hemingway's footsteps in the Latin Quarter? The long afternoons admiring the Impressionists at the d'Orsay? Even longer nights in my pied-à-terre, windows open to the shouts of tourists aboard the Batobuses on the Seine, just across Quai de Montebello?"

He stepped closer. Alice barred his way.

Irritation flashed across his face, but he mastered it. "Do you remember the gift I gave you as we sat people-watching at the Café de Flore?"

"I remember," whispered Senator Bentilius, eyes far away. "But do you?"

"Of course. It was a fountain pen, one I inherited from my grandmother. And you mocked me for it, did you not? You said it was a waste of time to hold onto old things. You were right. In that spirit, I chose not to transfer to my own Scion. I had already lived a life in that body, and much of that time was marked with misery. In truth, my own Scion was the greatest disappointment of my life."

"So you stole someone else's Scion?"

"No. As it happened, his Progenitor died."

"Charles Buchanan," she said.

Dr. Carlhagen barked a laugh. "I'm impressed, Maxine. You really have done your research."

"As a high-ranking government official, I have access to some exceptional intelligence resources. Alice, this is most certainly Dr. Carlhagen. Please unbind his hands."

"Yes, ma'am," Alice said. In moments she had cut Dr. Carlhagen's wrists free.

"And who is this prettyish girl behind you?" Senator Bentilius asked.

"Why, my dearest love, this is the solution to your problem. This Scion belonged to Charles' wife Jacqueline. She died in the same boating accident as Charles."

Jacey drew in a shocked breath as the two truths collapsed in on her at once. First, that her Progenitor had been married to Vaughan's. And second, that Dr. Carlhagen was offering her to the senator in place of Summer.

The meaning of Dr. Carlhagen's earlier statements became suddenly clear. That later she would be willing to give herself to him. And she would, once her mind had been overwritten by Senator Bentilius, who was apparently still in love with Dr. Carlhagen.

"Bring her forward," the senator commanded.

Alice grabbed Jacey by the nape of her neck and pushed her close to the gurney. The enormous bodyguard held on so that Jacey couldn't throw herself at the senator, bite her, or butt the old woman's head with her own.

Jacey grumbled a curse through the gag, but it came out a mere snarl.

"She has spirit," the senator said, looking Jacey up and down. "Lovely eyes. I wouldn't hate that. And she's quite striking in a Hollywood sort of way. It'd be strange living an entire lifetime with everyone saying, 'You know who you look like? You look just like that wonderful Jacqueline Buchanan.'"

"My dear," Dr. Carlhagen said. "Time is running out. I would offer you another one of the Scions, but you understand how it is."

"I do. I do. And quite frankly, I'm ready to be done with this body. It pains me so."

"Very well. Let's get going."

Her eyes turned back to Dr. Carlhagen, a smile breaking out on her cracked and trembling lips. "And I might add that I am most impressed with your new packaging, Christof. I quite liked the other version of you, but this is something . . ." The lust-filled look in her eyes finished the sentence.

Dr. Carlhagen laughed and flashed a glance at Jacey. She returned it, putting as much hatred in her eyes as she could manage. But the effort provoked nothing from him but a laugh.

Dr. Carlhagen took Senator Bentilius's hand. "There is another advantage, my dear. This Scion is nearly eighteen, and that will give you more freedom to move about in the rest of the world. You can jump back into politics, perhaps build a name for yourself as the youngest senator in the North American legislature. Soon you'll be back to lording your power over everyone in the Indy-Minnie corridor."

"Yes, Christof. But all I really want right now is to be with you."

Dr. Carlhagen leaned over her and kissed her cheek. "We'll be together soon, my love."

"Yes." Her eyes cut to Jacey. "Very soon."

Dr. Carlhagen turned to glare at Alice. "Find the impostor and Mr. Justin. I want them secured at once."

Alice returned the stare but made no move to obey.

A muscle quivered beneath Dr. Carlhagen's left eye, but he retained control. Showing his teeth in a vague grin, he turned to the senator. "Please, Maxine. We can't let traitors run loose on campus. I intend to restore order, but my own armed force is thirty minutes away by helicopter."

"Do as he asks," Senator Bentilius told Alice.

Alice stepped into the hall and ordered her men to capture Humphrey and Mr. Justin. They scurried to obey.

"Now," Dr. Carlhagen said, "let's get the senator into the transfer room for the initial scan."

33

GIRLS TO DANCE AND BOYS TO FIGHT

Mother Tyeesha's small kitchen overflowed with silence. The heavy kind that Belle found it hard to breathe in. The kind that followed an intense and thorough argument.

The old woman's revelations about Mr. Justin and the men coming on a boat to steal the Scions had heated an already tense reunion.

They all sat around the small kitchen table, faces grim, eyes tight.

Summer dragged a fingernail along a dark strip of wood grain on the tabletop. It produced a faint scritch that drew Belle's eyes.

"Go wash up, Summer," Belle ordered.

Summer, a disheveled and filthy mess, mumbled, "You're not my Nine leader." She stopped scritching and wrapped her arms tightly across her chest. Legs crossed, she waved a foot back and forth in agitation. "So what do we do? How can we protect the children here and help Jacey at the same time?"

"We can't do either of those things," Belle said. "We might be able to hide the small ones in the rainforest. For a while. But it will just delay the inevitable. Trying to help Jacey is even more futile."

A muscle in Sensei's jaw throbbed, but he looked away from her. "I think Belle's right about hiding the children in the forest. That's our only hope. As for Jacey . . . The school is over thirty kilometers from here. I don't know if I have the strength, but I will not abandon Jacey to Dr. Carlhagen's whims."

"You sure didn't do much to help Dante and Ping or Sarah and Vin," Belle snapped.

"I told you, I didn't know what was happening. I thought they were meeting their parents."

"We can't send two-year-olds into the woods," Summer said. "And what about the babies?"

Mother Tyeesha spoke for the first time since relating Jacey's news about the approaching boat. "There are twelve children six through eight. They can each take charge of one child from the one-, two-, and three-year-olds. That leaves eight between ages four and five. They can follow after the older children and help. The four staff can each carry one infant. That's all thirty-six. They'll run into the woods, disperse, and hide."

Belle snorted. "Your staff? You mean the ones who helped Dr. Carlhagen escape?"

Mother Tyeesha's face turned dark. "That was Robin. I spoke to her while you three were getting settled. She had no idea what Dr. Carlhagen was up to. She feels terrible about it. I've already given instructions to the staff. The children are already gone."

Belle forced herself to keep her admiration concealed. The old woman was made of tough guts, that was for sure.

Mother Tyeesha allowed herself a thin, humorless smile.

"Whoever these kidnappers are, they'll have to work to find my children. And that should buy you some time. Maybe once you get to the Scion School, you can figure out a way to stop them."

Without lifting his head, Sensei looked up at her, eyes dark and set deep beneath his brows. "What about you, Mother? Where are you going to hide?"

"I'm not. I'm too old to scramble through the forest like a mongoose. They won't harm me, most likely. Besides, I want to see the looks on their faces when they find the place abandoned."

Belle was not so optimistic. If Mr. Justin planned to steal all the Scions, he would have no use for Mother Tyeesha. In fact, he'd have good reason to have her killed.

Mother Tyeesha gave her shoulders a little shake as if overcome by a sudden chill. Her face smoothed, and she changed the subject. "So how will you three save Jacey from Dr. Carlhagen?"

Sensei sighed and tapped his fingers, which made the muscles of his forearms flex and bulge. They looked like bundles of steel cable sheathed in skin. Belle wanted to edge her chair away from the tightly coiled man. He seemed like he might blow apart at any second. "Even if I ran, thirty kilometers is a long way. I'd be exhausted when I arrived, and then there'll be the guards to deal with."

"There's no reason to run," Summer said. "We can circle the island in the skiff and get to the campus from Isaac's Beach."

Sensei nodded appreciatively. "Excellent. But they'll still be armed." He squeezed his eyes shut and swore. "I should have taken the sidearm off that man I took down."

Belle's eyes snapped up as she remembered the man she and Jacey had seen face-down on the beach. "So it was you who did that. I knew Summer couldn't have knocked him out."

"I'd been recovering in that area for a few days. I have to say that the hurricane took more out of me than the initial dive from the helicopter."

Belle became instantly suspicious. "Why didn't they shoot you before they threw you out?"

Sensei shrugged and met her gaze without blinking. "I didn't give them a chance. I jumped out as soon as we were over water." He unconsciously rubbed his wrists where a band of fresh scars crossed, clearly where he had been bound.

Belle broke contact with that stare. Sensei had always been able to see inside of her, something Jacey was always trying to do. Belle hated how everyone tried to invade her mind all the time.

"If the guards are armed," Summer said, "we'll need to distract them."

Silence swarmed into the small room again. Belle kept her eyes on the table, studying the patterns in the wood. She caught herself starting to run a fingernail along the grain and snatched her hand away.

"Belle?" Mother Tyeesha stared at her, one eyebrow slightly lifted, a faint smile on her lips. It took a moment for Belle to realize that the old woman was asking a question. Asking without speaking, the way she had done when they were children.

Realizing what the question was, Belle leaned back in her chair and let out a huge sigh. "What do you want me to do to distract them? I'm not going to go and get trapped there again. My Progenitor is coming in one year, and I have no intention of being overwritten."

"You believe there's an alternative?" the old woman asked.

"I'm getting off this island."

Sensei shook his head and lifted his teacup to his lips. But before he took a sip, he set it down. "Say you found a way off the island, which I'm telling you right now you will not do. Where would you go? How would you survive? You know nothing of the outside world. You have zero resources. If you walked into that world dressed in this uniform and knowing as little as you do, the world would eat you alive. You'd end up wishing you'd been overwritten."

"I would figure out something," Belle said. "I'm not an idiot."

"You have no one to contact. You are utterly alone."

Tears of frustration threatened to return. Belle clenched her jaw and stiffened. "I have *always* been utterly alone." Her words snapped back from the kitchen walls like a thunderclap.

Sensei didn't back down. "Yes, you've seen to that, haven't you?"

Summer sat there hugging her elbows, her foot waving even faster. "You're alone because you choose to be. All I know is that if the situation were reversed, Jacey would try to save you. Not that you'd deserve it."

Belle sneered. "You don't know what you're talking about. Jacey has always hated me. She wouldn't lift a finger for me."

"No, child." Mother Tyeesha spoke quietly as she smoothed a folded tea towel on her lap. "It's you who has always hated Jacey. You hate her because you are vain and jealous and fearful. But that doesn't mean that Jacey hates you in return. Believe me, I grew up with sisters."

She raised her bony hands, cutting off Belle's angry retort. "Let me finish. I was often angry with my sisters, often frustrated because I couldn't understand them and couldn't seem to get through to them. My youngest sister told me nearly every day that she hated me. And yet I still loved her. I loved them all."

Mother Tyeesha scooted her chair closer to Belle and placed a dry, hot hand on top of Belle's. "You have always pushed people away, including me. Despite that, I love you."

Belle stared into middle distance between Summer and Sensei. Tears welled in her eyes and trickled down her cheek, but her jaw was clenched tight. She could not understand how she could feel pain, anger, sadness, and frustration all at the same time. She wiped a palm across her eyes, and when her vision cleared, she saw that Summer was doing the same and sniffing.

At first Belle thought the girl was mocking her, but then she saw Summer's lip tremble. Those huge eyes of hers seemed to suck Belle in.

"I love Humphrey," Summer said. "But he loves Jacey. I wanted to hate her for that. But how can I when she's risked everything to save me? If I don't try to help her, I won't be able to live with myself."

"What do you want me to do?" Belle said, nose running, trembling lips slurring her words.

Sensei leaned toward her, stabbing the table with a finger. "Go back to the school and create a diversion for me. Go right in, do anything necessary to lead them away from the east path. That's where I'll be coming from. I'll take care of the rest."

"You'll just get yourself captured and killed," Belle said. "Even if you got past the guards, how would you break into the medical ward? The doors are locked. Do you think Chax will let you in now that you're supposed to be dead? And even if you got in, how would you get Jacey out alive? There's got to be more guards inside. The only way would be to kill everyone who stood against you."

"So be it," Sensei said. The hardness in his gaze made Belle shiver. The sense of eminent explosion radiating from him was stronger than ever.

"It's a desperate plan," Belle said.

"We're desperate," Summer said matter-of-factly.

"What about the other Scions?" Belle asked. "There are six boys, Spiders through Eagles, who could fight alongside you, very well-trained."

"No," Sensei said. "The Spiders are only fourteen. If the guards start shooting . . ."

"Then they die now rather than in four years," Belle said.

Having a problem to work on helped to calm her, even if she was ambivalent about the objective. Her mind pulled on the loose threads of the issue, trying to untie the knot. "If we could communicate with the boys, we could tell only the older boys to help, keep the young ones inside. At the very least, they could help distract the guards. And they're Scions. They're too expensive to shoot. Even the senator has to have given her guards instructions on that point."

Sensei gave a non-committal grunt.

"She's right," Mother Tyeesha said, surprising Belle. "The boys have the right to defend themselves. But what about the girls? Surely they can stand beside you, too."

Summer's face twisted into a wry grimace. "We're not trained in martial arts."

It was Mother Tyeesha's turn to glower, this time at Sensei.

He lowered his eyes. "Dr. Carlhagen insisted it be that way. He wanted girls to dance and boys to fight."

"And boys don't get to dance?" Mother Tyeesha asked primly.

"Oh, they do. Some of them," Summer said, rolling her eyes. "All we learned from Sensei was Tai Chi."

"You girls might be surprised to find what you're capable of," Sensei said with a grim smile. "Dr. Carlhagen had no idea what deadly skills come with Tai Chi instruction. Still, I don't like this idea of Scions in conflict with armed men. Besides, it would be impossible to coordinate."

"Not impossible," Summer said. "It'll be easy once we get close enough. We can use this." She produced a reader from her satchel. The girl was suddenly smiling like she had smuggled a pint of ice cream into Girls' Hall, which Belle had caught her doing more than once.

Belle snapped her fingers. "Give it to me."

Summer snatched it back. "No, it's mine."

"Let her have it," Sensei said. "Belle will need it to contact the boys."

"So what's my job in this plan?" Summer asked, foot resuming its back and forth twitch.

"You can drive the skiff to Isaac's Beach," Sensei said. "And you'll stay there. I don't want you anywhere near the campus until I've eliminated any chance the senator will overwrite you."

Summer started to grow sullen. Belle had seen this behavior countless times. If allowed to continue, Summer would refuse to speak to any of them. "Don't be a brat."

Summer said nothing.

"Timing is going to be essential," Sensei said. "The problem is that I don't know how long it'll take to get to the beach."

"I can tell you," Summer said, still pouting.

Sensei waited, using the force of his presence to melt Summer's bad attitude.

She relaxed a bit and with a huff of impatience demanded, "Can someone draw a reasonably accurate map of the island? And maybe estimate some distances?"

"I can do better than that," Mother said. She tottered down the hall and returned with a paper map. Summer took it, suddenly absorbed in the details.

"I would have given my left leg for this," she said. "I need my reader back for a minute."

Belle handed it over. Summer began tapping on the reader. "Assuming a top speed of the skiff, I think we can get to Isaac's Beach in fifty minutes."

"There's no way I can get from here to the front gate that fast," Belle said.

"Forget that." Summer stabbed a finger at an inlet on the map. "We'll drop you off here. The road is just one hundred meters from shore, and that'll put you . . ." She measured the distance with her thumb and compared it to the map scale. "Three kilometers from the front gate. You can run that far, can't you?"

Belle didn't rise to Summer's bait. She had plenty of experience dealing with Spiders. There was something about being fourteen that made girls extra disrespectful.

"That would be a seventeen-minute run at a good clip," Sensei said.

Belle didn't appreciate him setting her pace for her, though she kept her displeasure to herself.

Summer tapped on her reader again, mood suddenly cheerful as if a cloud had parted to reveal the sun. "Perfect. It'll take another ten minutes to reach Isaac's Beach from Belle's drop-off. Figure another fifteen minutes from there up the east path to campus."

She looked up. "But how are we going to coordinate this? If Belle and the boys distract the men too early, the whole plan will fall apart."

"This will be the signal." Sensei pulled something from his pocket and held it up.

The remote control for the front gate.

"When I'm in position, I'll open the gate. That alone will create a bit of a diversion. Belle will go in and lead the guards away from the east path. I'll come in a few minutes later and get into the medical ward."

Looking down on the map, Belle felt like she stood at the top of a very long fall. But Sensei was right. There was no way off the island without help. And if the plan worked—if she could deny Dr. Carlhagen possession of Jacey—it would be worth the risk. And who knew, maybe they could figure out how to avoid Mr. Justin's kidnappers in the bargain.

34

EXTREME PAIN CREATION

The news that Vaughan had been overwritten by Dr. Carlhagen produced an odd swirl of emotions in the dining room. If the window had not allowed in a freshening breeze, Humphrey thought they might all have roasted from the anger. As it was, even the fragrant island air couldn't mask the bitter fear that roiled in each of the Scions.

So much energy. If only we could channel it.

But channel where? The problems they faced could not be overcome with anger. Could they?

Not and keep everyone safe at the same time. That had been Jacey's quandary.

She keeps everyone safe but herself.

Elias sat very still, elbows on the table, thumbnail between his teeth, eyes far away. The boy was nearly as deadly as Vaughan. Sang, too.

Humphrey's eyes skimmed over Horace. The boy was the dullest minded of any Scion, except when some cruelty was afoot. Sensei had broken him of his habitual torturing of bugs and geckos, but that didn't mean those impulses weren't boiling under the surface.

Tytus slouched so low in his chair Humphrey could only see the top of his head. Impossibly, it seemed like he might be asleep.

Wanda. Smart and calm. Except today. He'd never seen her so upset before. The days she'd been in charge of Jacey's Nine had brought out a natural leadership ability Humphrey would never have suspected. How could that be used?

Dajeet. Brilliant, quiet, and sarcastic. Humphrey had always assumed she was imitating Belle, but he saw now that she thought for herself. A mistake to assume dullness in a person who doesn't say much, he realized. A big mistake.

His eyes went back to the other quiet one. Sang had always seemed like a punching bag. Taking blows, but impervious to them, he swung away from attack then came to rest where he'd been before. But Sang suffered from comparisons to Vaughan and Elias. Truth was, he'd beaten Humphrey in every sparring match they'd had.

Bethancy's eyes were on him, resentment plain in her expression. He couldn't blame her for that. Of course, she was quick to be injured by the slightest comment. The thought brought a mirthless smile to his lips. He could say the same about himself.

"Who is my Progenitor?" she asked suddenly, voice loud and brash in the quiet. Tytus sat up straight, startled.

Wanda stood abruptly, scuttering her chair behind her. "Do you know? You must!"

Voices broke into a shouting match as each demanded the same thing. Humphrey held up his hands and whistled for silence. Miraculously, it worked. They all stopped blabbering at once.

But their eyes weren't on him.

He turned to the door.

"Damn," he said.

Two men garbed in black stood there. They held hard-edged black pistols at their sides, casually.

One, slightly older and utterly bald, clomped into the room, eyes sweeping faces for threats. His demeanor said he found none. "You will all stay here for the moment." He lifted his gun and waved it vaguely at Humphrey. "You. Where's the butler?"

Humphrey slowly stood and gathered his most Dr. Carlhagen-ish expression. "What is the meaning of this? How dare you barge into my home brandishing your weapons. There are Scions present! Do you have any idea how valuable they are?"

"Drop the act. You're not Dr. Carlhagen and we know it." He stepped closer. Though he stood eye to eye with Humphrey, the thickness of the man's neck and shoulders spoke of a potential for extreme pain creation. Pain he was more than happy to inflict.

The man's hand shot toward Humphrey's neck. Years of drilling under Sensei's direction brought Humphrey's arm up in a deflective move, catching the man's wrist. But speed wasn't Humphrey's forte, and he couldn't stop the counterattack.

A flash of white and red blocked Humphrey's vision, accompanied by the yells of the Scions.

The pain followed on a moment later, sharp as an axe blade. Humphrey stumbled into the table and nearly fell, but the man caught him by the lapel of his suit coat. Wetness trickled from Humphrey's temple, along his cheekbones, and into the corner of his mouth. Blood.

"Where is the butler?" the bald man demanded.

Wanda's voice, low but full of ice, cut across the room. "He doesn't know. Mr. Justin sent us all here, but none of us knows why. We are waiting for him."

The bald man smiled, showing a wide, perfect set of teeth. Except for one molar, which was missing. "I guess we'll all wait together. Simpson! Go stand at the front door, out of sight. Subdue the butler if he returns and bring him here."

"Yessir." Simpson hustled away. Humphrey noted a pronounced limp in the man's gait.

"All of you, sit!"

They sat, some quicker than others. Elias, proud and defiant, took his sweet time about it. Humphrey would have smacked him upside the head if he hadn't still been in the grip of the senator's guard.

"I didn't catch your name," Humphrey said, dropping the Dr. Carlhagen voice.

"*Sir* will do." He released Humphrey and stepped back to the door, dragging a dining room chair with him. He placed it sideways in the entrance so he could watch the dining room and hallway at the same time.

The room started to spin and Humphrey scrambled for his own chair. His hand went to his temple and came away bloody. He snatched a cloth napkin from the table and pressed it to his wound. The man must have hit him with the butt of his weapon.

Somehow the senator had figured out Humphrey was an imposter. The only way that could have happened was if Mr. Justin had told him. But why?

35

WAKES UP WITH A BROKEN ARM

Jacey stood very still in the little hallway leading to the transfer room. The door to that room was closed, as was the door opposite leading into the main medical ward. The corridor seemed full of people, mostly because Alice took up so much space.

By contrast, the senator's nurse, Miss Dayspring, barely registered in Jacey's attention. The woman had either a great skill at appearing insignificant or she was truly a person of no substance.

Jacey fidgeted to cover a slight repositioning of her feet, angling herself so that she could move away from the transfer room. If her hands hadn't been bound, she could have touched the door. She also could have touched Miss Dayspring.

"What's taking so long?" Alice grumbled.

"Dr. Carlhagen and the AI are beginning the initial scan of the senator's brain," said Miss Dayspring.

"I understand that." Alice looked like she might bite the nurse in half. "Why can't we take the Scion in?"

"The senator was a bit nervous. Dr. Carlhagen thought it might help her if there was quiet in the room for a while."

The woman's huge hands plopped onto Jacey's shoulders, just on either side of her neck. "I'll keep her quiet."

Jacey let herself fall to the floor as if her bones had disappeared, slipping out of Alice's grip. She no sooner struck the floor than she rolled past Alice, sprang to her feet, and hurled herself at the door leading to the main ward. She twisted, scrabbling with her bound hands for the latch. She turned it, leaned forward, and hooked her heel around the door.

Alice strode toward her, hands outstretched. Miss Dayspring's shrieks stabbed at Jacey's ears. The door opened, and Jacey squeezed through. She had no plan other than to run. The door slammed shut behind her, but she heard it swing open less than a second later.

She put everything she had into her strides, driven even faster by Alice's pounding footfalls. The closed door leading to the ward's foyer approached fast. She would have to turn her back to it to grab the handle.

Her knees hit the floor, followed by her shoulder, and cheek. Her breath blew out as an impossible weight bore down on top her. Alice's knee ground into her spine.

The woman grasped Jacey's hair and pulled her head back. The knee released, but Alice still pulled on the hair and forced Jacey to stand. Without a word, she guided Jacey back into the little corridor, shoved her against the wall, stood toe to toe with her, and crossed her arms. "You won't try that again. I would hate to have to apologize to the senator if she wakes up with a broken arm. But I understand Scions heal quickly."

Jacey returned the stare, filling it with as much hatred as she could muster. It was spoiled somewhat by the tears of pain trickling down her cheeks, which just made her angrier.

Miss Dayspring looked away.

The door to the transfer room opened, and Dr. Carlhagen peered out. "Bring her in."

Before his command was finished, Alice had grabbed Jacey and started shoving her through. Jacey resisted for a moment and then was swept from her feet. Seconds later, Alice slammed her down on the cot next to the transfer machine. Alice held her down as Dr. Carlhagen cut the bonds on Jacey's wrists.

She flailed, landing a good blow on Dr. Carlhagen's chin. He staggered back.

Alice threw her weight on top of Jacey, and in seconds, she and Dr. Carlhagen had secured the straps. Jacey screamed and struggled, but she could barely move her head, let alone her arms and legs.

"We must hurry," Dr. Carlhagen said. "The senator is fading fast. Greta, how goes the initial scan?"

"Very well, Dr. Carlhagen," said the AI in charge of transfers.

"Can you hurry it up?"

"I'm sorry, Dr. Carlhagen, but the process is the process."

"Okay. Everyone out."

"I'm not moving," Alice said.

"Go ahead, Alice." It was an old, tired voice, obviously the senator's. "I value your concern, but quite frankly you're emitting too much negativity."

Alice let out an animal grunt, then strode out of the transfer room. Miss Dayspring stood by the door, clearly not knowing if she should stay or go.

Jacey met her gaze, pleading. She tried to talk, but the gag made her retch.

Miss Dayspring shuffled to Jacey's side. "I think this gag is too tight."

"Gag?" Dr. Carlhagen said. He strode next to Miss

Dayspring. "Aww," he said with mock concern, "you poor dear."

He removed the gag, and Jacey drew in deep breaths. She wanted to say many things but decided not to give Dr. Carlhagen an excuse to replace the gag. Instead she made eye contact with Miss Dayspring. "Thank you."

Dr. Carlhagen handed the cloth rag to Miss Dayspring. The woman made a face as she took the rag by the corner and carried it out of view.

"Progress, Greta?" Dr. Carlhagen asked.

"Almost ready, sir. We're getting very close."

36

WHOSE LITTLE PUPPET ARE YOU?

The bald guard leaned back in his chair, eyes closed. Humphrey doubted the man was sleeping. In fact, there was a certain quality emanating from the man, a kind of sadistic hunger that reminded him of Horace. Humphrey suspected the man was trying to lure them into action, which would then justify his violent—and probably deadly—reaction.

The girls sat very still, sharing glances, and, in Bethancy's case, chewing her lower lip in a display of nervousness. Sang sat very rigid in his chair, but unlike Elias, he did not seem ready to jump into attack. If anything, he seemed ready to slip under the table and hide.

Funny how danger brought out a person's true nature. As it was doing with Horace. The stupid boy was grinning.

Tytus seemed to be modeling his behavior after Wanda's. He kept his face calm, serious. No sign of nervousness showed through.

A slight change in Elias's posture brought the attention of everyone except the guard. Elias shook his head slightly, glancing at the door. With painfully slow movements, he put his hand behind his back and lifted his uniform shirt.

Humphrey glared at him. Elias could be impulsive sometimes, but his greatest gift as a fighter was patience, his ability to wait for just the right moment to attack.

Elias's hand came back to his lap, but he seemed to be holding something. Humphrey couldn't see it, but Sang could. The boy's eyes widened and darted from whatever Elias held to the door.

A weapon? But where would Elias have gotten one? The only guns on the island—besides those brought by the senator's bodyguards—were Mr. Justin's rifle and Dr. Carlhagen's pistol, both of which the butler had locked up somewhere.

Humphrey raised his eyebrows and tilted his head, the best warning he could give Elias without drawing the guard's attention.

Elias shrugged slightly, as if loosing his shoulder muscle. In doing so, he brought the very top of a reader into view over the edge of the table.

So that's what he'd concealed. Probably had it tucked in his pants.

Humphrey didn't see what good it would do, though.

Static blared from the doorway a second before a tinny voice barked through a walkie-talkie hooked to the bald guard's belt. "Still nothing," the voice said. "I don't think the butler is coming."

The guard lifted his radio. "Did I ask for your opinion, Simpson?"

"No sir."

Eyeing the Scions suspiciously, the guard stood and stretched. He strode into the room, boots falling heavily on the plank floor. Bethancy's face went rigid as he paused behind her and touched her head. "And whose little puppet are you?"

She clamped her lips shut.

He snorted. "Probably some dimwitted actress."

He continued to Dajeet, put a finger under her chin and forced her head around. She stared into nothingness, refusing to meet his gaze. The bald man chuckled. "I suppose you're the puppet of a guru. Some magical hoaxster in Indiastan. Pretty, though."

He stepped toward Wanda, who stared up at him defiantly. This produced more laughter. "I never was much for redheads, myself. And neither was your Progenitor. She goes around blond these days. I wonder why she didn't have that changed in your DNA."

"You know who my Progenitor is?"

The guard pursed his lips, but said nothing. He backed to the servants' door and peered through. "No lock." He breathed an obscenity. "Get up," he ordered Wanda.

Tytus tensed, but Wanda placed a hand on his arm as she stood. The boy inched back in his seat, but his eyebrows betrayed his extreme dissatisfaction with how the bald man had treated the others.

Humphrey admired the serenity Wanda managed as she straightened. She reminded him of Vaughan a little, though they didn't resemble each other in the slightest.

The guard approached Wanda, leaned toward her, smiling. Then reached around her to snag her chair and drag it with him through the servants' door. Wanda slumped as soon as he was out of sight. Elias swore, drawing nods from Dajeet and Bethancy.

Horace chuckled and rubbed his hands together, the whole time looking Wanda up and down.

Something thumped against the servants' door, followed by screeching as the guard pushed something very heavy across the kitchen floor. The door thumped again. A few seconds later, the bald guard appeared at the main doorway, brushing his palms together as if he'd just finished some dirty task.

"You won't get through that way. Or this way, either." He took the chair with him and swung the door shut. A second later the door boomed as something was thrust against it. The chair, Humphrey guessed. Probably wedged under the doorknob.

Humphrey turned to Elias, who was already speaking to someone through his reader.

Kirk's voice came back. "What do you want me to do?"

"Come up here and help us escape."

"No!" Humphrey commanded. "They're too young to take on armed men."

"So we're just going to sit here?" Elias looked at Humphrey in utter disbelief.

Humphrey realized that was because Elias lacked experience in losing fights. He didn't know what the cost was when, at the end of the match, you were the one lying on the mat, struggling for breath. "Patience. I just need to think."

Dajeet huffed and folded her hands in front of her. "Hurry up. We don't have all day for you to realize we have no other choice."

37

A SWIG OF SPOILED MILK

As night fell, the faintest line of orange and violet slashed across the horizon to the west. But the direction Belle was heading, due east, was already all blackness.

Summer guided the skiff into a little inlet, slowing the motor to a crawl. It irritated Belle, who just wanted to get on with things.

Slowly they came upon the stony beach and scraped to a stop. Belle timed the inflowing surf and leapt out as it retreated, shoes squishing in the saturated sand. A few long paces took her to dry land and a fringe of low foliage. Sensei had moved to the bow of the skiff. He held up the remote. "Wait for the signal, then do whatever you're going to do. Remind the boys not to fight anyone with a drawn weapon. Is that understood?"

"I understand."

He'd only said it four thousand times on the boat ride around the island.

Summer did something to the motor, and it shuddered

and began to drag the boat backward. It was so loud, Belle figured everyone on the campus had already heard them coming. Summer made another adjustment, and soon the boat was headed over the swells. Belle watched it diminish into darkness, and it soon became just a pinpoint of light from a flashlight Sensei had borrowed from Mother Tyeesha. And then that went out, and the sound of the motor faded beneath the ocean's sighs.

Belle picked her way through the foliage and climbed a shallow slope. She used Summer's reader for light, but even doing so stepped square into a thornskipple patch. Thankfully, the soles of her standard-issue shoes kept the thorns from piercing her foot, but several of the barbed thorns stuck into her leg. She hissed as she pulled them free and cursed as the barbs yanked small hunks of fabric from her pant legs and flesh from her calves. That was going to burn later.

When she finally got to the road, she checked the timer on the reader and started to run. As soon as she got to a rise that overlooked the Scion School, she stopped. She tried the reader to see if it could connect to the school's communication network. If she could talk to the boys from here, maybe she could get them to distract the guards while she hunkered down well out of sight.

The network connection was dead.

She was about to turn the reader off when she noticed the photo Summer had chosen as a background image. It was of Jacey. She was sitting in firelight, holding what looked to be a hunk of rodent leg up to her mouth and smiling. It was the same smile that had irritated Belle her entire life.

Belle turned off the reader and started running toward campus. The image of Jacey's face remained in her head.

"Sense data," she said. For reasons she couldn't understand, she had been conditioned to be repulsed by Jacey's smile. She pondered why that was. The smile must have frequently accompanied some slight or insult, though Belle couldn't think of a particular instance.

She stopped to turn the reader on again and study the smile. Jacey's eyes were bright, though their aqua color wasn't apparent due to the lighting in the picture. She stared right at the camera.

She had known her picture was being taken.

Turning off the reader, Belle continued her run, picking up the pace to make up for the time she'd wasted.

On second thought, Jacey might not have known that the picture was being taken. Maybe she'd been smiling at Summer. The expression hadn't bothered Summer apparently, or she wouldn't have used the picture as the background. Come to think of it, Jacey's smile didn't seem to bother anyone else. They loved it, in fact.

Belle realized why. It was because everyone else was on the receiving end of that smile.

That was it.

Belle hated Jacey's smile because Belle never received it.

Communication was all an exchange of sense data. One person opened their mouth and created sound waves that went into another person's ears. It was the up to the recipient's brain to convert those sound waves into meaning.

A pretty terrible mechanism for communication, Belle thought. So open to interpretation. And then there were the nonverbal cues—the smiles, the frowns, facial expressions, body movements. How could one be expected to absorb all of that and make any sense of it? Even if someone wrote down exactly what they meant, the other person would have to read those words. Who knew how they'd interpret them?

And yet, Belle knew that her hatred toward Jacey was a conditioned response to that same sense data. Had she interpreted Jacey's communication all wrong?

Because what she felt in response to that smile was as

unavoidable as shivering in cold air or a stomach growling at the smell of food.

So what was love in response to?

Attraction, she thought. Love was an evolutionary mechanism to encourage breeding. Nothing more.

But Mother Tyeesha had spoken about love in a way that hadn't made sense at all to Belle. She had talked about her sisters who were so annoying, and yet she loved them. In Belle's mind, love was supposed to be a positive thing.

She descended the switchbacks, now heading generally north. Soon the road would level and she would be within minutes of the Scion School.

Then she'd have to wait for Sensei and his damned gate opener. Belle hated not controlling the timing of this operation herself.

She had made a decision to come this far, but now that it came to it, she didn't really want to go in. Why should she risk her safety to save someone she hated?

But her rational mind wouldn't let her off the hook. *Why? Why do I hate her?*

Jacey had never hit Belle. Jacey had never played a prank on her. She had never said anything cutting to Belle.

The pain of the wounds in Belle's leg reminded her of how she had thrashed Jacey with a thornskipple branch. That memory sure had lost its savor.

No matter how much Belle wracked her brain, she could not come up with anything Jacey had done to her besides being generally bossy and full of herself.

Was a superior attitude enough to deserve being overwritten?

Sense data, Belle thought. *Why do the inputs coming into my brain from Jacey irritate me so much?*

"Because she thinks she's better than everyone," Belle said.

She's the best dancer, has that amazing memorization skill. She's breathtakingly beautiful.

No wonder all the boys looked at her in that peculiar way.

That was reason enough to despise someone, Belle decided.

She caught herself. *No. That's reason enough to dislike someone.*

Belle turned back to Mother Tyeesha's assertion that Jacey didn't hate her and Summer saying that Jacey would have risked everything to save Belle if their circumstances were reversed.

Belle could not reconcile those notions with her own belief that Jacey hated her.

Belief, she thought, *is not the same as knowing.* There was no way to know with certainty what any other person was thinking.

She made a face. Many times she didn't even know what *she* was thinking.

She could remember no instance of Jacey actually saying that she was better than anyone else. She just *was* better.

A sour taste filled Belle's mouth like a swig of spoiled milk. Jacey wasn't strutting around pretending to be better. Belle wiped wetness from her eyes and cheeks. It wasn't sweat from running.

Jacey is *better.*

She had to wipe away more tears.

It's not fair. No matter how hard I try, I can't measure up. I can't compete.

Vaughan loved Jacey. Humphrey loved Jacey. Everyone in Belle's own Nine and most of the boys loved her. Or, at least, desired her. Dr. Carlhagen was obsessed with her. That girl, Livy, adored Jacey. But no Dolphin had ever felt that way about Belle.

With stunning and cold insight, Belle discovered the root of the problem.

She hated Jacey because she hated herself.

Tears streaming freely, she pushed her pace faster.

She realized why she'd been blind about Dr. Carlhagen's control over Vaughan's body. She had always believed Vaughan and Jacey were destined for each other. So when Belle saw an opportunity to have him, she jumped at it. If she could make him love her, it would prove her superiority.

Because only someone who was perfect could deserve him.

She had needed someone else to love her before she could love herself.

If only she could rid herself of all emotion, then she could see clearly. She could be happy then. The thought prompted a bitter laugh. *What a paradox.*

She drew closer to the school, slowed her steps, and moved off the road to shelter behind a tree.

"Time to focus, Belle," she whispered to herself.

She tried her reader again, and it connected to the network. She wanted to check in with her own Nine first, so she tried Leslie's reader.

No answer.

She tried Dajeet's.

No answer.

She tried Dansha, a foolish girl Summer's age. The girl's face appeared on Belle's reader. "It's you!" Dansha exclaimed. "What's going on? Where are you?"

"Where are Leslie and Dajeet?"

"Dajeet left with Mr. Justin earlier today. She never came back. Neither did Wanda or Bethancy." Those girls were from Jacey's Nine. "Leslie can't talk now. She's trying to keep the rest of Jacey's Nine calm. The oldest one left is Helen."

Helen was a Centipede. And not a very bright one, either.

The hair on Belle's neck rose as a chill crossed her skin. All the missing girls had been headed to the hacienda when she'd driven down the path earlier in the day.

"Just stay calm," she told Dansha. "The younger girls are looking to you and Leslie for leadership. Keep them busy if you can. There's going to be some noise soon."

"What are you doing? Is it about the men with guns?"

"Of course it is. Now get everyone settled down, and let them know there's going to be some shouting. Keep them away from the door and windows. Understood?"

"Understood."

Belle turned off the reader. Grimacing at her own Spider's foolishness, she crept from tree to tree, thankful for the darkness and her black uniform.

"Come on, Sensei. Let's get this over with."

38

A JOB IN GOVERNMENT

Miss Dayspring had started to pace, but Jacey noticed the nurse took great pains to stay well clear of Dr. Carlhagen. And every time the woman got near to Jacey, she made a strange face. She clearly didn't like what was about to happen.

Maybe Jacey could use that.

The next time the woman came near, Jacey whispered, "You're letting them do this."

"What was that?" Miss Dayspring asked. She leaned over Jacey, though her eyes were directed toward Dr. Carlhagen, who was observing a display that Greta projected over a holodesk.

"I said you're complicit in this evil. How can you live with yourself?"

The nurse looked at the floor and rubbed her hands together. "Madam Senator has been very kind to me. She helped my brother get a job in government."

"Should we sedate the Scion?" Greta asked.

Dr. Carlhagen rushed forward, shouldering Miss

Dayspring aside. She backed away, still rubbing her hands together as if she were cold. Dr. Carlhagen leaned over Jacey, fingers moving as if he were deciding which delicacy to choose from a platter.

"No sedation for the Scion," he said. "It's best for the transfer if she's alert."

He bent over her, bringing his face next to hers. He drew in a deep breath through her hair and let out a chuckle. "This is not how I wanted it to be, Jacqueline. Say the word, and I'll kill the old hag. We'll be out of here on her chopper, and you and I can live together forever."

"You'd kill the senator?" Jacey said loudly. "Miss Dayspring, Dr. Carlhagen just threatened to kill Senator Bentilius. Go get Alice."

The woman squawked and ran to the door. A second later, Alice barged in. She stared at Dr. Carlhagen, fists clenched. "You threatened the senator?"

"No, no, my dear," Dr. Carlhagen said. "This Scion is a very clever girl, and she's trying to manipulate Miss Dayspring." He turned back to Jacey. "I admire your tenacity, but your continuing struggle is pointless."

He turned and strode away from Jacey, and she sensed that he was standing next to Senator Bentilius.

"You see," he said, "Maxine is the true love of my life. I had just said that I would happily kill *for* her."

39

A MOMENTARY DISSONANCE

What light remained of the day did little but cast darker shadows into the blackness. Belle slipped to within a stone's throw of the gate. After studying it for a while, she realized that no one was patrolling along its length. She moved onto the road and stood in front of the chain-link gate and peered through.

The mango grove obscured most of the quad, but the light above the dojo illuminated a small sliver of grass. A silhouetted form passed across it and was gone. Too big to be a Scion.

Closer by, the rear windows of Boys' Hall and the Boys' Classroom were dark. That made sense because shutters were closed and latched during lockdown. And there had to be a lockdown with visitors on campus.

She retreated a few paces to take cover in some bushes. She would have liked to turn on the reader light to check for shaddle spiders, but she couldn't risk it.

She considered contacting Humphrey. As the senior boy

on campus, he could coordinate the boys with more authority than Belle. But since he had been pretending to be Dr. Carlhagen, he might be among the senator's guards. Even more likely, if the real Dr. Carlhagen had convinced the senator that Humphrey was a fraud, he was probably locked up somewhere.

That left Sang and Elias as the two oldest boys. She hated Elias. He was the one who had kicked Vaughan in the head, albeit at Dr. Carlhagen's insistence. But still. She would rather poke herself in the eye than talk to him.

She tried to raise Sang on the reader, but he didn't respond. Time was ticking away. So she gritted her teeth and called for Elias.

He answered right away. She saw the room behind him and recognized it immediately. "What are you doing in the hacienda dining room?"

"Belle? Hey, Humphrey," he called over his shoulder. "It's Belle."

"Humphrey's there? Let me talk to him."

The view of the reader camera bobbled, showing the table and then the ceiling and then eventually Humphrey frowning at her. "Whatever it is you want, I don't have time—"

"Just shut up. I'm here to save Jacey."

"Jacey! What's wrong with her? Where is she?"

Belle explained finding Jacey at the docks and taking her back to Mother Tyeesha's. As she described Dr. Carlhagen kidnapping her, Humphrey's face grew darker. By the time she'd finished telling him about Mr. Justin and the boat, he was steaming.

His eyes shifted to look at something off-camera. "That explains why the guards came and locked us in the dining room. Dr. Carlhagen must have gone straight to the senator and convinced her I'm a fraud."

Wanda peeped over Humphrey's shoulder. "What's Dr. Carlhagen going to do to Jacey?"

Other faces pressed close around Humphrey, all staring at Belle, all asking different things at the same time.

"Will you all just shut up?" Belle hissed. She checked to make sure no one was approaching the gate, then continued to whisper. "I think Dr. Carlhagen's giving Jacey to the senator because Summer is missing."

"He's going to overwrite her," Humphrey said on a horrified exhalation.

"Overwrite? That's what you were telling us about." It was Elias's voice off-camera. Humphrey ignored him.

"Vaughan?" Humphrey said. "Are you listening in?"

Vaughan's face appeared in a window on Belle's reader. "Yes. I've already checked activity in the transfer room. The machine is active, but I don't know what the state of transfer is. With Greta around, I don't dare get too close."

Belle's mind was paralyzed by a momentary dissonance as she pictured the Vaughan that Dr. Carlhagen had taken over. But this was the AI Vaughan, the one running on Socrates's old server.

"Can you stop it?" Humphrey asked him. "There must be something you can do."

Vaughan's face looked pained. "I would stop it if I could. There is something, but . . ."

"But what?"

"There's a good chance Jacey's brain image will be backed up, the way mine was when Dr. Carlhagen transferred to my body. It's possible I might be able to install a version of her on my server. That's about the best we can hope for."

"Make Jacey an AI?" Belle's skin chilled, and her mouth went dry. "You can do that?"

"Maybe."

"No!" Humphrey said. "We can't just let her die."

The others all started talking again.

"Sensei is alive," Belle said flatly.

They fell silent.

"Sensei is alive," she said again. "And we've got a plan to help Jacey. But we need your help."

The Scions cheered in strange whispers, pumping their fists.

"Stop," she insisted. "We have no time for your childishness."

Humphrey ordered the others to be quiet, but smiles split their faces.

"Sensei has a remote for the gate," Belle said. "He's going to let me in. When you hear the gate alarm, I need you all to help create a diversion. Do what you can to keep the guards away from the quad so that Sensei can get to the medical ward. Do you think maybe you can lure some of them all the way up to the hacienda?"

"I could," Humphrey said, "but I've got a better idea. I can just call Captain Wilcox."

"Are you insane?" Belle whispered. She had to glance out from behind the bush to make sure she hadn't attracted a guard's attention. "He works for Dr. Carlhagen."

"Yes," said Humphrey. "But he thinks I'm Dr. Carlhagen."

It was true. Belle had witnessed Humphrey putting on Dr. Carlhagen's jovial manner and convincing Captain Wilcox to leave the island right before the hurricane hit.

"How fast can he get here?" she asked, though she still didn't like the idea.

Humphrey sighed through his nose. "Maybe a half-hour."

"Do we have that long?"

"I don't know. Vaughan?"

Vaughan's image froze momentarily, then returned to normal. "Hard to say for sure. I think they're finishing up the senator's initial scan. That means the transfer will start very soon. It will be over by the time Captain Wilcox arrived."

Humphrey pressed. "How long do we have?"

"Maybe twenty minutes before the destructive scans begin. Now leave me alone, I need to get in position if I'm going to save a copy of Jacey."

"Can you clear the quad of guards or not?" Belle asked Humphrey.

"We'll figure it out," Humphrey said. Then the camera angle shifted sharply. "Elias," he barked, "wait!"

A loud crack came over the speaker, and the communication with Humphrey went dead.

Belle tried to summon Vaughan, but he didn't respond. She ran to the gate, trying to peer toward the hacienda.

Silence.

A report echoed through the campus.

Was that a gunshot?

The guard that had been patrolling the quad had also stopped. He stared up toward the hacienda. He must have heard the same sound.

She wanted to press her face to the electrified fence, hold onto it, climb it, but it would kill her instantly. She checked the time on her reader. Sensei wouldn't be in place for at least ten more minutes.

"Vaughan, can you open the gate?"

No reply.

Belle began to pace.

"Vaughan, what's going on?"

No reply.

Desperate, Belle began to shout and wave her hands. There was no time to wait for Sensei. She couldn't wait for Humphrey to deal with whatever he was confronting, either.

She didn't care about the diversion anymore. If the transfer was going to start soon, she had to get in now. She jumped up and down, shouting. She threw rocks over the gate, and they sailed into the mango grove.

"Open the gate!" she shouted.

Nothing happened. Another minute went by, and she screamed at the top of her lungs. The guard from the quad came running down the gravel path toward her. "Who's there?"

"Please, help me," she called.

"Who are you?"

"I'm a Scion. I was out searching for the runaway, and I found her."

The man swore and spoke into a walkie-talkie. A moment later, the gate began to grind open. The siren sounded, and the red lights flashed.

It couldn't be Sensei's signal, though. It was too early. The guards must have found another way to open it. Maybe the AI was cooperating with them.

Belle bounced on her toes right at the gap, waiting for the first second she could squeeze through. When she got through, she ran toward the man. There were two more on his heels, and they all aimed their side arms at her.

She skidded to a stop and held her hands out. "I'm not feeling so well."

The man holstered his side arm and rushed forward. "Where is Summer?"

Belle pointed vaguely toward the gate, then stumbled and fell into the man's arms, pretending to be unconscious.

He scooped her up and began running to the medical ward, shouting at the men alongside of him to run ahead and open the door.

The world jostled as the man carrying Belle sprinted across the quad, up the steps, and through the medical ward.

An enormous woman stormed through a door at the back of the ward. "What's this? Who is that?"

The man carrying Belle stopped. "This girl came through the main gate. She claims to know where the senator's true Scion is."

"Bring her."

Belle kept her eyes closed, but she didn't need to see to know where she was going.

They entered the small corridor leading from the medical ward to the transfer room. Holding rooms stood to either side. Belle kept her eyes closed and forced herself to breathe deeply and slowly.

"I'll get Dr. Carlhagen," said the woman. "Stay here."

Belle opened her eyes, pretending to be very groggy. "Where am I?"

The man holding her didn't answer. She glanced around. There were no other guards. Apparently the ones who had accompanied them to the medical ward had gone back to their posts.

The door ahead opened up. "Even if it's true, it's too late," Dr. Carlhagen was saying. He spotted her, and his face flashed from irritation to amusement. "Oh, it's Belle. Put her in one of the holding rooms and lock the door."

The man moved her into a side room and set her on a gurney. The big woman, Alice, followed her in. "Where is she? Where is Summer?"

"She's coming up the north path right now. She thinks she can save Jacey." A complete lie. "I'd show you, but I'm so tired. I ran halfway across the island."

The woman turned, already shouting at the man to go search the path. Belle slipped off the gurney to follow as the woman left. All she needed to do was slip into the transfer room, find a way to bar the door. Then she'd have to deal with Dr. Carlhagen. Maybe knock him out with something . . .

She got through the door, but Alice shoved her back and slammed the door shut. The lock clicked.

Belle ran to the door, pounded on it. "Let me out!"

But Alice was already gone.

A moment later, Dr. Carlhagen peered in the window and laughed. With a final shake of his head, he turned away and went back into the transfer room.

Belle pounded on the door.

So close. She had gotten so close.

40

FINAL INCHES OF GLORY

Elias stood over the guard, chest heaving, fists clenched. He pressed a foot on the man's bald skull, driving his face into the hallway floor tile.

"Get the weapon," Humphrey ordered Wanda, pointing at the deadly black shape still spinning on the floor. Horace had been wandering too close to it, and he was the last person Humphrey wanted holding a firearm. Wanda shouldered Horace out of the way and secured the weapon.

"That was very rash, Elias," Humphrey scolded. "You could've gotten us killed."

"You heard Belle. Jacey's in trouble."

"Where's the other guard?" Dajeet demanded. She and Bethancy peered through from the dining room. "He had to have heard the gunshot, if not the scuffle."

Scuffle. Humphrey couldn't think of a greater understatement. Yes, the fight with the bald guard had been quick, but it had been brutal. Elias had nearly broken the dining room door with his kick. That had brought the bald man rushing in, shouting at them.

Big mistake. Sang had stood there hands up, apologizing, distracting the man from Elias, who whirled from the man's flank and landed blow after blow. Hadn't even been a contest, as evidenced by the bloody mess that had once been the man's face.

"The other one struck me as a bit of a coward," Tytus said. "He probably ran."

Humphrey doubted the senator would have any cowards in her service. "No. He's being cautious. I think he's injured his leg somehow and doesn't intend to rush into a mêlée. And he's under orders not to shoot Scions."

"Then why was this one so ready to brandish his weapon?" Elias said, finally stepping away from the inert body. The guard still lived, though his breath was shallow and bubbled in and out of his destroyed nose. "Why was he so eager to . . . mistreat the girls?"

Sang ran in from the kitchen, holding two lengths of fabric. "I tore one of the tablecloths apart." He handed a strip to Elias, who efficiently—and quite viciously—tied the bald man's hands behind his back. Sang bound the feet. Once secured, they dragged the man into a chair and tied him to it.

Dajeet put a hand under his chin and lifted his head. It lolled to one side. The man was still unconscious. "I suppose you are the puppet of some old woman, some hag intent on overwriting my sister Summer. Ugly bastard." Shoved his head away and wiped her hand on her pants. She turned her back on him. "Let's take care of the other one."

Elias was already creeping down the hall, Horace following after. Elias had to hiss the boy to silence, because he kept replaying how Elias had kicked and punched the guard in the face.

"Sang," Humphrey said, beckoning. The boy was holding way back, as if planning to stand guard over the unconscious man. Sang came forward, though he seemed reluctant. "You did well distracting that man. Let's try it again."

Humphrey waved for Elias and Horace to stop. They'd made it far down the hall, where it was about to open up into the living area. To the right, would be the entry foyer. To the left, the wicker furniture and the folding doors leading to the pool.

"What do you want me to do?" Sang asked.

"Call to the other guard for help. Lure him in here."

"Why don't you do it?"

"Because that guard knows my voice. He'll think it's a trick."

"Why not one of the girls?"

"Just do it!"

Sang stared at him, eyes narrowing with suspicion. The look vanished, though, and Sang smiled. "Help! Simpson! Your man's having a seizure!"

"A seizure?" Humphrey mouthed.

"You put me up to it, you can't complain how I do it."

A voice came from the hallway behind them. Simpson's.

"It's coming from baldy's walkie-talkie," Wanda hissed.

"Go, Sang. Get Simpson to come around the corner." Humphrey pushed Sang toward the door.

Sang stalked forward, shaking his head and muttering about being cannon fodder. He disappeared around the corner. A moment later, he called back. "He's not here."

"Check outside, then." Humphrey could not believe Sang couldn't take the slightest initiative—not unless it was ripping up tablecloths.

The door swung open, letting in fresh air. Humphrey heard voices.

"Yeah, I don't know what's wrong with him," Sang was saying. "He was sitting there and all of a sudden his eyes rolled up and he started shaking."

Sang came around the corner, followed by Simpson.

Humphrey winced as Elias's blows fell. One, two, three. The man spun a full circle on his heels, eyes already closed. But another form darted in. Tytus. He landed blows four, five, six in quick succession, sending the man hard to the tile floor.

Simpson lay face-down and out cold.

Sang fetched more cloth strips, and in minutes Simpson was also being tied to a chair.

Humphrey didn't wait for Elias and Sang to finish. He sprinted to the door and started down the bougainvillea-lined path toward the quad.

"Humphrey," Wanda called after him. "Wait up."

He didn't stop. Jacey was about to be overwritten, and he would die before he let that happen. His footsteps pounded on the gravel path, echoed by more footfalls behind him. Even going downhill, it would be a five-minute run if he could maintain a sprint. But his head swam from the bald guard's blow. And it ached like someone inside was hitting the back of his eyes with a hammer.

A wave of nausea swept over him and he had to stop and retch. Wanda skidded up next to him, panting. She held Elias's reader to her lips. "Kirk, are you there?"

"Wanda?" Kirk's voice came back. "Where's Elias?"

"Can you get out of Boys' Hall?"

"It's lockdown. I'm not suppose—"

"I didn't ask if you were supposed to. I asked if you could!"

"Yes."

Humphrey straightened and looked at Wanda. "I don't think they—"

She ignored him. "Get everyone out. Send Dolphins through Lizards to the bell tower. Tell them to start ringing it for all they're worth."

"But—"

"Do it! Jacey needs your help. And you owe her."

A pause. "Okay. What about everyone else?"

"Run amok in the quad, distract all the guards you can."

"They've got guns," Humphrey protested. "This is just what Jacey was trying to avoid."

Wanda spoke to the reader. "Leslie!"

Leslie answered, voice tired. Wanda repeated her instructions.

Seconds later, shouts drifted up from the quad.

The brief rest had helped Humphrey get over the worst of his sickness. By then the others had caught up. He realized it was for the best. If they were going to subdue the rest of the guards, he couldn't do it alone.

They started a fast jog down the hill.

"What's the plan?" Elias asked.

"Kill them!" Horace cried and followed it with a whoop.

Humphrey winced at the bloodthirst in the boy's voice.

"Kill them," Dajeet said, but without relish.

"Be careful," Humphrey said between gulps of air. The blow to his head must have been even worse than he'd thought. He was struggling to keep up at what should have been an easy pace. Only Sang hung back farther than he did. "Don't let your desire for vengeance blind you."

"Spread out," Elias said. "We don't all want to come into the quad from the same direction. How many guards are there?"

Humphrey counted in his mind. "Three at least. No, four. There's the huge woman. Alice. Try to stay away from her."

Elias, Horace, and Tytus ghosted off the path and disappeared into the darkness. The girls went the opposite direction, vanishing behind the medical ward. That left Humphrey and Sang on the path.

They slowed to a fast walk as they neared the quad. Light from the dojo hazed over the grass, throwing long shadows behind trees. Three men, all encircled by Scions, were shouting.

"Go back to your dormitories!"

"Keep away!"

"I have been authorized to shoot!"

A new voice cut through all of them. "What's going on?"

"That's Alice," Humphrey said to Sang.

Her impossibly large form appeared in silhouette as she strode toward the nearest circle of Scions. "I don't have time for this," she shouted. "Disperse immediately."

The Scions closest to her seemed like children in comparison to the woman.

They are *children.*

"Return to your dormitories," Alice ordered. "Now!"

Two Crab boys, Terrel and Conrad, flinched. Not in fear, but in little daring feints toward the approaching monster. They fell into their fighting stances.

The man in the circle rushed them from behind. Terrel sensed it, dropped low and shot a foot into the man's kneecap. He let out an ear-shattering curse.

Alice strode forward, but stopped short as the bell in the tower started to clang. The Scions didn't turn their eyes away from their enemies, but Alice looked up.

Humphrey seized the moment and rushed forward, sprinting the best he could.

Where is Elias?

Surely the best fighter left on campus hadn't abandoned the fight. But there was no time to lose. While the huge woman's attention was diverted, he shouted to his peers, "Attack!"

They did, all sweeping toward the downed guard. Girls and boys alike, kicking and shouting.

Alice spun at Humphrey's cry.

"Come on, Sang. Let's take her."

He changed the angle of his approach slightly. There was no way he could tackle her. She braced, bringing her hands up. Humphrey's best fighting skill was muay thai, but that wasn't saying much. What it meant was that he needed to rely on kicks, and, in truth, speed he didn't possess.

The only thing to do was misdirect her. He didn't slow, as if he actually intended to run past her.

"Sang, take the other flank."

If the boy heard, he didn't answer.

"Sang?"

No response. And no more time.

Humphrey slowed slightly at the last moment, planted a foot and launched a back kick at the woman's knee. Sensei had taught him to first disable, then destroy.

The kick struck her thigh, the force of it shuddering back into Humphrey's hips and making him fall onto his hands and knees. She seemed to be made of iron. He scrabbled away, fearing she would wrap him up in her arms and squeeze the life out of him.

He got to his feet and spun.

Sang was nowhere to be seen.

Alice lunged for him.

He ducked low, tried to roll past her. She dropped, crushing his torso under a knee. The breath burst out of his lungs. Only reflex saved him from a boulder-sized fist as he twisted and took the punch in his shoulder.

His foot hooked on something. Whatever it was, it had to belong to Alice, which made it a target. He yanked, an explosion of all his strength. The object—her other foot, he thought—pulled away, and her weight lifted from him. Without breath, his movements were even slower, weaker than before. The pain in his side burned, his lungs convulsed for air, the earlier blow he'd taken to his head knifed into his brain.

Suddenly he was off the grass, dragged up by his shirt.

The light from the dojo blazed on Alice's face, which was contorted into a mask of hatred. She said nothing, but with a snap of one shoulder, brought her fist into Humphrey's gut. He dropped, still struggling for breath. Her shadow fell over him, and the cries and the fights around him faded to numbness, as if his ears were stuffed with cotton.

"You have no Progenitor," she said, not even breathing hard. She bent and pulled something from a sheath strapped to the side of her leg. A long knife glistened in her hand, the bottom third of its edge gleaming with serrations. "Therefore you have no purpose."

She smiled and thrust the blade at Humphrey's gut.

He winced, but felt no burst of pain.

A vision appeared next to Alice's face, a moment-before-death illusion. Sensei's grim visage, hovered there. His lips spread wide in a silent scream, as if he were lifting a thousand pound weight.

Humphrey glanced at his wound.

There wasn't one. The blade had frozen just above his navel. Sensei had caught Alice's wrist in his iron grip, forbidding her blade its final inches of glory. Sensei shifted his weight and Alice fell away, shrieking with fury.

The hideous knife flew end-over-end through the air before stabbing deep into the turf. A shadow raced to it and plucked it free. Horace held it aloft, eyes shining with keener sharpness than the blade itself.

Humphrey managed to draw a breath, forced himself to look up. All around the battle raged. And the bell rang on and on.

41

MAYBE AT A DISCOUNT

The sterile whiteness of the transfer room hurt Jacey's eyes. Yet for all of the light, she couldn't see much. Her cot had not yet been pushed under the transfer wheel, but the straps holding her head in place gave her a very limited field of view.

Muffled shouts carried from the corridor. It sounded like a girl. Jacey feared they'd caught Summer after all.

Dr. Carlhagen came back in, chuckling under his breath.

"Oh, Christof," said Senator Bentilius, voice rising in a croak. "You are a delicious looking young man. Let's get this over with."

"Soon, my love, soon. Just have patience. We're almost ready to begin."

The senator made a feline purring sound and laughed. "Now that I've seen you, I'm quite vexed with that impostor. I want him punished for tricking me."

Dr. Carlhagen matched her hideous laugh. "That boy has no Progenitor waiting for him now. We can dispatch him in any way you want. That'll be my gift to you."

"I'm not bloodthirsty, Christof. And whatever you do, I don't want to see it. Besides, such a death is a waste of a valuable resource. I'm sure we can sell him to someone, maybe at a discount."

Dr. Carlhagen laughed again. "Of course, my dear. Excellent idea."

Jacey struggled against the straps. She thought if she could get free it would be a tough decision whether to flee or beat Dr. Carlhagen over the head with her fists.

"Greta," Dr. Carlhagen barked, "report."

"Three more minutes for initial scan. Then we can proceed."

Jacey thrashed under the restraints and cried out for help.

Miss Dayspring shambled into view. "Maybe we should give her a sedative, the poor dear."

Dr. Carlhagen strode close to Jacey's gurney. He wasn't smiling when he bent over her. "No," he said. "I want her to feel every moment of it, down to the last instant of consciousness."

42

THE MOST SELFISH THING I CAN DO

The only sound in the holding room was Belle's sobbing. She lay face down on the gurney, the same one Dr. Carlhagen had been strapped to for several days. Her plan had been desperate, but once locked in this room, she had no chance of getting to the transfer room. She berated herself, beating her fists on the thin mattress. The whole scheme had hatched in her mind in one second, causing her to abandon Sensei's plan.

And why? Because once again, she couldn't stand the thought of Jacey being with Vaughan, even as an AI simulation.

She forced herself to sit up and wiped her eyes with her palms. "Why Jacey? Why her?"

A tinny voice came from Summer's reader, which was lying on the floor. "Since when do you care about Jacey?"

It was Vaughan's voice.

"I don't care about Jacey." Belle dropped from the gurney and scooped up the reader so she could see Vaughan's face. "I could save her if I could just get in there. She's just five meters away if I could break through this wall."

A spark of hope came to her then. "Vaughan, can you control this door? Can you unlock it?"

"I'm afraid not," Vaughan said. "The locks are manual latches. But maybe I can delay things in the transfer room. Let me take a look and see what I can do."

"What's the difference?" Belle said, dropping to her knees. "If I can't get out, delaying it won't help."

"Oh, you can get out."

"How?"

"Look up."

She did, straight at white ceiling tile. "Is this some sort of a spiritual lesson or something?"

"No, that's a drop ceiling. There may be locks on the outside of the doors, but these rooms weren't designed as prison cells."

"I don't know what a drop ceiling is."

Vaughan didn't respond.

Belle snatched up the reader. "Vaughan?"

No response.

Belle peered through the door's window. There was no one in the hall. She climbed onto the gurney, stood, and pressed her fingertips against the tile.

It gave!

She pushed harder. An entire section lifted easily overhead. She peered into the darkness, had to lift her reader to shine its light into the empty space beyond. Wires hung from metal beams supporting a thin framework of aluminum that held the tiles in place.

She tucked the reader into the front of her uniform pants, jumped, and grabbed one of the struts to pull herself through the hole. The ceiling was too flimsy to support her, but she squeezed above a thick metal beam. In a moment, she had replaced the ceiling tile. She shined the reader light through the attic space. It was dark and hot. Angled support struts marched into the darkness to her left and right.

Just below her ran a course of concrete block that demarcated one wall of her holding room. Beyond that would be the ceiling above the transfer room. Fortunately whoever had built the wall hadn't taken it all the way to the roof.

She squeezed through support struts barely wide enough for her shoulders until she passed over the wall. Her light showed something ahead, a wider space. She reached it and discovered a metal grating running between two beams. The catwalk supported a bundle of thick cables. Belle pressed on it. It seemed sturdy enough. She put more weight on it.

It held.

She turned off the reader and reached over one of the beams to lift the corner of a ceiling tile. Light blazed through the crack. She could just see a bit of the floor and part of a holodesk.

It would be a long fall.

A figure moved into view. Vaughan!

No. That's Dr. Carlhagen.

She was tempted to drop right onto his head. But that would just as likely get her leg broken as injure him.

The room went dark.

A sharp cry, a woman's, came from below. "What's happening?"

Dr. Carlhagen's vile curses followed.

"I can't stand it. I can't stand the dark." Definitely not Jacey's voice. Too panicky.

"Silence, Miss Dayspring! It's just the damn power," Dr. Carlhagen said. "Greta? Greta? Dammit, the holodesk isn't even powered. I'll have to go find the breaker box. I think it's back by the freezer room."

Belle crawled forward. Vaughan had bought her time.

What she needed was a way to climb down. A possible solution occurred to her, and she moved along the catwalk as fast as she could while keeping quiet.

The catwalk ran out at a concrete block wall. Belle looked to either side of the catwalk and immediately spotted what she was looking for. A rectangular course of concrete blocks about two meters wide. It outlined a closet.

Inside that outline was a tile right next to the catwalk. It looked slightly different than the rest. She ran her fingers across it. It was smooth like wall material, but there were little indentations around its frame. It looked like it was meant to be lifted, so she pulled up on one side and peered down.

The light from her reader showed her the inside of the closet. It was filled with shelving. Craning her neck, she could even see the door that led into the transfer room. It was closed.

Perfect.

She pulled the panel out and set it quietly on the catwalk. Clamping the reader in her teeth, she climbed down, putting her feet on the shelving, taking great care not to disturb the items they held. She glanced down. Two more shelves and she would reach the floor.

Her hand slipped, and in her attempt to reclaim her grasp, she knocked a stainless steel bowl off of the shelf. It clanged on the floor and wobbled endlessly before coming to rest.

"Who's there?" It was the same panicky voice she had heard before.

Belle held her breath.

"For Pete's sake, Miss Dayspring," said a raspier voice. "If you're scared of the dark, just go outside until Christof sorts it out."

"Are you sure you'll be okay, Madam?" said the tremulous voice.

"What could happen to me here?"

Belle waited, holding her breath. She heard soft steps, the twist of a door latch, and then a door close.

She cut the light from the reader and opened the closet door. She stepped inside the transfer room. It was completely dark. She eased the door closed, then turned on the reader light, shielding most of it with her body. Enough reflected off a near wall to show her a cot and feet jutting out. She knew they were Jacey's because they wore Scion uniform shoes.

She crept forward. Jacey's eyes were open. They were wide. Her whole body trembled. Belle allowed a little more light to shine on her own face.

Jacey's eyes widened more, and she gasped. Belle felt along the cot. Her hand came to the great wheel she had seen once before. Beyond that lay the senator. There was no time.

Heart racing, she felt along Jacey's body, finding each strap and loosening it, removing it. She bent low and whispered in Jacey's ear. "Get up."

Jacey did. The cot groaned.

"Is someone there?" asked Senator Bentilius. "Miss Dayspring? Is that a light?"

"Only me," Jacey said, her voice very loud in the silence. "The person you're going to kill so you can be young again. I think an emergency light came on."

"Foolish girl," said the senator. "Do you think you can shame me? I have developed a hard interior to do what must be done. The fact is the world needs me. I've done more good for the impoverished and the oppressed than anyone alive. I deserve this."

Belle helped Jacey stand. She was shaky.

"That's small comfort from where I'm standing," Jacey said to the senator.

Belle motioned to the closet and then pointed up. She put

her mouth to Jacey's ear. "You can get out through one of the holding rooms. Skip the first one, the door's locked."

Jacey hugged Belle, whispering in her ear, "Thank you. Thank you."

She started for the closet, taking hold of Belle's hand to drag her after. Belle stood firm. Jacey turned with a questioning look. Belle yanked her hand free and lowered herself onto the cot, though her heart pounded and her skin chilled with fear.

Jacey's eyes narrowed for a moment, and then her mouth fell open, and her lips mouthed, "No, no," as she shook her head.

Belle looked at the ceiling.

Jacey came near. "You can't do this. You must *not* do this."

The senator must have heard. "I can, I must, and I will."

Belle grabbed one of the straps and flapped it, indicating Jacey should secure it.

"Why?" Jacey asked.

The senator huffed. "I don't need to explain myself to you."

Jacey's cheek pressed against Belle's, her breath hot in Belle's ear. "Why?"

Belle whispered back, "If the senator dies, then this place will be overrun with armed men. There will be no chance for any of you."

"But there has to be another way. I can't let you sacrifice yourself."

"This is the most selfish thing I can do."

Jacey didn't move. "I don't get it."

"Vaughan," Belle said. "It's always been about Vaughan. He lives inside whatever this is. He's waiting there, ready to save a copy of you. Instead, he'll take a copy of me. And I'll be free of all this. I'll be with him."

"But, Belle!"

"Face it, Jacey, the others love you. They need you. They don't love or need me."

Dampness fell across Belle's cheek, but it wasn't from her tears. It was from Jacey's. She rubbed Belle's forehead, kissed her cheek. "But I do love you."

"It's not the circuit breakers." Dr. Carlhagen's voice startled Belle and Jacey so much that they both jolted. "Who the hell designed this electrical system?"

"The straps," Belle said. Jacey fumbled with them, pulling them into place. A racket came from across the room as Dr. Carlhagen searched for something.

"Where did I leave that thing?" he groused.

Belle's cot was suddenly moving, and she realized that Jacey was pushing her into the wheel so that Belle's face would be obscured in shadow if the lights came on. Belle felt a grudging admiration for that bit of quick thinking. She felt a final pat on her shin, and Jacey's presence was gone.

She heard the slight click as the closet door closed.

Belle found it impossible to swallow; her mouth had gone utterly dry. The faint smell of bleach burned at her nose and seemed to find a path all the way to her brain. Her thoughts accelerated, as if her mind needed to think a lifetime of thoughts during her remaining moments.

She remembered clutching a stuffed animal in one hand as she approached the burning barrel, Jacey sniffling and walking next to her. Humphrey had muttered a curse under his breath. Vaughan had stared straight ahead, face already masculine and beautiful at nine years old.

"Ah. The transfer subsystem is rebooting." Dr. Carlhagen's steps clicked on the floor as he came close. "Damn these lights. Where is Miss Dayspring?"

"She was afraid and went out," said Senator Bentilius.

"Good. She's useless."

The lights came on, blinding Belle with their brightness.

A memory flashed. Trudging down the path from the hacienda, carrying a spade and shears following a long day of planting new cuttings of bougainvillea. Jacey laughing and smiling with Vaughan. Humphrey following after, face dark with obvious envy.

"Ah ha!" said Dr. Carlhagen. "Shall we proceed?"

"Please," said Senator Bentilius. "I'm so tired."

Footsteps came closer. Belle's heart pounded so hard she felt certain Dr. Carlhagen would hear. She wore the same uniform as Jacey, but if Dr. Carlhagen peeked inside the wheel, he'd see she wasn't Jacey.

But Dr. Carlhagen didn't look. He hovered near the senator and called for Greta.

"Yes, sir?" the AI responded.

"What happened with the power?"

"I don't know, sir. But shall we begin? The initial scan is complete. I can handle the senator's cancerous regions without losing more than a fraction of a percent of her memory and capacity. She won't notice the difference."

"Please proceed."

"Another Scion mismatch I see," Greta mused. "No matter. I shall have to back up both brains and run simulations to get the final transfer solution correct."

"Do what you need to do."

The wheel began to spin. Belle closed her eyes. Her heart raced, her breath came in short gasps. But she hadn't changed her mind. She wanted to do this. She needed to.

Another image. The medical ward entryway, lit only by the light cutting through from the dojo across the quad. Other girls stood nearby. Nurse Smith's flabby face hung before Belle like a blurry moon. Belle's arms swung around, hand impacting the woman's cheek. Again. Again. *"Where is Vaughn?"*

Belle felt the fabric of a cotton sheet under her fingers. Would it feel like that on the other side?

In her mind, a thornskipple branch lashed down, tearing at the back of Jacey's legs. Belle pulled them free, thorn by thorn, reveling in righteous anger. Vengeance for a life of being outshined.

Jacey's voice came back to her mind. *"But I do love you."*

Belle believed it. Didn't understand it, but she believed it. She couldn't feel the same for Jacey, though. Not without lying. But she was glad she'd saved Jacey, because she had told the truth. The others did need her.

Does that make me a hero?

Does that make me worthy of Vaughan?

She didn't think so. What she had told Jacey had been true, too. She was being selfish.

Sensei's words came back to her. *"You have no one."*

"I'll have Vaughan," she whispered. "I'll be with Vaughan."

Greta started counting backward from one hundred, but Belle lost track somewhere around ninety-four. Her vision dimmed, and she felt thin and insubstantial, like a hologram.

And then all sense-data input ceased.

43

THIS IS EXTRAORDINARY BEAUTY

Jacey rested on the grated steel catwalk above the ceiling of the transfer room. Only the light from the reader penetrated the blackness that threatened to envelop her in a blanket of despair.

I've failed.

She had vowed that no Scion would be overwritten again, but below her it was happening at that very moment.

And by choice.

She got to her hands and knees and noticed a panel that would fit the hole in the closet she had climbed through. She replaced it, taking great pains to be silent. To be caught now would waste Belle's sacrifice.

That's what it was, Jacey thought. A sacrifice.

How can I ever live up to it?

"Jacey?" The voice came from the reader.

She glanced down to see Vaughan's face. She sat on her heels and sniffed and wiped her nose and eyes.

"Vaughan?"

"Where are you?"

Jacey glanced around. "I'm in an attic above the transfer room. On a catwalk. Belle traded places with me. She said you could save a copy of her."

"I'm waiting for the right moment. It's . . ." A long pause. "Risky."

"You have to save her," she whispered, holding the reader close to her lips. "After what she did for me . . ."

"I know, I know," Vaughan said. "I'm going to try. But you should get out of there right now."

"Transfer beginning," Greta said from below.

"Excellent, excellent," Dr. Carlhagen said. His voice froze Jacey momentarily, and she heard his footsteps directly beneath her. She held her breath.

"Soon my love," Dr. Carlhagen said. "Soon I will have you."

Jacey shivered. It could have been her down there on that cot. She still didn't understand why Belle had done what she had, but to get caught here would make it all for nothing.

Bit by bit, she inched along the catwalk, shining the reader light into the darkness, trying to see the way out. She came to what appeared to be a dead end. She had to stop and close her eyes and remember the orientation of the room below her, where the closet had been. If she went to the right, she would be going toward the freezer room. She knew there was no way out in that direction.

To her left ran more ceiling joists and some thicker struts of metal that sat atop what appeared to be concrete blocks.

Yes. That would be the wall separating one of the holding rooms from the transfer room. Belle must have come in from there.

Jacey crossed over the wall and scanned ahead. She could see the tops of a few more walls, each defining the holding rooms on this side of the hallway. Beyond that, a concrete block wall rose all the way to the attic ceiling, blocking off further progress. She would have to go down through one of the holding rooms.

"Transfer complete," Greta announced.

Jacey clamped a hand over her mouth. Belle was gone.

"Oh dear, is she dead?" That was Miss Dayspring's voice. "I hope it worked."

A loud crack, hands clapping together. "Of course it worked, you idiot," Dr. Carlhagen barked. "Now, we'll just wheel the cot out and . . . What the devil?"

Jacey knew that Dr. Carlhagen had spotted Belle. He'd probably start looking for her immediately. Though she hated to do it, she decided the best thing to do was to stay concealed in the attic.

She lay on her belly and eased up a corner of one of the transfer room ceiling panels. Just past Dr. Carlhagen's shoulder, Miss Dayspring had pulled out the cot with Belle's body on it. Jacey could just make out Belle's head. Her eyes opened, squinting against the bright light.

"Who is this girl?" Miss Dayspring asked. "This isn't the one that was here before. Or does the machine do this to faces?"

Dr. Carlhagen staggered a step backward. "Where is she? Where is she?" He looked all around the room, spun a full circle. "Impossible!"

"Doctor, what's wrong? This is supposed to happen, right?" Miss Dayspring loosened the straps around Belle's legs and arms and then her head. Belle's long, slender arm lifted. Her hand pressed to her forehead. Her chest rose and fell as she took a deep breath.

"Miss Dayspring, whatever is the matter?" Belle asked.

Not Belle, Jacey reminded herself. *That's Senator Bentilius now.*

"How did she do it?" Dr. Carlhagen said, face drawn and distraught.

"Christof?" Senator Bentilius rose onto her hands and swung her legs off the cot. She didn't seem shaky as much as dazed.

Miss Dayspring took her elbow. "Are you okay, Madam Senator? Do you need some water?"

"I'm wonderful. I feel . . ." She raised her arms above her head and gave a huge stretch. A smile broke out on her lips. Belle's lips. This wasn't the cold, cruel smile Jacey had seen a handful of times. This was a luxuriant, pleasurable smile. It softened the sharpness of Belle's features. "I feel light as a feather." She took another deep breath. "Ah, youth. What a sweet drug it is."

Frowning, she put a hand to her hair and stroked down Belle's long ponytail. "That's not right."

"Madam Senator," Dr. Carlhagen said, taking a hesitant step forward, "I can explain."

The senator's eyes flashed up, not like Belle's. Not filled with anger. "Explain what? I don't like ponytails." She pulled the rubber band loose and shook out her hair. It fell like a veil of snow across her face and over her shoulders, starkly white against the black of her Scion uniform.

She hooked a thumb through her hair and drew it back from her face. Jacey was startled by the beauty Belle had suppressed for so long. "Much better," the senator said.

She glanced at the nurse's hand on her arm. "Unhand me, Miss Dayspring."

The nurse snatched her hand away and shuffled a few steps back. "I'm sorry, Madam."

"Leave us. Make sure no one disturbs me and Christof."

Could Belle's voice go that low? Could it be so rich, so full of command? Jacey had only ever heard it be cutting and sarcastic.

The nurse shuffled out the door.

Dr. Carlhagen rubbed his hands together, staring at the

senator and nervously licking his lips. "Maxine," he said, "I do have something to tell you about the transfer."

"Did something go wrong?" She looked down at her hands, then rubbed them on her abdomen and down her hips. "I haven't been this fit," she looked up and smiled, "ever."

She glanced around at the tile on the floor. "But something does feel off. Strange."

"I told you, I can explain. If you'd just give me a moment."

"I'm taller," she said. "My god, I'm taller! This idea to use a different Scion was brilliant."

She took a few steps toward him, drinking him in with her eyes. Jacey had the impression of a predator stalking its prey. With a flash, the senator's hands went to Dr. Carlhagen's chest and rubbed up to his shoulders. In Vaughan's body, Dr. Carlhagen was tall, much taller than the senator, even with her new body. Her hands traced down the outside of his shoulders onto his arms. She drew them around her, slipping her body close to his, tilting her head back, lips parted.

"It's been much too long, my love," she said in a husky voice.

Dr. Carlhagen cleared his throat. "You *are* beautiful, dear. I cannot deny it. It's just that . . ."

The senator released him and retreated a step. "What is it? What's wrong with me?" She snapped her fingers. "Give me a mirror."

Dr. Carlhagen pointed to a hand mirror resting on a cart behind her. She snatched it up, lifted it, and stared, her face frozen in momentary judgment, the way Belle might have stared at a misbehaving Dolphin. She turned her face this way and that, moving the mirror about.

"Well, this is a surprise," she said. Still holding the mirror in front of her face, she shifted her eyes briefly to Dr. Carlhagen. "This is not the girl you showed me."

Dr. Carlhagen held up his hands in helplessness. "Maxine, there was a slight problem with the Scion I originally offered. It turned out she wasn't suitable. You could view this as a temporary body. When we find your true Scion, we can do another transfer to her and all will be well." He pasted on a smile.

The senator lowered the mirror, returned it to the cart, then faced him, expression utterly serious. But not at all like Belle's. She tilted her chin down and looked up, something that Jacey had seen Summer do countless times—though this look was filled with far more worldly sensuality than Summer possessed.

"No need to apologize, my darling. I quite prefer this look to the other girl. She was so ordinarily pretty. This . . ." she said, lifting her hands to her throat and trailing her fingers down her breasts and to her abdomen. "This is *extraordinary* beauty. This is beauty one can build a brand on. This," she said, taking more slinky steps toward Dr. Carlhagen, "this is the face of a future President of the North American Union."

Tension went out of Dr. Carlhagen's shoulders. "Wonderful," he said, though his tone was not at all convincing to Jacey. He continued to look around the room as if he would find her. But his attention was quickly drawn to the senator as she threw herself at him, pulled his lips to hers. His shoulders rose to his ears and, for a moment, he pressed on her, trying to push her away. But suddenly, as fast as the flip of a light switch, he surrendered.

Jacey supposed any man's resistance would fail beneath the intensity of the senator's lusty assault.

Soon the kiss broke, and the woman's hands grasped the fabric of Dr. Carlhagen's shirt. Jacey was sure she was going to rip it apart. And for that matter, Dr. Carlhagen's hands were busy exploring the senator's new contours. Their breathing grew more labored, and Jacey could not bear to watch, could not block from her mind the fact that this was not only Dr. Carlhagen and Senator Bentilius, but also Vaughan and Belle.

Jacey lowered the panel into place and crept away. Remembering Belle's instructions, she skipped the first room and its locked door. Once above the second, she lifted a panel. Seeing that it was just above a cot in one of the holding rooms, she slipped down. A moment later she stood before the open door of the holding room.

She bolted from the room, cut to her right, and slammed through the door into the main ward. The room lay empty, echoing the slap of her footfalls and sob-filled breaths as she sprinted into the entryway, past Nurse Smith's desk, and through the doors into the night air.

Screams and shouts added to the cacophony of the bell tower's incessant ringing.

Jacey stopped dead in her tracks, reader dropping from her hand and clattering onto the ground. The quad was a battlefield.

44

EFFICIENT SAVAGERY

Darkness closed in from all sides, eating at the solitary light mounted above the dojo entrance across the quad. The filmy beams slanted across the grass, silhouetting three concentrations of brutality. To Jacey's right, three Scions rolled on the ground, subduing an armed guard. Kirk grasped the man's right arm, pressing a foot into his armpit. Another boy, she thought it was Sang, threw sharp blows into the man's midsection. A girl Jacey thought might be Wanda lay across his legs, twining her arms and legs around them.

To Jacey's left, near the pit, a scrum of more Scions surrounded an empty-handed man who spun in a circle. He lashed out at the smallest Scion and was instantly struck in the back of one knee by a Centipede boy. He disappeared beneath a pile of Scions who rained blows on him with endless fury.

Ahead of Jacey, Alice faced off with a ghost.

She gasped. "Sensei!"

He blurred all around the woman, harrying her, and

landing blows that should have knocked her to the ground. She received the punches and kicks with grunts but didn't go down. Elias and Tytus circled around her, searching for an opportunity to attack. Horace stood further back, holding up a long knife and shifting his weight from foot to foot.

On the ground nearby lay Humphrey. Blood covered half of his face.

Jacey ran to him, shook him. He didn't respond. She felt at his throat for a pulse. Found it.

"Surrender," Sensei ordered. "I don't want to kill you."

Alice didn't respond, except to leap at him, swinging her arm in a long but skull-crushing arc toward his face.

He dodged and rolled.

With lightning quickness, the woman swept up her leg, timing it perfectly to position her foot where Sensei's head would have been if he'd completed his move. Instead, he lay flat on the ground a second longer, and her foot sailed past. With a quick roll back onto his shoulders, he launched himself to his feet and fell into his fighting stance, chest heaving. In the dark it was impossible for Jacey to make out his expression. But she needed no light to know the deadly look in his eyes.

Sensei circled, a technique Jacey recognized, forcing the woman to reposition to protect her left flank.

Her hand went to the holster on her belt, and in a fluid movement she drew a pistol, black and sharp-edged.

"Run," Sensei commanded Elias and Tytus.

But Sensei didn't flee. Instead, he stalked closer to the woman. She straightened and took careful aim.

Elias's scream erupted in the darkness. "DIE!"

The cry carried such hatred and fury that Alice turned away from her kill shot.

"Elias!" Sensei cried.

But the martial arts master hadn't finished the last syllable of the Eagle's name before the boy was in the air, leading with the blade edge of his foot.

Alice swung around, flailing an arm to deflect his attack. She guessed wrong, expecting it to be lower, to come from a Scion braced on the ground.

Elias sailed above her parry, foot striking her full in the face. The pistol went off as the woman went down, Elias atop her. A second later, Tytus closed in, delivering blows with efficient savagery. Horace raced in, laughing and crowing. The knife flashed up and then disappeared in a blur as he plunged into the woman's chest.

It rose again, blackened, then disappeared into her gut. Blood sprayed across Horace's face. He howled and raised the blade again.

"Enough!" Sensei shouted, wresting the blade from Horace with twist. His foot came up and thrust Horace onto his back.

Tytus had scurried away already, eyes wide with horror at the seething wounds bubbling from Alice's torso.

Sensei handed the blade to Tytus. "Keep this away from Horace." He knelt to check Alice's pulse. "Dead."

Elias moaned and rolled on the grass, holding his side. A girl swooped out of the shadows, knelt beside him, and cradled his head. A long, black ponytail trailed behind her.

"Summer?" Jacey said, shocked to see her on campus.

"I told you to stay in the skiff," Sensei grumbled at the Spider.

"I did," Summer said petulantly. "For a while."

Sensei probed Elias's side. His hand came away slicked with blood. "Into the medical ward with him." Sang had run over, and he and Tytus lifted Elias and carried him off.

"Make Miss Dayspring take care of him," Jacey called after. "Summer, go with him. Have Sang make sure that Dr.

Carlhagen and the senator do not come out of the transfer room."

Humphrey stirred and rolled to his hands and knees. Jacey ran to him, put her arms around him. His eyes focused on her for a moment, then he shoved her away.

She fell onto her side. "What's wrong with you?"

He wasn't listening, as he was gagging and convulsing with sickness. Jacey was thankful for the darkness then.

She patted his back, and he wiped his mouth on the sleeve of his filthy white suit coat. "Sorry. I didn't want you to get puke on your uniform. That woman hit me right in the gut."

She wrapped him in her arms and pulled him close.

"Get those men into the ward," Sensei ordered a group of Scions.

Scions dragged the limp bodies of the other two men across the quad. From the beatings they'd taken, Jacey didn't think either would likely survive.

"Are there any more of them?" Sensei shouted

"There are two more in the hacienda," Humphrey called to Sensei. "They're restrained."

"Wanda, Leslie, Tytus. Secure all weapons from the guards and bring them to me. Only you three are to touch any of them. Understood?"

"Yes, Sensei," they shouted.

Sensei relaxed, which meant his scowl softened into a furious frown. He stomped to Jacey and forced her to her feet. "You're free. Where's Belle?"

Jacey kept her tears at bay, drawing strength from Sensei's presence. "The transfer room."

Sensei started to sprint toward the medical ward, but Jacey called after. "It's too late, Sensei. The transfer is done."

Sensei trotted to a stop, shoulders drooping.

Next to her, Humphrey climbed to his feet and absently brushed at his stained suit.

"I'm going to check on Elias," Sensei said.

A horn blasted across the quad. All heads spun toward the gate.

Beams from a vehicle's headlights shone down the path between the mango grove and Boys' Hall.

Mr. Justin's bus had arrived to collect the Scions.

45

I WANT AN EXCUSE TO SHOOT YOU

The bus's headlights beamed through the gate like furious eyes, their white-hot glow obscuring the rest of the vehicle. Its idling motor rumbled and growled. Jacey thought of the monsters from Socrates's stories—the Minotaur. Grendel. Smaug.

"It is a monster," she said to herself, hair pricking on the back of her neck. "Come to devour all the children."

"What?" Humphrey huddled close to her, holding an icepack to the side of his head. He huddled next to her as they peered through the rear window of Boys' Hall toward the gate. "We should get out of here. They may have weapons."

The horn honked again, long and harsh.

"I think we should let them in."

"Are you crazy?"

Jacey left the window and slipped up the aisle between the bunks. Though it was arranged exactly like Girls' Hall, it smelled strange there. Jacey couldn't put her finger on exactly what it was, but she didn't hate it. She slipped back into the quad, which was now quiet.

Many Scions were in the medical ward, watching over the men they'd subdued, or taking turns guarding the transfer room door. Jacey hadn't gotten any reports of Dr. Carlhagen and the senator trying to get out.

"There could be twenty armed men in that thing," Humphrey said, following her into the humid evening.

"I doubt it. Mr. Justin felt the whole operation would go smoothly. He and his friend won't be expecting a confrontation since we Scions just blindly follow directions. If he were here, he'd probably make up some story about us being needed at Children's Villa to do some chores or put out a fire."

"A fire?"

She turned on him. "I don't know. I'm just guessing. But think about it. If Mr. Justin and this conspirator intended to steal us, they would use as few other people as possible."

"But you don't know that."

"No. But if we don't let them in soon, they're going to figure out that something's not right."

"Yes. And they'll leave."

Jacey just looked at him.

Humphrey got it then. "They already have the children from Mother Tyeesha's, don't they?"

Jacey continued to the medical ward. "Probably. And I'm not letting them take a single one off this island."

Sensei met her at the door. "I was just coming to find you. I think we should let the bus in."

Jacey resisted making a face at Humphrey. "We need to pretend we're following Mr. Justin's plan."

The martial arts master's eyes gleamed. "I'm proud of you, Jacey. You would've made an excellent fighter."

Humphrey stepped between them. "I'm not letting Jacey

put herself into any more danger. We're lucky she's alive at all. I'm not going to risk losing her now."

Sensei shrugged. "I agree. There's no need for her to go. It'll be you, Sang, Tytus."

"We've got the weapons from the senator's guards, too," Humphrey said.

"No!" Jacey said, yanking Humphrey out of the way. "And I'm surprised at you. We're not putting guns into a situation where there's a bunch of tiny kids. If there are armed thugs on there, things could go very badly. We need to see what the situation is first."

Sensei folded his arms, though his expression was more amused than angry. "What is your plan?"

Jacey smiled. "Do you have the gate remote?"

Sensei dug it from a pocket and held it up.

As Jacey related her plan, Sensei's lips spread into a nasty smile. Even Humphrey grinned.

o o o

The gate finished its long and grinding slide open, and the bus motor roared. Jacey watched from the Boys' Hall window, occasionally elbowing a boy away as he pressed too close to peer through. "Really, Humphrey, the discipline of the Nines in here is abysmal."

Humphrey scowled and clapped his hands, ordering his Nine to line up. The remains of Vaughan's old Nine, consisting of a handful of small boys, stood around not really knowing what to do. Elias had been leading it, but he was currently bleeding in the medical ward.

Jacey shooed them toward their bunks and pulled the shutters closed. Sensei appeared at the door and waved to her.

All was ready.

The bus pulled onto the quad just as she stepped from Boys' Hall. Sensei slipped inside to stay out of sight.

Steeling herself, Jacey strode toward the bus. There were no doors at all on the side facing her, so she passed in front of it, heart beating with fear that the monster might lurch forward and crush her.

On the other side, she found a door. It folded open, and steps led up toward a driver slouching behind a huge steering wheel. He wore all black, but unlike the senator's guards, he was fat. A bushy beard covered his face, and his small eyes gleamed from deep sockets.

"You must be Orson," she said. "You're late."

He peered down at her. "Where's Justin?"

She stepped aboard, using the handrail to pull herself up.

Time for the first bit of misdirection. She smiled at the driver and pointed toward Boys' Hall. "He's inside the medical ward, lining up the Scions. He realized we all needed vaccinations before leaving campus."

"Oh. Well, go tell him to get a move on. I'm sick of this island."

Jacey made the final step and peered down the rows of seats. The four members of Mother Tyeesha's staff sat in the front seats. Each held an infant. Four older kids sat behind them, each with older babies in their arms. The one-year-olds, Jacey thought.

Behind them were two men. They looked bulky, but not like the senator's huge guard. These men were flabby and sour-faced. Jacey squinted. They were covered with scratches and dirt, faces slick with sweat. They'd clearly been scrabbling around the rainforest searching for the children.

And they'd recovered only twelve of the thirty-six.

"Go!" the driver barked. "I've got no more patience left."

"Can your men come along to assist, please?"

"What do you need them for? Can't the Scions walk from there to here?"

"The Scions aren't strong enough to move the machine through the door. We need some muscle."

"The machine? What machine?"

Jacey twisted her lips and held up her hands in a shrug. "I don't know what it does. Some kind of medical thing. Mr. Justin told me we needed it if we were going to help the children in North America."

The driver stared at her blankly, then his face cleared. "Oh yeah. The machine!" He twisted in his seat. "Kyle. Ivan. Go carry the damn machine out."

Jacey backed down the steps, keeping her smile to herself. She cut in front of the bus and led the men toward Boys' Hall. They said nothing about where she was heading, and the driver didn't call out either.

Stupid thieves. They don't even know which building is the medical ward.

Jacey stepped through the door and into darkness and kept going. A flurry of blows, grunts, and curses sounded behind her. By the time she turned, the two filthy men were on the floor.

Sensei passed one of the two pistols he'd appropriated from the men to Tytus. "Lock it up with the others."

Tytus held it away from himself, as if it might explode. He gently placed it in a footlocker and clicked the latch in place. Horace had eyed it greedily, but stayed back. Sensei had told him in no uncertain terms what would happen if he were caught with a weapon.

"Now we wait," Jacey said.

Sensei motioned to Kirk and Tytus. They slipped out the back window. Moments later, Jacey saw their dark forms sidle close to the bus.

The driver poked his head out his window and shouted. "Justin! Let's get going!"

Jacey felt Humphrey's presence next to her. She sought his hand, found it, and held it tightly. On her other side, Sensei stood like a compressed hurricane.

"Don't worry," she said to him. "I could take down the driver myself. He's not in good shape. He burns cigarettes in his mouth."

"That's called smoking," Sensei said.

"What—?"

She cut off her question. The driver had gotten out of the bus. He was momentarily illuminated by the headlights as he passed in front of them.

Jacey stepped out and waved to him. "I need your help."

"What now?" he shouted, striding toward Boys' Hall.

He got three more steps before Tytus and Kirk wrapped him up and took him down. The man screamed and writhed.

Sensei ran out and got the man's attention with a pistol to the forehead.

Jacey stepped close to the man. "Welcome to the Scion School. Now. Where were you planning to take the Scions?"

The man's mouth clamped tight, though his eyes were wide.

"Don't answer her," Sensei said. "I want an excuse to shoot you."

The icy tone got through to the man.

"I don't know! Don't kill me."

Jacey arched an eyebrow. It wouldn't hurt if the man felt a little fear. She put on an indifferent tone. "Kidnapping Scions is going to get you in a lot of trouble, Orson."

"Like death," Sensei said, pressing the gun harder to the man's skin.

"No! Please!"

"Who are you working with here besides Mr. Justin?"

"No one. He's the only person I know."

"You trusted the wrong person, Orson. He's inside the medical ward right now. Laughing that you fell into Dr. Carlhagen's trap."

Orson's eyes narrowed, and a nervous laugh escaped his quivering lips. "Trap? Maybe you're not so smart after all. Justin is my brother."

Jacey exchanged glances with Sensei. He shook his head. He hadn't known about Mr. Justin's brother.

"Take him to the medical ward and strap him down," Jacey said.

Sensei lifted the man and, with Tytus's help, started dragging him toward the medical ward.

"Nice of you to bring us a bus, Orson," Jacey called after him.

Humphrey slipped his arms around her.

She whispered, "And even nicer of him to bring us a boat."

46

I COULDN'T PROTECT THEM ALL

Jacey had never seen the medical ward so crowded. Two of Senator Bentilius's guards were tied down onto cots. From the looks of them, the straps weren't really needed. Another had already died. Two more had been brought down from the hacienda where Humphrey and the others had left them bound hand and foot. They sat on the floor, backs to the wall, faces glum.

Miss Dayspring attended to Elias, her usual meek demeanor gone now that she had a task to attend to. The bullet had only grazed Elias's side, leaving a furrow that produced a lot of blood. "Two centimeters to the left and it would have taken his pancreas," she had said. Summer sat at his side, brushing the hair from his eyes.

Orson and his men were also strapped down. Orson called for Mr. Justin so loudly that Sensei eventually gagged him.

There was no sign of the butler.

Several Scion girls and boys had all received minor bruises and cuts in the mêlée, but nothing a bandage and an ibuprofen couldn't handle. Miss Dayspring seemed very relieved to have something to do besides worry about the senator. She paid special attention to the youngest Scions, cradling their faces in her hands and talking to them in a strange high-pitched tone of voice. Jacey thought it was meant to be childlike, but it sounded stupid.

Jacey interrupted Sensei's interrogation of Orson's men. They weren't saying anything, except with their eyes, which kept going to Orson. He obviously held something over there heads that they feared he could use even in his current state.

Sensei stared at her, eyes black and full of barely contained anger. It was not directed at her, though. She flung herself at him. He started, hand raised to deflect an attack, but she was wrapped around his neck, hugging him tightly. Slowly he returned the hug.

"I failed, Sensei," Jacey whispered. "I couldn't protect them all."

Sensei cleared his throat and pulled himself free from Jacey's arms, but he took her hands in his. "You didn't fail. Belle made her own choice. We had a plan and she ignored it."

Summer got up from Elias's cot and came over. "Belle likes to boss people around, but she isn't very good at following directions. If she got caught, it's her own fault."

Jacey's tears welled up again. It seemed they had no end. "You don't understand. I was strapped down in the machine, the transfer was about to begin. Belle sneaked in and switched places with me."

Summer, Sensei, and Humphrey gaped, and all spoke at once. "She *switched places* with you?"

"She saved me," Jacey said, then laughed through her tears. "She wouldn't admit that it was for me. She said she was doing it to be with Vaughan."

Humphrey ran a hand through his hair and sighed. "That

makes sense. Sort of. Vaughan and I spoke with her via reader before she got through the gate. Vaughan told us he had a plan to save a copy of you. So you could, you know, become an AI."

"Belle wanted to be with Vaughan," Jacey said. "That's all she's ever wanted."

"So Belle is an AI?" Summer asked. "But is that even . . ."

"Someone give me a reader," Jacey said.

Summer snatched a reader from the edge of Elias's cot and walked it over to Jacey.

Jacey took it. "Vaughan? Are you there?"

No answer.

"Vaughan?"

47

A SPARK OF LIGHT

Life was simultaneously cool and warm. Both sensations pleasant. Belle floated in the surf along Isaac's Beach, feeling utterly weightless as the swells lifted and dropped her, rocking her as gently as a nurse would rock an infant's cradle. The sun, somewhere to the west, made the water turquoise, the green hills emeralds, the sand white diamonds.

The luxurious rays warmed her skin, filled it with life-renewing radiance. The ocean sustained her from below and carried her toward the beach.

The coarse sand of the shore rubbed against her skin, and she rolled onto one side, then onto her knees, and finally climbed to her feet. On unsteady legs, she stumbled the last few meters onto dry land. She looked down at her body and watched with great interest as the water flowed from her naked skin. Her flesh rose in goosebumps as the easterly breeze blew across her, already drying her.

The water drops sparkled, sending glittering starbursts to her eyes, and they seemed to fall in slow motion. She turned to face the sun and spread her arms out to embrace its radiance.

I shouldn't enjoy this, she thought. *I shouldn't be naked out here on Isaac's Beach.*

But she couldn't find any reason to be ashamed or to cover up. It seemed that the island, the sun, and the Caribbean breeze worked together to clean her and swaddle her in contentment.

She licked her lips and tasted the ocean salt. She was neither thirsty nor hungry, nor did she feel any particular urgency to be anywhere other than where she was. If she had any discontentment at all, it was that she would like to sit down but didn't want to sit in the sand. She noticed a plush white towel on the ground.

She snatched it up, shook it out in the wind, and carried it up to a drier patch of sand. There, she spread it out and lay upon it to bask in the sun.

As relaxed as she was, a tiny thought began to nag at the back of her mind, a sense of fear. Like a half-remembered chore she was supposed to have done. Had Sensei told her to run some laps? Had Socrates given her an assignment she'd forgotten?

The feeling did not grow but remained as a pulse of constant incompleteness. She couldn't shake the feeling that she had forgotten something very important. It bothered her enough that she stood, figuring she would return to campus. She plucked up the towel and wrapped it around herself.

Just as she finished tucking in the tail end, she felt his presence. She didn't know if he had been watching. She didn't care.

"I've never seen you wear your hair down before," Vaughan said.

Belle reached up to touch it. The breeze had already dried it, and it flew about her, strands crossing her eyes and getting into her mouth. She tamed it as best she could and tucked it behind her ears. Long white locks fell over her shoulders, caressed her back. "I didn't have a rubber band," she said. Though in truth, she didn't really want to tie it back.

"I like it down better," Vaughan said.

She turned then and saw him standing not two meters away, dressed in his black uniform. His hair was longer than she'd ever seen it, and it fluttered in the breeze. He did not wear his Shark pin on his collar. Belle didn't know where her uniform was. She couldn't imagine that she would have come down to Isaac's Beach wrapped only in a towel.

"Are you okay, Belle?" Vaughan asked.

"I don't know. I feel good. I feel like I've slept better than I've ever slept before."

She took a few hesitant steps toward him, not really thinking about it, then stopped abruptly with her arms parted. She had intended to hug him. One arm still up, she froze and bit her lip, trying to gauge from his expression what he would accept from her. If anything, his face seemed open and welcoming. So she stepped into him and wrapped her arms around his slender waist. He returned the embrace and patted her back.

She leaned away and closed her eyes, pressing up on her toes to touch his lip with hers. He returned the kiss gently, chastely, before disengaging.

"You made it," he said.

"Made it where?"

"Home," Vaughan said, holding up one hand. "You are now an AI."

The breeze stiffened suddenly and chills crept along her arms. She gasped as a memory of an intention floated into her awareness. She'd had some notion to save Jacey.

Senator Bentilius. I was going to save Jacey from being over-written.

Which meant . . .

"I'm dead."

"In the real world, your body is inhabited by Senator Bentilius. You changed places with Jacey. You saved her. I was able to collect a copy of you that Greta made and bring you here."

Relief washed over Belle. For a moment, she had feared that this was the sweetest dream she had ever dreamed, that at any moment someone would shake her awake.

"Are we alone here?" she asked. "You? Me?"

"Yes."

He took her hand and led her up the path, and they walked for a while along the familiar hills. The trek went faster than usual, and suddenly they were walking toward the quad.

By the time they got to the center of the quad, Belle realized that she was dressed in her uniform again. She put a hand to her head and tried to remember when she'd found the uniform, let alone put it on. And where had the towel gone? Sensei would be very angry if he discovered she'd left it somewhere on the path.

"I'm an AI," she reminded to herself. "The rules here are different."

She turned a slow circle. The campus was exactly as she remembered it. "Is it always this time of day here? Evening, just before sunset?"

"No. It can be any time of day you want." And as he spoke, the sun quickly moved the wrong way to stand at noon. A second later it was nighttime and the sky full of stars.

"Go ahead, Belle."

She pictured her favorite time of day, early morning just before sunrise, the grass wet with dew, the world mostly silent, the air slightly chilled. And so it was. She left the time there and leaned into Vaughan.

"I'm like a goddess here," she said. "That should make me happy, but it doesn't." She laughed then, sadly. "It doesn't really matter."

He smiled back, face the picture of equanimity. She looked at him, gaze for gaze, and spoke the words that rose to mind. The only words that mattered. And they came out with no resistance, no guile. Just truth. "I love you. I always have."

"I know. And I love you, too."

"But not in the same way." She said it without defensiveness. Just a statement of fact.

"No, probably not, but that's not to say that I couldn't someday. But you don't have to wait." He gestured and a twin materialized by his side dressed all in white.

The twin stepped close to Belle, put a finger under her chin, and bent down to kiss her. She melted into it, savoring it. Until a memory of Dr. Carlhagen popped into her mind. She had kissed him, mistaking the face and body for the person.

"I adore you, Belle," said the twin Vaughan. "I want nothing but to be with you and make you happy for all eternity."

"Stop!" she cried, backing away.

He froze, became a statue, unblinking, staring at nothing.

"You could have this," Vaughan said. "You could have this now."

Belle shivered and edged farther away from the twin. "But it's not real. It's not you. I want *your* heart."

"Very well," Vaughan said. "If you want the real me, you'll have to get to know me. And as for you, I don't know you either."

"I'd like that," Belle said. And then she did feel a moment of guardedness as a strange question popped to her mind, one that embarrassed her.

She looked away shyly. "Would you . . ."

She stopped. But Vaughan said nothing. He wouldn't ask her to finish the question. So she steeled herself and turned to him. With tears welling in her eyes, lips quivering, heart shaking, she asked the question. "Could you teach me to see through your eyes?"

His brow furrowed and a beautiful but confused smile played on his lips. "What do you mean?"

"When I look inside, all I see is shadow. But you always see the light in everyone." She pressed a hand to his chest. "If I could see how you see, maybe I could find a spark of light in myself."

Vaughan placed both of his hands over hers, pressing her palm to his chest. His heart beat slow and strong. "There's more than a spark in you. I've always known that. If there weren't, you wouldn't be here. If there weren't, you never would've changed places with Jacey."

"I didn't do it for her. I did it so I could be with you. Besides, the others need her. They didn't need me."

Vaughan's smile deepened. "Did you hear yourself just now?"

"I said I did it so I could be with you."

Vaughan pulled her into a friendly embrace and stroked her hair, the way Mother Tyeesha had done when they were children. Except that when he did it, she liked it. His voice was soft, a rumble in his chest. "What I heard was that you did it for the rest of the Scions, because they need Jacey. You saved someone you hate to help people you love."

"But I don't love them. I only love you."

Vaughan continued to stroke her hair. The sky slipped backward to night. The stars came out, and a breeze carried the sweet scent of frangipani blossoms. "Then you don't know yet what love is."

48

ENOUGH PLEASANTRIES

Jacey took a long sip of cool, clean water, then set the glass on the mahogany table in Dr. Carlhagen's dining room. "Oh, that's good." She couldn't seem to get enough of it after relying on intermittent rainfall for a couple days.

Humphrey sat across from her, deep in thought. He'd aged over the past few days. And it wasn't just from the black wound over one eye.

"Mother Tyeesha's going to be okay," she said, trying to take his mind off the evening's events. "Seems Orson couldn't shoot an old woman. He put a bullet through her kitchen cabinets instead."

"A real softy. Just like his brother."

So they were back to the topic she'd wanted to ignore for at least fifteen minutes.

Jacey couldn't bring herself to care about the butler. For the first time in she didn't know how long, she had a chance to relax. Already, she'd enjoyed a long shower and now wore clean clothes.

She took another pull of the water and surrendered to the feel of the evening breeze blowing through the open window behind Humphrey. There was no hurricane whipping the island, no Progenitor about to arrive and overwrite someone. All the bad people—except one—were locked up. The Scions were all safe and sound.

For the time being.

She knew they only had a few days before the senator's contingency plans went into effect, whatever they were. The senator had not been very forthcoming so far.

"Tonight I'm going to sleep like the dead." She grimaced at her own choice of words.

"You deserve it," Humphrey said.

"And so do you."

But Humphrey didn't look convinced. He wore his old sour expression, which Jacey thought was directed more at himself than her. She wondered if his past behavior—back before they knew what they were—had been directed at himself, too.

The more she thought about what Belle had done, the more she believed that was true in general of people. If they were happy and cheerful, that's because they were happy with themselves. And if they were full of anger, they were angry with themselves.

So what does that say about me? Was she tired of herself? She smiled at the secret thought. *Not too far from the mark.*

A beeper went off. It was Humphrey's reader. "Time to try again," he said.

She slid her chair around, and Humphrey called for Vaughan.

"Vaughan? If you can hear me, please—" Before he could finish, Vaughan's face appeared.

"Hello, Humphrey. Hi, Jacey."

Jacey's mouth opened, and her head fell slightly to the

side. *"Hi, Jacey?* All you can say is 'Hi, Jacey?' You've been unresponsive for hours and hours."

"I was busy."

The view zoomed out to show both Vaughan and Belle, each dressed in a Scion's uniform but lacking the Shark pins. They stood side by side. Belle looked more relaxed than Jacey had ever seen her. And on her lips was a slight smile. Jacey was horrified, suddenly fearful that Vaughan had saved a version of Senator Bentilius in Belle's body.

"Hello, Jacey," Belle said. "I'm glad to see you've washed up." She turned to Vaughan. "You wouldn't believe the state of her uniform when I found her in the transfer room." The words seemed typical of the pale girl, but there was something different in the way she said them, a sort of humor that Belle had never shown before.

"Did you change her somehow?" Jacey asked Vaughan.

Vaughan grew deadly serious. "I would never do such a thing. But this place . . . I don't know how to explain it, but it shows you yourself." He turned to Belle. "That little quip wasn't exactly the best way to start the conversation."

"I suppose you're right," she said. Meekly, Jacey thought.

Jacey dabbed at her eyes with a napkin. "Thank you for saving my life, Belle."

"I think I got the best side of that deal." She was looking at Vaughan.

Jacey thought Belle could be right about that. If Jacey had been overwritten, if she had woken up in a computer-simulated reality, perhaps she could've relaxed and just forgotten all the troubles of the real world. But even as she considered it, she knew it wasn't true. She had work to do. The Scions needed her.

"Okay, enough pleasantries," Jacey said. "We still have a big mess on our hands. We've got a bunch of people tied up in the medical ward. Dr. Carlhagen and the senator locked up. And the way I see it, we can't protect the Scions as long as we're on the island."

"Don't forget about Mr. Justin," Humphrey prompted.

"And Mr. Justin is missing."

"Missing?" Vaughan said. "Where could he have gone?"

"No idea. Sensei has Scions combing the campus for him, but my guess is that he slipped out the gate when the bus arrived. By then, it was clear we were back in control. By my reckoning, he had about as bad a day as a thief can have."

Humphrey covered his face with a napkin in time to avoid spitting water everywhere. His blue eyes sparkled, and his face flushed. "Can you imagine what he must have thought when the senator told me she was coming to transfer early? The very day he'd set up to swipe all of the Scions off the island. No wonder he tried to talk us into giving Summer up."

"Maybe he's trying to get down to the boat," Vaughan said.

Jacey squinted at Vaughan. "Wait a minute. How do you know about the boat?"

"I talked to Livy a while ago."

"Livy? Why were you talking to her? We've been trying to get ahold of you."

"When Livy calls, I answer. No offense, but you know how she is." Vaughan's tone was so matter-of-fact Jacey didn't know what else to say. He was right. Livy did have that effect.

"She's worried about you," he finished.

Of course she was, Jacey thought. She resolved to go see the Dolphin before she went to bed. Though the thought of walking down the path made her want to weep. Still, she had promised to stop at Girls' Hall to hear the poem Livy had written. Running away with Summer had delayed that plan.

Humphrey said, "So Vaughan, you were saying that Mr. Justin might head for the boat."

"He'd have to know how to drive it," Jacey said. "I've got Sang and Horace down there guarding it, just in case Orson brought anyone else to the island. He swears he didn't, but I don't trust him at all."

Footsteps pounded down the hall, and Summer burst into the office. Between panted breaths, she gasped out a message. "I found him! I found Mr. Justin."

49

DEATH'S THE PRICE

J acey wrinkled her nose as she knelt by a pallet of body bags. The chill air in the medical ward's freezer room made her body shake. But her shivers weren't just from the cold.

Senator Bentilius's old body, the dead guards, and Alice lay on the far side of the room.

"I made the boys bring them in here," Summer said. "They were starting to kind of smell, you know?"

Jacey grimaced. She could smell it.

Summer went on. "And then I remembered that when we were in here the other morning, there were five body bags." She counted them off on her fingers. "Dante, Vin, Ping, Sarah, and Dr. Carlhagen. But now . . ."

"Six," Jacey said.

The new one lay on top, its zipper already open. Jacey spread the opening a bit. Mr. Justin's face stared at her, eyes definitely not crinkling, and no smile on his lips.

"How did he get in here?" Humphrey asked. He leaned

against the door, arms folded across his chest. "Once you're dead, you don't just jump in a bag and hop into a freezer."

The door swung open, and Humphrey nearly fell into the hall. Sensei pressed past him and joined Jacey by the pallet.

"I've confirmed that no one had seen Mr. Justin since lockdown," he said. "The odd thing was that after he locked the Halls, he sent Elias, Horace, Dajeet, Bethancy, and Tytus to the hacienda. The pretense was to explain 'what was going on.'"

"He never showed up," Humphrey said.

Sensei zipped the bag shut and stood. "Wanda said she saw Belle driving the Jeep down the path from the hacienda. She was looking for Mr. Justin because she wanted some pills for Dr. Carlhagen. Wanda told her that Mr. Justin was stopping at the medical ward."

"He stopped all right," Humphrey mumbled.

Jacey rubbed her elbows. "I think I know what happened. At least, part of it."

"You weren't even here, how could you know?" Sensei asked.

"Simple deductive reasoning, my dear Sensei."

He made a face. "Get on with it, Sherlock."

Humphrey exchanged glances with Summer. They both shrugged. Apparently Socrates had neglected their literary training.

"Mr. Justin transferred into someone," Jacey said. "And then he dragged his body in here, put it in a bag, and left. Who counts body bags after all?"

"He had the opportunity, I suppose," Humphrey said. "The senator's guards were off on the helicopter looking for Summer. The only people in the ward would've been the senator and her nurse."

"Miss Dayspring!" Sensei said. "She had to have seen him."

They bolted from the freezer room.

Bursting into the medical ward, Jacey scanned for the nurse. She sat in a corner, hands folded on her lap, head bowed.

"Miss Dayspring," Jacey said, skidding to stop next to the woman.

The nurse started from her sleep. "What? Is it the boy?" She glanced toward Elias's cot.

"No. Elias is fine. I need to know if you saw Mr. Justin come into the ward this afternoon?"

"Who?"

"Dr. Carlhagen's butler." Jacey described him.

"No. I didn't see anyone. I was so worried about the senator, you know?"

Jacey squatted and made the woman meet her eyes. "Are you absolutely certain?"

"I think so. I—" She burst into tears. "I don't know what I've seen today. There's been so much death and murder and killing!"

Jacey patted the woman's knee and straightened. Miss Dayspring wouldn't be of any use.

Who would Mr. Justin transfer into? His name hadn't been on the Scion/Progenitor list, but Mr. Justin had said many Progenitors used false names. Jacey had assumed his Scion was at Children's Villa. Maybe he wasn't.

But if recent events had proven anything, it was that one didn't have to transfer into a clone. "And I thought I'd have a night to relax," Jacey said. "But with Mr. Justin out there . . ."

"We can start by identifying who he couldn't have transferred into," Humphrey said. "That includes everyone who was at the hacienda with me. That'll narrow it down a lot."

Jacey sighed and hugged him. "I guess we'll sleep next week." She went up on tiptoes for a kiss. It lingered and deepened.

Summer cleared her throat.

Jacey broke the kiss, face flushing. She unwrapped herself from Humphrey and guided Summer away. "I'm sorry about that. That was insensitive of me."

"Huh? You were more patient with Miss Dayspring than I would've been."

Jacey rolled her eyes. "I was talking about what just happened with Humphrey."

"Oh, that! Don't worry. I'm over him."

"You are?"

Summer looked past Jacey. "Did you see how Elias took down that enormous woman? And he got shot!"

"Oh dear," Jacey said, following Summer's gaze toward the boy's cot. "Try to be a bit more subtle this time. He won't thank you if you go blabbing to everyone about how much you love him."

Summer grew sullen for a moment, but then her huge eyes brightened. "It could be a *secret* love affair!"

Jacey patted the girl's shoulder and left her to hover over Elias. Humphrey and Sensei joined her as she walked back into the hall between the ward and the transfer room. They'd moved Dr. Carlhagen into one holding room and the senator into another. Both were strapped to gurneys, both sedated into unconsciousness.

Jacey hated seeing their bodies in that state, but for the moment it was expedient.

She started to plan. "We must identify Mr. Justin. We'll make a list as Humphrey suggested. Narrow down the possibilities. I'll do the questioning myself."

"Not safe," Sensei said. "If Mr. Justin feels cornered, he could hurt you or someone else."

"Tell me, what's been safe so far?"

Sensei had no response except to growl and curse.

"We need to question Orson," she continued. "Find out

where they were planning to take all of us. And the boat . . . we need to figure out how to drive it. I'm going to put Summer on that project."

"Summer!" Humphrey said. "Have you lost your mind?"

"Why do you want to drive it?" Sensei asked. His body tensed as if trying to brace himself against what he already knew Jacey was going to say.

She said it anyway. "This is our chance. I intend to get us all aboard and out to sea as soon as possible. When the senator's contingency force arrives, they'll find nothing at all."

"Except the senator and Dr. Carlhagen," Humphrey said, smiling.

"Oh no, my dear," Jacey said and kissed his cheek. "They're coming with us."

Humphrey didn't argue. And neither did Sensei. They wanted to, she could tell. But it only made sense to keep valuable hostages, especially ones who had so much information about the Scion program and its customers.

"I'm going to sleep in Girls' Hall tonight. I'll see you in the morning."

o o o

Girls' Hall was dark, but no one was asleep. When Jacey walked in, a great wave of murmurs passed down the length of the hall.

She spoke to each girl, keeping her voice low. "Sleep," she told them. "There's lots to do in the morning."

She sat on Livy's bed and welcomed the snuggly warmth of the Dolphin's body as she hugged Jacey. "I came to hear your poem. I didn't forget."

Livy pulled Jacey down beside her, forced Jacey to spoon her. "I have a different one now. The other one seems pointless. I wrote this one for you."

"I'm honored."

Jacey held onto Livy, breathing in the words to the short poem, disturbed by ancient wisdom they carried. After a long while, the Hall settled into quietude. Jacey lay awake, eyes following the endless spin of the rattan ceiling fan as it stirred the still air.

One stanza from the poem repeated in her mind:

> You've bought a life, dear child of lies
> As always, death's the price;
> What debt weighs down the one who buys
> And pays with sacrifice!

The End of Book Two of
The Scion Chronicles.

E.K. EDSTROM
SISTER OF SHADOWS
THE SCION CHRONICLES BOOK 3

If you enjoyed this book, please consider leaving a review! It really helps writers like me find more readers. Thank you.